Treasure was...
ing at her bare...
whisper, she sl...

How many ...
other?

The huge mother-of-pearl sphere above her illuminated her skin with an ethereal silver sheen. She began walking toward him.

He could see her soul in the depths of her eyes, looking for his.

How many days have you been mine?

She stood before him, a heartbeat away.

How long have I known I love you?

He touched her.

His fingertips swanned her face, her throat, explored lower to her shoulder. . . . Passion burst inside him like a madness. With a strong will, he buried it deep, but the echo of it was a hunger, begging to be sated.

Reaching out, feeling powerful, yet uncertain, he brushed the damp hair at her temple. "I realized long ago if I were blind . . ." He slid fingertips to the fine line of her cheekbones, caressed the curve of her mouth, the stubborn lift of her chin. ". . . if I were blind, I would still know you."

She thought his voice as warm as the night air. "Would you?"

"Always."

Always.

Donovan cupped Treasure's face between his hands, as he softly kissed her parted lips. Her eyes fluttered closed, and her breath escaped on a sigh. He kissed her again, deeper, hotter, longer, kindling her desires until they were a match for his own.

Then, sweeping her into his arms, he carried her back to the balcony, no longer hearing the siren serenade of the sea . . .

PINNACLE BOOKS HAS
SOMETHING FOR EVERYONE—

MAGICIANS, EXPLORERS, WITCHES AND CATS

THE HANDYMAN   (377-3, $3.95/$4.95)
He is a magician who likes hands. He likes their comfortable shape and weight and size. He likes the portability of the hands once they are severed from the rest of the ponderous body. Detective Lanark must discover who The Handyman is before more handless bodies appear.

PASSAGE TO EDEN   (538-5, $4.95/$5.95)
Set in a world of prehistoric beauty, here is the epic story of a courageous seafarer whose wanderings lead him to the ends of the old world—and to the discovery of a new world in the rugged, untamed wilderness of northwestern America.

BLACK BODY   (505-9, $5.95/$6.95)
An extraordinary chronicle, this is the diary of a witch, a journal of the secrets of her race kept in return for not being burned for her "sin." It is the story of Alba, that rarest of creatures, a white witch: beautiful and able to walk in the human world undetected.

THE WHITE PUMA   (532-6, $4.95/NCR)
The white puma has recognized the men who deprived him of his family. Now, like other predators before him, he has become a man-hater. This story is a fitting tribute to this magnificent animal that stands for all living creatures that have become, through man's carelessness, close to disappearing forever from the face of the earth.

Alabama Twilight
Danette Chartier

PINNACLE BOOKS
WINDSOR PUBLISHING CORP.

PINNACLE BOOKS

are published by

Windsor Publishing Corp.
475 Park Avenue South
New York, NY 10016

First Printing: March, 1993

Printed in the United States of America

To Al and to Jeff,
and to yours, mine, and ours,
for putting up with us over the last four years.

Special thanks to our dads,
Ted Fertig and R. C. Chartier,
for patience, priceless advice,
and for always being there,
and to our agent, Joyce A. Flaherty,
for your support and encouragement,
and for giving us a chance.

Chapter One

Treasure McGlavrin wound slender fingers around the smooth column, squinting a little into the late afternoon sun as she followed the distant figure of the rider. White-gold heat pummeled the long stretch of road leading to the plantation house, rippling and shifting the silhouette of horse and man in a brown dusty haze.

Treasure brushed wayward, pale red tendrils from her forehead, wide, gray-green eyes wary as she watched the rider near Rose of Heaven.

She couldn't imagine anyone calling for pleasure on such a day. Since early morning, the heat had crushed sound and motion, settling in with oppressive stillness. No breeze stirred the leaves; even the cattle and horses clustered under the lean pine shade, silent and still. The sun burned relentlessly, alone in the sharp blue sky.

Crazy heat, Bettis called it, so hot you eat and breathe it, bringing the worst out of even the best. He muttered and stumped around the just plowed fields of corn and cotton, cursing the dryness and short tempers, adding creases to his weathered dark face. *Change is comin', Miz Treasure. This weather bringin' a change.*

Bettis and his witch man's predictions stirred an

7

odd restlessness in her. Shaking the notion aside, Treasure brushed her skirts down primly. It didn't matter. The change had already come and gone. Nothing coming could make it worse; nothing could make it better.

Her papa was dead.

The clop of the horses' hooves neared and slowed. Treasure looked out over the faded lawn fronting the sprawling white house and tried to trace features on the ebon shadow of the man. Before the man pulled his brindled stallion up short at the curve of the long drive, Solomon scrambled down the steps to greet the newcomer.

Dwarfed by the size of horse and rider, the young slave waited while the man reined the horse in, swung off, and tossed him the reins. Soloman gave the man a tentative smile and began tugging the horse toward the stables.

Treasure waited. But instead of walking toward the big house the man held still a long minute, staring, watching as if he wanted to look his fill endlessly.

Uneasiness crept up Treasure's neck. She slid her hand up and down the familiar wood, trying to soothe the disquiet away with the rhythmic motion.

Finally, he started up the circle drive leading to the house. "Afternoon." The word slid off his lips in a deep, suggestive voice that made it sound more like an invitation than a greeting. He touched two fingers to his black slouch hat.

"Good afternoon, sir," Treasure said, then waited for him to state his business. She wanted to see his eyes, but his hat sat low over his face. Treasure was inclined to think he was a drifter, maybe looking for work. Long and lean, in faded black trousers and a sweat-damp, dingy white shirt, he reminded her of the trappers who sometimes dared to trespass on the timberland overlooking Rose of Heaven — dangerous and hungry.

8

She watched as he studied the grand white elegance of the big house, the gem in a ring of green and cream magnolias that separated it from the vista of russet brown fields fanning out far behind it. His gaze was intense, almost possessive. It fed her unsettled feeling and she thought of the muzzle loader standing just inside the door.

"This is Rose of Heaven," he said, satisfaction evident.

Treasure stepped square in front of the door, her eyes steady on his. "Yes, sir, it is. And any business you have here, you have with me."

He swept her with a glance. "Who are you?"

"I own Rose of Heaven." Her eyes dared him to deny it.

"This" — He gestured to the house and fields — "is yours?"

Treasure paused before answering. There was no clue in his manner or his appearance to explain his odd questions. Even the elusive quality of his voice guarded his identity. His accent was strange: not Southern easy, but not quite as fast-talking as the few Yankees Papa had ever allowed on Rose of Heaven. Of course those men were Northern businessmen, not at all of the same breed as this intruder.

"What business do you have here, sir?" she finally asked, wanting to be done with his evasions.

To her annoyance, he laughed, a throaty amusement as tantalizing as an unexpected cool breeze in the heat. "All the business in the fine state of Alabama, mistress of Heaven."

He took the first steps of the porch in two easy strides, and leaned insolently against one of the pillars. A patch of leaf-patterned sun touched him and Treasure traced with her eyes a hard angled face, straight nose, the sharp line of a jaw. Under the shade of his hat, his eyes looked black.

"Your humble servant, Donovan T. River, pretty

9

lady," he said, making her a half bow. "And I'm here to collect what's mine."

Treasure started. "Yours?"

"Mine. You see, all this"—he spread out both arms in a wide sweep—"all this belongs to me."

Caught between fury and laughter, Treasure stood motionless for a long moment, unable to express either. Finally, she blurted out, "I don't find this amusing, sir."

"It's true. Seamus McGlavrin—"

"My papa is dead," Treasure said flatly. With a quick sweep of gray skirts, she yanked open the front door and snatched up the rifle. Eyes defiant, heart trembling, she leaned the butt against her shoulder, a finger hovering on the trigger. "I'm certain Colonel Stanton sent you here to do his dirty business, but you are wasting your time, sir. I have made it quite clear I do not intend to sell Rose of Heaven. I'm going to keep this plantation if I have to take on the entire valley to do it."

Donovan crossed his ankles and pushed back his hat, his expression unreadable. The eyes steady on hers were dark misty gray. "I don't need to pay for what's already mine."

Treasure kept the rifle securely against her shoulder. Cold sweat trickled down her back and she was acutely aware of the hard butt of the rifle biting her flesh, the hot, slick iron under her finger. "If you don't get off my property, sir, I'll have you carried off."

"Strong words, pretty lady. But the truth is Seamus McGlavrin—your father—deeded Rose of Heaven to me." Donovan stroked a finger over his jaw, his eyes softer as they studied her. Whether with sympathy or pity, Treasure couldn't tell. "When was the last time you saw him?"

Treasure gritted her teeth against the surge of anger. Her eyes flashed fire. "That is hardly your business, sir. And you are sadly mistaken if you expect me to believe my father turned over Rose of Heaven to some low drifter."

"I've got the proof."

"Then you murdered Papa to get it. He would never give up Rose of Heaven."

He was standing straight now, the insolent curve of his body replaced by a menacing poise. Treasure stood her ground, not willing to give him any advantage. "I suppose you and Colonel Stanton expected me to accept your lies like a poor lamb led to slaughter. You underestimated me, sir. And you can tell Colonel Stanton the like."

"Look . . ." Donovan held out a hand, frustration darkening his eyes. "If you would just listen—"

"I am through listening." Keeping the rifle pointed at him, Treasure stalked to the side railing and shouted in the direction of the woodshed, "Elijah! Elijah!"

There was a rumble inside the tiny building and then a man emerged, shirtless, his deep, golden mulatto skin gleaming with sweat in the sun. Short, but broad and muscled, he lumbered to the porch, sky blue eyes narrowing when he spied the newcomer.

"Elijah, this gentleman needs escorting back to the road," Treasure said, looking directly at Donovan. "He has made a terrible mistake, one I am sure we can rectify."

Elijah motioned to Solomon. The boy, drawn to the commotion, darted off toward the stables. Elijah then moved threateningly toward Donovan, who threw up his hands in a gesture of good-natured surrender, favoring Treasure with a raffish grin. "You win, pretty lady." His eyes meandered over her with slow appraisal. "This time." He sauntered down the steps, touching his hat to Treasure, and then Elijah.

Solomon, breathless from his run, led the stallion to the base of the stairs and waited for Donovan to

11

mount. "But you better start packing your trunks," Donovan said as he tossed a long leg over the saddle. "Because I intend to have what's mine. And if you won't leave, I'll consider you part of the bargain."

Wheeling the horse around, he urged it into a gallop down the path, kicking up a swirl of fine red dust. Treasure watched him disappear down the road before she eased the rifle down with a trembling hand.

"Miss Treasure . . ." Elijah watched her, his hooded eyes liquid sky, betraying nothing.

"It's all right," Treasure said. "He won't be back." She said the words firmly, forcing a smile.

But as she turned back into the house, Treasure wished she believed them.

Treasure eased into the willow-wood rocker, her favorite retreat on the back kitchen porch, and pictured her fields beyond the dense barrier of pines and oaks — cotton, corn, a few acres of cane, and the pastures, farther out still — all tinged with the peach and scarlet glow of the sunset. They were newly planted, loamy, river-rich soil thick with seeds of promise, waiting for languid heat, tempestuous summer storms and sure hands to bring them alive.

And at the center of it all, Rose of Heaven. Whitewashed pine and oak, a foundation of stone, eight grand pillars to make it stately; touches of ornate scrolls and glass to soften it. Even when the fields waned, and fortunes were uncertain, Rose of Heaven weathered the discord with stoic endurance.

From behind her, the salty tang of Orange Jane's supper ham wafted out to mingle curiously with the sweetness of early honeysuckle and musty damp earth. Treasure leaned back, her eyes half closed, listening to the faint familiar sound of Orange Jane singing, honeyed and low.

"Der's a man in de sunshine,

12

comin' here for me
Der's a man in de moonlight,
   sure to pass me by
Der's a man in de mornin',
   I can never see,
Der's a man in de evenin',
   come to make me cry.
But de man in de shadow,
   standin' lone, apart,
Dat's de man o' twilight,
   come to take my heart."

For long moments, Treasure let herself be lulled by the throaty voice. Orange Jane was accompanied by the occasional cry of a night bird, the mournful lowing of the cattle. Sultry evening air draped over her. Fog began to creep over the fields in a spreading haze. A fat ivory moon hung low on the horizon.

Treasure nearly succumbed to the urge to drift into a pleasant half-sleep, when the discordant yap of Bonny, her father's terrier, shattered her peaceful respite. She immediately felt a twinge of guilt for allowing herself the reprieve. Eura Mae could use help with the twins, the account books needed tending, and she'd promised to see to the hem of Spring's rose lawn where it had caught on a nail in a loose floor board on the back porch.

And none of it was closer to being done because of him.

Donovan T. River.

Knotting her fists into a tight ball, she cursed the offending name. His claims were ludicrous. Weren't they? Ever since he'd heard of Papa's death two months ago, Ira Stanton had been pestering her to sell Rose of Heaven. Seamus McGlavrin would never give up his plantation to please the likes of Ira and his grand plans to lumber her mountain, but apparently Ira had convinced himself that Seamus's daughter,

13

alone and beleaguered by her new responsibilities, would welcome the opportunity to sell.

You've more chance of owning the governor's mansion, Ira Stanton, Treasure silently thought *You can send all the Donovan T. Rivers you like, but I'll never change my mind.*

Papa had loved Rose of Heaven. And since as far back as she could recall, Treasure had shared his joy in the land, feeling she belonged more to the plantation than she did to herself.

But Papa was made for good times. When his second wife died a little more than a year past, Papa had taken to spending long days alone in the woods or by the river, his nights in the valley, lost in cards and bourbon.

Many dawns, Papa's slurred curses and pounding at the door would rouse Treasure from an exhausted slumber. She would tumble out of bed, calm his temper, and lead him to his room, her slim shoulders draped with his heavy arm.

And always, always, she listened to his regrets, his sorrows made blacker by long hours of liquor.

"I dinna know what went wrong. I had me bonny Claire—puir, puir lass, she woulda made some fine sons. I had me town and had the best bit of Heav'n in Alabama—river to mountain top. It well nigh breaks my heart to think of it."

She soothed him, praying he would sleep. Because she knew what he would say next and each time made it harder to bear. But the words always came before she could escape, finding her heart with cruel accuracy.

"Puir, puir Claire. No finer lady to be found. You're nae like her, lass. None of me sweet Claire in you. And you lived. She, puir Claire, she died. I mighta seen reason for it if my bonny Claire had left me a son. But 'tis no use now. Dinna matter anymore . . . none of this means anything to me."

14

"It matters to me, Papa," she chanted to deaf ears. "It all still matters to me. It always will."

Treasure wore herself ragged each day, but Rose of Heaven languished under her inexperienced hand.

Papa's jaunts to the river lengthened. Then one day, eight months ago, he didn't come back.

But Treasure never stopped believing he would. And to prove her faith she devoted herself twice over to his once cherished Rose of Heaven. She nurtured it, fussed over it, worried and fretted over the smallest details. Papa *must* have trusted her to leave her mistress of one of the biggest estates in Alabama.

"I won't disappoint you, Papa," she recited her nightly vow. "I'll work harder and longer. I'll make you proud."

She would never be a graceful plantation mistress the way her stepmother was, but she was determined to make her land prosper.

You're all legs and arms, just like sticks and twigs, Treasure. Red hair, and those freckles—hopeless. You'll never be a lady, Treasure, with your head full of numbers and your hands and nails ugly and stained from digging in the dirt. Maybe Seamus is right. You should have been born a boy. At least then you'd have a future.

Lettia McGlavrin always delivered her observations with a tinkling laugh and a helpless wave of a long white hand, as if she were merely teasing her stepdaughter. But the cultured, drawling tones never failed to cut and wound.

Why, darlin', if you don't improve, we'll have to pay the overseer to make you his wife! You'll never be fit for a real gentleman.

Papa shrugged the slights away. "Lettia is a real lady. If anyone can teach you fine ways, she can. Dinna disappoint me, lass. A daughter is no good to me if she's not a lady."

She did try, from the time she was four with a new

15

mother and sister, until she was eighteen and Lettia died of fever.

But Treasure supposed she was still a disappointment: too thin from long days and short nights, skin dusted with fawn freckles, gold-red hair a thick unruly mass. She talked too sharply, worked too hard, and became awkward and fumbling every time she walked into a room full of people.

But if she could make Rose of Heaven a success, no one would ever dare call her a disappointment again.

"Lord, Treasure, with your face all screwed up like that you look like you're ready to swat someone." Spring McGlavrin swished out onto the veranda, perching on the edge of the long chaise near Treasure. Having Spring sit next to you was like having a wood fairy alight for a moment, quivering and eager to flit away, and the impression always afforded Treasure a smile. "You must have had a trying afternoon."

There was prompting in Spring's voice and a wealth of sixteen-year-old curiosity in her dark eyes. Treasure sighed, certain that news of the intruder had already spread over the plantation. Sometimes she marveled that Spring was Lettia's daughter. She'd inherited all Papa's mischievous humor, his bold, laughing manner, and the rich auburn hair Treasure envied beyond hope.

"Well?" Spring demanded. "Is it true? Did Papa really give him Rose of Heaven? Are we going to have to go and live with Aunt Valene? Say we won't, Treasure, *pleeease*. She never visits. Why, she hardly feels like family." Spring wrinkled her nose. "And—oh!, did you really point the rifle at that dangerous man? You're so daring, Treasure, I wish I had your courage!"

"Spring!" Treasure, with a choice between laughter and exasperation, picked a smile. "How did you manage to find all that out in one afternoon?"

"Elijah, of course." She flicked a corner of her

16

white flowered muslin, her eyes dancing. "He'll tell me anything if I ask him sweetly enough."

"Spring, I've warned you . . ."

Spring waved aside the admonition. "Never mind about that. Tell me—does this stranger really own Rose of Heaven?"

The note of anticipation in Spring's voice annoyed Treasure. Spring loved spontaneity and excitement; Treasure much preferred order and everyday routine. "Of course not. Why, I can't believe you'd put any faith in such a frightful lie."

"What a change it would be." Spring sighed. "You could use some excitement, Treasure. Since my mama died, you've done nothing but worry away your days in the cotton fields—with the slaves, really!— and scribble in Papa's account books. And now that Papa's gone, and having to sell so many of the slaves, it's just been so much worse. And so boring!"

"I don't find the notion of losing Rose of Heaven exciting," Treasure admonished. "Boring or not, it is my responsibility, just like you and Emmaline and the twins, and—"

"Camille?" Spring shook her head vigorously. "Camille's eighteen. She doesn't care for you telling her what to do. Besides . . ." Spring twinkled at her. "She thinks you're boring, too!"

"Spring!" Treasure knew her sister was teasing, but she couldn't stop the faint color from flushing her face.

"Oh, Treasure, I'm sorry." Spring flung herself at Treasure's feet, laying her head on her sister's knee. "You hurt so easily. I'm the worst sort of idiot. Please, please, please, say you forgive me."

Treasure smoothed the dark red hair in her lap, smiling a little. "How silly—I'm not that tender and there's nothing to forgive. You're so dramatic, Spring. I worry one day you'll run off and become a bawdy house actress or a saloon singer or some such entirely unsuitable thing."

Giggling, Spring looked up at her, her contriteness vanished. "Don't laugh at the idea. If your mysterious Mr. River is telling the truth, I may have to!"

In a dark corner of the nearly empty salon at Johnson's Hotel and Boarding House, Donovan River slouched in a chair and glowered at the bottle of bourbon on the table in front of him. Lamp flame danced through the brown liquid and teased the planes of his face, rearranging light and shadow. Near his table, twilight crept in behind the bright calico curtains, leaving a dewy mist on the window glass.

He had found what he came for. But—as usual—it wasn't what he expected.

From Seamus McGlavrin's avid descriptions, he had seen McGlavrin's Valley in his mind as it was—wide dusty streets lined with buildings of pine plank and whitewashed wood, lying in the palm of lush northern Alabama hills. Wrapped like a ribbon around a picturesque package, the Tennessee River turned the bottom land soil to gold in the pocket of any man lucky enough to tame it with fields of cotton.

Seamus McGlavrin had been that man. Donovan could recall every story the old man told, from the time he had found him delirious in a Louisiana swamp, until the day he died after playing his last hand of five-card draw, still rambling about his Alabama heaven.

Donovan listened partly because curiosity drove him to wonder what it was like to belong so thoroughly to a piece of land, partly because he was intrigued by Seamus McGlavrin himself, the big, bluff Scotsman who forged a town and built a plantation and then threw it all aside when a black mood struck him down.

They formed a curious friendship, and it stood them even in the end when the old man was crazy enough to try to bluff a card sharp with nothing but a pair of deuces and a promissory note for his plantation. Damned fool, old Seamus, thinking he could stare the table down. Knowing he had the Scotsman beat, Donovan took the game—and the note, promising himself he wouldn't keep it. The old man had laughed in his face, swore at him for being so damned stupid, and made sure he had the note in hand. Then Seamus McGlavrin had the audacity to die.

Donovan had taken the note for Rose of Heaven, he admitted it, partly because in all the hours spent listening, he became entranced with Seamus's "wee farm." The old man talked about it as if it were a woman—beautiful, giving, but needing an understanding hand to teach her joy and bring her to life. *My Southern beauty,* Seamus called it. *She owns me more than any flesh woman ever could. Even now.*

How did it feel? He hadn't belonged anywhere in the thirty-two years he'd been alive. Hell, his name didn't even belong to him. But for the first time in all his rambling, Donovan considered stopping long enough to get a taste of having roots. He often wondered if Seamus had insisted he take the plantation knowing just that.

It all seemed a great adventure, one in a long series of escapades that had taken him from north to south. The idea of owning a bit of a plantation intrigued him. Alabama. Why not?

Except Rose of Heaven hardly fit the description of "wee farm." And not once during the long winter had Seamus ever spoken of a family. He'd mentioned no one, in fact, except when he was dead drunk. And then it was his "bonny Claire, gone now these twenty years."

But Rose of Heaven's fierce little guardian couldn't be a wife of twenty years past.

She had to be his daughter—she had Seamus's eyes, the color of a river before a rain, and his red hair, though his had been a rich autumn auburn. Hers was a morning sunrise, pale, glimmering red, kissed with gold. A willow wisp of a girl, her face delicate, yet fresh and vibrant, with a poignant touch in the trembling mouth, the faint violet hollows under her eyes.

She'd looked ready to fight him claw and tooth. Pointing a damned rifle in his face—Donovan threw back another jigger of bourbon, slapping the shot glass back down on the table. From the resolve in her eyes he was convinced she'd have pulled the trigger and damn the consequences. One thing was certain: Seamus McGlavrin's daughter was nothing like the fragile rose petal beauties he'd expected from the fine state of Alabama. His capricious luck had found a briar in the garden.

Donovan rubbed a finger over his jaw, trying to think. What in damnation was he supposed to do? He couldn't just set her at the side of the road, trunks at her side. And yet he wanted that plantation—damn it! It was his! Wanted it for reasons he knew and some he couldn't guess at.

But her . . . hell, he didn't even know her name. Only the way she'd faced him, not a quiver in those slender, capable-looking hands. Something in her river green eyes—a child's bravado, uncertainty—aroused a treacherous tenderness in him.

He'd never forget it.

He was trapped.

Donovan River snared by another impossible cause.

A long line of a shadow suddenly darkened the table. The fire in the lamp flickered in a draft of sour whiskey. Donovan slowly looked up.

An imposing man stood there, dressed in immaculate sand-colored coat and a jade and burgundy brocade vest, hung with a heavy gold watch and chain.

The man grinned down at him, thin lips pulled back in an imitation of genteel hospitality. He swept his hat aside from slick fair hair, and offered a slight bow.

"Good evenin', suh. Let me be the first to welcome you to the valley."

Donovan acknowledged the greeting with a nod. "Nice to be welcomed by somebody."

"Well, suh, we are normally kindly folk, but I understand you did not meet with much goodwill at the McGlavrin plantation."

Donovan was deliberately slow to answer, sizing up the man with a practiced eye. Tall, broad-shouldered, with small wandering eyes, beetle dark, looking for an advantage, a glib refinement in his manner. "Word seems to get around pretty fast," he said at last.

"Why, down heah, suh, you can't spit on Sunday without folks knowin' it twenty miles away. Mind if I join you?" He pulled out a chair and dropped down without waiting for a reply. "Colonel Ira Garrison Stanton, mayor of this fine valley," he said, eyeing the half-empty bottle of bourbon. Donovan half expected him to lick his lips. "And I do believe we can do a little business. That is"—the mayor scraped his chair closer—"if you're tellin' the truth."

Ira Stanton. She had spat out his name, making it sound as if he were consorting with the devil. Donovan's eyes narrowed, but he kept his voice bland. "The truth about what?"

"Why, owning Rose of Heaven. Let us say, suh, that poor Seamus, God rest his soul, did give it to you. And I can't see why he shouldn't." Ira's smile said he didn't believe in Donovan's luck, but it didn't matter. "A plantation like that needs a man's hand. Now Miss McGlavrin . . ." The smile soured. "Miss McGlavrin she does her poor best, I'm sure. But the ladies have no head for that kind of work. And I can't see why a traveled man like yourself would want to be tied down. And that's where we can do some business."

Donovan's fingers played over his jaw line. "Hmmm. Business?"

"Certainly." Ira leaned over the table. "I'm willin' to pay you a fair price. It's no good to you as it is. You can pocket the profit and be on your way. No bones broken."

"What do you intend to do with it?"

"That's my business, suh." His expression lost some of its careful polished charm. "Why should that matter to you?"

Donovan answered with a shrug. "And what about the lady of the house?"

"Treasure? A lady?" The colonel gave a hoarse laugh. "You'll forgive me for plain speaking, but Treasure McGlavrin is no lady. I have tried, since her papa died, to be a friend to that girl, to relieve some of her heavy burden. But she has been most ungrateful. Nothing the least well bred about her. As a man of good sense, I'm sure you can see the reason of the situation."

Treasure. Donovan tried the name in his mind. Treasure McGlavrin. Treasure of Heaven. *Damn you, Seamus, you crazy old fool. Why didn't you tell me?*

"So—are we agreed, suh?" Ira watched Donovan with eager eyes.

Donovan looked at him straight, a hard smile curving his mouth.

"No."

The colonel shot back in his chair, faster than if he'd been punched, a dumb blankness on his liquor-reddened face. "Wha—?"

"No." Tension darted up the veins in Donovan's neck, but his pose remained smoothly unflinching. "You don't seem to understand the word, so I'll make it clear." He waited, prolonging the silence with the slow tap of his fingers to the side of his glass. He leveled the colonel a dark stare. "Miss McGlavrin has no intention of selling and neither do I."

22

"You're making a mistake, suh," Ira jerked out as he got to his feet. "A most serious mistake."

"Probably, but why stop now?" Donovan leaned his chair back against the wall, hands linked behind his head. "Besides, I'm looking forward to becoming a Southern gentleman of leisure."

Ira yanked his hat down low on his brow. "I wouldn't get too used to it. Things have a way of not lastin' sometimes. Especially in these parts."

"Maybe."

"Just remember the offer stands — but not for long." Whipping around on his heel, Ira stalked out of the salon flinging the door closed behind him with a resounding crack.

Twitching the curtains apart, Donovan watched Colonel Stanton stalk off down the street, feeling a grim satisfaction as the square figure was eaten by the fog. As he turned back to his table, Donovan met another set of watching eyes, appraising him with a thoughtful expression.

Large and lumbering, the man was straightening one of the salon tables. "You'll pardon me for sayin'," he said slowly, "but you don't appear to be makin' many friends today."

Donovan gave a terse laugh. He poured out another shot of bourbon and swallowed it in a gulp. "Yes, sir," he muttered. "The local favorite."

His companion ran a hand over grizzled nut brown hair. He hesitated as if weighing his words then said, "Treasure McGlavrin has had an unfair share of trouble lately. If you're thinkin' about bringin' her more, might be best you reconsider."

"I'd like to oblige. I certainly would. But . . ." In a languid motion, Donovan got to his feet and retrieved his hat, settling it low to shade his eyes. "I can't. Like it or not, Treasure McGlavrin is stuck with me."

* * *

23

Colonel Stanton slammed his way into the sitting room of Gold Meadow hard enough to shake the furniture. Launching his hat into a convenient corner, he snatched up a bottle of whiskey from the liquor cabinet and dropped into a chair, not bothering with the formalities of a glass.

"Don't look like you had any luck with the new master," a voice sneered from the doorway. Jimmy Rae Stanton leaned against the pine-timbered archway and eyed his brother with malicious satisfaction. "I told you—"

"Yeah, ain't you so smart? You told me." Ira took a long draft of the liquor, wincing as it burned a trail to his stomach. "You've done your share of telling. But what you haven't done, little brother, is come up with any better ideas."

Jimmy Rae shrugged, lazily trailing a lean hand through too long, brandy-colored hair. A stubborn wave refused to cooperate, falling over his right eye. "Leave it. Unless you like the idea of stirrin' up trouble." A malicious gleam sparked in his dark, deep-set eyes. "And that's fine by me."

Trouble. Yes sir, trouble to spare. Ira knew it, and it turned his gut sour. Gold Meadow was a damned mess. Had been for years. The cotton crop had struggled; a body couldn't make enough in cane and corn to live easy. Ira hated the land and it returned the favor.

He'd nearly decided to chuck the plantation and take his chances with some new venture. And then Seamus McGlavrin turned up dead and he'd seen a chance finally to get something out of the valley besides a fancy chair at the town hall. Snuggled up close to the river, Rose of Heaven was wed to some of the finest timber in the state. Ira itched to plow down the fields and turn the whole thing into a gold mine in lumbering.

Nearly everyone in the valley would thank him; he'd

be assured the prestige of the mayor's seat for a lifetime. All it would take was a little starting capital, discreetly borrowed from the valley's taxpaying citizens. A fine, tidy plan.

Except for little Miss Treasure McGlavrin.

She spit in his face every time he set foot on the plantation. When he'd gotten the news of the stranger and his wild claim, he'd thought a back door had opened. But the stranger had slammed it shut and shot the bolt.

And now what was he supposed to do? Forget the whole idea? Stay here, pretend to like being a damned dirt farmer? Watch his hard-earned reputation erode like the fields of Gold Meadow?

All Jimmy Rae was interested in was gettin' folks riled up. At seventeen, his worthless kid brother only wanted a thing as long as it was easy or fun. Never did care for waiting and working at it.

But for a prize as golden as Rose of Heaven, Ira was willing to do labor, long and hard.

He could feel Jimmy staring down his neck. "You ain't gonna give it up, are you, Ira?"

The colonel smiled, a vicious twist of the lips that made Jimmy grin. "You know something, little brother," he said, holding up his bottle in a silent toast. "You're damned right."

Chapter Two

"Treasure! Always Treasure! She can do without if she pleases, but I refuse to give up the few luxuries I have left in this house just because she insists on living like a slave!"

"But Missy Camille, Missy Treasure say—"

Poor Solomon, Treasure thought. Her stepsister's tirade reverberated through the parlor walls into the study where Treasure was struggling to catch up on her ledgers. *She's missed breakfast again, no doubt. Please, Camille, just once, let it rest.* Treasure clamped her hands over her ears. *I don't have time for another interruption this morning.*

"Stop prancing about like a spooked horse!" Camille yelled at the nervous house boy.

Lord above, she'll be at him all morning if I don't put a stop to it. Treasure slammed her ledger closed, pushed away from her desk, and left the room.

"I'll take my biscuits and coffee in here today. Oh, bring me extras with jam, too. I'm famished." Camille placed her order, unaware Treasure stood in the parlor doorway watching.

Treasure sighed and shook her head. On the settee in front of the window Camille basked languorously in the warmth of the late morning sun. The day wasn't advanced enough to be stifling hot, but it was too late for breakfast, and too late to be lounging around in her nightdress.

A feathery breeze drifted off the verandah through the open French doors, fluttering the chiffon froth of Camille's nightdress, the ivory silk confection she'd made haste to adopt after her mother's death. Her dark hair flung artfully over the arm of the settee, Camille wound the ribbons at the low neck of the gown around her finger, slowly letting the thin silk uncurl and then curl against milky skin.

Solomon cleared his throat and ducked his head. "You heared what de mistress say 'bout missin' breakfast."

"Just do it!"

The house boy skittered out, nearly bumping into Treasure.

"I done try to tell her, Missy Treasure—"

"I heard, Solomon. Go ahead, bring her a tray. But this is the last time. Is that clear?"

"Yes, missy," the gangly youngster said, and bowed out of the parlor.

"How dare you dictate where and when I will eat!"

"You will eat when the meal is served, or you will not eat, Camille."

"Just who do you think you are! You may run everyone else's business around here, but you won't run mine."

"As long as you live in this house you will live by my rules, like it or not."

"Well, I don't like it! Just you wait sister, dear, one way or another I'll snatch myself a man who'll give me every fine thing I deserve. And for all I care, you can rot away into an old spinster out here all alone if you please!"

Solomon, balancing a laden tray in his hands, trotted in and set it down on the low table in front of Camille. She scrutinized the offering and frowned. "Where is the cream for my coffee, Solomon? You know I take cream."

"Missy Treasure say save de cream fer churnin'.

Hard times, she say, missy." Solomon nodded vigorously. "Ain't dat de truth, Missy Treasure?" His large round eyes reflected his distress.

"Absolutely, Solomon. I've measured the morning buckets. I know precisely how much we have and how long it will last."

For a moment, Camille looked as though she would fling the breakfast tray at Treasure. Instead, she sucked in a breath and flashed Solomon a coy smile. "Now, Solomon, you can see this is important to me. Treasure, poor dear, doesn't have to worry about preservin' her figure. But I can't please the gentlemen if I let myself dwindle to that" — she pointed an accusing finger at Treasure's thin frame — "now can I?"

Solomon ducked his head. "All I knows is Missy Treasure say — "

"You aren't getting your way this time, Camille." Treasure stepped past Solomon, the relief on his face evident. "That will be all, Solomon," she said. "I think Aunt Orange Jane needs your help in the kitchen.

"How dare you humiliate me like that." Camille glared up at her, dark eyes narrowed dangerously, her face flushed. "You treat the slaves better than you do your own family and I for one am quite tired of it."

Treasure gave her a pointed glance. "You don't appear to be suffering the deprivation."

"You're just jealous. It's so obvious. I've got my mama's face and my mama's figure and you . . ." She laughed. "From what Seamus used to say about your mama, seems the only thing you ever got from her was to live in her shadow. I declare, Treasure, from that cameo portrait of hers your papa so loved, you might be a changeling. You know, I do think he loved that portrait better than he ever loved you. He took that with him. And what did he leave behind?"

Anger and pain struck with such force Treasure was sure Camille could see them burn in her eyes. Her

28

hands clenched at her side, opening and closing with her attempt to remain calm. She would sooner die than show Camille how deeply her remarks wounded.

"I refuse to discuss Papa with you. But I will admit you are like your mama. She never had any sense of shame either."

Camille bowed her head in a mockery of abasement. "No, I fear I have no shame at all. You, sister dear, are prudish enough for us all."

"Please get dressed, Camille. Anyone might come calling and see you in your nightdress. It's scorching hot already; the day is half gone." Treasure sat down in one of the chairs by the fireplace ticking off the day's chores in her mind, speaking aloud more to herself than her stepsister. "We've near fifty sets of socks to finish knitting for the slaves before fall, and the down in those milkweed pods out back has to be spun into wicks before I can restock the candles, and the twins' shoes. . . ."

"Are positively unsightly. I won't have my little sisters seen one more Sunday in those." Camille delicately nibbled at one of her biscuits, then immediately slapped it down with a grimace. "My breakfast is ruined."

A sudden spate of determined yapping quelled Treasure's urge to tell Camille exactly what she thought of ladies who slept away the morning and demanded more than their due. She decided it was a well-timed interruption since confrontations with Camille tended to yield only headaches.

Hearing footsteps in the hall, Treasure called out, "Solomon? Has someone called?"

"You might say that."

That voice. . . . Smooth and dark as the best Kentucky bourbon, Treasure saw its owner in her mind before he appeared in the doorway.

Donovan River.

He hadn't picked up any respectability during his

29

night in the valley. His clothes fit loosely, and he wore them negligently, as if they were of little consequence. Leaning against the door jamb, he tugged at one corner of his black slouch hat and flashed her a disarming smile. "Good morning, Miss McGlavrin."

A strange uncertainty suddenly clutched Treasure. Her fingers tightened convulsively against the rough cotton of her skirts. She knew she must look a sight after working all morning dressing out the strawberries and raspberries. But until today, it never occurred to her to care if callers found her in such a state.

She could imagine Donovan's thoughts as he glanced around the parlor. What was she—a drab wren in scruffy brown, her hair untidy, wound with a ragged scarf—doing in a room appointed for a peacock? The parlor was cool ivory and rose, with fat chairs, marbled fireplace, and an intricately carved grand piano dominating the center. It was made for Camille in her frothy confection of a gown, not Treasure in faded utility cotton.

Treasure, pushing aside her discomfort, faced him with aloof disdain. "I thought I had made it very clear we had nothing further to discuss, sir. You are not welcome at Rose of Heaven."

"Now, Treasure, that is certainly no way to treat a caller." Camille unwound herself from the settee, measuring slow steps to Donovan and offering him her hand. "Treasure has the most frightful manners, Mister River. But I can remedy that. I'm Camille McGlavrin, and of course, I know who you are."

"Camille!" Treasure drew a breath. "Camille was just leaving to dress," she said evenly, with a hard stare at her stepsister.

"Why, sister dear, I'd rather be introduced to a gentleman as handsome as Mr. River here in my nightdress, than looking like a field hand." She glanced up at Donovan through a billow of lashes. "You appear

30

to be a discriminatin' man, Mr. River, which do you prefer?"

Donovan eyed her figure and said with a hint of a smile, "It's been my experience, ma'am, the real beauty is under a woman's trappings. It often takes a time to uncover it."

The words were honey in his mouth, but the hard glint Treasure saw in his expression added an edge to them, Camille she knew, was oblivious. His cool smile had been enough.

"Well, how interesting," she said. "But I do believe I can change your attitudes. If you'll excuse me, I'll stop embarrassing my poor sister and change my attire. Then you won't have to work so hard to make a choice."

"Oh, I doubt it'll be much of a choice, Miss McGlavrin."

Camille glowed. "I shouldn't think so." Brushing past Donovan, she kept her eyes fixed on his until she was well out the door.

"I'm sorry you won't be here to enjoy the results of Camille's transformation, sir," Treasure said tightly once Camille was gone. "If you think you can bully your way onto my property, you're sadly mistaken. I've asked you to leave. Next time, I'll save you the trouble of making any choice."

Instead of the expected retort, Donovan rubbed a hand over his jaw, giving her an odd look. For a moment, Treasure thought he might turn and leave. But finally, he sighed and pulled a crumpled envelope from his shirt pocket. "I brought my invitation with me this time," he said.

Treasure looked at the envelope then at him. Why did the strange expression on his face suddenly arouse a feeling of unease? Her fingers brushed the proffered paper. Then she pulled her hand back, uncertain. "I don't care to see whatever it is you've concocted to make me believe your lies."

31

"Come now, Miss McGlavrin. I wouldn't have taken you for a coward."

His tone, half-teasing, half-challenging, spurred Treasure to snatch up the letter. She held it in her hands, rubbing her fingers over the yellowed paper.

"I'm not leaving until you read it," Donovan said, folding his arms across his chest. "Besides, I think you'd rather settle this between us. A courtroom can be very humiliating. I'm certain we would both rather avoid it."

The quiet authority in his tone gave Treasure pause. He sounded almost like a completely different person, a man accustomed to giving orders and having them carried out without question. And one thing rang certain — Donovan River didn't appear a man who made promises lightly.

"I might have guessed a man of your stamp would use threats to get his way," she said.

Donovan shrugged. "Call it what you will. I'll do whatever it takes to get you to listen."

Treasure glared at him. "Fine. I will read it, but after I do, I expect never to see your face at Rose of Heaven again."

Her finger had slipped under the flap of the envelope when a flurry of petticoats and high-pitched squeals burst into the parlor.

"Sissy! Sissy! Don't let her make us do it!"

Two small pairs of hands clung to her legs, looking up at her with pleading faces. In the wake, a stout woman, her hair in disarray, came scuttling through the doorway.

"Spoiled rotten potatoes! You two is nothin' but."

Treasure shushed the two youngsters holding on to her knees as if their lives depended on it. "Abigail! Erin! Whatever are you going on about now?"

"Mammie Eura Mae is gonna make us wear those awful dresses to town," Abigail wailed.

"It hurts my stomach," Erin added, nodding vigorously.

Twin faces looked at her hopefully. At times, Treasure could scarcely tell them apart. Their strawberry curls, freckled noses, and huge green eyes were a matched set. But Erin was slightly thinner and taller than Abigail. And in her five years of growing up next to her aggressive, self-confident twin, none of it had rubbed off.

"We just won't put them on." Abigail stomped her feet. "You won't do it and we won't either. We want to play in the dirt with you."

Treasure blushed under Donovan's smirk. Of all the times for Erin and Abby to be difficult.

"You shoulda knowed lettin' deese chillun out in de garden were a mistake, Miz Treasure. Now dey nebber gonna put on der fancy dresses 'cause dey say big sissy don't wear 'em." Eura Mae clucked her tongue and shook her head at the twins.

Donovan laughed outright, and Treasure wished herself elsewhere. She smothered her embarrassment under a stern dignity. "Erin, Abby, you two listen to me. It is not the same for me. I've told you two many times you must pay mind to your mammie. Haven't I?"

The twins nodded solemnly, but from the mischief in their eyes, Treasure knew her familiar lecture went unheeded again. "Erin and Abigail—you two march up those stairs this very minute with Mammie Eura Mae or I'll take a switch to you both."

"I don't think that's necessary," Donovan said, casting a frown in Treasure's direction. Ignoring Treasure's attempt to protest, he bent down on one knee, giving the twins his beguiling smile. "So you're going to town, are you?"

Intrigued by a new face, the twins released Treasure and turned, hand in hand, to Donovan. "Yes, we are," Abigail said.

"Do you like to go to town?" he asked, receiving enthusiastic nods in response. "I see. I'll bet there's one special store you like best. The one with the lemon drops and hard balls, maybe?"

"And red licorice and taffy," Abby said. "Erin likes chocolate, too," she added graciously.

"Well, then, I'll make you a little deal. You be good girls and do as your sister asks and you can each have one of these to spend on your favorite candy."

Before Treasure could see how he had done it, Donovan made two shiny coins materialize, one in the palm of each hand.

The twins squealed with delight. But when their eager fingers grasped for the coins, they magically disappeared.

"Wait a minute," Donovan said, eyeing them with mock severity. "We have to shake hands on this deal. And then I'm going to give your coins to Mammie Eura Mae. When you keep your bargain, she'll give them to you. Agreed?"

The girls looked at each other then back to Donovan. His expression was strictly business. Abigail thrust her plump palm out to him. Cautiously, Erin followed suit.

"By the way, my name is Mr. River, and it certainly is a pleasure to do business with such lovely young ladies."

That oddly refined voice again. It struck a strange discord with his appearance, Treasure decided.

"Thank you, Mr. River," Abigail chirped, nudging Erin in the ribs. Her twin mumbled her thanks as well, then both scampered out of the parlor and up the long staircase to their rooms.

"Lawdy be." Eura Mae looked after them. Turning back, she stared hard at Donovan and then at Treasure. Finally, with a wide smile and a shake of her head, she followed her charges upstairs, humming to herself.

34

Treasure faced Donovan, not certain whether to be angry or relieved at his interference. She lifted her chin, affecting a self-righteous attitude she did not feel. "You bribed them," she said tartly.

"You would have had them beaten."

"My, but you have a vivid imagination, sir. I wouldn't have had them tied to a whipping post, you know. I just don't believe in spoiling them."

Donovan got to his feet, his face serious. "And I don't believe in frightening a child into obedience."

Stung, Treasure snapped, "Perhaps you'd like to take over the rearing of my family along with the running of my plantation?"

"No, actually I wouldn't." He glanced to the envelope still in her hand. "You were about to open that, I believe."

Treasure had hoped he had forgotten the missive. But there was no avoiding the moment now. She cursed the slight tremble in her hands as she tore open the envelope and unfolded the worn sheet of paper.

Having no other means by which to pay my debt, I deed my plantation, Rose of Heaven, all properties and holdings included, to Mister Donovan T. River, Twenty-fifth day, February, 1839. New Orleans, Louisiana.

Treasure didn't need to see the signature to recognize the awkward slant of the *t*'s, the exaggerated capitals.

Lord in Heaven, he did it!

She blinked, trying to think and see clearly enough to discover it was all a mistake. It couldn't be Papa's scrawling all over the paper, Papa's writing facing her with the bitter truth.

Pressing a shaking hand to her forehead, Treasure felt the room lurch around in a sickening wave. The paper slipped from her hand.

35

Donovan's hands touched her waist, her arm, guiding her through a strange mist to the settee.

"Should I throw him out now, Miss Treasure?" Elijah's deep voice cut through the fog, bringing the room back into sharp focus.

"No. Elijah — wait." Treasure sucked in a steadying breath. She looked up and realized Donovan sat next to her, his hand still curved around her arm. He was close. Too close. Close enough for her to be aware of the scent of him, musky, sun-warmed, very male. She moved away, to the far side of the settee, trying to gather her wits about her.

This can't be. Papa, you wouldn't have done this, not to me, not to Rose of Heaven.

"Treasure . . ." He said her name and his dark voice stroked her as surely as if he'd touched her. "Treasure, I'm sorry. I didn't realize . . ."

"That I'd care so much? Think nothing of it, sir. I suppose you expect me to accept that — that piece of nonsense as proof."

"It's your father's hand. Admit it. You wouldn't have been so upset if it hadn't been."

"Even if my papa did write that, you must have somehow forced him." Treasure fixed him with a hard stare. "But since he is dead, I suppose you believe there's no way I can prove that."

Donovan rose, ignoring the threatening ripple of muscle in Elijah's shoulders. "I'm no murderer, pretty lady," he ground out derisively. Then the ire in his voice turned to menace. "But don't push me too far."

Standing also, Treasure bit back the sudden surge of fright rushing through her veins. "Your threats won't change my mind. I'm not given to swooning."

"Spoken truly enough," he remarked wryly. "Woman, you're not given to anything but your own blind, obstinate will — "

"And you're the lowest, most despicable bounder I've ever had disgrace my parlor!" she railed.

Their eyes met like thunder and lightning, the strain of barely suppressed fury etching a deep furrow in Donovan's brow. Treasure's breath came fast and short and she watched the quicksilver tightening of his lean jaw muscle. Angry as she was, their argument filled her with a strange thrill. She was so used to holding back her feelings, maintaining a calm exterior, that giving vent to such strong emotion was an exhilarating experience.

To her surprise, Donovan smiled, a sardonic expression. "You're enjoying this, aren't you?"

His perception startled her. "I'd enjoy it if you left. Elijah, wait by the front door. Mr. River is leaving."

"Mr. River is not leaving," Donovan said. "No matter how many times you repeat it."

"Why, I certainly do hope not." Camille swept into the room, a vision in a violet lawn gown that favored her exotic beauty. "Treasure, I am surprised at you, speaking to our guest in such a horrld manner."

Treasure ignored her stepsister. She was watching Donovan. He watched Camille, but he seemed distracted, as if she were not at all what he expected. And no wonder, Treasure thought, a bitter twist in her heart. Few men could withstand Camille at her determined best.

"Well, Mr. River" — Camille whirled once around — "have I succeeded? Or do you still contend a woman's virtues are hidden from view?"

"I'll admit, I may be forced to reevaluate my conclusions," Donovan said with a polite bow.

"I don't believe I'll be satisfied with that. Perhaps you would care for a walk around the grounds while we discuss the matter."

Donovan shot a look at Treasure. She met his gaze, stoic, unmoved.

Keeping his eyes on Treasure, Donovan said, "A little air is what we need right now."

"You're quite right," Camille purred, laying a hand on his arm.

Treasure refused to react as she watched them walk away, Camille's dark head bent to Donovan in intimate invitation. As soon as she heard the click of the front door, she dropped onto the settee, haunted by the echo of Camille's low, sultry laugh, but more by the lingering presence of Donovan River.

No sooner had they gone than Elijah returned to the parlor with a tall glass of lemonade and a plate of Orange Jane's cinnamon cakes.

"It's near enough to supper," he said, setting the tray on the table in front of her. "Aunt Orange Jane sent this along."

"She certainly is thoughtful," Treasure said, knowing Orange Jane had done nothing of the kind. Elijah never failed to appear just when Treasure needed him, often before she realized she did. It was a comfort of sorts, knowing she had at least one ally at Rose of Heaven. Purchasing Elijah had been a risk at the time — she'd been warned a slave with an education, and white blood in his veins, would be trouble. But so far, he'd proved to be nothing but faithful and honest.

"You can go now, Elijah," she said, smiling. "I'd like to see those railings for the new porch finished today."

"Yes, Miss Treasure. But I'll be close by."

"I know, Elijah. I can count on you."

When he had gone, Treasure made a pretense of nibbling at her cakes, too restless to be hungry.

Everything seemed to be going wrong at once. The difficulties of planting. Her sisters. Problems at the bank. And now Donovan River.

Could Papa have done such a thing? Treasure tried to consider the possibility reasonably, but her emotions defied her. Abandoning her meal, she curled up on a corner of the settee, hugging a pillow to her chest, her chin buried in its goose down softness.

"A chance, Papa, I just need one chance to prove to you I can do it."

The whispered resolution held no comfort now. Treasure suddenly ached to cry, to loose the emotion coiled inside her.

But she had forgotten how.

Eight-year-old Treasure lay in her narrow bed, too excited to sleep. She tried to imagine animal shapes among the shadows on her ceiling, but all she could think about was it. The gift.

Finally, unable to stand another moment, she tossed the bedclothes aside and retrieved her package from its hiding place in her wardrobe. No matter what Mammie Eura Mae said about waiting, she just had to give Papa the picture tonight.

Papa and Lettia's room was quiet and Treasure slipped in. She went straight to Papa's pillow, smoothing her hand over it. Before she laid her present there, she hugged it to her chest, kissing it for luck.

This was the perfect picture. One Papa would cherish always and hang proudly on the wall of his study. She had been so careful, painstakingly drawing the old magnolia, Papa's favorite, then working each stitch like Lettia had taught her, making them all perfect.

It had taken ever so long. When she tied the last stitch today, Mammie Eura Mae had helped her dig through the attic for a frame, and then she'd decorated paper with colorful flowers and wrapped it up for Papa.

Papa wanted her to be good at ladies' things, like needlework and talking prettily, things Lettia was forever nagging her about. This would prove to him she could do something besides follow him around the fields, dirtying her best frocks.

Treasure turned to go, but on impulse she decided to hide behind the big dressing screen. She nearly giggled aloud, thinking how surprised Papa would be when he found her gift.

Heavy footsteps sounded in the corridor and Treasure crunched behind the screen, a hand on her mouth.

"Lettia," Papa boomed as he threw open the bedroom door, "dinna forget that damned lamp tonight."

A little of Treasure's excitement dimmed. Papa sounded as if he was in a temper. She hoped he hadn't been drinking bourbon again.

"Certainly, suguh, anything you want." Treasure could hear Lettia move about the room, rustling back the bedclothes.

"What the devil is this?" her father demanded.

"I don't know, honey. Looks like somethin' one of the girls made."

Papa gave a grunt and Treasure heard the paper rip. Now he would be happy.

"Satan take me, I dinna know what I did to deserve this. 'Tis another damned bit of useless clutter." Treasure's picture hit the floor with a loud crack. "Aren't these cursed daughters good for anythin' else? 'Tisn't fair, Lord in Heaven, it isn't fair!"

"Now, Seamus, honey . . ."

Treasure barely heard her stepmother's attempts to soothe and cajole. She squeezed her eyes tightly shut. She had done it now. Papa was mad. She had upset him again. Treasure wanted to run, to fade away. But she was trapped forced to listen to every hurtful word.

"Easy, suguh," Lettia said. "It must have been Treasure. The girl has no better sense than to leave a thing like that lying around. I'm sorry, honey, but I have tried to teach her. She just doesn't have the talent to be a real lady."

"She nigh well breaks my heart. She shoulda been a son. 'Tis a fine curse on me, havin' all these daughters. No man should have to bear it. A lass is worthless to me."

"Now, Seamus darlin', there is one thing a woman is good at givin' you." Treasure thought Lettia's voice sounded extra smooth, like the times when she wanted a present from Papa.

"And what have I gotten from it?"

"I can still give you what you want, Seamus. If you give me somethin' in return. Come on now, darlin'."

Treasure heard the bed creak and groan and then Papa mutter, "You do it right this time, Lettia."

Her natural curiosity about their exchange muffled by her hurt and fear, Treasure began to feel strangely panicked about being trapped. She hugged her arms to her body. If Papa caught her, she'd be blue for weeks.

Gradually, though, the strange sounds and murmurs from her father and Lettia started her wondering. What could they be doing? Unable to stay motionless a moment longer, Treasure crept to the edge of the screen and peeked around the edge.

The scene in the room stunned her into a frozen figure, small hands clutched to the screen. Papa was lying atop Lettia, and from his fierce movements, Treasure was sure he must be killing her. Lettia was squirming, as if she wanted to get away, but Papa didn't stop.

Suddenly sick to her stomach, Treasure flattened herself back behind the screen, trying to keep from retching.

The minutes seemed to go on forever. Treasure, her eyes pressed tightly together, prayed over and over that they would stop. At last, a long groan filled the room and then, there was silence.

After a moment, Lettia gave a low laugh. "That's right. Sleep, you old fool. I don't need to be a man to control you and your money, Seamus McGlavrin. All I have to do is part my thighs."

Treasure waited until Lettia dimmed the lamp and she could hear nothing but Papa's rhythmic snores. Then on wobbly legs, she crept out of their bedroom and scurried back to her own.

Curled in a ball on her bed, Treasure thought about the picture she'd been so proud of. She hated it now. Lettia could beat her black, but she'd never pick up a needle and thread again. She'd find a better way to please Papa, something that boys, not girls, were good at.

Treasure wanted to cry remembering Papa's painful words. But she kept back the tears even when they burned at her eyes. Papa hated crying.

And if nothing else, she could do this right.

A soft heated breeze, redolent with the heady perfume of magnolia, drifted through the open French doors, and played with wisps of red-gold hair. The slight motion tickled Treasure's nose, coaxing her awake. She brushed at the errant tendrils and realized her head had slipped to the arm of the settee.

Stretching the stiffness from her neck, she slowly sat up, knuckling her eyes like a sleepy child.

"Did you enjoy your nap, pretty lady?"

Treasure started. Seated in the chair across from her, Donovan smiled at her wide-eyed surprise. "How long have you been there?"

"Not long. I didn't want to wake you. You looked as if you could use the sleep."

Unable to think of a reply, Treasure rose and began brushing out her skirts. "I see you've found another hostess," she said, annoyed to notice Bonny stretched out over his boots in apparent canine contentment. Bonny who made it a point of ignoring or detesting nearly everyone else. "Did you lose your little wager with Camille?"

Stirring Bonny from her resting place, Donovan

42

eased out of his chair. "I'm not in the habit of losing, Miss McGlavrin."

"Precisely what are you in the habit of doing, sir?" Treasure asked pointedly. "So far all I know about you is that you are not above stealing a woman's home and land. I can't help but wonder what past treachery you might have been embroiled in. Tell me, could it be the timing was fortuitous for you to leave Louisiana when you did?"

Donovan's eyebrows knitted together. "You wound me." Treasure was almost tempted to believe he meant it, until she saw one corner of his mouth curl into a teasing smirk. "I didn't leave Louisiana to escape the law, and while I don't lay claim to sainthood, I've never done anything to anyone that they didn't deserve."

"What did my papa deserve?"

The smile vanished from his lips. "I'll tell you what he *didn't* deserve, whether you want to hear it or not. After coming here and seeing what he did to you and your sisters, I know he sure as hell didn't deserve my help."

Treasure tensed from head to toe. "If you ever speak of Papa in that manner again, I'll see to it those are your last words."

"I'm sorry. I didn't say it to hurt you. And I didn't come here today to argue." An easy, soothing smile slipped across his face. "And I didn't come for a tour of the roses and violets, no matter how charming they may be. I'd prefer to have you guide me through the fields."

"Unlike my sister, I don't have time to waste strolling through the magnolias," she said, realizing it was futile to question him further about his mysterious past. "I've wasted too much time already, so if you'll do me the courtesy of leaving, I'll return to my business, sir."

Treasure turned her back on him, walking out the French doors to the verandah. Her hands on the wrought-iron railing, she pretended to ignore him. In truth, she was filled with nothing but him.

43

The parlor seethed with the hot silence of the afternoon; only the murmured rustle of a sheet of music as it was lazily stirred by the breeze disturbed the quiet.

He was watching her. She felt the heat of his eyes on her neck. Her nerves screamed with the tension of waiting. Her hands balled at her sides.

At last she heard Donovan's footsteps. Was he gone?

Treasure turned and discovered him the space of an outstretched hand away from her. Looking up, she saw herself mirrored in his remarkable gray eyes.

Slowly, Donovan raised a hand and brushed two fingers over her cheek, drawing them down lower to whisper against the corner of her lips.

Without pausing to consider, Treasure stepped backward and slapped him. Her reaction came so swiftly that she was as startled as he. "Oh!" Her eyes flew to his in sudden consternation. "I didn't mean—"

"I'm sure you did," Donovan said, rubbing the side of his face. He held up his fingers, now stained with distinctively red Alabama soil. "I have this habit of acting before thinking. In this instance, I didn't like to see a pretty face smudged with dirt."

Clasping tense fingers behind her back, she squeezed out a stiff apology. "I'm sorry. It's just—I don't like to be touched—like that."

Donovan frowned. "Like what? With gentleness?" He paused, then added softly, "As if you're an attractive woman?"

"Yes. No. Please . . ." Treasure straightened her shoulders. "I think you've overstayed your welcome, sir."

"Maybe." Donovan strode to the front door, stopping to look back at her. "But I'll be back this evening, baggage in hand. And this time, Treasure McGlavrin, I'm staying."

Chapter Three

One knee in the soft russet loam, Donovan let a fistful of soil sift through his hand, stroking it between his fingertips. It was damp with the dawn's dew, warm and pliable to his touch.

The simple earthy scent — summer and rain and wind held in his hand — evoked an image of Treasure McGlavrin, her slender fingers stained with the same soil, rubbing it in careless abandon across her cheek. He imagined her in these fields, now, at sunrise, her hair a match for the fire on the horizon.

She fought for the right to walk these fields everyday, yet didn't seem comfortable with the privilege. A child-princess struggling to fit the role of queen of an Alabama kingdom.

Except neither the kingdom nor the princess seemed to have yet been awakened by the magical kiss.

"Be hot again, near too hot. But sometime she like de heat, if it come gentle and slow."

Donovan twisted quickly to meet steady black eyes squinting down at him. The man, built low and wiry, nodded several times, his dark, wizened face creased with lines of humor and temper. Straightening, Donovan offered him a wry smile. "I've got quite a lot to learn about her," he said, not certain if he meant Rose of Heaven. "I'm —"

"I knows who you are." The man's eyes narrowed a little more in frank scrutiny. "And you's not what I expected. No suh, you isn't." He stared again, then shook his head. "Hmph. Well . . ."

"I hope I'm an improvement."

The man tilted his head to one side. "Dat may be so. But it's early yet."

Donovan laughed. "So it is. You have me at a disadvantage, I'm afraid. You know me, but I can't return the compliment."

"Bettis. I been helpin' Miz Treasure since d'overseer quit her dis past month. He say he ain't takin' orders from no woman, 'specially no shrew." A crooked grin split his face. "You, suh, is now livin' in his cabin."

"So she doesn't do everything herself," Donovan said, half-aloud. He glanced over the freshly turned field. "I was beginning to wonder."

Bettis gave a derisive snort. "You does have lots to learn. Miz Treasure have a hand in near all things, especially lately. Not like her papa, no suh. Now dat gentleman, he be content to let dis girl find her own way. But she need a sweet hand to turn her to a fine lady."

"I can't see Miss Treasure ever being content."

"No, no suh." Bettis stroked his grizzled jaw. "She love dis land. Here be her heart."

The curious note in Bettis's voice caught Donovan's notice. His words went deeper than their surface meaning. "I don't understand."

A chuckle from Bettis told Donovan he'd spoken his thoughts aloud. "No suh, I don't see as you would. But if a body wants to belong on de land, he got to make it his woman. Got to know how it feel, what it need, when it achin' fer mo' and tired from too much. Can't expect her to give to you less'n you leave somethin' behind. No suh."

Something told Donovan he didn't want to forget what Bettis had just said. He reached into his hip

46

pocket, pulled out a battered, leather journal and scribbled a note to himself.

Bettis tipped his head to the sky, shaking his face at the sun. "Well, suh, I best be gettin' to work fo' Miz Treasure catch me wastin' time." He turned and stomped off toward the barns, calling over his shoulder, "Miz Treasure be settin' out dose snaps today. Best do it fo' noon, I says."

And that, thought Donovan with a rueful grin, is obviously my cue to report to the mistress. He only hoped a night's sleep had soothed her temper.

But recalling the heat in her eyes, Donovan decided he'd be more likely to draw four aces on his last dollar.

"Emmaline, how many times have I told you? You are here to collect eggs, not sketches of chickens."

The stub of charcoal skittered nervously over the paper and Emmaline turned dismayed brown eyes to her sister. "I am sorry, Treasure. I only stopped for a moment. The Emperor stood so quietly today, I didn't dare miss him."

Treasure followed Emmaline's point to where a large red bantam rooster sat perched atop a post of the poultry yard fence, eyeing them with regal disdain. "He is a sight, but you can't be forever drawing in that book when there's work to be done. Sometimes I believe those sketches of yours are more real to you than reality itself."

Emmaline's thin fingers fidgeted with her charcoal stick. She was silent, but the contrition on her pale, innocent face softened the hard line of Treasure's mouth. "I didn't mean to snap," she said softly, brushing her fingers over her sister's head. Emmaline was so quiet, so sensitive, it pained Treasure to say the slightest unkindness to her. But Emmy's complete disinterest in the day-to-day goings-on of the plantation tried her patience. She would send Emmy out to fetch eggs or mend the button on a dress and, more likely

47

than not, find her propped under a tree, sketching whatever had caught her fancy.

"It's all right," Emmaline said, then added, nodding solemnly, "I know you're just worried about taking care of us."

"For a thirteen-year-old, you understand more than is good for you, I do believe." Treasure tucked an errant strand of sienna hair back into Emmaline's unruly braid. "Now, I'm afraid the Emperor is going to have to wait for his portrait. Aunt Orange Jane is expecting those eggs."

With a sigh and a wistful glance at the Emperor, Emmaline struggled to her feet, tucking her charcoal and tablet into one of her sagging apron pockets. She tugged up the enormous willow basket abandoned earlier. It rocked precariously in her arms, threatening to dislodge the windfall of brown and white eggs.

"Be careful, Emmy, or you're going to scramble those eggs before they ever get to Aunt Orange Jane," Treasure said, already striding up the narrow path that led from the chicken yard to the kitchen and its attached garden.

"You know," Emmaline said as she paused by the garden where Treasure was returning to her morning planting, "I really don't like beans, especially snaps."

Treasure glowered at the seeds in her hand, drawing a giggle from Emmaline. "They aren't my favorites either."

Emmaline brightened. "Then just throw them over the fence and forget them. I would. Then you wouldn't have to spend all morning in the sun, poking them into the dirt."

Treasure shook her head, exasperated. She bent back over the neat soil row to push the seeds in one at a time. "If I did that every time I didn't care for a task, we'd surely starve."

"And never let it be said a body starved on Miss McGlavrin's plantation."

48

Startled, Treasure darted up and was greeted by Donovan's amused gaze. "You've got quite an armful there," he said to Emmaline, ignoring Treasure's frown. Gently, he disengaged the basket from Emmaline's arms, his smile charming a blush to the girl's face. "You must have a hundred chickens," he added, peering at the eggs.

"Forty-two, Treasure says," Emmaline said. "I've never bothered to count them."

Donovan laughed. "Wise child. A taxing occupation, if ever there was one."

"Emmaline . . ." Treasure gripped the handle of the hoe, forcing calm into her voice. "Aunt Orange Jane is waiting."

"Then let's not keep Aunt Orange Jane in suspense," Donovan said. "Lead the way, Miss Emmaline."

You could probably charm fish from a pond, Donovan River, Treasure thought as she caught the look of intent interest on Emmaline's face. *And a place at Rose of Heaven from you,* she reminded herself.

How easily she'd succumbed. Those compelling gray eyes caressed hers until finally she had let him bully and cajole her into allowing him to take up residence in former overseer's cabin yesterday. If only he had remained the Donovan River who'd shown up on the doorstep of Rose of Heaven: insolent, disreputable, dangerous.

But as quick as a summer storm, he had conjured honey from vinegar and became the smooth, sweet-talking gentleman that nearly convinced her he was innocent as a babe and genuinely concerned for her fate and the future of Rose of Heaven. Thinking now of how expertly he had manipulated his way into her life, how carefully he had evaded her questions about his past, her mistrust of him returned and multiplied.

Treasure consoled herself with promises he would

49

be gone just as soon as she proved the note he had produced was a fake, a clever ruse on his part.

Only getting the proof seemed, at the least, a monumental task. The truth was in Louisiana, where Papa had met his death, and she couldn't pack up and leave without abandoning Rose of Heaven and her sisters to the mercy of Mr. River.

If I could just figure out his plan, what he really wanted out of Rose of Heaven. Donovan River didn't strike her as the kind of man who stayed anywhere for long. From what she'd observed so far, hard work was as foreign to him as Alabama soil. He must be an outlaw, or a gambler at the very least; surely he was the lowest form of Yankee. He was sharp enough and handsome enough to make a living by his wits, that was certain. Did he plan to revive Rose of Heaven, then sell it off for a quick and tidy profit? Or would he bother to work that hard?

The back door of the kitchen slammed shut, scattering Treasure's thoughts. She looked up and her eyes were drawn inexorably to him.

Donovan walked slowly toward her, lean muscles savoring each fluid movement. Stopping at the corner of the garden, he rested his back against a fence post, a smile playing at the corner of his mouth. From the expression in his eyes, Treasure didn't need to guess at his thoughts.

Donovan River was trouble.

"Were you looking for something?" he asked, all innocence.

Flushing, Treasure nonetheless answered coolly, "Nothing you might have."

"Don't say no until you've heard my offer."

"I wouldn't be so quick to waste my breath, sir. You'll need it quite soon to talk your way out of a hanging."

Touching two fingers to his forehead in a mocking salute, Donovan's smiled widened into a raffish grin.

"Yes, ma'am. I'm duly warned."

Treasure resumed her planting with a vengeance, determined to ignore him.

"You know, Miss McGlavrin, you seem to have a fascination for soil. I'll admit, I wonder what you look like without it covering you from head to toe."

"I am hardly in the mood for your observations this morning. Unlike Emmaline, I don't have anyone to do my work for me."

Donovan raised a brow. "Seamus told me he had nearly one hundred slaves working Rose of Heaven," he said, doubt evident in his voice. "Surely on an estate this size, there's one who can tend the kitchen garden."

"Since Papa left, we've had to make some allowances." Treasure couldn't meet his eyes.

"Allowances?"

"Nothing to concern you, sir." Turning her back, she whacked at the row under her feet, venting her churning emotions on the soil.

He watched her. She felt it as surely as if his gaze was a caress. Treasure forced her attention to the work at hand, but her senses stubbornly ignored her mind's commands. Her eyes had ruthlessly memorized the lazy slant of his muscular body against the post, his gaping shirt. She inhaled him, felt the heat of him, trembled with her own sudden agitation.

She hated it. She was exhilarated by it. Groping for a measure of reasoned control, Treasure bent to push in another seed. It tumbled off her quivering fingertips. "Damn!"

"Treasure." Donovan's voice savored her name.

She didn't dare look up. "Yes?" was the only word her lips would form.

"Treasure, I've never known anyone so anxious to win the honor of toiling all day in the sun, and worrying about seeds and chickens and a house full of sisters."

51

Treasure straightened, meeting his eyes. He looked honestly perplexed, as if she truly were a new experience. She answered solemnly. "Then you've never met a woman who loved her home as I do."

"I've never met a woman like you, Treasure McGlavrin, that's for certain," he said softly.

There was no trace of mockery in his manner, but Treasure hesitated to believe him sincere. He was a liar, a thief, and possibly a murderer. No matter how gentle, how tender he seemed at times, he was what he was, and she'd be a fool ever to forget it!

Donovan tilted his head to one side, studying her with unnerving intensity. "Tell me—why didn't you just find an accommodating relation to take you in and leave all of this to someone else?"

Her mouth set in a defiant line. "You mean leave it to you."

He shrugged. "To anyone. You could have sold out a long time ago. I've only been in town two days and I've already had one interesting offer."

"Let me guess—Ira Stanton. Well, let me tell you something, sir, I'll burn in hell before I let that miserable bounder set one foot on Rose of Heaven!"

"Why, Miss Treasure"—Donovan slapped a hand to his chest in mock horror—"that's surely no way for a lady to speak."

Irritation struggled briefly with unexpected amusement. The engaging humor in Donovan's eyes and his roguish grin won the fight. Treasure's mouth twitched into a small smile. "I suppose it isn't. But as you have so kindly pointed out, I am no lady."

"You underestimate yourself."

"I'm honest," Treasure said firmly, recalling his admiration for Camille and her lady's charms. "I hardly think most ladies of your acquaintance wear garden soil and dare to speak in such a bold manner."

The laughter on his face was replaced by an unfathomable expression. Donovan hesitated a long moment, then with deliberate slowness, straightened and stepped over the low garden fence.

He walked toward her, not stopping until he was close enough for Treasure to see herself mirrored in his clear gray eyes. Slowly, he reached out and took her hand, bringing it to his lips. He brushed his mouth over her dirt-stained fingers, his warm breath caressing her skin. "There's more to being a lady than wearing silk and making polite conversation," he murmured.

Confused by his unexpected attentions, Treasure gazed wide-eyed at him, her fingers lingering in the gentle embrace of his.

In the next instant, Treasure's cold reason asserted itself. What was she doing, letting him befuddle her this way? Yesterday she had been ready to see him hang, and today . . . Pulling her hand away, she said, her voice unsteady, "I must finish setting these out. It's getting late and I —"

"Late?" Donovan laughed. "It's barely light."

Treasure scooped up another handful of seed. "I have to get these cabbages and early snaps planted. And then there's the salting. . . . And if I don't get to the stockings today, there won't be enough for winter and —"

Donovan wrapped a hand around her wrist, letting the seeds in hers drop one by one into his own palm.

His touch excited her pulse. And it frightened her. "Stop it," Treasure said through gritted teeth.

"Stop what?" His inscrutable gaze seemed to peer down to her soul.

"Stop that! I have work to do."

He let the last seed fall into his hand and released her wrist, letting his fingers drift over hers. "I'll help." Following her example, he used one finger to slide each seed into a hole, pressing it in firmly, drawing his finger out to plant the next. "You're allowed a rest from all this every now and then, you know."

53

"No, I don't know," Treasure said, hating the prim sound of her voice. She began working the opposite end of the row. But her eyes were fascinated by the hypnotic rhythm of his hands. She burst into sharp speech, trying to cover her confusion. "If I don't work, none of us eat or are clothed. It's obvious you know very little about managing a plantation. If you expected a life of easy luxury, I fear you're going to have your proper share of disappointment."

"I'll take my chances. And I'm not easily disappointed. There's always a way to turn the odds in your favor, if you're willing to take a risk."

"And how much did you risk to get Rose of Heaven?"

The quick stab didn't ruffle him. "My neck. A certain group of gentlemen wouldn't have been too pleased to discover I stacked the odds in my favor during a high stakes game to back your father out of a corner."

The seeds she held dropped from her hand unnoticed. Treasure stood staring at him in disbelief. "Are you telling me you won Rose of Heaven in a card game?"

"Not exactly. Your father deliberately lost it to me." He finished his task and moved to her, resting his hands on her shoulders. "I'm sorry, Treasure, but it's the truth. Seamus didn't want Rose of Heaven, and for some reason, he was determined I have it."

Shaking free of his hold, Treasure stepped back, eyes cold. "I must say, your stories are becoming more creative, sir. But you can hardly expect me to believe Papa was a low gambler who gave you Rose of Heaven out of the goodness of his heart."

"He left you here, alone, without once looking back," Donovan said, his voice taut. "Did he ever contact you — even once — in the entire time he was gone? Did he?"

"He wanted to. I know he wanted to." Treasure

whirled away from him. She wouldn't let him shake her. She wouldn't. Her hands knotted into fists at her sides. "I warned you not to talk about Papa—"

"Treasure—"

"No." She turned on him in a rush. "No, I will not listen anymore. You think you can confuse me with your lies and accusations, but I won't let you trick me into giving up Rose of Heaven. You may be here for the moment, Mr. River, but don't become too accustomed to it. You won't be here much longer!"

"I'm afraid, Miss Treasure, Donovan River may be here for a long time." Rader Johnson carefully set his glass of strawberry tea back on the low table, sizing up his young hostess's reaction before he went on. Typically thoughtful before action, he chose his words with extra care. "I know," he said holding up a hand as Treasure's lips parted in protest. "I know what it seems. But I would swear this note is your father's hand. I'm not an attorney, but without proof otherwise it does appear he has a legitimate claim."

"It can't be. I can't conceive of Papa doing such a thing."

"If it is true, Seamus surely had his reasons, Treasure," the woman seated beside Rader said gently. Eliza Johnson's dark blue eyes reflected compassion and concern. "Perhaps he only wanted to relieve you of the burden of having to manage this entire plantation on your own. It is quite a task for anyone, especially a woman alone."

"Papa knew I loved Rose of Heaven, and he did leave me to care for it. Why would he give it to a stranger?" Treasure fixed her eyes on her hands clenched in her lap. "If he truly wanted to quit his family and plantation, he could have sold Rose of Heaven and sent us to my aunt's home. But losing it in a card game—it doesn't sound like the sort of thing any reasonable man would do."

The Johnsons exchanged a glance. Treasure knew they thought Papa, with his wild, volatile moods, might have done just that. She had called them to Rose of Heaven, hoping a discussion of the situation might give her new ideas about how to get rid of Donovan River. Normally, she shunned help from anyone. But handling human problems had not been a part of Papa's lessons about the plantation.

Rader and Miss Eliza were her closest friends and best allies in McGlavrin's Valley. Childless themselves, they had taken Treasure and the younger McGlavrin girls under wing when Seamus disappeared, and Miss Eliza had quickly become Treasure's trusted confidant. Treasure welcomed her warm sympathy and generosity, admired her practical common sense, and envied her loving marriage. Eliza had become a wife at seventeen and the only blemish on her happy twenty-one-year alliance had been her inability to conceive a child.

The couple had made themselves content with nurturing their two prospering enterprises, the valley's general store and only hotel.

"It's a sad thing," Eliza said, moving to sit beside her friend. "But some men just cannot bear disappointment. Perhaps — "

Treasure rose stiffly from the settee, crossing to the French windows at the end of the parlor. She stared out over the stretch of green lawn, seeing nothing. "I know Papa longed for a son. Something I could never be."

"Oh, Treasure, I didn't mean that, honey. Mercy, child, you're falling into such a maudlin state. This Mr. River of yours must be quite a treat to put the cool and controlled Miss Treasure McGlavrin into such a stew."

The teasing tone produced the desired effect. Treasure realized she'd said more than she'd intended to. She covered her embarrassment with a chuckle. "I do sound like a heroine from one of those melodramas Spring is so fond of, don't I?"

"I must say, you have me most anxious to meet your mysterious guest. My heart is all aflutter," Eliza crooned in an affected falsetto voice, touching a coy hand to her flaxen curls.

Rader and Treasure laughed, and Treasure felt a renewed sense of balance. She was glad she had called the Johnsons. Seeing them made things seem easier.

"From what I've seen of the man," Rader said, sobering, "he means to pursue his claims, even if it means trouble."

"Oh, I think Treasure needs a little trouble in her life," Eliza said. "She is entirely too serious."

"It's a serious matter, Liza. We don't know anything about this Mr. River and his dealings with Seamus. I don't care for the thought of leaving Miss Treasure and the girls alone on Rose of Heaven with him." Rader shook his head, concern furrowing his brow. "Your nearest neighbor is too far if there is trouble."

"Elijah is here. And the rest of the slaves," Treasure said, trying to put a reassuring confidence into her voice. "I can handle Mr. River for the short time he'll be here."

"I'm sure you think you can, honey." Eliza laughed, and tossed a mischievous glance at her husband. "Mr. Johnson, you are quite missing the opportunity of this situation. This might be our chance to at last find someone who is man enough for our Treasure." She wagged a finger at Treasure's scowl. "Oh, I know you better than you know yourself. Why, you'd run every last one of these dull-headed roustabouts right into your precious ground in no time. No, only one kind of man will ever tame you, honey; one who can keep pace with you in mind and body. And believe me, unless this Mr. River is the exception, there isn't another man up to the task in this town."

"Honestly, Miss Eliza. Just wait until you meet Mr. River. He's . . ."

Eliza raised a brow. "Yes?"

"Mr. River," Treasure said firmly, "is the worst sort of scoundrel."

"Mmmm . . . well, we'll see, won't we?" Eliza rose, flouncing her skirts into place. "By the way, honey, I missed you at the church social last Sunday."

Treasure avoided her friend's eyes. "Miss Eliza, you know I don't care for that sort of thing. I don't even have a proper dress."

Eliza studied her for a moment, then smiled. "I'll have to set my mind to remedy that. And in the meantime, don't you be fretting about this scoundrel of yours. I'm sure it will all straighten itself out in time."

Eliza gave her a warm hug and Rader patted her shoulder with awkward affection. "I'll be checking in on you. If there's anything crooked about this business, we'll uncover it soon enough."

Treasure walked them to the door, watching as their buggy slowly wound its way down the long drive to the road. She wanted to believe them both, that it would all sort itself out. But Treasure had the feeling she had started down a tangled path, fraught with secreted dangers, and with no way of turning back.

She paced the parlor, turning the matter over in her thoughts, searching for some way to outwit Donovan River. Eliza meant well, but Treasure couldn't afford to wait for matters to smooth themselves out on their own.

She walked the sunny room for nearly an hour before something Miss Eliza had said sparked an idea. Treasure culled it over in her mind, at first rejecting, then warming to the notion, until at last, she settled herself to it.

Straightening her dress, she smoothed back her hair and tucked in the loose strands of auburn. Defiance glittered emerald in her eyes. Shoulders thrown back, small chin in the air, she swept out of the room in a proud stance.

"Let's just see how you like this, Mr. Donovan River."

Donovan paused, curry brush half through a stroke. Amusement and suspicion divided his expression. "You've become quite accommodating all of a sudden. Forgive me if I wonder why."

Afternoon had faded to evening by the time Treasure had found him at the stables. He had lighted a single lamp to chase the twilight gloom and was brushing down the big black stallion in the end stall. Bonnie lay at his feet, wrapped around his heels. Treasure, perched on a bale of straw outside the stall, watched his hands as he talked, liking the deft way he drew the curry comb over the stallion, using the distraction to avoid his eyes.

"I don't see why it should surprise you. If you're determined to stay here, I think you should be willing to earn your keep. I don't intend to support you. And after all," she added, "I'm certain you want to know something about running the plantation you went to so much trouble to get."

Resuming his steady strokes, Donovan smiled. "Now I know you've devised some clever plot. You're never this polite to me."

"I do hope you're not telling me you're adverse to work, Mr. River," Treasure said sweetly.

"Only if it's too long and too difficult." He rested tanned forearms against the stallion's back for a moment, regarding her. An unnerving intensity replaced the amusement in his eyes. "What do you really want?" he asked, his tone low and demanding.

"I've told you." She struggled to maintain the flip note in her voice. "You want to learn about running Rose of Heaven. Working on the plantation is the best way to learn. You could, I suppose, attempt to find someone else to teach you." She drew in a breath, knowing she was wading in dangerous waters. "But there aren't many who can or would, especially if they knew you turned five orphaned girls from their rightful home." Donovan scowled, but Treasure plunged ahead. "And even with the finest overseer, you must know the land or you'll ruin it with neglect and bad management. It only gives back what you put into it."

"You talk about this plantation as though it was a beloved companion rather than a piece of land. Just like your father."

"He loved Rose of Heaven," Treasure said quietly, and for a moment her face softened as she remembered days spent with Papa in the fields. "The work can teach you to love it also. That is what you want, isn't it?"

Donovan started currying the horse's legs, his motion hard and fast: "What I want and what I'm likely to get from you I assume are two vastly different things."

Treasure held her tongue. If she wanted this scheme of hers to work, she had to convince him to go along with her suggestion. "It depends on what you were hoping to get. I thought you wanted Rose of Heaven."

With a final flourish, Donovan finished his task and ran a hand over the stallion's back, smoothing the sleek ebony coat. The stallion nickered softly in response, nudging at Donovan's arm with his nose. "You might be surprised at what I want," he said, leveling her a smoky stare. "I accept your offer."

"Tomorrow then." Treasure's small smile reflected an ambiguous sense of triumph. "At five, in the south field. You can be there at five, can't you?"

"I'll do my poor best, Miss Treasure."

There seemed to be nothing else to say, but Treasure lingered, feeling strangely unsatisfied with her little victory. "Belial seems to like you," she said, as the stallion nudged Donovan's arm again.

Donovan accepted her change of front without comment. "He's just looking for his promised carrot." He fed the stallion the treat then rubbed his ears. "He was in dire need of a good brush-down, so I obliged him."

"No one ever gets near enough to him to curry him down properly. He has a devilish temper—that's why Papa called him Belial. You're the first he's allowed so close."

"He just needed a little sweet-talking," Donovan said, giving Belial a final pat on the flanks. Easing out of the stall, he latched the low door behind him. His face, thrown in shadow, reminded Treasure of the first time she saw him—a dark, enigmatic stranger bringing tumult to her carefully ordered life.

For a moment, he stood in front of her and said nothing, only watched. Then he murmured, "You've got dirt on your face again."

Treasure didn't move as he raised a hand to brush the smudge on her cheek. His fingers trailed over her cheekbone and teased a wispy curl at her temple. Slowly, as if he were coaxing a frightened creature, he slipped his hand to her nape and loosed the hair coiled at her neck, letting the fiery tangle sift through his fingers.

Donovan stared, mesmerized at his creation. Lantern light caught her hair afire with gold and red and favored her face with a warm apricot glow. She looked at him, her deep river eyes secreting her feelings from him.

Treasure tentatively tasted new sensation, for the first time indulging a desire to experience a man's touch. She wondered what he saw when he looked at her so intently. A stern, dowdy slip of a girl? Or something else, something she had yet to discover. She wanted to ask him, but didn't dare for fear of hearing the truth and shattering the fragile enchantment enveloping her.

His fingers tightened in her hair, and for a moment, he hesitated, as if struggling with a choice. At last, he let his hand fall away and stepped back.

"Sweet dreams, pretty lady," he murmured, then slipped out into the twilight before she could rally a single thought.

When she did think, it was only to wonder at the sweet warmth his touch left behind.

Chapter Four

As he smacked at the sun-hardened soil, chipping another portion of row into place, unrelenting heat branded Donovan River's bare back. Taking a moment's respite, he crossed his palms over the scarred wooden handle of the hoe and tried to recall the days when the nearest he'd gotten to being up this early was the end of an all-night poker game. He wondered if he'd ever stand straight again after bending over hoe and being dragged behind a mule and plow six days a week, ten hours a day, for nearly three weeks.

In the distance he caught sight of Treasure leaving the dairy barn, her slender arms carrying the weight of two large buckets. She kicked the door closed behind her and started back up the hill to the big house, bent a little by her burden.

He watched her with both compassion for her situation and irritation knowing she was the cause of his own predicament. "Who'd have thought I'd ever let a slip of a girl order me around like a damned bondsman," he muttered, sending a scowl in her direction.

As fragile-looking as a willow sapling, she hardly seemed old enough or strong enough to care for herself. Yet, not only was she mother to five sisters and a small army of slaves as dependent upon her as her own flesh and blood, but as both master and mistress, she ran the largest plantation in northern Alabama. She awed him. And she frustrated him to delirium.

Donovan swiped the back of his hand over his brow as his eyes followed her struggle up the hill to the kitchen building behind the big house. Did she ever slow down? Would she know how to enjoy a moment's rest if she afforded herself one? Somehow, he doubted it.

Treasure disappeared into the kitchen, and with a resigned sigh, Donovan resumed the rhythmic clap of his hoe into the stubborn red clay. If she kept working him nearly to death every day, he'd learn to hate this land long before he had a chance to find out if he could like it.

No doubt that was precisely what Miss McGlavrin had in mind. The dawn after their meeting in the stables, he'd known exactly how she planned to oust him from Rose of Heaven.

Well, two could play her game. He'd conned better players than Treasure McGlavrin when the stakes were considerably higher. And just to spite her plan, he'd get used to working for a living—sooner or later.

Later, most likely, he thought, envying the silent, mulatto slave toiling without pause at the next row. Huge drops of sweat rolled off his broad, chestnut shoulders. Elijah had been in the field at dawn, working with hardly a word uttered, and no more than a few brief moments of respite. It wasn't only Elijah's stamina that intrigued him, though; Elijah obviously claimed a different background than the other slaves on Rose of Heaven. Someone had taught him to speak correctly, a fact that caused Donovan to wonder if Elijah's education extended to reading and writing. Not likely, he mused, since planters considered even a little learning in their slaves a treacherous luxury.

His insatiable curiosity urged him to ask questions; his intuition suggested caution.

"This does get easier, doesn't it, Elijah?" he ventured, not certain he wanted the answer, but deciding it was an innocuous enough query.

"Yes sir, it does. Time'll come when you won't hurt no more; won't feel anything."

Donovan grimaced. "That's not encouraging."

"Not meant to be," Elijah said with a shrug.

"No one's meant to be out in this horrid sun," a light voice called from behind them. Balancing a brimming bucket, Spring sidestepped row after neatly mounded row. "My, but you two look as if you've just stepped out of the bath."

"Miss Spring, if that's water, I'll believe you're an angel sent to deliver me from your sister's tyranny," Donovan said with a hopeful smile.

"The whole bucket — just for Elijah and you." Spring set the pail down and fished out the ladle. "Mercy, I simply can't imagine why Treasure put you to work in this field. It's the most frightful of the lot. In fact, Papa hadn't used this in, oh, three years, I'd say. You know" — Spring moved a step closer and glanced over her shoulder, — "sometimes I think she's just turned plain mean!"

Elijah abandoned his hoeing for a moment and turned his liquid eyes on Spring. "Miss Treasure has worked mighty hard to keep this place goin' since her papa left."

To Donovan's surprise, there was no jaunty retort from Spring. Instead, she suddenly found the ladle in her hand immensely interesting.

Without a word, she scooped it full of water and handed it to Donovan.

"Why Miss Spring, I do think you've set a personal record — a full minute without uttering a sentence," Donovan teased.

Spring, her somber mood flitting away, laughed up at him. "Really, Mr. River, I can go twice as long as that! And I wasn't being catty about Treasure. I do love her better than anything." She sobered a little. "It's just that since Papa died she's been so — so hard. Mind, she's always been serious,

65

but — mercy! — now, at times she is downright severe."

Donovan rubbed a hand over his shadowed jaw, thinking before he responded. "Your sister is under a great deal of pressure."

"I know," Spring agreed with a hint of remorse. "She always fusses at me for being too carefree. But I do help as much as I can. I just hate being reprimanded like some child!" Spring shot Elijah a direct glance. "I'm a full-grown woman now, and I know exactly what I want."

Donovan intercepted her look and smiled a little at the defiance in her eyes. Spring might resent her sister's tendency to domineer, but they shared that same expression of stubborn rebellion. Lord help the man who crossed the McGlavrin women. "In any case, Elijah's right. Regardless of her indelicate methods, your sister is a devil of a worker."

"Well! I see I'll find no sympathy in the company of you two. Elijah is utterly loyal to Treasure. Aren't you?" Beneath her playful sauciness, Donovan quickly discerned a grating note that gave him pause.

He watched Spring as she passed the refilled ladle to Elijah. When their eyes met, she let her fingers linger on the handle while Elijah grasped it. His large brown hand moved briefly to cover her delicate white one.

Donovan looked away, suddenly feeling like an intruder.

"Spring!"

The sharp call startled all three of them. Spring jumped back and nearly stumbled over her bucket. Elijah resumed his work with alacrity.

Only Donovan remained slouched over his hoe, coolly unconcerned as Treasure advanced on them.

She gave him a hard glare then turned on her sister. "Spring, it's not time for supper yet. Leave these two alone or they won't finish before sundown." Treasure pulled Spring aside for a moment, and Donovan could imagine the words behind her harsh tone.

"You're right, Spring," he muttered to himself. "She needs to learn a little sweetness goes a long way."

"Do you know someone who could teach her, Mastuh River?"

Donovan noted the twinkle in Elijah's clear blue eyes. "Maybe I do," he said. "And do me a favor, stop calling me Master River, master anything for that matter. I figure any two people who've spent this much time working the same ground ought to know each other's first names."

Elijah paused as though weighing the suggestion against its consequences. "That wouldn't be proper," he said finally.

A spurt of irritation sobered Donovan's expression. "It would be if I say it is."

Elijah studied him, no hint of emotion on his face. "Then you don't think like other folks—do you?"

"No, I don't. At least not like the ones here."

Something flickered across Elijah's face, a fugitive emotion Donovan might have called wonderment if it hadn't been so quickly masked. He began hacking at the soil again, his strokes short and choppy. "You best keep that to yourself, Mastuh River. Unless you want more than your share of trouble."

After dismissing Spring with orders to take water to the slaves in the north field, Treasure redirected her displeasure at Donovan. She didn't intend to let him think he could charm either her sisters or her slaves into letting him worm his way out of working.

She strode straight to him, her face set in familiar severity. "Your break is over. I advise you to finish this before supper, Mr. River. Otherwise, I fear you'll be doing it alone tomorrow. I need Elijah to begin repairs on the pasture fence."

With an exhausted sigh, Donovan closed his eyes

and let his head fall back against his sore neck. Treasure tried to look away but failed as slowly he smoothed his hand over sweat-damp ripples of muscle at his abdomen, up through the soft mat of curls on his chest to the back of his neck. Then, with a languid motion, he massaged his sunburned neck and shoulders.

Treasure memorized the path of his hand over his sleek body with her eyes. His sensuous movements distracted her for a moment — until she realized he'd opened his eyes and was watching her with undisguised pleasure.

Their eyes met in a heated clash. Reason told her she should be put to shame for staring so blatantly. Instead, she felt only an odd fascination with the strange, intimate silence lingering between them.

The first times she'd seen Donovan working, shirtless, pants rolled up to his knees, she deliberately turned away, stricken with embarrassment. She couldn't understand her own discomfiture — during the summer, many of the slaves worked in the fields without a stitch. She'd grown up with it, been taught to accept it. Yet for days, just the thought of seeing Donovan half-clad unnerved her.

But not this time.

She felt a wanton delight in the sight of his strong body. She'd secretly anticipated the pleasure of seeing him this way. For the first time, she allowed herself to revel in it, to experience sensations she long denied she could ever have; would ever want. It was something aching, intense yet tender. A feeling she wanted to last.

Donovan broke the strange spell between them with a smile. "You know," he said softly, "your sister thinks you intend to be harsh. I think you're just afraid."

Treasure stiffened. "Afraid? Of what, sir?"

"Of someone else gaining an advantage over you."

68

"What a thing for you, of all people, to say."

"Before you skin me alive, hear me out."

Teeth gritted, Treasure reluctantly complied.

Donovan searched her face for a moment before continuing and Treasure felt he was carefully balancing his next words. "I think I understand you better than you might imagine—or want to imagine. I know what you're trying to do, and it's time you knew I can hold out as long as it takes. Although"—he flashed a rueful smile—"there have been days when I've been a heartbeat from walking down that drive and never looking back."

"Then why didn't you? And pray don't tell me you enjoy the work," Treasure added smartly.

"Damned if I know," Donovan said with a soft laugh. His voice then lowered to a smooth easy pitch. "When I find the answer, you'll be the first to know. But in the meantime"—he slapped the handle of the hoe—"in the meantime you're going to have to try to work the life out of me to get me to leave. Something inside me is compelling me to stay." He shrugged, then added offhandedly, "So, I'll stay—for now."

Treasure smothered jitters of anxiety with the firm grip of self-control. "And what is it that's keeping you here?"

In a breath, he changed into the Donovan River who made her heart pound with a disconcerting mixture of fear and anticipation. Tossing aside his hoe, he stepped closer, slowly circling around behind her. Treasure's senses quivered as he drew near enough for her to feel his breath at her nape; to brush his warm, moist skin against her.

"It might be you, Treasure McGlavrin." His deep voice taunted her ear, a hushed breath of sound.

Chills shot down her spine and Treasure jerked away. *Was he trying to scare her?* She refused to flatter herself into thinking he sincerely was taken with her. But how easily he might believe he could manipulate her into succumbing to his will by tossing his charm at a plain woman. Undoubtedly by now he realized she'd had little experience with men, other than as adversaries. It followed he might assume that same smile that set all the belles in the valley into a tizzy would work on her as well.

And yet, the sincerity in his voice, and his eyes, so soft and yearning, tempted her to believe he actually . . .

No, I can't let him do this to me!

She had to get away from him, had to clear her reason, purge her senses of him. "Stay then," she said sharply. "Stay and work until you drop." She turned to Elijah. "I've a number of errands to run in the valley and it's quite late. Tell Bettis this field must be ready by sundown."

"Yes, Miss Treasure."

Retrieving his hoe, Donovan frowned at her. "Are you going alone?"

"Yes." Leaving no room for rebuttal, she whirled and hastened to the stables, the disturbing notion that his eyes stalked her haunting her all the way.

Treasure paced the richly paneled office of the president of First Valley Bank, waiting for Mr. Clement to keep their appointment. Her back rigid, she twisted and untwisted the cord of her bag.

Outside the half-shaded windows, activity in McGlavrin's Valley had slowed in deference to the scorching afternoon heat. A handful of wagons and surreys rattled their way down the dusty, tree-lined street; a few sign boards creaked with the slight push of the breeze. Across the street, the barber's hound lay stretched out in the shade of a shop overhang.

The lazy quiet did nothing to soothe Treasure's nerves. When the door opened and Mr. Clement entered, she nearly started out of her skin.

70

"Ah, Miss McGlavrin, I'm glad you were at last able to make a sojourn into the valley to visit me. I had begun to fear I would have to come to Rose of Heaven personally to speak to you about this—delicate matter." Mr. Clement cleared his throat several times.

"That won't be necessary now, sir. I am sorry for the delay."

"Please, do make yourself comfortable," the banker urged, as he moved behind his desk.

Treasure lowered herself to sit at the edge of the chair opposite his desk. She tried to adjust the wide sweep of her skirt to the best advantage, hoping she looked the part of the proper, responsible estate mistress.

Eura Mae had chosen her dress, a deep indigo cotton, stiffly pressed, the simple square neckline flattering her slender shoulders. Her hair had been persuaded into a sweep atop her head and she had added a wide-brimmed hat of fine straw.

The hoop felt clumsy, the petticoats hot and scratchy, but Treasure decided she could endure anything if it would win her an advantage with Mr. Clement.

"Miss McGlavrin," he said, clearing his throat again. "As you know, your papa and I were friends from the start of this town. Why, in those days, Seamus was like a brother to me. Yes, yes. But, well, time passed and things grew more complex . . ." His voice drifted off. Recalling himself with a small cough, he continued. "Despite the differences Seamus and I may have had before his tragic death, I have not forgotten our friendship. What I'm trying to say, Miss McGlavrin, is that I have now stretched that friendship to its very limits."

Treasure breathed in deeply. She willed calm into her voice. "I do thank you for your patience concerning our accounts, Mr. Clement. And I assure you, after the harvest I will be able to settle Papa's debts once and for all." Her unflinching outer confidence didn't shelter the frightened girl inside who quaked at the regret on Mr. Clement's face and at the very real possibility she could not make good her promises.

What if the crops failed? What if a drought stole her harvest? What if all her back-breaking work came to naught, and she lost Rose of Heaven to Mr. Clement's bank, or worse yet, to Donovan River?

Mr. Clement sighed. "That would be the best solution, of course. If — I say, if, Miss McGlavrin, I could wait out the months to harvest. Unfortunately, that decision is not mine to make alone. I have obligations to meet as well."

"But it's only a matter of months — "

"It has been three months already. I am sorry, but I must inform you that if payment is not made by the end of this month, I will be forced to take your property to satisfy your papa's debts."

Treasure's heart pounded so hard it hurt. Her hands clenched the handle of her bag. She began to feel light-headed, but fought away the urge to swoon to win Mr. Clement's sympathy. Other women might use such ploys, but she would save or lose Rose of Heaven on equal ground with any man.

She gathered her wits and steadily met Mr. Clement's owlish gaze. "There is no other alternative?"

"I'm afraid we've exhausted them all."

"Very well." She rose with dignified grace. "Then I will have your payment by the deadline. Good afternoon, Mr. Clement."

"Have a pleasant visit with our friendly banker, Miss Treasure?"

Ira Stanton's caustic insinuation interrupted Treasure's daze. Startled, she suddenly realized she'd been standing in front of the bank for an indefinite period of time captive to the turmoil of her thoughts. Lifting

72

her chin, she squared her shoulders and started to move past the mayor. He was the last person she wanted to confront today.

"If you'll pardon me, Colonel Stanton, I am in a hurry."

Ira positioned his large frame directly in her path. He slid the thick chain of his watch between his fingers, toying with the links. "Now, now, it's not polite to hurry off when a gentleman wants a word. What I have to say is certainly more important than any other little errand you may have."

"I sincerely doubt it. Now get out of my way."

"In a minute," Ira said with a sneering smile.

Treasure glared at him. "I'm through listening to your nonsense. Now let me pass or I'll make a scene and tarnish that reputation you're so at pains to preserve."

"You're going to lose Rose of Heaven. Yes, ma'am, that's a promise. So why not pretend to be a lady and surrender it graciously?" Ira leaned forward. "I can think of several ways to express my gratitude, Miss Treasure."

Without a word, Treasure tried to shove past him, but his hand bit into the soft flesh of her arm, holding her firm.

"Your beloved constituents are watching, Colonel Stanton," Treasure hissed, refusing to give him the pleasure of seeing her cringe at his force.

"And I, for one, am sorely disappointed in what I see."

The hint of menace in the voice behind her was— for once—extremely welcome. Donovan stepped forward and took Treasure's arm. His free hand closed around Ira's wrist.

The hard set of Donovan's jaw told Treasure his volatile temper was sorely agitated. Beneath the brim of the hat drawn low over his brow, she saw only a dark, narrowed gaze riveted on Ira.

Ira immediately released Treasure's arm. "This isn't your business, suh," he spat, rubbing at the wrist Donovan reluctantly let go. A venomous anger seethed in his eyes.

"You have this annoying habit of repeating yourself, Colonel Stanton. I wasn't impressed the first time, and I'm certainly not now." Flicking a dismissing glance over the colonel, Donovan looked into Treasure's eyes. "I believe we have supplies to buy." He gently lifted her hand and slipped it through the crook of his arm.

Awash with relief, Treasure allowed him to guide her away from the bank.

"Our business is just beginnin', Miss Treasure," Ira called after them. "Just beginnin'."

Donovan said nothing as they walked down the sidewalk toward the Johnsons' general store. Treasure was grateful for the silence. She wanted to thank him, but at the same time, she was annoyed at both his unexpected presence and his witness to her confrontation with Ira.

She was still struggling with her feelings when she reached to open the door to the store.

"Allow me," Donovan said, beating her to the polished brass knob.

Treasure darted a look at him, somewhat taken aback. "I'm not accustomed to—"

"Perhaps it's time you were accustomed, Treasure."

"I'm content to rely on myself, *Mr.* River." With a toss of her head, Treasure stalked inside the store, Donovan's murmured "yes, ma'am" teasing her ears.

"Why, Treasure, what a surprise to see you." Eliza backed down the ladder away from the bolts of brightly colored fabric she'd been arranging on a high shelf. She took Treasure's hand in a friendly squeeze, then turned with twinkling eyes to Donovan. "And you must be the notorious Mr. River."

74

"I confess, ma'am." Donovan swept his hat off and deferred to her with a deep nod.

Treasure, with stiff politeness, made the introductions.

"You've already met my husband, I believe," Eliza said, making no attempt to hide her appraisal of Treasure's unwanted guest. "And I'm pleased to meet you myself. I certainly have heard a great deal about you. Why, it seems you're all Treasure can talk about."

"I do no such thing," Treasure said, a blush heating her face as Donovan glanced at her and raised a brow in amusement.

"It's most interesting," Eliza went on, ignoring Treasure's discomfort. "Because Treasure doesn't have time most days for gossiping. But then I'm certain you're well aware of that already, Mr. River."

Donovan laughed. "That's quite an understatement, Mrs. Johnson."

"Miss Treasure, is that you?" Rader Johnson stepped out of the counting room. "I'd almost swear my eyes were deceiving me. I began to think you'd given up coming to the valley for good."

"Not quite." Treasure conjured a smile for him. "But only when I have to."

"Well, I'm glad the necessity arose today," Donovan said. "It gave me the perfect excuse to get out of that blasted field."

Treasure turned to him and said sweetly, "I'm surprised you were able to finish the south field so quickly. You did finish—didn't you?"

"No," Donovan answered matter-of-factly.

"How typical of you. You knew I wanted that finished by tonight. I suppose you expect me to take everyone else away from their other duties just to finish your work."

Rader and Eliza exchanged a knowing look. "We still have a room at the hotel, Mr. River," Eliza said with a wide smile.

"Thanks, I'll remember that. But for now . . ." He tipped Treasure a mocking salute. "The boss lady has given her orders, and so finish I will."

Treasure planted her hands on her hips. "How? By starlight?"

Donovan grinned. "Why not? I've had enough Alabama sun to last me through winter. Which reminds me, do you have any salve for blisters? I seem to be having a disagreement with the hoe."

"Over here," Rader gestured to a far corner beyond a shelf of brogans.

Immediately, Eliza pulled Treasure aside. "My, my he *is* devilish handsome, isn't he? A little rough at the edges perhaps, but—mercy!—if you must have an enemy under your roof, why not that one?"

"Miss Eliza, I've told you, he's nothing but a clever scoundrel. I cannot understand your blind acceptance of that man! He's a stranger who may well have murdered my papa. And he is not and will never be living under my roof."

"Oh, come now, child, even you can't convince me you haven't noticed how attractive he is."

"Not in the least," Treasure said firmly. "He may be more charming, but I don't trust him any further than I do Ira Stanton."

Eliza's expression turned solemn. "Is Colonel Stanton still trying to convince you to sell?"

"Every opportunity he can make for himself, including this afternoon. I must admit, Mr. River did pick an opportune time to forget his work." Treasure's faint smile held malicious satisfaction. "After tonight, though, I believe he'll regret it. And if he plans to make up for lost sleep tomorrow, I'll be quick to prove him wrong."

"Treasure, honey, I don't mean to meddle—"

"But that never stopped you before."

"I only have your best concerns at heart."

76

"I know that. That's why you're the only person I listen to."

Eliza patted Treasure's hand. "Then listen now. Did it ever occur to you that Mr. River abandoned his work out of concern for you coming into town alone?"

Treasure blinked. "No. Why should it? He simply took the first opportunity to escape work. I don't think he's ever worked a full day in his life before now."

"If you say so," Eliza said sweetly, shaking her head.

Treasure pretended not to understand the implication in Eliza's voice. "Here's my list. I know it's quite lengthy, but—"

"Don't fuss about it, honey. I'll just put these on your account."

"I'll settle with you as soon as the harvest is in," Treasure said, not quite able to meet Eliza's sympathetic gaze. "You have my promise."

"Liza is right—don't fuss," Rader said, returning from his errand with Donovan. "Your credit is good. For as long as it takes. Always has been. You know that."

To Treasure's chagrin, Donovan said, "That's very generous of you."

Rader, his eyes thoughtful on Treasure, brushed aside Donovan's thanks. "Nothing generous about it. Miss Treasure always keeps her promises."

Warm under Rader's protective kindliness, Treasure avoided Donovan's curious glance and bustled about the store after Eliza, gathering up sundry supplies. When they had found everything, Donovan insisted on helping her load her purchases into the back of her surrey.

"Do you usually drive out alone?" he asked, tying down the final bundle.

Treasure struggled to think of an excuse to keep him

from offering to travel back to Rose of Heaven with her. "Ever since Papa died. Despite common opinion, a woman can manage one horse and a surrey quite easily, without a chaperone."

"Then you can make it back by yourself?"

Expecting to feel relief, Treasure forced herself to quell a wash of irrational disappointment. She balled her fists at her sides. "Of course," she snapped, adding stiffly, "Thank you for your help."

He touched a finger to his hat. "My pleasure, pretty lady. I'll be a while behind you. Don't forget to save me supper. Emmaline has an irritating habit of stealing the last biscuit."

Treasure wanted to ask why he was staying in the valley, but didn't. "Maybe I'll even rescue a scrap or two of ham from the twins," she answered lightly. Climbing up onto the driver's bench, Treasure took up the harness leathers. She was about to slap them against the horse's back when an impulse took command and she turned back to him. "Mr. River—I hope you don't have a notion to confront Colonel Stanton. He's my problem, not yours. Let's keep it that way for both our sakes."

Without waiting for his reply, she gave the leathers a quick smack and the surrey jerked into motion, leaving Donovan standing at the curb, watching until she disappeared from his sight.

Treasure stole another glance out the kitchen window, her mouth pursed in a tight line. No matter how many times she looked, the drive to the big house stayed empty.

Turning away from the fogged glass, she picked up another supper plate to wash. Nearby, Emmaline began to lift a stack of delicate china plates to their shelf in the large oak hutch.

Treasure cringed. "Be careful Emmy, those were my mama's—"

"I know. They were part of your mama's wedding china. You tell me that every time we use these plates."

"Do I? I didn't realize . . ." Treasure snatched another look at the drive.

Noticing her sister's preoccupation, Emmaline tried to offer a word of comfort. "Don't worry, Treasure. Camille has stayed out long past supper before. She always comes home, though."

Spring, absently polishing a linen cloth over one of the bucket ladles, smiled faintly. "What makes you think she's watching for Camille, Emmy?"

"Well, who else? Oh — Mr. River." Emmaline turned to Treasure. "You're waiting for Donovan, aren't you?"

"You've become quite familiar with Mr. River," Treasure said, sidestepping Emmaline's question. "You should know better than to address any gentleman by his Christian name."

Emmaline shrugged and studied the dish cloth in her hand. "He doesn't mind. And I've just talked to him some," she mumbled. "He likes to look at my sketches. And he understands about — things. You know."

"I see," Treasure said, although she didn't understand at all. What could Emmaline and Donovan River have in common?

"You didn't answer Emmy's question."

Treasure scowled at the mischief on Spring's face.

"I am concerned about both Camille and Mr. River."

"Being together, I suspect," Spring teased.

"That's absolutely absurd, Spring. You know my feelings for Mr. River. And I just don't trust Colonel Stanton. I fear Camille is with him again tonight even after I told her to stop allowing him to pay her court. He's so much older than she. I fail to see why he caught Camille's fancy."

Spring sighed, her fingers tracing over the ladle. "He's the only man in the valley with tolerable looks and passable manners with money in his pocket. Besides Mr. River, of course. Would you rather see Mr. River pay her court?" Her expression was guileless as she turned wide sparkling eyes on her sister.

"I think Mr. River is far more handsome," Emmaline said. "Don't you Treasure?"

Slapping down the plate in her hand, Treasure snapped, "Have you two forgotten that man is trying his level best to take away our home? Have his good looks charmed that little detail from your minds? And besides, from all appearances, he hasn't a penny to his name."

"There's no need to get angry, Treasure," Spring said with a pretty pout. "You take things so seriously. We were just funning you."

"I prefer you devote your energies to getting these dishes finished. And I do believe that is quite dry." Treasure nodded at the ladle in Spring's hand.

"Oh!" Spring flushed. She shoved the ladle in the pocket of her dress. "I'll put it away when I've finished."

"I'm certain you will," Treasure said, glancing curiously at her sister.

"Dat's de last of 'em, Miz Treasure." Orange Jane reached around behind and untied the strings of her apron, her long, delicate hands neatly refolding it into a square. With a sigh, she smoothed her mass of silver-laced ebony curls, tucking a few troublesome wisps back into her bright red headscarf. Treasure always admired the cook's ability to maintain her stately dignity, whether scouring cooking pans or managing a last-minute meal. Watching Orange Jane fold her apron into a drawer, Treasure wished she possessed even a spoonful of the cook's gentle grace.

Moving casually to Orange Jane's side, Treasure glanced at her sisters, then lowered her voice.

"Where's the plate I asked you to set aside?"

Orange Jane leaned close to Treasure and winked, the sparkle of a shared secret in her eyes. "In de larder, Miz Treasure, just like you says. I saved a bit for Miz Camille too, but as she be meetin' dat gentleman in town, I don't rightly know if she'll be wantin' it."

The question hovering on Treasure's lips was stilled by Bonnie's furious yapping, followed by the slap and click of hooves and wheels in the front drive.

Silence hung heavy in the kitchen. Treasure glanced at the inquiring faces of her sisters and Orange Jane. "I'll see to it," she said, forcing herself not to walk too quickly. When she reached the front hall, she stopped, staring in stunned surprise. Camille leaned heavily against the staircase rail, tottering, Donovan's arms the only barrier between her and the floor.

For a moment, they all gaped at each other. Then Treasure found use of her voice. "What have you done to Camille?" she demanded.

"Rescued her doubtful reputation, if not her pretty neck, Miss McGlavrin." Donovan spat the words at her, hard fury striking steel in his eyes.

"What are you talking about?"

"I found her with Stanton at the hotel salon in the middle of a rousing fight. She was going for his throat when I pulled her off him."

"I don't believe it!"

"Take a look at Stanton's face tomorrow, then. Camille managed to do a little damage with her nails. Although from the amount of whiskey Stanton looked to have put away, I doubt he felt it."

Treasure stared at him, anger mixing with the shame she felt seeing Camille in this state. Suddenly aware Emmy and Spring were witnesses to the humiliating scene, she turned quickly to summon Eura Mae.

"Mammie Eura Mae! Take Miss Camille upstairs at once," she ordered when the mammie scuttled in, dogged by Spring and Emmaline.

Treasure looked at her sisters and pointed to the stairs. "Upstairs. Now."

Both moved slowly, Emmaline wide-eyed with curiosity; Spring looking as if she smothered a laugh.

Camille waved them up with a limp hand then turned bleary eyes to Treasure. "Such authority, sister dear, it quite makes my knees quake. A pity that particular trait has nothing to do with being a *real* woman." Camille giggled, clinging to Donovan's shirt to keep from falling. She leaned toward Treasure, leering at her dress. "You're not still wearing that horrid old scrap of homespun, are you? I do declare Mama was right about you — poor little Treasure. You will be lucky to marry the overseer. If Aunt Orange Jane doesn't snag him first!"

Eura Mae clucked in disapproval. Hurrying forward, she detached a wildly laughing Camille from Donovan. "You done sharpened your claws 'nough for one night, missy. Too much cream for dis little cat tonight, I say." Ignoring Camille's pouting protests, Eura Mae led her up the staircase.

Treasure summoned as much dignity and self-control as she could muster before turning her attention back to Donovan. Expecting anger, she shrank back at the tenderness of his expression. Had she misjudged him? She suddenly wanted to apologize, but pride held her tongue. "It's late," she said finally. "We can discuss this tomorrow."

A chill settled in his eyes, pulled his mouth into a hard line. "As you wish." Turning on his heel, Donovan strode out the door, leaving it hanging open behind him.

Treasure took several steps in his wake. But she stopped in the open doorway. She wanted to call him back, but he disappeared into the night, leaving her alone with the echo of his fury.

Chapter Five

Treasure dropped her pen on the ledger in front of her, pressing her fingers to her eyes. The figures on the pages were beginning to wobble and dance in the dim lamp light. Their balances leered at her. No matter how many times and ways she totaled them, they remained woefully short at the end.

Two days. She had two days to find the means to satisfy Papa's debts. Mr. Clement had been regretful, but firm. He would take Rose of Heaven if she could not pay.

And even if somehow she found the money, Donovan River remained with his promissory note and his determination to claim her plantation. She had worked too hard to let either Mr. River or the bank succeed. But how could she stop them?

Shoving the ledger aside, Treasure got up and paced to the long window at the far end of her bedroom. She stood in front of the open panes and let the night's breeze gently fan her face. It was near midnight, but the air was still hot, laden with a clinging dampness. Under the waning moon, fog curled silvery fingers around shadowed images of magnolias and pines.

She leaned on the sill and looked out over the plantation. From her second-floor vantage, the southern vista of Rose of Heaven stretched, it seemed, to infinity. It stirred in her a fierce sense of possession. Here, she belonged.

Treasure felt she had sowed her heart and soul in the soil. Now she waited for it to give to her in return.

In his teasing moods, Papa had often compared her to the land. All the promise buried deep, stubbornly refusing to let it show until a body sweated and fussed over it long enough to get through the hard rocky crust and find the heart sheltered beneath.

The fanciful notion usually gave her comfort. To-night, even the serenity of Rose of Heaven at rest failed to calm her careening thoughts, and after a few moments, Treasure reached up to close the window, deciding a few hours' sleep might clear the confusion in her mind. As she did, a glow of amber caught her eye.

The small spot of light hovered near the slaves' compound. Then, bobbing and wavering through the dense grove of trees, it moved toward the south field.

"What on earth . . . ?" Treasure craned out the window, watching until, at last, the dot of light reappeared in the field, hopping along then seeming to hesitate, finally stopping.

Her first thought was Colonel Stanton. If he was up to some mischief . . .

Treasure tried to reason out all the possibilities. If it was the colonel, what was he doing in the middle of the field this time of night? She wouldn't put him above trying to frighten or sabotage her into leaving. But he could do precious little damage in the south field and a single light was poor help if he was trying to cause trouble.

And Mr. River? He'd disappeared after their confrontation over Camille. She assumed he'd returned to his borrowed cottage.

Treasure briefly considered summoning Elijah or Bettis, but decided against it. Surely whatever—or whoever—it was, she could resolve it alone.

84

Darting down the stairs, Treasure paused only long enough to snatch up the rifle. She walked quickly toward the south field, still culling over likelihoods in her mind in the time it took to trek from the house through the trees to the fields beyond.

As she neared the edge of the field, she could make out a solitary figure silhouetted against the backdrop of starry sky. Land and sky coupled in a single blackness and the figure—seated on a box, a lantern beside burning like a tiny sun in the night—might have been the only person in the world.

The scene gave Treasure pause as an impression of isolation swept over her. She carefully moved closer, almost hesitating to disturb the solitary midnight sojourn.

Yet common sense argued that no one with any legitimate business would spend the night sitting in a field. It was long past the hour for honest labor.

Stopping close enough for a clear aim, far enough away to avoid inviting trouble, Treasure firmly shouldered the rifle. "Who is it?" she called out. "If you're up to no good . . ."

With a familiar languid ease, the broad-backed figure turned. "You're going to have to shoot me this time, pretty lady." Treasure immediately recognized Donovan's deep, mocking voice. In her mind, she clearly saw his familiar, provoking smile, the glint of amusement in his eyes.

"Damn," she muttered under her breath. Lowering the gun, Treasure strode up to him. "I've a mind to do just that. What are you doing out here? Do you know the time?"

Donovan glanced up at her, his head tilted to one side. "No. Do you?" Dim yellow light flickered over his features, illuminating the angles of his cheeks and jaw, leaving his eyes a mystery, dark rounds, unreadable through night's changing shadows.

"Of course. It's past midnight." She hoped he heard

confidence instead of anxiety in her voice. "For someone who promised to be up by five, you don't seem too concerned. And you didn't answer my question. What are you doing?"

With a slow, stretching motion, Donovan came to his feet. "I finished the work you said had to be done here." He held up his battered journal. "And now I'm doing a little work of my own."

Treasure raised a brow. "In the middle of the night? There aren't too many lessons to be learned about crops and planting at this time of the evening, Mr. River."

"Depends," Donovan said, his voice husky and low, "on what you're trying to learn. I felt like being here, so I came."

"That seems to be your excuse for a number of things. Don't you ever have a reason for what you do?"

Shoving the journal in his back pocket, Donovan propped one black boot up on the chicken crate he'd used for a chair, resting his arms on his knee. "Sometimes," he said, leveling her a stare. "But more often I just have a feeling."

Treasure stared back at him through the amber haze, trying to imagine what it would be like to act impulsively, guided only by instinct, without taking time to consider. She failed. The notion was too alien; and, somehow, frightening. "I don't understand you," she said finally.

Donovan shoved his hat back from his forehead a little. "That's all right, pretty lady, neither do I." He straightened, massaging a hand over the back of his neck. His shirt hung open and Treasure's eyes were drawn to his taut chest muscles, flexing copper-brown in the lantern's glow with each rhythmic move of his fingers. "What are you doing up so late?" he murmured.

The easy question made her realize she'd been staring. "I was working, too." Quickly, she glanced away. "The ledgers needed to be finished. I saw your light and I thought someone might be trying to cause some trouble."

"So you dashed out armed with your trusty rifle. Didn't you think to call Elijah?"

Treasure threw her chin in the air. "I can handle a gun as well as any man and better than some, Mr. River."

"I've no doubt of that," Donovan said with a laugh.

Despite herself, she liked the sound of his laugh, rich with unbridled feeling, as beguiling as his smile. Sometimes, she thought, it was hard not to like Donovan River—whoever he was. But it is easy to mistrust him, another voice reminded her. Abruptly, she turned from him. "It's late. I'm going back to the house."

Donovan bent and picked up his lantern. "I'll walk with you."

"That's not necessary. I'm perfectly able—"

"To take on Satan in Hell, if need be. I know."

The gentleness in his voice, a softness as dark and heated as the night itself, stilled Treasure's reply.

Donovan stayed motionless for a long moment, watching her. "I know you're independent," he said finally, "and capable and eminently reasonable. But there comes a time when everyone needs to be taken care of. Even you, Treasure McGlavrin."

Treasure tried to answer and couldn't. She shook her head, uncertain what she tried to deny.

Donovan smiled, slow and easy. With a languorous motion, he reached out and took the rifle from her unresisting hand, resting it against the crate. When he turned back to her, Treasure's breath caught in her throat. Reason told her to walk away. But the words in her mind were hard to hear over the pounding of her heart.

She felt as if she were suddenly caught up in the

87

movements of a dangerous dance. And even uncertain of the steps, she was driven to join in the treacherously seductive glide and sway.

Donovan took one step closer, then waited, searching her face. Treasure wanted to read the expression in his eyes, but they were liquid silver in the moonlight, compelling, concealing. At last, as if he had infinite time, Donovan took one of her hands in his. He slowly raised the other and pulled the end of the ribbon that confined her hair, until it slipped free. Loosed waves of auburn slid around her face.

Treasure tested each new sensation as if it would be her last. The rough firmness of the hand enclosing hers. The earthy scent of him. The singing in her ears.

Donovan's hand savored each movement as his fingers sifted through her hair, then brushed her face. With an exploring touch, he gently traced her cheek, the soft line of her jaw, and then drew his thumb over her lower lip, parting her mouth.

His hand drew her a step nearer. Treasure looked up at him. She tried to think. Her mind was a riot of clashing emotions and thoughts, none of them clear.

One finger tilted her chin. Donovan let it pause there for a moment, then bent and brushed his mouth against her forehead. He kissed her temple, her cheek — soft, lingering caresses.

At last, looking into her eyes, he touched her lips with his.

Her first kiss. Treasure quivered with the sweet heat spreading over her. It was nothing harsh, nothing frightening, nothing like Papa's assault on Lettia. Instead, it was a gentle dawning, a trembling in her blood. She tasted the honey of his mouth as his lips coaxed her into a tentative response. Timidly at first, her fingers tightened around his.

Donovan returned the pressure as he slowly lifted his head. Treasure waited for him to draw her back. But he only smoothed a few wisps of hair from her forehead, a smile playing over the sensual line of his mouth. Easing her hand upward, he touched a kiss to her fingers, then released her.

"It's very late, pretty lady."

Treasure stared. "Late?"

"Only a few hours until dawn. I wouldn't want to encourage you to oversleep."

Was that all he was going to say? A stiff demeanor crept over her, dispelling the softness in her eyes. "How kind of you, Mr. River. You needn't be concerned. I'll be in the pasture at five. I expect to see you there."

Donovan moved toward her, pulled back. "Treasure . . ."

"If you'll pardon me, I must get back to the house." Retrieving the rifle, Treasure turned on her heel and started back, back straight, eyes fixed forward. She refused to let herself feel anything except annoyance and humiliation at her own weakness. How foolish and naive she must have seemed, swooning beneath his practiced seduction.

But when dawn came, she was still sitting at her bedroom window where she had ended up, staring, unseeing, toward the south field.

Donovan lay on the narrow bunk, watching the night fade to a muted early morning gray. The pallid light was unkind to the dim interior of the cabin. Dusty and rough-edged, the few bits of furniture resembled old bent figures, long forgotten; even the air seemed musty from neglect.

The bleakness, Donovan thought, was oddly appropriate. He had tried to sleep, but had finally given it up when it became obvious he couldn't.

Wakefulness, though, was a painful experience. Remembrances of Treasure McGlavrin plagued him, and for no good reason, he told himself. She was just another woman. Little more than a girl, really. And

89

hardly the prettiest, the most sensual, the most willing he'd ever kissed.

Yet she clung to his thoughts like a burr, tenacious and just as irritating.

More often than not, he wanted to throttle her. But he kept coming back when he should have been saying good riddance.

Why?

Slowly sitting up, Donovan rubbed a hand over his jaw, wishing he had the beginning of an answer. The scruffy terrier sleeping at the end of the bed lifted his head and slapped his tail against the covers.

Maybe because I can't let go of Seamus's gift. "Or maybe I'm just tired of roving," he muttered, scratching Bonnie behind the ears. *And maybe I don't want to leave her,* he thought, unwilling to let the possibility escape his lips.

Last night. . . . His fingers remembered the soft planes of her face. Even now, if he were struck blind, his hand would recognize her by touch; his mouth would recall the sweet tentative innocence of hers.

Her guileless response to his caresses had been more provocative than any artful embrace. He had pulled back, afraid of his own wellspring of feeling, of frightening her with the undisciplined strength of desire. In consequence, he had wounded her touchy pride.

Donovan jerked on his boots and shirt, trying to vent some of his pent-up frustration. There had to be a way of reaching her, some compromise in this situation. But he was damned if he knew what it was.

He was rummaging through a cabinet in a vain search for coffee when a raucous pounding rattled his door. "Mastuh River," Bettis called. "You alive in there, Mastuh River?"

Donovan ran a hand through his hair, knowing he probably looked as if he'd spent the night with a bottle.

Bettis came in grinning, shaking his head at Donovan's rumpled clothes. He proffered a steaming mug of fragrant black brew. "Hot as hell, sweet as love, and black as night—jus' as a man should have it," Bettis said with a wink. "I done sweet-lipped Miz Jane outta dis. Miz Jane, she be a hard woman when it come to her kitchen, but"—he smiled broadly—"Miz Jane and I has an understandin'. I figured you would be needin' it dis mornin' and, suh, you does look like you do."

"Thanks," Donovan said, with a grimace. "I may need the entire pot to convince me to go back to that field. I can't find anything that doesn't hurt."

"Some days de work does dat, suh, yes it do. But . . ." Bettis held up a finger and then began scrabbling in his pockets. After a thorough search he at last produced a small linen pouch. With careful ceremony, he extracted a small pinch of powder and sprinkled it in Donovan's cup. "Fix it right up. I done used it more dan a time or two."

Donovan eyed the brew with suspicion, sniffing at it. "What is it?"

"Willow bark, yessuh. No better cure for aches— 'cept maybe those of de heart."

Avoiding the question in Bettis's voice, Donovan cautiously took a sip. "I'm willing to try anything this morning."

"I'd say you might," Bettis said. "But take a piece of advice from a man with plenty experience." He grinned. "I'd do my romancin' at a more kindly hour. Yessuh, I surely would."

With a wink, Bettis disappeared out the door.

Treasure had been pacing the pasture for fifteen minutes when Donovan arrived. He picked up the hammer she'd hung on a nearby fence post, grabbed a handful of nails, and swung his powerful arm. One by

91

one, he pounded, beginning repairs on acres of broken fence railings. She barely gave him a glance. But she knew he watched her.

"Be too hot again today, Miz Treasure." Bettis glanced at the horizon then at the dirt under his feet. "Yessum, be a mighty hot one today." Scuffing the dry soil with his boot, he bent and poked at it, shaking his head. "If we don't get no rain soon, be bad trouble."

"I'm well aware of that," Treasure snapped. Bettis raised a brow. She drew a breath and said, "You and Elijah make sure the last planting gets done in the south field today. The ground's ready," she said, picturing Donovan working by moonlight to finish the work as promised. "So, it looks as though we can stay on schedule. I'll check back with you at noon."

Without a word to Donovan, Treasure left them to their work.

Walking quickly, she headed toward the small work shed situated at the edge of the north field. She planned to finish the candle making today, a task she hoped would divert her mind for at least a few hours.

And it would keep her away from Donovan River. Treasure dreaded the notion of speaking with him. Even seeing him had been a trial.

She imagined he was probably laughing at her shameless abandonment or, what seemed worse, he regretted the entire incident in the field.

Treasure didn't want his mockery, his recriminations, or his apologies. She wanted him to leave. Mr. River had completely upset her ordered life, inflicting chaos on both her routine and her emotions.

Before he came, she'd walked away when emotion tried to touch her, keeping her heart safe from the pain of feeling, staying strong and in command of herself. But when he touched her, she couldn't run from her heart. He aroused feelings she didn't want, didn't need. It frightened her. At the same time, like a taste of heaven, it left her hungry for a nameless satisfaction.

She wanted him to go.

Her idea of working him off Rose of Heaven had backfired. Instead of pushing him farther away, Treasure was constantly aware of his presence at her every turn. When he wasn't engaged in some task, he followed her around, making endless notes in his ever-present journal, asking questions even the youngest of slaves on her plantation should know the answers to.

What would happen if he stayed?

Absorbed in her thoughts, Treasure failed to see the two riders until they were nearly upon her. Their shadows crossed her path and she looked up, squinting into the sunrise.

With the sun behind his head, the lead rider's face was thrown in black shadow. Treasure, though, didn't need light to recognize Ira Stanton. Behind him, Jimmy Rae reined in a snorting black stallion, a sneer curling his mouth.

"Why good mornin', Miss Treasure," the colonel said, flicking a finger over the brim of his hat. "You are just the person I came to call on."

Four ragged, red weals marred his face and the edges of two more poked above his stiff shirt collar. Donovan had, for once, apparently been telling the truth, Treasure decided. The thought of Camille with Ira Stanton leant her an extra measure of anger.

She slapped her hands to her hips. "It's too early for a social visit, Colonel Stanton," she said, her voice devoid of the least hint of politeness. "As there's no one to receive you, I'll ask you to leave. We have nothing to discuss. Especially after your shameful treatment of my sister."

"Miss Treasure, I do regret allowin' Miss Camille to be seen in that unfortunate condition. But your sistuh can be a hard woman when she doesn't have her own way. I am sure she's willin' to forget the entire incident." Ira gave her a condescending smile. "Now I know you can't yet consider me your friend, but I think it would be in your best interest to heah what I came to say."

Both Stantons slid off their horses. Ira sauntered to her, gracing her with a courtly bow. The salacious glint in his eyes mocked any notion of civility on his part and Treasure stiffened. Unease, like nervous spiders, crawled on her skin.

She moved to step backward, but Jimmy Rae stood in her path. Arms folded, he rocked back on his heels, menace implied in the smug stance.

Treasure refused to bow to the threat. "I sincerely doubt anything you have to say is in my best interest, sir," she told Ira, squarely meeting his gaze. "Now if you will pardon me, I do believe you can find your own way back to the road."

Ira smiled tightly. He fingered the watch chain looped over his vest with jerky movements. His eyes challenged her. "I'll say what I came to say, Miss Treasure."

"Please yourself. I don't intend to listen."

"Even when it concerns your late daddy's business? Business it seems he cared to keep secret from certain folk."

Treasure knew the sly thrust of his words. She smiled coldly, twisting their meaning. "Only with those he didn't trust, sir."

"I'm truly pained at the inference, Miss Treasure. But no matter. As I have been reliably informed, Mr. Clement will soon be taking Rose of Heaven to pay your poor daddy's debts. I'm prepared to spare you that humiliation."

Treasure fought an uprising of anger. How could Colonel Stanton have known about Papa's debts? Someone had betrayed her, either unwittingly — or purposefully. "How kind. But I have no intention of

94

accepting any offer from you, Colonel Stanton. I think I have made that quite clear. You will never own Rose of Heaven."

"Don't be so sure of yourself." Ira smiled. The gesture held no mirth, but a crafty malice. "In two days, I'll be the one payin' your daddy's debts. Which means I'll own Rose of Heaven — and you, Treasure McGlavrin."

Knowing the Stantons relished any sign of distress from her, Treasure forced a mockery of a polite smile. "I'd never be so bold as to debate a gentleman. But until you hold the deed, Rose of Heaven is mine, and I want you to leave."

"I'm only lookin' out for your best interest, Miss Treasure. You should know that by now." Ira reached out and slid the back of his hand over her face.

Treasure slapped it away. But Jimmy Rae, with a quickness she didn't anticipate, caught her wrist from behind in a bruising grip, yanking her against him. "Didn't your papa never teach you any manners, little Miss Treasure?" he purred in her ear. "That's no way for a lady to show her gratitude."

"Jimmy Rae." Ira scowled at his brother. "I told you, boy, I don't want none of your kind of trouble. Not now."

"And I'm tired of waitin' for you to romance your way onto this piece of land. I can convince Miss Treasure to show her thanks." A sneer curled his mouth. Treasure twisted her arm. He tightened his fingers. His free hand, resting against her hip, began to climb her waist, groping against the curve of her breast.

A sick disgust choked her. She squirmed to one side and then kicked out at his legs with as much strength as fury could muster. Jimmy Rae grunted in pain, and Treasure jerked her wrist from his grasp. She stumbled back out of his reach, her eyes afire with anger. "That's how grateful I am, Jimmy Rae Stanton. Now get out. Both of you. Unless, of course, you'd like

95

your constituents to know just how you conduct business, Colonel Stanton."

"No one in town would believe a word you say," Ira growled. For a moment, Treasure feared he would damn the consequences. Instead, he whipped around and climbed back on his horse. "You don't have a handful of friends in that valley. You've made sure of it the way you treat this place like it's some goddamned kingdom. Just you remember that, Miss Treasure."

Jimmy Rae, nursing his shin, made no move to follow his brother's example. "You remember something else, Miss Treasure—"

"Treasure, is something wrong?"

Treasure's heart leaped at the soft query. Whirling around, she met the startled eyes of Emmaline, poised a few feet behind her, her small wedge face pale. "Of course not, Emmy. The gentlemen were just on their way." She turned to the Stantons. "Weren't you?"

"For now," Ira snapped. "Get movin' Jimmy."

The command went unheeded. Jimmy Rae was staring at Emmaline with undisguised interest. Emmy, suddenly flushed, looked back. Mingled with fear and uncertainty, Treasure recognized a gleam of familiar fascination in her expression. The expression Emmy reserved for interesting objects and animals who caught her fancy.

"Emmaline," she said sharply, "you have chores to do." *That boy means ruin to any decent girl's reputation,* Treasure silently fumed. Oh, how she wished she could pack her sisters up and send them away—to Aunt Valene in Atlanta, anywhere, to protect them.

With reluctant slowness, Emmaline started toward the big house. "Good mornin', Miss Emmaline," Jimmy Rae drawled after her. When Emmaline darted a glance at him, he smiled, easy and knowing. Emmaline bit her lower lip, fidgeted with the skirt of her apron, then turned and ran up the path.

Jimmy Rae, the cocky smile still plucking at the corners of his full lips, swung back onto the stallion. With a smirk, he tipped his hat to Treasure.

Jerking the horse into a turn, Ira kicked it into a gallop toward the road, his brother following. Treasure watched the Stantons disappear in a cloud of red dust before she took pity on her starved lungs and drew in a long tremulous breath.

She had no doubt Ira Stanton meant every word. She was in a corner, just where he longed to have her. With the slightest of opportunities he would take Rose of Heaven. And Jimmy Rae . . .

Treasure shuddered at the memory of his hand against her. But even more repulsive was the way he had openly scrutinized Emmaline. Sweet, innocent Emmy, who had little defense against Jimmy Rae's brand of bold sexuality. Her fists cinched into tight balls.

She had to get that money somehow.

Forcing her legs to move, Treasure resumed her trek to the woodshed, deliberately drawing out the walk.

Her options were dwindling fast. She was expecting a letter any day now, that might mean salvation. And perhaps Rader and Miss Eliza could help. There was always her mother's jewelry, yet Treasure doubted the sale of the few remaining baubles would be enough even to dent the enormous debt Papa had managed to incur.

When she reached the work shed, Treasure paused outside the door a moment, absently rubbing her bruised wrist. She hated to wait. But until the post arrived with her anticipated news, wait was all she could do.

The acrid smell of hot tallow greeted her in a heated rush when she pushed open the door. This was one task she hated, but today she welcomed the detested labor. If it couldn't let her forget, at least it would keep her from remembering for a while.

She was busying herself with tying the cotton wicks to the dipping stick when a sharp kick flung the door open.

Donovan strode in, his face set in hard lines of anger. "What happened?" he demanded.

Treasure calmly knotted another wick end to the stick and reached for another, pleased her fingers didn't betray the tremulous quiver in her heart. "Exactly what are you talking about, Mr. River?"

"You know damned well what I'm talking about. And stop calling me Mr. River like I'm your hired help."

"My, we are in a temper today. You should spend more time sleeping, instead of spending your nights in the fields." Treasure refused to show him how much his unexpected presence disconcerted her. He might believe his charm could win wars, but this was one battle he was destined to lose. In some ways, he was no better than Ira Stanton.

Donovan scowled at her. Before she could protest, he plucked the dipping stick out of her hand and, taking her hand in his, pulled Treasure to her feet. "I know the Stantons were here."

"Really? Do you have spies?"

"Emmaline told me. She was upset and wanted someone to talk to."

So she ran to you. The thought stung Treasure's heart. Emmaline—none of her sisters—ever confided in her. Donovan had been here less than a month, and already he had won over at least one of her young siblings. "They were here," she said, turning aside to study the kettle of wax beside her.

"And?" Donovan growled. "Am I going to have to beg for the story?"

Treasure snapped back around to face him. "And Colonel Stanton wanted the same thing he always wants. Rose of Heaven. The one thing he is not going to get no matter how many threats he makes."

"Threats?" Donovan poised, very still.

"Nothing to get in a fuss over," Treasure said, then added, trying to cover her slip, "don't let it concern you. I handled the Stantons long before you came."

She turned to resume her work, hoping to dissuade any further questions on his part. As she did, Donovan caught her bruised wrist and Treasure, startled, sucked in a sharp breath.

"What in . . . ?" Donovan raised her hand. His face darkened like a midnight storm when he saw the blue marks already beginning to shadow her fair skin. "Stanton? Which one?"

"Mr. River—"

"Never mind. This time I know the answer." For a moment, his hand gently loosened around her arm, softly caressing the tender bruising. Then, abruptly, he let her go, and without a word, strode out of the shed.

Treasure took a step forward. The urge to follow him was strong. For several suspended moments, she stood riveted in place, emotion fiercely warring with her reason.

She had work to do. The thought made her choice.

For the long morning she worked alone, kept companion only by the cold emptiness in her heart.

"I'm sorry, honey. We surely would help if we could. You know that." Eliza set down her glass of tea and laid a sympathetic hand on Treasure's arm. "It's just times are hard in the valley right now. Such a hard winter and now the drought. We've extended so much credit . . ."

Treasure smiled with more confidence than she felt. "Don't fret about it. I shouldn't have even asked. It's just I'm at my wits' end today."

And out of time. She'd spent the past two days searching for a miracle. Now, with her deadline only hours away, none seemed likely.

99

Eliza's delicate features puckered in a frown. "I thought perhaps that letter—"

"Aunt Valene sends her regrets, but," Treasure quoted from the letter in her lap, *"I regret at this time I simply cannot lend even the slightest of assistance, my dear,"* but that *"Ransom and I will certainly do our best to come lend our support at the earliest juncture possible."*

Treasure touched a finger to the heavily scented paper. Two days ago she had anxiously awaited its coming. Today it was just another reminder she was about to fail in her promise to Papa to keep Rose of Heaven safe.

Aware of Miss Eliza's questioning gaze, Treasure hastened to explain. "Aunt Valene and her son haven't come here since I was a child. There was bad blood between Mama and her sister, you know. It will be wonderful to renew their acquaintance, but I fear it may be us traveling to Atlanta unless I can convince Mr. Clement to give me more time."

Eliza paused a moment before answering, busying herself with refilling Treasure's glass. "He knew your papa well, Treasure," she said. "Perhaps you could use that memory to coax him into waiting until harvest for the money."

"I've tried. But Papa's debts are so deep, I can scarce blame Mr. Clement for not waiting. As it stands, I'll need a promise year of harvest to make good on what papa owes and still have enough left to keep Rose of Heaven running."

"Treasure . . ." Eliza smoothed a hand over her skirts. Her eyes were thoughtful on Treasure. "I don't want to cause you any more grief, but have you discussed the matter with your Mr. River? Perhaps he could be of some help."

Treasure's mouth set in a defiant line. "No, I haven't. And I don't intend to. Why ever would you even suggest such a thing? It's not his business."

"You have let him stay."

"Only because I have no other choice at the moment. But once this matter with the bank is settled, Mr. River will be my foremost concern."

"Is he?"

The soft query, although she knew Miss Eliza only pried out of caring, made Treasure feel hot and uncomfortable. "Of course," she said, fidgeting with her purse strings. "I want him gone as soon as can be managed. Isn't it natural I should?"

"I suppose. Although . . ." A wicked gleam sparkled in Eliza's eyes, belying her elegantly proper appearance. "Those eyes alone might be enough to make me forget my good intentions."

"I hadn't noticed," Treasure said, bravely meeting her friend's gaze.

"Forgive me, Treasure, but you're either a nice little liar or blind. Why, there isn't a woman in the valley who wouldn't trade places with you right this moment, regardless of Mr. River's questionable past. In fact, there have been whispers that you and he aren't the great enemies you seem." Eliza laughed at Treasure's outraged expression. "I for one never pay heed to such claptrap. But if you should care to confide in someone . . ."

"I'll remember your kind offer," Treasure said, smiling stiffly at Eliza's teasing. She gathered up her bag with a determined air. "Unlike those women, Miss Eliza, I cannot afford to allow myself to succumb to a handsome face and a kind word. Frankly, I am shocked you think I would even consider such an alliance. I must be on my way now. Thank you for the visit."

"Honey, come anytime. And don't mind my catty tongue. It's just sometimes you're so serious you invite me to try and tease you into relaxing that guard of yours." Eliza saw her to the door, and as she watched Treasure start down the street toward the bank she called out, "Keep that chin in the air, Treasure. No matter what."

Treasure tried to heed Eliza's advice as she walked into the bank. And she tried to forget her friend's comments about Mr. River. Surely no one would think—

The idea—and a sudden remembrance of a night two days past—returned the heat to Treasure's face. She couldn't think about that now. She had to be calm and collected to meet Mr. Clement.

It became more difficult with each step that brought her closer to the bank. As she walked into the neat brick building, a thousand doubts massed against her. What could she say to him that she hadn't already said? What new pleas could she appeal to him with? What would she do if he said no, a very final no?

She was in the midst of trying to rally her thoughts when the door to Mr. Clement's office came open and Mr. Clement himself walked out, greeting her with a broad smile. "Why, Miss McGlavrin. I didn't expect to see you here today. Is there something else you needed?"

"Something else?" Treasure stared at him, puzzled. "We had an appointment today, Mr. Clement." When he looked back blankly, she insisted, "About the payment of the debts."

Mr. Clement's face relaxed. "Ah, I see. You wanted to make sure everything was in order. Yes, yes. Well rest your mind, my dear, it's all taken care of."

Treasure stared. "Taken care of?"

Bobbing his head with cheerful assurance, Mr. Clement said, "Yes, yes. Quite nicely too.

The new owner made certain of that."

Chapter Six

Eura Mae, Solomon, Spring, and Emmy descended upon Treasure in succession when she strode through the front door. She passed them all without a word. She had no more solutions to their little problems, no more answers to their ceaseless questions.

No more courage.

For the first time in her life, she pushed aside her responsibilities, dropping them outside the door to Papa's study. She turned the key, locking out her shattered world. She had to be alone. She longed to pretend she wasn't Treasure McGlavrin. That, instead, she was a stranger, free from the burdens of caring, and planning, and scrimping, and worrying.

She headed straight for Papa's liquor cabinet. For a moment, her hand tensed on the cold brass handle. Papa. This had been Papa's comfort, his relief. And the whip flogging his demons. Yet it helped him forget. And God, she needed to forget.

With a quick yank, she opened the cabinet and pulled out one bottle from his vast supply of Scotch whiskey, untouched since the day Papa left. This had been Papa's solace, and now it would be hers.

As fast as her burning throat would allow, she gulped the liquid fire. Then she waited for the magic Papa promised, the magic that would erase the memories.

She'd lost Rose of Heaven.

It hurt, how it hurt, even to think of it. A deep, unrelenting pain. She squeezed her eyes shut and tried vainly to wish it away. She'd lost Rose of Heaven, and in losing that she lost everything that gave her reason to fight, to hope for a future for herself and her sisters.

She had tried — *fool!* — and failed.

She ached for tears to bring her release, the way they availed other women in times of need. But, no matter how her insides might flame with anguish, her eyes burned dry.

Throwing back her head, she held her breath and swallowed another long draught of whiskey. Nothing was happening the way she'd planned. After Papa died, she knew what must be done to save Rose of Heaven. She'd ordered her life, step by painstaking step, to bring Papa's dream to fruition; made his lost ambition her sole aim. It was all so logical. Why did things go wrong? Why was nothing working the way it was supposed to?

Her steps faltering, she paced the floor. Lost in a state of shock and confusion that grew murkier by the moment, her mind became a courtroom playing out defenses and judgments for her choices and actions.

Treasure's legs grew suddenly annoyingly heavy, refusing to obey. Bottle in hand, she tottered to the huge old desk where Papa always sat to finish the last of his liquid salve, and dropped into his battered leather chair.

"Wretched books," she muttered, glaring with bleary eyes at the records of daily accounts in front of her. Solid, square symbols of reason, they seemed to mock her failure. How many hours, how many nights had she pored over the numbers in those books, reassuring herself against hope she could make them balance one day?

"You're a damned fool, Treasure McGlavrin." She tipped the bottle to her mouth, then slammed it against the books' unyielding covers. Someone else understood the numbers on those pages as well as she did. Seeing the moment was ripe to gather the spoils of her financial ruin before anyone else seized the chance, the traitor betrayed her, feeding the information to a waiting scavenger.

Another thief (worse even than Donovan River, if her suspicions proved true), had bought her home and land as easily as Donovan flashed his roguish smile.

She had left Mr. Clement's office in a blind daze of shock, not even bothering to ask the banker to tell her the name of the new owner of her plantation. She didn't want to hear the name spoken aloud. The hateful shame of losing Rose of Heaven overwhelmed her, eclipsing everything else.

The sound of the handle impatiently jiggling, then the door being eased open, turned Treasure's head. But her eyes refused to focus. Shelves of books lining the study walls began to circle her, looming, closing in on her, dark and predatory, leather-backed vultures.

Someone was talking to her, close to her ear. The voice sounded too loud, and she winced.

Fighting a wave of dizziness, Treasure cautiously looked up. Familiar gray eyes seemed to be laughing at her.

"Donovan River? Is that you?"

"Lucky for you, pretty lady, it is."

"I hate you."

"I know."

"Good. Now, would you care to help me to my feet. My legs don't seem to be co-coop—oh hell! They just won't do what I want."

"My pleasure."

Treasure was vaguely aware of being scooped out of Papa's chair into Donovan's arms. "This isn't what I meant. Put me down."

Donovan gathered her closer. "I don't think I will. But it would expedite matters if you'd put your arms around my neck."

Unable to think of a reason why she shouldn't, Treasure obeyed. Her head rested naturally against his hard chest, the rhythmic sway of his body as he walked upstairs lulling her into a sleepy daze.

Her last remembered thought was a mild surprise at the sweet pleasure of knowing Donovan had been her rescuer.

"It's a damned good thing the rest of the household gave up and went to bed hours ago," Donovan muttered as he entered her bedroom, "or my impetuous rescue might be the end of your virtuous name."

"Hmmm . . ." Treasure murmured as Donovan laid her atop her bed. She curled into a snug ball, nestling her face against the soft down pillow.

"Woman, you aren't making this any easier. Where is your night dress?"

"Night dress? Mammie Eura Mae, you're teasing me. Why it's in the armoire, like always." Treasure giggled and pointed across the room.

"Mammie—hell, it's just as well you don't know who I am." Staring down at her for a long moment, Donovan drew in a breath. He reached out and brushed damp strands of auburn from her forehead before gently loosing her hair from confining pins and combing it through his fingers until it twined in a halo of flame around her face. "That was the easy part."

Working quickly, he tugged free the row of buttons on her dress, tossing it aside, then struggled with her petticoats. "You never wear these damned things any other time." He fingered the intricacies of her stays, feeling unaccountably ill at ease. The practical solution was Eura Mae. But Treasure wouldn't thank him

106

for exposing her weakness. Or for taking the liberty to conceal it.

Treasure, her eyes closed, stretched like a lazy cat. "Feels so good," she murmured. She lounged, deliciously relaxed, tempting his hands to stray.

"That's a matter of opinion," Donovan grumbled.

Treasure's eyes slowly opened and she looked up at him with a guileless gaze. "I suppose I could help."

He sighed, thrusting a hand through his hair. "Please do."

Clumsily, Treasure unfastened the first stay of her bodice. Inch by inch, the tight garment loosed down her front, gradually revealing more of the creamy swell of her breasts as each stay snapped open. When she finished, Treasure threw aside the restraint and breathed a contented sigh. She raised her arms, as if signaling her imagined mammie to drop the nightdress over her head.

"My God . . ." Donovan stared at her, dumbfounded. Underneath the drab frocks, the smudges of dirt, "You're beautiful," he whispered.

Her hair licked fire against the cool silk of her skin. The slender strength of her body lent her a sensual grace, and there was more allure in her artless stretch than any practiced pose he'd ever been enticed with. Desire struck him weak. She was no girl, but a woman, with a body that begged to be touched, caressed . . . everything lovely, everything desirable, every bit the epitome of his fondest dreams . . .

You bastard, don't even think about it.

Commanding his hands not to wander, Donovan slipped the filmy nightdress over her bare breasts. With trembling fingers trailing down her sides to her waist, he settled the fine cotton around her, brushing it over her legs. Her skin was intoxicatingly fragrant and silky smooth beneath his hands.

"Ooohhh, that tickles." Treasure wiggled like a

107

child being teased. The motion tugged the thin material tantalizingly close to each curve of her body. "Your hands feel so nice on my skin. They're so warm."

Donovan jerked back as quickly as if she'd slapped him. "That's enough. If I don't leave now, I'll hate myself as much as you do." Easing her back against the pillow, he pulled the quilt over her, tucking it under her chin. Hesitating a moment, he bent and brushed a soft kiss on her forehead. "Sweet dreams, pretty lady," he murmured, allowing himself a small satisfied smile. "Because I've got a feeling waking up is going to be a nightmare."

Dawn came much too early. Donovan, certain Treasure would be in no condition to make her usual rounds, went in her stead. Outside the kitchen behind the big house, he came across Bettis straining his ax over a stubborn log. Sweat rained down his face and chest and he was huffing so hard with each swing, Donovan worried he'd collapse.

"Aren't you out of your domain?" Donovan put a friendly hand on the older man's shoulder, startling him. "Where's Elijah?"

"Yes, suh. Mornin', Mastuh River. Elijah be tendin' de hole in de barn roof where Missy Treasure be puttin' up de South down sheep fer fattenin'."

"The wind brought that winged elm down on it yesterday, didn't it?"

"Sho 'nough did," Bettis said absently. Donovan noticed his attention shifted to follow Orange Jane as she swayed down the kitchen stairs, a spot of color in a bright red and yellow-striped shift.

Her voice, sweet and rich, carried over the sounds of morning activity, and Donovan couldn't suppress a smile when Bettis added his lusty bass to the last phrases of her tune.

"I'se got a thousand ways,
   to makes my love love me.
A song in de evenin',
   a stolen kiss by day,
And a hundred other things,
   dat I may never say."

"You ain't et none o' my fresh orange blossom muffins yet, Bettis, and I knows dey's yo' favorite," the cook said smiling broadly. "You neither, Mastuh River. Come to think, Miz Treasure ain't been in to breakfast yet neither. Best muffins I ever made 'n' not a soul done tasted hardly a one!"

Orange Jane laughed at Bettis's appalled expression. Turning coyly aside, she called out to the one remaining scullion at her disposal to bring in fresh water. Donovan took advantage of Bettis's distracted state and lifted the ax from his hands.

Bettis turned and shook his head. "Whatchu doin', Mastuh River? I be cuttin' de wood today."

"You won't get much chopped on an empty stomach. Get to those muffins before you offend Orange Jane." Donovan gave a conspiratorial wink. "You can have your job back after breakfast."

"But Miz Treasure —"

"Won't know the better. Trust me."

Bettis tipped his head to one side and studied Donovan for a moment then grinned widely. "Well, suh, I do think I'll take that offer, I does. Thank you."

"I should be thanking you," Donovan muttered to himself after Bettis had gone. He wielded the ax with unusual fervor. After the trial Treasure gave his mind and body last night, the physical exertion felt releasing. Each slam of the ax deep into the wood eased the torment of frustrated desire.

The first log splintered into kindling. He stacked it nearby and vented his pent-up longing onto one log after another until the pile he heaped up was enough

109

to last for days. He sliced the ax into the chopping stump and loaded his arms with wood to restock the huge andirons.

"Ain't you gonna set and join us?" Orange Jane asked as Donovan unburdened himself of the wood.

"No, thanks, not this morning. But I will take a few of those muffins along if you don't mind."

"Well, it ain't a proper breakfast, but you kin take what you like."

Donovan was stuffing several muffins into a linen when the twins tumbled into the kitchen, Abby chasing Erin. They gathered about Donovan's pant legs.

"Peek-a-boo." Abby hid behind Donovan's leg, poking her plump face out to tease her sister.

"I see you! I see you!" Erin cried out.

They squirmed and squealed with abandon and Donovan laughed along good-naturedly. The clamor drew Orange Jane, who caught hold of their skirts.

"Where's your Mammie Eura Mae, you two? Whatchu doin' 'round my kitchen? You know what I does t' chillen comin' in here uninvited?" Holding the squirming trespassers by their petticoats, she pulled them to her work counter and grabbed two dish rags to pin to their clothes.

"No, Aunt Orange Jane! No, please!"

The game amused Donovan almost as much as it did the twins. "That ought to keep you out from under your Aunt Orange Jane's feet," he teased.

Orange Jane popped them on their bottoms and sent them giggling and scurrying out the door back to the big house.

"Bettis, you wouldn't happen to have any of that fine morning-after cure, would you?" Donovan asked, suddenly reminded of Treasure. "I could use a pinch or two this morning."

Bettis offered an empathetic smile. "Yessuh, I do. Come see me in an hour. It'll be waitin' fer you."

110

Smiling his thanks, Donovan left him, deciding to vent his unspent energy helping Elijah.

As he passed the north field, now dotted with perfectly lined rows of green, Treasure's moonlit face came to mind. And though she'd kill him without a care if she ever remembered, his memory of the night before let him paint a vivid portrait of her lying bared to his hungry gaze; of her skin separated from his fingertips only by thin cloth. His hands burned to embrace her. His loins ached to feel her body inflaming the passion he struggled to bank. Where had he found the will to resist the demand of his body? Lesser temptations than Treasure McGlavrin had led him to satisfy an impulsive desire. Why not now?

A bead of sweat trickled down the cleft in his shirt. He shrugged out of the damp material and pulled his hat out of his back pocket, tugging it low on his brow to shade his eyes. "Damn this heat," he muttered.

If I had touched her, one night wouldn't have been enough. And more than one night is impossible for either of us.

An echo of hammer to wood cracked in the distance, recalling him to his errand. Raising a hand to shield his eyes, he picked out Elijah on the barn roof beyond. He climbed the rolling slope to the sheep stalls, then swarmed the ladder to the barn's roof. "Need a hand?" he asked the bare-backed man straddling the pitch on the far end.

"You serious?"

"Wouldn't offer if I didn't mean it." Without waiting for an invitation, Donovan hefted a hammer in one hand and set to driving nails.

The two men worked in silence, the sun's relentless heat beating down fiery bullets on their backs.

All the while Donovan couldn't keep his gaze from wandering off the hole in the roof. He'd never had so clear a view beyond the fields to the densely wooded

111

forest that was all part of what was—or ought to be—his land.

"Those pines are packed in so thick out there, it's a wonder any of them can get light enough to grow."

Elijah glanced over his shoulder. "I know. Best not say anything about it to Miss Treasure, though, Mastuh River, or she'll be accusin' you of siding with Colonel Stanton."

"Why's that?"

"Colonel Stanton'd like to harvest that timber. He'd make a fine profit now in Birmingham and Atlanta."

Donovan shot Elijah a curious look. "You keep abreast of lumber prices, do you?"

Elijah shrugged. "Before I came to Miss Treasure, I did the books for Mastuh Jordan, just north of here. He dammed the river where it branched off to run the wheel of his sawmill. Had customers for every log he felled."

"I see." Elijah's stiff stance told Donovan not to pursue the questions he itched to ask. Not yet. "Well, I have to admit, much as I'd like to hang that bastard Stanton by his purse strings, with the river just down the other side of that slope, a lumber mill is a tempting proposition."

"You and Miss Treasure don't think the same."

"That seems to be my problem around here."

"Seems to me"—Elijah pulled another nail from his pouch—"you don't hold much in common with her thinkin' on most things."

Donovan pried his eyes from the rich forest to focus on Elijah. "And?"

"And from what I've seen, seems you might just be more North than South, that's all."

"What if I am?"

Elijah focused on the nails in his hand. "Suppose you knew something about who a man might talk to if he was thinkin' about travelin' north."

Donovan considered his words carefully. "I do

know anyone willing to risk heading north right now better understand his chances of making it there alive are slim at best."

"Not if he knows the right people."

"Maybe. Maybe not." He paused. "It could be dangerous—knowing the right people."

"Some people might not mind."

"Some people." There was a shared moment of silence then Donovan clasped Elijah's shoulder. "We're done for now. Go on and get some water."

"You coming?" Elijah asked as he stood to a precarious stance atop the roof's pitched center.

"In a minute." Propping one foot on the roof slant for balance, Donovan pulled his journal from his back pocket and stared off into the distant woods.

Treasure groaned and burrowed deeper into the downy softness of her mattress. Where did that relentless pounding come from? It throbbed with cruel intensity, refusing to wane in the slightest. Wherever—whatever it was, Treasure prayed it would cease.

It didn't. Instead it grew louder, accompanied by Eura Mae's maternal admonitions outside her locked bedroom door.

"C'mon, open up dis here door. I knows you's awake in daire. You open dis door, chile, right now!"

She was awake. Sort of. She'd gotten up on wobbly legs at the first hint of daylight to draw her drapes tighter and lock her door. Now she lifted the corner of her coverlet. "Go away!" she moaned, each word careening painfully inside her head.

A sliver of yellow light sliced through the center of her drapes. From its brilliance, she knew the sun had been full up for hours, but she'd kept her drapes closed to block it out. Light, reality, even moving—she couldn't face them today.

113

"I jus don't understand you dis mornin'," Treasure heard Eura Mae grumble on. "You ain't never stayed abed past sunup. Is you sick?"

"No. I want to sleep in for once. Just leave me alone."

"Sleep in? You? You's sick, sho' 'nough, one way or 'nother."

Eura Mae probably suspected her and Donovan of having another quarrel, and for an instant Treasure wished he had caused her black mood. She heard the floor boards creak as Eura Mae finally gave up and shuffled away, muttering to herself.

She knew she was surrendering to a damning self-pity. She despised the whimper in her voice. But she couldn't summon the strength to stop. Like a child escaping a nightmare, she groaned and yanked the coverlet back over her head. She just couldn't face Ira Stanton today, his feigned sympathy a thin disguise for the gloating sneer she knew he wouldn't bother to hide.

And Donovan . . . was there a strange sort of justice in this for him? He had tried to steal Rose of Heaven out from under her, and now it had been taken from him. Try though she might, Treasure could derive no satisfaction from the thought.

The idea of Donovan River walking the corridors of her home, the paths of her grounds as master, had devastated her enough. But to think of Ira Stanton and his deceitful younger sibling in the same role. . . .

It was too much!

Finding no release in sorrow, her pain and frustration suddenly gave way to rage. She sat bolt upright, threw the quilt to the floor, and hurled her pillows one by one against the far wall, knocking a vase to the floor in a shattering crash of water, wilted roses, and china splinters. As she continued her tirade, her nightdress wound taut about her body. The final pillow thrown, she twisted to tug at the infuriating piece of cloth.

And looked directly at Donovan. Leaning against the door frame of her open bedroom door, he put two fingers to the brim of his hat, smiling slow and easy.

Eura Mae bustled past him to take a robe from Treasure's wardrobe. But Treasure felt his eyes touching her body before Eura Mae tossed the covering over her shoulders and bosom. For as little as her nightdress concealed, she might well have been naked to his suggestive gaze.

Treasure, lacking anything solid to throw, tossed a bevy of angry words at Donovan. "How dare you burst into my bedroom! I've a mind to—" Her eyes flew open and she clapped a hand to her mouth. The combination of the night's folly and her morning tantrum churned and soured in her stomach like a foul witch's brew in a searing cauldron.

"I—I'm going to be sick." She clutched her middle and would have toppled to the floor if Donovan hadn't caught her. Gently, his hand supported her waist from behind while Eura Mae snatched a basin from the wash stand.

Her chest heaving from the nausea, her breasts brushed his arms again and again as she bent forward. She leaned over the basin and he followed her motion, wrapping his body around her for support. His comforting warmth enfolded her, his broad chest and arms encircling her back, her hair gathered in his hands.

Despite her illness, the caressing heat where his body met hers felt oddly familiar instead of foreign and intrusive, as she expected it should.

"You might as well get it over with," he whispered against her cheek. "You'll feel better."

How he understood exactly what she felt, she had no idea. Somehow he made her unafraid. She should be dying of humiliation, yet his simple acceptance of

115

her, even in this horrid state, eased her thoughts—if not her stomach.

She retched until she gasped for air. Her last heave finally spent, she collapsed back against Donovan. He traced feathery, hypnotic patterns up and down her bared arms, soothing her into relaxing against his strength.

"Can't no one know nothin' 'bout you bein' up here wit' her. Never!" Eura Mae glared hard at Donovan.

"Don't worry," he said softly. "I don't intend to do anything to hurt the lady."

Eura Mae set her hands to her hips and lifted her chin to him. "Never said you did." She looked at Treasure, her mouth sour. "I dunno who else to call dis mornin'. Lawd, I ain't never seen Missy Treasure do nothin' like dis! Sho 'nough couldna let no one else find out. I kno'd was you who done broke de lock in de study 'n' brung her up here early. Don't you be lookin' at me dat way, Mastuh River, I knows everyone's goin's-on in dis house."

"I'll remember that, the next time I have to perform a similar rescue."

"You do dat, Mastuh River." Her eyes softened. "Now daire, po' chile . . ." Treasure, wearied by the noise of their conversation, pushed close to Donovan's chest, drawing a frown from Eura Mae. "Hurry now. Outta dis room, fo' someone come and sees you and her together."

Donovan grazed his fingers over Treasure's damp brow. "Give her plenty of water. She'll be better by afternoon." With special care, he eased her back onto the bed, tucking the quilt back around her.

Treasure opened her eyes enough to see him standing over her, gazing down, his expression inscrutable. She half heard him murmur something, but her mind couldn't make sense of the words.

"How could I have thought it would make you happy? Whether Rose of Heaven ends up in Stanton's

116

hands or mine makes no difference, does it? Bettis was right — your heart belongs to this land, and nothing and no one else, doesn't it?"

She dreamed she heard a catch in his tone, saw a flinch of pain on his face. But it was so difficult to tell. Too tired to fathom it all, Treasure let the velvet whisper of his voice lull her into the twilight of sleep. And as she drifted into blessed darkness, she imagined the soft touch of a kiss against her face.

It was suppertime before Treasure managed to dress and drag herself from her room and downstairs. Her sisters had already begun their meal when she shambled into the dining room.

"Come and sit next to me," Spring beckoned. "Mercy, you look so pale."

"Are you sick?" Emmy reached out to touch her fingertips to Treasure's forehead.

"Why, I do declare, you're green in the gills." Camille's eyes narrowed. "Here, have my plate," she said, stuffing the dish under Treasure's nose.

Treasure wanted to sit down and eat with her family, make amends for yesterday's rude behavior. Certainly she owed them an explanation. She stared down at the plate of food, tried to force herself to eat.

But her stomach refused to submit to reason. If she took even one bite . . . "I don't feel quite well. I'm sorry. I believe I need some fresh air. You all go ahead now and finish supper." She was still apologizing as she hastily backed out of the room.

Seeking the refuge of her willow rocker, Treasure retreated to the kitchen porch. Sitting gingerly, she rocked back. Once.

She didn't dare move, even to turn at the clap of the screened door. The click, click of Bonnie's nails against the pine planks told her who it was. She groaned inwardly, humiliated by her disgusting display earlier.

Donovan, an empathetic smile playing with his mouth, looked down at her from under the shadow of his hat. He handed her a glass of strange brownish liquid. "Here. Drink this."

"I would fear it was poison, but that isn't necessary now, is it?"

Donovan either pretended not to hear her jab or chose to ignore it. "Bettis made it. Believe me, it's effective."

"I suppose you should know." Reluctantly, Treasure took the glass. "I must thank him."

"What about me?" His smile melded into a half-smirk.

"You! Thank you for trying to rob me? Not I, Mr. River." The edge in her own voice sliced through her head. She paused, imposing an inward calm. "But you didn't succeed, did you? He won. We lost. Both of us. Where does that leave you, Donovan River?"

Donovan knelt in front of her. Pushing his hat back, he locked the arms of her rocker firm in his palms and stared her square in the eyes. "What in the ever-loving hell are you talking about? Did you pull the cork on another of Seamus's bottles?"

Treasure felt the heat of shame surge to her cheeks. The warm hands on her back, her arms, the kiss to her forehead last night—suddenly it struck her who had undressed her and tucked her into bed the night before. Her first instinct was to flee in shame. Her second was to slap the knowing amusement from his face. But she quickly managed to suppress both impulses in an effort to salvage what she could muster of her pride.

"Oh my, you haven't heard? I am sorely disappointed, sir. I should have expected you to have better informants by now."

"I could do with a little less sarcasm, and a little more fact."

Treasure fixed on a point over his shoulder. "It seems Ira Stanton has bested me. He's managed to learn every bleak detail of my finances and used that knowledge in the most unscrupulous manner to buy my home and land."

"Stanton bought you out, did he?" Laughter overcame him, and Donovan released the chair he had inadvertently pulled forward, sending it rocking back and forth.

Treasure's stomach reeled in response. She slammed her feet into the planks to break the motion, grasping at her precious dignity. "I cannot fathom what humor you find in this."

Donovan answered by scooping her into his arms like a weightless bundle. He danced across the porch, Treasure clinging to his neck in self-defense. "Stanton didn't buy Rose of Heaven."

"Wha—" Treasure gaped at him. "Are you mad or am I?"

"Both. Neither. It doesn't matter. I'm the one who paid your wretched debts, pretty lady, not the despised Colonel Stanton."

"Donovan—Mr. River—p-please, I *really* don't feel at all well. Put me down."

"Here," he said, gently setting her on a cushioned chair, "finish this. It's magic, I promise."

Treasure sipped from the glass he proffered, trying to rally her thoughts. "You're lying," she said at last, more to herself than to Donovan as she tried to reason out his claim. "You must be lying. You have to be. You came here with nothing. I don't see how you possibly could have paid those debts, as deep as they were."

Donovan shrugged. "I had a few dollars hidden for deserving situations."

Suddenly the impact of Donovan's gesture—if it proved true—slapped Treasure. "Then that means . . . you really do own Rose of Heaven." She fell

119

against the back of the chair. Things didn't seem to be improving.

Donovan sat down next to her and took her hands between his. "I paid your debts to keep Rose of Heaven from Stanton. And I don't have to buy Rose of Heaven."

"No one else knew that! Now Mr. Clement will surely have it spread all over the valley."

"Treasure, he's a banker. I paid the debts. I have the note. To him, I've long been the new owner."

"So, not only have you won the bank's favor, but the respect of the valley as well. Congratulations. You've accomplished more in your short time here than I have in a lifetime."

"I don't give a damn what this town thinks of me." He shoved a hand through his hair, frustration darkening his eyes. "I did it for you."

"Don't try to use that manipulative charm of yours on me, Donovan River. I know why you did this. To gain the upper hand. Everyone will think my plantation does belong to you. I'm the only one who knows you probably couldn't afford to leave now if you wanted to."

"Oh, I could." He leaned back, pulling his hat back low. "But I won't. I have no desire to leave. And, broke or not, I feel it was money well invested."

"And how about when you awake one morning and decide you've had your fill of playing the planter? When your fingers are itching to hold a smooth hand of cards instead of the handle of a hoe? Or didn't you think about that?"

"Dammit woman! You just don't understand, do you?"

"Understand what, Mr. River?"

"Sometimes you just have to do something because it seems right at the moment. And damn the consequences!"

"No, I don't understand that kind of impulsive, thoughtless behavior, and I never will!"

"It may have been an impulsive gesture to plunge my last dollar into this miserable land, but it wasn't thoughtless. My concern, whether you care to believe it or not, was for you."

Taken back by the intensity in Donovan's words and in the depths of his eyes, Treasure was momentarily speechless. *He's telling the truth!*

The realization astonished her, because her mind had no intention of believing anything Donovan River said. But she couldn't wish away his straightforward gaze, the sincerity in his voice.

"I — I don't know what to say . . ." she stammered at last. "I should . . ."

Donovan cocked his head, staring at her with unnerving candor. "Should what?"

"I suppose I should — thank you. Somehow."

"Kiss me."

Treasure stared. "What?"

"You wanted to thank me, didn't you?"

Taken back at the bold suggestion, Treasure stiffened automatically. But she yearned to experience what he knew so well, to act on her heart's whim this once; she longed for nothing more in that instant than to kiss him in a way he could never forget. To give him the same feeling he'd gifted her with when he kissed her the first time.

Yet when it actually came down to touching her lips to his, naiveté and pride blocked her action. She glanced about self-consciously to see if anyone watched them. Could she really do it?

Yes. No. Treasure nearly decided to refuse him. The amusement tugging at his lips changed her mind.

A militant set to her mouth, she leaned over and gave him a chaste peck on the cheek. "There. Thank you."

"You're not quite welcome," Donovan said, the

devil in his eyes.

Before she could object, he rose then reached out and swept her into his arms. His hands were sure yet searching against her body, as if discovering a precious possession feared lost.

His mouth tasted hers, slowly at first. With a gentle touch, his lips teased a smile to the corners of her mouth. Her fears began to ease, her body surrender in his arms as he courted her hidden desires, brushing soft kisses over her chin, her cheeks, down her throat.

Then, without warning, as though he sensed her longing, he deepened his kiss. She didn't cower now, but met his demanding lips, learning to return the warm, moist probing until their play took her breath with a lightning thrust of desire. Donovan held her close against him as he felt her answering shudder.

Instead of releasing her then, though, he drew her to him again, this time with hunger in his eyes and fire on his lips.

Her anxiety seared away in a passion that pulled them together. She felt strong with the power of it, weak from her own mystifying desires. She groped for reason and found only feeling, letting it draw her nearer, clinging to him with a need so powerful it eclipsed everything but the desperate, demanding longing between them.

He moved his hands to hold her face, stroking her skin with his thumbs while his mouth devoured hers.

Treasure clung to him, tasting the sweet depths of his kiss. Her body molded to his, and her mouth was a being of its own. One sated yearning created another. Something deep inside her wanted to taste more than this kiss, more than this closeness satisfied.

As if responding to her body's nameless plea, Donovan's fingers slipped to her throat. Sliding one hand to her nape, he let the other wander her shoulder, then lower, until his fingertips grazed the curve of her breast.

Treasure started in surprise and discovery as his palm molded to her soft flesh. She reeled with a surging need to reach out to this man in a way so intimate, so compelling, it overtook her senses, her thoughts, until she succumbed to the pure sensation of him, a prisoner to the new passions Donovan evoked with his touch.

Lost in the sweet escalation of desire, she forgot herself, where they were, until Donovan stiffened.

Words, agitated, deferent, registered in her mind. Solomon's voice. With a nervous jump, she pulled out of Donovan's arms.

Solomon scuttled backward at her sharp motion and hung to the doorway. "Sorry, Missy Treasure, but someone be wantin' Mastuh River in de parlor."

Treasure and Donovan exchanged a confused glance.

"I'll be along in a moment," Donovan answered. When the house boy scurried away, he turned back to Treasure.

"I'm going with you," she said, not certain exactly why it mattered.

She sensed he struggled over a reply. But in the end, he merely trailed a soft, exploring finger over her face, his eyes searching each plane as if he intended to memorize them. An eternity passed. He bent and brushed a lingering kiss against her mouth, then wordlessly turned her toward the house.

Treasure felt a skitter of foreboding as they walked in silence to the parlor. And when she saw their visitor, she knew it was justified.

Skinny as a snake and twice as mean-looking, the man waiting in the parlor greeted Donovan and Treasure by spitting tobacco at their feet.

Treasure's heart contracted painfully when she saw the grim recognition on Donovan's face. Every muscle tensed. "Gunter. I should have guessed you'd show up sooner or later."

Treasure looked from one man to the other. "We haven't been introduced," she said at last.

The man's eyes crawled over her body in a leer. "Well there, River, you done mighty good with my money, looks like. Slade Gunter, ma'am, willin' to service."

Treasure recognized the dark fury gathering on Donovan's face. "Get to the point, Gunter. Then get out."

Slade spit out another sloppy, brown wad. His scratchy bark and slick dirty black hair reminded Treasure of a mangy mongrel cur. "That's exactly what I come to do. I come to claim what's mine, River."

"I don't owe you a damned thing," Donovan said, his voice dropping to a menacing pitch.

"You do by my book. You managed to kill off old man McGlavrin before I could get my due, but you ain't gonna get by so easy with me. You owe me a hell of a lot and you're gonna pay every last penny of it." Slade's mouth curled in an angry sneer.

"You don't cheat a man at cards without payin' in blood."

Chapter Seven

The front foyer door slammed shut with an angry crack, as sharp and sudden as a shot from a sniper's pistol.

Poised at the open French windows between the parlor and verandah, Treasure started. Only her fingers conveyed any emotion, tightening convulsively for a moment on the edges of the windows. Searing late afternoon air hung deadly still around her. She watched Slade Gunter toss a last snarl over his shoulder, his thin lips curled in sneering menace.

Snatching up the reins from Soloman, he flung himself on his horse, wheeled it about, and viciously spurred it into a gallop toward the road. Treasure followed his retreat until horse and rider disappeared into the dusky early evening haze.

So this was Donovan River's past. It had stalked him all the way from New Orleans to take its revenge. Small wonder he declined to discuss it.

She supposed she should feel some measure of triumph—she had pegged Donovan River a charming scoundrel, not to be trusted, and if this Slade Gunter were to be believed, he was that and worse.

But instead of triumph, a sensation, perilously akin to panic, surged up within her, demanding control. It was as if she were suddenly aware she balanced on the edge of an abyss, a step away from falling. She shivered and hugged her arms to herself, mentally grappling against the intangible foe. But logic proved a weak opponent against the force of emotion. Her reason cowered then fled.

The sound of her own quickened breath, her heart in her ears, left her shaken. With deliberate effort, she forced her arms to relax, flexing the tension from her fingers. She tried to think of nothing, to feel nothing.

Donovan's firm tread in the hallway reminded her that was impossible. Treasure waited, resigned, knowing he would come to . . . what? Explain? To try to placate her with more lies?

She refused to turn around when he came into the room. But his image haunted her thoughts: his eyes, soft and seducing, storm gray with mystery and passion, touching her everywhere. One glance could breach her defenses and tempt her heart into believing in him.

There was a long silence before Donovan's low voice stroked her nerves. "He's gone."

"So I see. But for how long?"

Donovan moved to her side. She heard his breath come slow and deep. His nearness did little to soothe her disquiet. "I'll make certain he doesn't cause you any more trouble. You have my word."

It was a dark threat and a silver promise; the former alarming, the latter infuriating.

"Your word!" Turning sardonic eyes to him, Treasure gave a short, derisive laugh. "And whose word shall I take that you won't cause me any more trouble, Mr. River?"

Donovan frowned, studying her as if trying to probe her feelings. "Just a short while ago I was Donovan."

Treasure's hands groped at her skirts. "Just a short while ago I nearly convinced myself I could trust you. I started to believe that you . . ."

"Cared?"

Indignation flared in her eyes. "No."

"Yes, Treasure." He didn't move, but the dark, caressing inflection of his voice was more potent than a touch. It revived memories so real, so vivid, her skin quivered. Unwillingly, her senses remembered his fingertips brushing her face, his powerful arm possessing her waist, his taste, the taste of honey and temptation, lingering on her lips.

In the same instant her reason marked her a fool.

"That's what you're afraid of, isn't it?"

His question intruded into her secret musings. She flushed. "I'm not afraid," she said, regretting the childish retort as soon as it had escaped her lips.

"You're afraid I might care, and that you'll have to admit you feel something for me besides contempt."

"You flatter yourself, Mr. River." Treasure swept away from him, unable to do battle with both him and her traitorous senses at the same time. With a trembling hand she busied herself with lighting the sconces, trying to still her churning feelings with the small ordinary task.

A draft suddenly rushed into the parlor through the French windows, whistling a melancholy tune. The candles' flames hovered and danced. Their shadows cast a wavering amber glow about the darkening room.

Donovan's gaze followed her every move. Treasure tried to ignore him, hoping he would leave her in peace. But there was no mercy in his relentless scrutiny.

Minutes seemed to stretch tortuously into hours before at last he stepped away from the windows. He left them open, creaking slightly as the wayward breeze tapped them to and fro. Moving with almost languorous ease, he sat down on the long piano bench and casually trailed a hand over ivory and ebony keys. The

127

single candle at his side shadowed his face, part in golden flame, part in twilight.

Treasure expected him to say something, but he stayed silent. Finally, she gathered her courage and took one step toward him.

"Is Slade Gunter telling the truth?" Treasure shot the question into the tense silence, defiantly, half-fearful of the answer, but unable any longer to stand not knowing.

"His version of it."

"And how many versions are there?" she snapped. "I'm becoming sorely grieved with low-bred ruffians who keep showing up on my doorstep to claim Rose of Heaven. Pray tell, Mr. River, how many more can I expect?"

Touching a discordant combination of keys, Donovan glanced up to her. "I own Rose of Heaven. And I cheated Slade Gunter to get it." He arched a challenging brow at Treasure's stunned stare. "Isn't that what you wanted to hear?"

Treasure reached to steady herself against the back of a chair. "Is it true?"

"It's true." He played out three long, low notes. "That's what you want to believe, isn't it?"

"Is it true?" Treasure repeated insistently, her voice harsh and unfamiliar to her own ears.

Donovan waited before answering. Without striking a sound, he slowly trailed his fingers up and down the keys.

Treasure searched his face for some hint of reaction. But his feelings were kept well in check behind an unfathomable facade.

At last he answered. "Yes, I cheated Slade Gunter, but only because your father wanted me to. Seamus was no match for Gunter, but your father never could resist a good gamble." His tone was cavalier, but his eyes were hard. Tensed, his hands poised over the piano keys. "He bet his pretty plantation, knowing damned well I'd be there to back him out of whatever corner he got himself into. Seamus knew I could never resist a fool's bet."

"Papa would never—"

"He did." Donovan's expression softened. "I'm sorry, Treasure, but he did. You have to accept it. Your father no longer wanted a plantation—or a family."

"You're lying!" Treasure cried out, then stilled the sudden pain welling up inside her. She clenched her hands at her sides. "I can't believe it. Papa . . . I—I don't know what to believe." Feeling defeated, she sank onto the settee, trying to unravel some comforting reason from her snarled emotions.

Donovan said nothing. He slid his fingers over the piano keys, testing a solitary note here and there. They rang out mournfully, without meaning by themselves. Slowly, with one finger, Donovan began to bring them together, at last joining the single notes into a melody.

It was a sad, sweetly haunting sound, the gentle music vaguely familiar to Treasure, although she hadn't the presence of mind to give it a name. Yet it stirred something inside her—a soft, heart-touching feeling between tears and poignant happiness.

Fierce longing sprang up in her heart. The music reminded her of something she wanted, something she had never found. Or had lost. . . .

Wind whipped through the open windows, banging them against the wall. It flickered the light at Donovan's side, and he stopped playing, letting the song drift away with the breeze.

"I should go," he said, looking at her, his face a mask of shadows.

Treasure hesitated, then ventured, "You never told me."

"Yes?" Smoky eyes met and held hers.

"I have to know."

Donovan stilled.

"Slade Gunter said you killed Papa."

Donovan's soft expression turned to steel. Rage, hot and savage, etched hard angles in his face. With unbridled anger, he crashed a fist down onto the piano keys. The room reverberated with the furious clash of sound.

The shock of violence sent Treasure, wide-eyed, shrinking back against the settee. In that moment, he looked capable of striking her — capable of murdering a man in cold blood.

In a visible effort to regain control, Donovan closed his eyes. He drew a harsh breath and slowly uncurled his fist. Moving stiffly, he shoved back the piano bench and strode to the door.

His hand gripping the door handle, he stopped. "I suggest you settle on your favorite version of the truth. Then inform me of the role I'm to play, and I'll graciously accommodate you." He fixed her with a stare so harsh, so foreign, Treasure scarcely recognized him. "But be sure to choose carefully, Miss McGlavrin. Cast me in the role of murderer and I'll be compelled to live up to the part."

Curled in her willow rocker, chin resting on her knees, Treasure scanned the early morning sky from her vantage on the kitchen porch. She had retreated to her favorite haven in the dark hours of the morning, unable to will away the inner chaos that stole her sleep. Anger, grief, doubt, and a nagging disquiet made it impossible to even close her eyes.

Dawn, just arrived, was in a sullen mood. It guaranteed to be the harbinger of a troublesome day. Violet-black clouds hunched on the horizon and a capricious wind buffeted Rose of Heaven from whatever direction whim commanded. Treasure could smell and feel the promise of rain.

"Be a mean one today, Miz Treasure." Orange Jane

130

stepped out onto the porch, an end of her apron wrapped around the handle of a coffeepot. Setting a cup on the low table next to Treasure, she poured out a measure of the steaming brew, and glanced skyward. "We do need de rain, but Bettis say dis be a wicked one. Come hard and fast it will." The cook slowly nodded. "Yessum', bad—bad dis one gonna be."

"Summer is like that," Treasure murmured. "Gentle one moment, temperamental the next." Blinking several times, she stretched her stiff legs and reached out for the cup. Hot liquid slid down her throat. The sensation was almost painful, and it seemed to underscore the harsh realities the day brought with it.

"Somethin' wrong, Miz Treasure? Lordy, you be makin' one awful face!"

"No—no, it's fine." The cup rattled against the saucer as she set it down. "It's just this weather, I expect. It's so uncertain, and with all I have depending on the right amount of rainfall . . . It gives me a turn to think I have no control over it."

Orange Jane slipped a thoughtful glance at her mistress. "Only d'Lord knows, ain't dat true." She played her fingers over the porch railing, gazing out over the misty gray-green meadow behind the kitchen. With unconscious habit, she began humming.

The first phrases of the soulful melody stirred a faded memory of Papa, at the piano, in a rare moment of patience, teaching her the notes of a favorite song. She recalled words she had thought long forgotten, remembering them with a mix of pain and pleasure.

" 'Tis a poem ne'er spoken,
a song with none to hear.
'Tis a dawn no eyes will ev'r see,
this love I hold so dear."

"Hadn't you better see to breakfast?"

Orange Jane started at the sharp command. Without a word, she picked up the coffee pot and Treasure's empty cup and disappeared into the sanctuary of her kitchen.

As Treasure pushed off the rocker, the wind licked at her skirts. She moved to the railing, leaning out over it for a better view of the sky. She knew the fury of a summer storm could kill her fledgling crops, crushing the heart of the fields. At the very least, it would set her back a day's work. Thunder rumbled above her, a faraway echo of the anxiety rolling over and over inside her.

"Treasure?"

Emmaline stood at the door, her tattered sketchbook clutched to her chest. She edged her way onto the porch, perching on the settee opposite Treasure's rocker. "May I sit for a while? I won't be long." The words rushed out. "I promise, I'll finish all the chores by noon and I won't be late for supper and—"

"It's all right, Emmy," Treasure said with a sigh. "There's not much work to be done outside in this weather. You can help with the knitting later."

With an uncertain glance at her sister, Emmaline settled onto the settee. She began scratching at her sketchbook with a charcoal stick and became so intently focused on her work that Treasure at last admitted a reluctant curiosity. "What in heaven are you scribbling at?" she asked.

Emmaline's hand abruptly stopped. Her fingers played with the charcoal. "Nothing," she muttered, avoiding Treasure's questioning eyes.

"Well, it must be something. Let me see."

"No! I mean . . . well, it's not finished."

Brows raised, Treasure stared at Emmy, starting to feel irritated at her sister's unexpected reluctance. "I have seen your unfinished drawings before. What in particular is special about this one?"

"Nothing." Sliding off the settee, Emmaline inched

toward the door. "I'd better go. I should see to my chores."

"Not until you show me that sketchbook." Treasure stretched out an open palm.

Her eyes lowered, Emmaline grudgingly handed her the book. With a stern glance at her sister, Treasure turned to Emmaline's handiwork.

It was a rough affair of black and gray line. But the likeness, drawn with feeling detail, was unmistakable.

It was a portrait of Jimmy Rae Stanton.

"Emmaline . . ." For a moment, all Treasure could do was gape at her sister.

Emmaline plucked the sketchbook out of her hand, a spark of defiance suddenly lighting her eyes. "After all, I can draw what I want."

"Emmaline, believe I told you—"

"You just don't understand!" Tears welled in her eyes and she rapidly blinked them away. "You don't know what it feels like. How could you? You never loved anybody but Papa and Rose of Heaven. That's still all you care about. So how could you understand?"

With a sob, Emmaline turned and dashed into the kitchen, slamming the door closed behind her.

Treasure took one step in her wake and then stopped. She stood frozen in silence for long moments then slowly turned back to the railing, her hands taut on the rough wood.

In the distance, lightening cracked against the clouds and thunder bellowed in a bass crescendo, the sound dying away with an ominous growl.

"I'll see who I please and there's not a single thing you can do about it, sister dear."

Camille preened in front of her full-length glass, turning from side to side to check the sway of her skirts against the wide hoop. The rich, honey-colored satin should have been a perfect foil for her dark hair and creamy skin. But her sulky mouth and the petulant lines around her eyes spoiled the effect.

"You've your pick of any man in the valley. Why does it have to be Ira Stanton?" In vain, Treasure tried once again to convince Camille not to allow Colonel Stanton to escort her to the valley. "A man like that will bring you to sure ruin." Treasure swept her heavy hair back over her shoulder. She hadn't taken time yet to pull it black. The day seemed destined to bring a plague of problems, first Emmaline and now—"Why him, Camille?"

"Perhaps just to rile you," Camille taunted with a smirk. "I daresay that's as good a reason as any."

"I was given to understand you and Colonel Stanton weren't exactly friendly anymore. After your disagreement at the Johnsons' salon—"

"Disagreement?" Camille gave a little trill of laughter. "My, what a proper way you have of puttin' things, Treasure. Your only real passion is this wretched land, isn't it? Well, never you mind about my little spat with Ira. He was just bein' difficult. But I do believe he's come to see things my way."

"If you intend to marry—"

"Oh, please do spare me the usual tired old lectures! You may be satisfied to work like a slave and live like a spinster, but I need a different kind of satisfaction." Camille smoothed her hands over her satin-covered breasts and down her waist and hips. The sensuous motion brought a blush to Treasure's face. Smiling maliciously at Treasure's hastily averted eyes, Camille added, "I wish you would simply leave me be. I intend to make my own opportunities and I surely don't need your advice."

Sounds of a visitor's arrival drifted upward, interrupting any retort Treasure might have mustered. Colonel Stanton's genteel affectations reached her ears, turning her attempt at reason to ashes. "Your

134

association with that man is destroying your chances of making a decent match. Can't you see that?"

"Maybe decent isn't what I want."

Camille was baiting her, Treasure knew. "Very well then," she said coolly, "if you must shame yourself, it will not be under this roof. After everything Ira Stanton has tried to do, I will not have him in my house."

Ignoring Camille's indignant gasp, Treasure swept past her and marched down the staircase, fire in her eyes. Colonel Stanton stood in the foyer, running the chain of his watch back and forth through his hand. Solomon hovered near, clutching the colonel's hat between his thin hands.

A gust of wind tugged at the corners of Ira's white coat and Treasure noticed the front door still hung open. Hurrying down the rest of the stairs, she was about to berate Solomon for his negligence when she realized the house boy wasn't the cause.

Donovan stood on the stoop, his hat slung low over his brow. Legs splayed, arms folded over his chest, he faced Ira, challenge glinting like flint in his eyes. The colonel hung back in the foyer, rocking on his heels. His fingers agitated the watch chain until Treasure was certain it would snap in two.

As she stepped into the foyer, both men turned. With a sharp jerk of her head she sent Solomon scurrying. Then, ignoring Donovan's dark glance, she fixed her attention on Ira. "I believe I made it quite clear the last time you paid an uninvited call, Colonel Stanton. You are not welcome here."

"Why, Miss Treasure." He dipped her a half-bow, his eyes mocking. "You and your—companion heah may have forgotten your manners. But your lovely sistuh, I am pleased to say, still knows how to extend civilized hospitality."

"How kind of you, Colonel Stanton," Camille's throaty voice floated down the stairs. She descended into the foyer with calculated grace. Casting a dispar-

135

aging look at Donovan, she laid a hand on the colonel's arm. "Really, you must forgive poor Treasure, sir. I'm afraid she never learned how to receive visitors in a ladylike manner."

Donovan strode inside. With an eye on Treasure, he removed his hat. "But she, at least, can lay claim to the title."

Treasure stared at him, stunned.

Camille blushed an unbecoming red. "Why I never!"

"Oh, I'm certain you have. Several times."

"Now then, suh. Now then," Ira blustered, taking a step forward. "Insultin' a lady . . . Those are fightin' words, suh, fightin' words."

Donovan raked Colonel Stanton with a steely glare. "Am I to take it you are going to defend Miss Camille's dubious honor?"

"Why . . ." The colonel sized up Donovan's implacable stance, then looked to Camille. "My deah . . ."

"Colonel Stanton, I must insist! You simply cannot allow this—this ruffian to slander my good name in such a manner. You would be no kind of gentleman." The rush of words ended on a dramatic sob, and Camille pressed an inadequate handkerchief to her mouth.

Colonel Stanton squared his shoulders. "Miss Camille is right, suh. I cannot allow—"

"What's it to be then? Something that won't sully your white waistcoat too much. Pistols, perhaps?"

"Enough!" Treasure suddenly found use of her voice. With a quick step, she put herself between the two men, glaring from one to the other. "I want you"—she looked at Ira—"off my plantation. Now! And you"—she turned to Donovan—"as far away as possible. If you are settled on spilling each other's blood, that is your business. But I won't have it on my doorstep."

"Colonel Stanton stays if I wish it," Camille said, all appearance of tears vanishing. "You aren't mistress of this house, and you surely aren't my mistress, little Miss Treasure."

Ira shifted back on his heels. "Perhaps I should take my leave, Miss Camille."

Camille's mouth set in a temperamental line, and Treasure recognized the signs of an angry fit. Colonel Stanton's beetle-dark eyes coveted the front door.

And Donovan—

Treasure controlled the nervous shudder skating along her nerves. That deadly look—contempt—silently straining every fiber of his being, terrifying in its serene dispassion. Treasure decided Donovan, at that minute, could kill without regret.

A still moment held them all in a tableau of unspoken frustration. Pressure bubbled and boiled up from the knotted little group, until, just before the impending explosion, Treasure abruptly turned and left them all.

She walked and ran toward the fields, instinct rather than sight guiding her path. Humiliation washed over her. *Damn them all!* She'd come so close, too close to freeing a tirade of cloistered emotion, to thrusting aside her reason, telling the whole lot of them exactly how she felt.

And it terrified her. She had no illusions; self-restraint was her anchor, sword, and shield. Surrender to her whims, her fears, her passions, and she destroyed her focus. Success cost dearly, and she was willing to pay any personal cost to make Rose of Heaven thrive again.

Why, suddenly, must she war against this longing to follow her heart instead of her reason? Why now, when she could least afford the luxury of indulging in personal desires and needs?

Treasure stopped at the edge of the great expanse of rusty soil with its carpet of new green, wind whipping back her skirts, slashing auburn streaks of hair across her pale skin. Above her, dark clouds rolled and grumbled. The air embraced her, warm and wet.

Turning her face to the sky, she closed her eyes. Mist kissed her bare skin like subtle temptation lingering sweet with promise. *A summer storm, desire in motion, coming strong and fast, striking with a sudden thrust — then leaving you empty.*

Was that love? she wondered. Gone as quickly as it came, leaving only its passionate echo and a restless longing for the next time? A longing never satisfied?

"I thought I'd find you here."

Treasure snapped around. "You followed me."

"No, pretty lady." Donovan offered her a hint of a smile, but it lacked its usual raffish sparkle. "I just knew you'd feel safest out here," he said, glancing up at the darkening sky. "Even in the midst of a storm." He had picked up a stone along the way, and he bobbed it in the palm of his hand, betraying a restless, unspent energy.

His tension fed hers. Shivering as she followed his skyward gaze, Treasure battled the strength of her unease, unable to find a source for it.

Donovan let the stone fall. "What is it?"

"Nothing." She willed calm into her voice. "Nothing at all."

Donovan began flicking a corner of the journal stuffed in the pocket of his trousers, worrying an edge of the battered leather cover. "Camille left with Stanton. Short of kidnaping — which I assume you wouldn't approve of — I couldn't stop her."

"I see." Treasure stared blindly at the horizon. "Is that all?"

"All?" He rubbed a hand over his jaw. "Well, Stanton wasn't about to —"

"No. Not that." Drawing in a breath, she asked bluntly, "Have you settled with Slade Gunter?"

Donovan's face hardened. "That's my business."

"You have managed to make it my business, too."

"Don't borrow trouble, Treasure. You've had your share today."

"You mean Colonel Stanton . . ." Treasure stilled the nervous clenching of her fingers against her skirts. "Camille simply enjoys provoking me. She isn't serious about encouraging him."

Donovan raised a doubtful brow, but said quietly, "She is serious about besting you. Even if that means she has to use Stanton to do it."

"Don't talk nonsense! Camille is my sister—"

"There's no blood between you."

"You can hardly understand the meaning of family. Where you come from—"

"Where I come from, *sisters* don't plot against one another."

"Camille is doing no such thing. She would never betray her family, no matter what her feelings for me."

"She would and she is. You just won't see it. You can't see anything—anything except your vision of your little Alabama kingdom."

"And nothing would delight you more than for me to abandon my plans for Rose of Heaven and leave it to you. Isn't that your fondest hope, Mr. River?"

They were both near to shouting when Donovan suddenly reached out and grasped her by both shoulders. "This plantation is not the center of the universe, Treasure McGlavrin."

Treasure stood rigid in his grip, meeting his gaze with angry eyes. The wind blew the first spatter of raindrops at them. "Do tell, what else is there? You're so worldly-wise, why do you stay here?"

"Because of this—"

Trapping her face between his hands, Donovan snared his fingers in her hair and jerked her mouth to his.

Their lips met in a heated clash. Struck senseless by

139

the alien fire between them, Treasure felt helplessly lost in a whirl of sensation.

None of the gentle, tender caresses they'd shared had prepared her for this passionate assault. She had no defense against the fiery demand of his lips and hands. Her resistance fled without even a whimper of protest.

She forgot she wanted to hate him. She only craved the rush of excitement she felt as Donovan's hand slid down her spine and claimed her waist. She curled into his body, and his mouth moved hotly over her face, tasted the slender length of her throat.

Rain sputtered and sprinkled. Suddenly, it showered over them, drenching them in a warm river. Treasure opened her eyes to his. She searched the silver flames smoldering with dangerous, feral desire. He moved to kiss her again, this time parting her lips under his. His tongue explored her mouth, its sweet probing caresses smothering her desperate gasp. Caught in the heat of a battle she was rapidly losing, she melted into his embrace.

Any attempt at reason deserted her when he pushed aside the shoulder of her dress and slid his hand over her wet skin. It glided over bare, slick flesh, unleashing a surge of something wild and hungry inside her. Boldly, Treasure skimmed her hands over his arms, pressed them against the thin fabric of the shirt plastered to his chest by the rain.

Lean, rock-hard muscles tensed at her fingertips; his rapid breaths brushed her cheek in rasps. Her fingers memorized each valley and plane until Donovan stilled them, wrapping her tightly in his arms.

Thunder resounded around them, dimmed to her by her pounding heart. It roared again, pulsing, throbbing. And faintly, she heard Donovan call to her, insistently, asking her to surrender what she longed to give him. . . .

"Miss Treasure — Miss Treasure! Mastuh River!"

140

The shout drove them apart, and Treasure whirled around.

A few feet behind them Elijah looked at Donovan, his fathomless eyes betraying nothing.

"He's here, Mastuh River. At your cabin."

Treasure called over the voice of the storm, "Who's here, Elijah?"

Elijah was silent. Donovan nodded at him. Turning to Treasure, he raised a hand as if to touch her, then pulled it back. "Go with Elijah," he said. "I'll deal with this."

"With what? With whom?" She stopped, suddenly knowing. "It's Slade Gunter."

"Go with Elijah."

"No!"

"You don't have a choice." Donovan's fingers gently brushed her face, and she glimpsed a fleeting sadness in his eyes. He smiled a little, a grim twist of the lips, then turned away from her, striding toward the cabin.

Treasure started to follow, but Elijah stepped in her path. Startled, she paused in midstep. "Let me pass."

Elijah squared his shoulders. "Mastuh River wants you to stay away from there, Miss Treasure."

Wind and rain swirled around them in a furious whirl, the pelting water blurring her vision. Treasure let it course over her, unheeded. "Mr. River isn't your mistress. I am."

Elijah, unmoved, stared steadily back at her.

His response put Treasure at a loss. None of the slaves had ever questioned her commands. Elijah's disobedience rankled, but the need to follow Donovan swept it aside. Disquiet rose in her to near panic. She swallowed hard. "Mr. River may need help. Your help, maybe mine. I am going."

Silently, their wills struggled as each weighed the other's resolve. At last, Elijah turned and began walking toward the cabin. Treasure, in his wake, tried to

141

keep pace with him. But the rain seemed determined to drive her back.

Too late. They would be too late. For what? She didn't know. But she sensed disaster hovered close.

When they reached the cabin, the clash of angry voices rose above the roar of the storm. She started at the splintering crash of wood. Glass shattered. A heavy thud against a wall vied with the thunder reverberating over her head.

The crack of a pistol shot answered.

Pushing around Elijah, Treasure pounded at the door with both fists. She wrenched it open.

Framed in the doorway, Donovan crouched against the fall wall. Blood from a gash at his temple spattered his face. Oblivious to her presence, his eyes were locked in a cold, metallic stare straight ahead. He held a pistol.

And as Treasure watched, unable to move or to scream, he pulled the trigger.

142

Chapter Eight

Donovan slumped against the wall, eyes closed. His right hand, still clenched around the pistol, dropped limply to his side.

Treasure stood transfixed in the doorway. Her mind refused to react. It was too incredible, too unthinkable. And yet she coerced her legs to take a few trembling steps into the room, forced her eyes to look at the slouched body in the opposite corner of the room. The sickly-sweet smell of warm blood mixed with sweat festered in the hot, thick air. Her stomach churned.

Slade Gunter stared at her with dead eyes.

For a fleeting moment she saw Papa. The vision was as clear as the image of death before her. In her mind she saw Papa and Donovan argue, envisioned Papa forced to write the note deeding his beloved plantation to Donovan, saw Donovan raise the pistol and—

She started as gentle hands on her shoulders turned her away. Elijah moved past her and knelt by Slade, running a swift hand over his blood-soaked shirt.

"Is he dead?" Donovan's voice sounded strangely flat.

Elijah slowly nodded. "Yes, Mastuh River, he is. Clean—through the heart."

"Of course he's dead," Treasure said, amazed at how calm and reasoned her own words came out. She

143

looked at Donovan, seeing a stranger. "You killed him."

Donovan stared at her and then at the pistol in his hand. With deliberate motion, he laid the weapon on the floor. He raised a trembling hand to brush at the gash on his temple. "Yes," he said at last. "I did."

The spate of defensive words Treasure expected never came. Donovan looked at her as if expecting her to produce a clean, clever remedy for the situation, the way she would for any other messy interruption in her prescribed agenda.

She hated the bewildered calm of his expression. She wanted to rail at him, to provoke some familiar reaction from him. His lack of response frightened her more than if he had been cajoling, threatening.

"We — I have to fetch Sheriff Axle," she blurted out. "We can't just leave — him here. Sheriff Axle will . . . he will — "

"Arrest me?" Donovan finished, with a faint ironic smile. "Your fondest wish come true."

"I am so pleased you find amusement in this situation. But perhaps you're used to settling your disputes in this manner. Or perhaps it never occurred to you murder might have its consequences."

Donovan slowly climbed to his feet. "There are worse things." He ignored the question in Treasure's eyes as she tried to find sense in his cryptic retort.

Treasure's tenuous hold on her emotions slipped when he stepped in her direction. She jerked a pace backward, unable to stop the nervous flutter of her hands.

Quickly masking a wince with a cool sardonic expression, Donovan held up both hands. "Don't worry. I have no intention of touching you." He kept a careful distance between them as he reached out and snagged a discarded coat from a nearby chair, tossing it to Elijah.

"What are we gonna do with him, Mastuh River?" Elijah asked as he draped the coat over the gambler.

Donovan turned back to Treasure. She easily read the clear challenge in his eyes. With the weapon in her hands, how far would she go to destroy him?

I don't know. I don't know! Are you a murderer? Now and before? Did you kill Papa like this? Treasure couldn't trust her reason to decide. She had precious few facts. And her feelings were a poor ally. Never relied upon before, they did nothing now but baffle and unnerve her.

"Leave him here," Donovan said abruptly. "You can take Miss McGlavrin back to the house and then fetch the sheriff."

Elijah hesitated. "If the sheriff comes—"

Donovan stopped him with a glance. "Yes, I know."

Treasure looked from one man to the other before fixing her gaze on Donovan. "You can't stay here."

"Afraid I'll bolt?"

Treasure stiffened. "Yes."

"Well, don't worry, sweetheart, I'll stay, if only to afford you the pleasure of finally getting your wish to see me escorted to the local jail. It's the very least I can do."

"You'll come back to the house and then Elijah can take the cart into the valley to get the sheriff." Her eyes challenged him to oppose her.

"Aren't you afraid of being alone, sharing the same parlor with a murderer?"

"Are you a murderer?"

"Am I?"

"I think you are, Mr. River. But that's for the sheriff to decide."

Without waiting for his reply, Treasure turned and walked out the open door. She knew the two men followed her—she heard the quiet closing of the cabin door, the soft slosh of footsteps in the wet soil—but she didn't dare look back. Instead, Treasure hurried her steps, feeling as if Satan himself chased her heels.

Spring met her at the front door of the big house. She opened her mouth, then shut it quickly. Bedraggled and pale, Treasure silently walked past her into the parlor.

She heard the urgent chorus of voices as Donovan and Elijah followed her into the house. Treasure walked to the French windows, trying to shut her ears to the insidious sound. It reminded her that, even here, she couldn't escape the nightmare left behind in the cabin.

Treasure glanced over her shoulder at the tentative tap on the door. "Treasure?" Spring came up behind her, brushing a touch against her shoulder. "Treasure, are you all right?"

"Of course. I'm not given to fits."

"I know, but . . ." Spring paused, then said quickly, "Elijah told me."

"I've no doubt he did." Treasure turned and faced her sister. Spring's expression caused her faint surprise. She expected curiosity, fright, uncertainty. Instead, Spring's dark eyes reflected a warm sympathy and a strength Treasure never suspected in her flighty young sister.

"I'm going to town with Elijah," Spring said. Her words tumbled out in a rush at Treasure's sudden frown. "Even if you write him a pass, he'll be in trouble with the patroller if he's out after the guardhouse bell rings, and you'll want to stay here with Mr. River. It's really for the best, Treasure. You never could tolerate having anyone about when you're upset anyway. You always keep to yourself. If I thought I could help—"

"You can't." Spring flinched and Treasure felt a stab of painful regret. But she couldn't begin to share her feelings with anyone, not even Spring. It frightened her to even admit she had them. To voice them aloud would be too shattering.

"I know," Spring said quietly. "I'm going. I'll be back as soon as I can."

Treasure didn't know how long she stood at the windows, her vision as blurred as the water-misted glass. Outside, the fury of the storm had waned to a soft pat-

146

ter of rain. Someone had lighted the lamps in the parlor, and they threw a muted light against the windows, taunting Treasure with a reflection of herself. She stood stiffly, hands knotted at her side, her face rigid with her effort to keep her control. Inside she felt as if she were collapsing. A cold, shaking fear lived in her heart, and she wondered if she could ever turn it away.

How could she have been such a fool? She had always prided herself on her reason, taken care to guard her heart against any intrusion of emotion that might cloud her judgment. Yet she'd allowed Donovan River's practiced charm to breach her defenses. And now the cost of her folly might be higher than she had ever imagined.

As if from nowhere, there was a motion behind her. Her image in the window glass blurred. When it cleared, she looked into a reflection of Donovan River's eyes.

Treasure whirled on him. She felt the wet hardness of the glass pressed against her palms as she backed up against the window. "What are you doing here?"

A long silence answered her. His eyes searched hers with unsettling intensity. At last, he turned away. Dropping onto the settee, he slouched in one corner, long legs stretched out in front of him. Treasure cursed the weakness in herself that felt a pang in seeing the exhaustion evident in the tired slump of his body. He had haphazardly swiped the blood from his face, and an angry gash marred his temple.

To roust the treacherous softness lodged in her heart, she snapped, "Do you intend to answer my question, or have you decided to renounce all notions of civilized behavior."

"Ever tactful, aren't you, Treasure McGlavrin? You wanted me here. You more or less ordered it, I recall."

"In the house. Not in the same room with me."

"There are plenty of rooms for you to hide in if you don't relish the company."

147

"I don't."

"Afraid?"

"Yes."

Donovan got to his feet. They faced each other, wary, uncertain. "Oh, I believe you. You are afraid. Afraid I might not be the blackguard you so desperately want me to be."

"We have had this conversation before, Mr. River, and your arrogance still manages to astound me." She gathered her courage, then added, "But you're right. I am afraid of my feelings for you. I'm frightened I can still feel so much even though I know what you are, what you're capable of."

Donovan took a step toward her. Treasure, unable to retreat, fought off an upsurge of alarm. Her hands tightened at her side. She was trembling and couldn't stop. Just as she couldn't stem the torrent of painful words. "I came so near, so near, to listening to my heart, to trusting you. It was the first time —" Her voice faltered. She willed firmness into it. "And it will be the last. I don't intend to let you come close enough to deceive me a second time."

"What you do intend may have nothing to do with your feelings for me, Treasure. You don't believe it now, but there are forces stronger than even your iron will."

Though Donovan's words sent an icy rush through her, chilling her blood, Treasure mustered the determination to banish the sensation and regain her stoic front. "You're right, Mr. River. I don't believe anything you tell me," she spat, and turned on her heel to retreat before he unmasked her uncertain heart once more.

Night stretched over McGlavrin's Valley, a velvet silence, quieting the streets and ushering the townsfolk home to their families.

As Elijah handed Spring up beside him in the cart, he relished the isolation. Out past curfew for only the third time in his life, he felt the strong surge of indepen-

148

dence. Freedom. Freedom was power. Power to choose your own path, his mama said. He wanted that power as surely as he wanted his heart to beat.

Spring pulled a shawl over her shoulders and smiled over to him. Elijah turned away to hide from her any trace of the rebellious thoughts that might be mirrored on his face. But his eyes stole a sideways glance at her. From his first day at Rose of Heaven, God help him, the beautiful, spirited Spring had charmed and captivated him. With each passing month, as she took on the shape of a woman, her harmless flirtations became ever more dangerous temptations. Now with her so near, bolder than any proper Southern miss ought to dream of being, he feared her beguilement as much as he feared his own weakening will.

"What a lovely night it is, don't you think so, Elijah? And I'm certainly in no hurry to get back to all that awful worry at home. Mercy! What a night. Let's take the long road over the creek. It's so much nicer."

Elijah hesitated. The girl's teasing and smiles, her innocent laughter and butterfly grace, were rapidly spoiling his desire for any other woman, even though his head warned him against the impossible. And worse yet, if she was toying with him, she could destroy him.

"Miss Treasure will be waiting for you," he said at last. "We best go on back directly, Miss Spring."

"Oh, honestly! Treasure won't miss me a minute. What with Mr. Johnson and Miss Eliza and Sheriff Axle, and of course, Mr. River, she's up to her neck in people wanting her attention." Spring caught her lower lip in her teeth, staring long at the horses' backs, then looked directly into Elijah's eyes. "I can't think of another person I'd rather spend this evening with than you, Elijah."

Elijah searched Spring's eyes for guile. But to his heart's surprise, he found instead in their dark depths a longing echoing his own. *It's impossible.* "Miss Spring, I don't think we ought to be alone."

149

"Well, I do." She flitted her fingers against his arm. "I'm not a child anymore."

"I know. That's why it isn't right. If anyone thought something happened to you here, with me, tonight . . ."

"Oh, Elijah." Tears sparkled like stars in her eyes. She drew a tremulous breath, straightening her shoulders, suddenly transformed with a woman's determination. "I would lie for you, steal for you, kill for you if I had to. You're the kindest, most giving man I've ever known. I don't give a care about your color, or my breeding, or right and wrong. No one knows our hearts but us."

Elijah didn't dare meet her intent gaze. "That's dangerous talk, Miss Spring. You best be careful. Don't ever say anything like that to another soul. Ever."

"I never have, and I never will. I know people think I'm simple because I prattle on. But I have strong thoughts." Boldly, she reach out and gripped Elijah's hand, forcing him to look at her. "And strong feelings. I would never betray you. I'd sooner die."

Lost in the depths of her eyes, risking all he dreamed of, planned for, Elijah trusted her. With a sharp slap of the harness leathers, he turned the cart in the opposite direction and headed for the long road home.

"We hoped you wouldn't mind if we came," Rader said as Solomon ushered him and Eliza into the big house.

"You two are always welcome." Treasure was hardly in the mood for company, but she reminded herself Rader and Eliza were near enough to family. "News certainly does spread through the valley faster than wildfire."

Eliza wrapped a comforting arm around Treasure. "No one's heard but us. Sheriff Axle was in the store picking up spools for his Myra when Elijah and Spring came looking for him."

Sending Solomon out for coffee, Treasure followed the Johnsons into the parlor. "Are they on their way back then?"

"Axle should be here any minute. Said he had to stop by the house first," Rader said.

"Spring told me to let you know they'd be back a little later. She had some errand, I do believe." Eliza smoothed her skirts with a thoughtful hand. "I think she simply wanted to wait out the storm."

Treasure perched on the edge of a wing chair, her hands twisting in her lap. "I do hope she is careful." Lord, she simply lacked the energy to deal with another problem now.

"Where is Mr. River?" Eliza asked.

Her face stoic, Treasure opened her mouth to begin recounting the past hour's horror, but Solomon, Sheriff Axle in his wake, interrupted.

The sheriff tipped his hat, his manner intended to reassure. "Evenin', Miss Treasure. I came up here fast as I could. Seems we've got us some ugly business to tend to."

"Yes, I fear so." She nodded to Solomon, who had just returned with the coffee tray. "Go and find Mr. River. Tell him—" She drew a steadying breath. "Tell him the sheriff is here."

Sheriff Axle dropped a meaty hand on the boy's bony shoulder. "Don't bother, Solomon. I'll go out and fetch him myself. You folks just carry on with your visit."

"But—" Treasure objected.

"I'll take care of it, Miss Treasure." With another tip of his hat, he disappeared after Solomon.

"Well, I never." Treasure flung up a hand. "I should be with him. I was there."

"Oh, honey, how simply awful." Eliza shook her head.

Treasure couldn't stop the words from spilling out. "I saw him, Mr. River, with the gun. He pulled the trigger

151

and . . . and that—that man lying in the corner. Dead. He was dead."

"There now, it's all over, child." Eliza moved next to Treasure and gently brushed tangles of hair from her face.

"Liza's right. It's up to the sheriff now," Rader added. "Who was that man anyhow? What did he want with Mr. River?"

"Some low gambler Mr. River knew from Louisiana. Mr. River cheated him out of—" She stopped. She just couldn't bring herself to tell them how Papa had lost Rose of Heaven. "He cheated him out of a huge sum, and this man wanted payment. In blood."

"Oh, my." Eliza rubbed fingers to her temple. "Donovan certainly has courted his share of trouble."

"Not quite the enchanting stranger you imagined, is he?" Treasure's bitter wounds were too fresh to hide.

Unruffled by her sharp tone, Eliza patted her hand. "I am sorry, honey. But surely there's been some horrid mistake."

"Oh, indeed there has. My mistake was to ever let him wheedle his way into this house. I should have kicked him back out into the swamp he slithered out of the first day he set foot on Rose of Heaven."

"As I recollect, you tried," Rader said. "He has a valid claim to this place, or you'd have been free of him long ago. We all know that."

"We still don't know everything about this evenin'," Eliza added. "I realize Mr. River appears in a rather bad light, but maybe there's a reasonable explanation."

"How can you say that!" Treasure jerked away from her friend. "I told you why Slade Gunter came here, and I told you what my own eyes saw. Donovan River killed that man. He is guilty. There is no other explanation."

"I'm afraid Sheriff Axle disagrees."

Side by side, looking to Treasure like friendly companions rather than law officer and prisoner, Donovan and Sheriff Axle stepped back in the parlor.

She slapped Donovan with a glare, then turned to the sheriff. "You cannot be serious."

"Yep. I don't see no reason to take Mr. River here into town with me. We got everything settled between us. He's free to stay in the valley long as he likes."

Heat rose to Treasure's face in a red flush of anger. She stood, hands balled at her sides. "Aren't you even going to talk to me?"

"Don't see as I need to."

"I cannot believe I am hearing this."

"Now, Treasure." Eliza came up behind her. "We've always trusted Sheriff Axle's judgment where the law is concerned."

"He's a reasonable man."

Treasure whirled on Donovan. His voice was bland, but she imagined a smug edge. His hat, pulled low, guarded any expression in his eyes. Her strained thread of patience snapped. "To a man who kills on impulse, the devil himself is the soul of reasonable behavior."

Her fury, tempered to cool sarcasm, swung to Axle. "Good evening, sheriff. Solomon will show you out."

"Well—er, good evenin' to you all." He turned to Donovan. "You know where to find me if you have any more trouble, Mr. River."

When he had gone, Treasure addressed Eliza and Rader, stiff politeness in her manner. "I thank you for coming, but if you will please excuse me, I should attend to my family. Perhaps you would come for supper tomorrow. I assure you"—she glared hard at Donovan—"the conversation will be more pleasant."

"Why of course we will, honey," Eliza answered, despite the clear hesitation on her husband's face.

With a sharp nod, Treasure strode out of the room, certain a single moment longer in Donovan's company would prove too burdensome for her frayed temper. She knew such rudeness to her fondest friends was inex-

153

cusable, but she also knew they would forgive her. This once, she felt compelled to presume on that friendship. Apologies could come later after she foraged the will to control her frustrated rage.

She couldn't recall a time when she had skated so near to losing her prized dignity, her leash on her emotions. Anger scorched her reason to ash. And the reason stood in her parlor. Donovan River. He provoked this chaos inside her, and she hated him for it. Hated the way he forced her to feel, to react.

As she rounded the doorway into the front hall, Treasure's inner warring nearly blinded her to the slight figure crouched halfway behind the parlor door, her head bowed deeply into her skirts.

"Emmy?"

Emmaline looked up, her eyes swollen and red from crying.

"You heard—everything. Didn't you?" Treasure took a step toward Emmy, who scrambled to her feet and backed away.

She sucked in a sob and swiped tears from her face. "You're going to send Donovan away, aren't you?"

"Emmy . . ." Treasure sighed. "I don't know what I intend to do yet."

"I do. You'll make him leave. I know you."

"I have our family to consider. I care about you all. I can't chance one of you coming to harm."

"Donovan wouldn't hurt us."

"He killed a man."

"Maybe Slade Gunter deserved to die!"

"Emmaline!" Treasure snapped, regretting it immediately when Emmy flinched. She softened her tone. "It's not that simple. People are not always as they seem. You don't know a thing about Mr. River."

"I know he's kind and fun to be with, and he takes time to listen to me. Which is more than you ever do!" Emmy cried. Her tears spilling over, she turned to dash for the stairs.

154

"Emmaline, you stay right here."

"No! Leave me alone, Treasure. I just want to be alone!"

Treasure heeded the urging of her heart as she rushed to follow Emmy up the stairs. It hurt to be reminded once more how easily Donovan had reached Emmy. She'd often noticed them chatting together, Donovan intent on one of Emmy's sketches. Each time the sight stabbed at her own sense of failure, her inability to give what Emmy so desperately sought.

Now, the memories compelled her to follow his example.

Once inside her bedroom, Emmaline flung herself on the bed, burying her face in the pillow. Pausing for a moment in the doorway, Treasure moved to the bed and sat down beside her sister.

"Emmy?" She reached out and touched Emmy's stiff shoulder with a hesitant touch. "I'm sorry I've upset you," she said softly, groping for the right words of comfort. "I'm only worried about you."

Emmaline sniffed loudly, her voice muffled by the thick down pillow. "You worry about everything, Treasure. It's all you ever do."

"I suppose it seems that way sometimes. But with Papa gone, someone has to be responsible for our family and Rose of Heaven."

"Why do you have to do it all the time? Donovan would help you."

"Emmaline . . ." Treasure bit back the lecturing words on her tongue. "Emmy, I know you like Mr. River and I'm trying to understand, but—"

"Then let him stay." Emmy scrambled up, wiping the tears from her eyes. "Please, Treasure. Please let him stay."

Treasure tried to stand firm against the hopeful plea in Emmy's eyes. "I . . . I'll think about it," she said at last.

"Do you promise?"

"Yes, of course. If you promise to get under the covers and get some sleep. We've a lot to do tomorrow."

"We always have a lot to do," Emmy said with a grimace. She complied with Treasure's request, though, crawling under the sheets and letting Treasure draw the light cover to her shoulders.

Gently brushing the tousled hair from Emmy's forehead, Treasure lightly kissed her cheek. She quietly closed the door behind her as she left the room.

Her steps slow, she retreated to the solitude of her own room. Sitting at her window, she stared out into the grim darkness, waiting for the light of day to bring her new answers.

Let him stay.

How can I? Yet given his claim to Rose of Heaven, how could she let him go?

The question haunted her well into the night.

Morning, when it came, found her still curled against the dew-misted glass. Aching from little sleep and a tired heart, she slipped on a work frock and went downstairs to begin her day's chores.

A night's worth of thinking and rethinking hadn't brought any solutions. Donovan River was a murderer. Once, likely twice. Why was she the only one to see that? It seemed he hypnotized them all with a carefree smile and easy charm.

Passing by the parlor, an image of him seated at her mama's piano, gently brushing his fingers over the keys, creating a sweet, melancholy tune, stopped her momentarily.

Yes, you almost had me convinced as well, Mr. River. Almost.

Treasure shook off the spell as quickly as it had come and delved into her morning chores, grateful he was nowhere about.

Orange Jane sent word out to the fields that the noon meal would be served outside on the picnic table, under

156

the spread of white-blossomed magnolias, the dining room table being in dire need of a good polish before guests arrived.

Treasure, having worked up an appetite at last, came up the back walk to the pine plank table set with fresh watermelon and berries, ham and loaves of freshly baked bread. The sweet-tart aroma of blackberry pie made her stomach growl in complaint for a missed breakfast.

Now well accustomed to sparse meals, Treasure thought the array of food looked like a windfall from heaven. Immediately, she fretted that her impulsive invitation to the Johnsons would severely strain her already depleted pantry. The feast incited a sudden suspicion of either Donovan's attempting a gesture of reconciliation, or Orange Jane's trying to kindle her mistress's waning appetite.

She decided it must be the latter, as much to avoid any more confrontation as to soothe her own disquiet. Wiping her hands on her apron, she strode up to the table. A huge magnolia trunk obstructed her view, but Treasure had no difficulty recognizing Camille's sultry cajoling and Donovan's bourbon-smooth reply.

"You have to eat something, sugah. Come on now, have a bite of my ham."

"I have no appetite for anything you have to offer, Camille. I thought that was clear." Treasure stepped around the tree in time to see Donovan push away the fork Camille held to his mouth.

Treasure smiled despite herself. She deliberately scuffed her feet in the stiff grass to announce her presence. Donovan looked up. They faced each other, a long, searching silence suspended between them.

"Afternoon," he said finally. With deliberate ease, He stood up, pinning her with his eyes as she struggled to maintain a cool facade.

"Good afternoon, Mr. River, Camille."

"I do declare, Treasure, after all the excitement

around here yesterday, I should think you'd be taking a day in bed."

"I thought I'd best leave that to you. I am certain you found the whole ordeal most taxing."

"I was only trying to be understanding, but I can see you are determined to think the worse of me. No matter." Camille gave a delicate shrug. "I'm going into the valley to distract my mind from all our worries." She bent close to Donovan, exposing the deep décolletage of her rose and cream neckline. "Care to join me, Mr. River? I dare say you would be the better for a little diversion after your trials."

"No, thank you. My reputation has suffered enough."

"Your loss then. There are plenty of men waiting to be seen escorting me." Camille, with a flounce of her skirts, left them alone.

Treasure sat down and helped herself to watermelon and pie, trying not to feel intimidated by Donovan's looming figure. "I shouldn't worry about your reputation. Everyone is convinced you are innocent."

"Everyone?"

Treasure glanced up from her watermelon. "What I think hardly matters." She shoved a piece of melon around her plate with the tip of her fork. Suddenly, it lost its appeal.

"It matters more than ever. Don't deny it."

Treasure shoved her plate aside. "You admitted you killed Slade Gunter. You were indebted to him. Whatever you've managed to convince the others your intention was, the reason is obvious to me."

"No more Slade Gunter, no more debt. Is that it?"

"Precisely."

"Life is always so neatly black and white to you. I'm envious. Nothing has ever been that clear-cut for me. I seem to wade through shades of gray most of the time."

Baffled by his meaning, Treasure pushed her plate aside. "I need to look over the corn crops."

158

"A welcome suggestion."

"It wasn't an invitation. I don't want your company."

"Too bad." He picked up his hat and tugged it low over his face. "Because like it or not, you've got it."

She stepped in front of him and their bare arms brushed. Her skin against his felt warm and slightly moist, like skin in the aftermath of love. A fresh, morning scent floated after her, swirling around him in her wake, binding him by an invisible chain he couldn't break.

It made no sense. She was hopeless; never believing a word he said, never trusting an action. Why in hell didn't he just give up on her and let her rot away on her precious land into an embittered spinster. Wasn't that what she wanted?

"Mr. River," she said suddenly as they wove their way out into the field of thriving green corn stalks, "this really must end. You have no place here. It is quite obviously you are unaccustomed to a life of civilized responsibility. And you can't expect me ever to trust you. Not after — yesterday."

She sounded so reasoned, so calm, as she made her little speech. Donovan heard her, but cared less what she said. Which was just as well, he decided, since Treasure McGlavrin's logic never failed to frustrate him.

But he did notice the way the sunlight separated her long waves of hair into glistening threads of copper and gold. He paused, captivated by the radiant glow of her sun-kissed skin, its faint dusting of freckles nearly blended by summer light into one apricot-gold shade. "Hardly the epitome of the milk-skinned Southern belle," he murmured.

"Excuse me?" Treasure turned, scrunching up her nose as she looked up at him.

He laughed. "You look about ten years old when you do that."

A hint of a smile almost touched her lips, but the straight-lipped look of the disgruntled mistress faith-

159

fully overtook it. "Don't even consider it, Mr. River. I allowed you along to ask you one final time to leave my land and my family alone." She fixed her attention on a corn plant, breaking a husk from its stalk. "Go back to your gambling and your blackguard companions. Leave us in peace."

"This subject is becoming too well worn. Let's try another." Aware he risked inciting a torrent of anger, Donovan reached out and covered her small hands in his, cupping the corn husk between them. When she didn't pull back he began, slowly, shedding layers of the stiff, green foliage.

"Please . . ." He felt her gaze on his face, searching. "Don't do this. Not now. I can't — I don't want to fight you anymore."

"Then don't." Stripping away the shimmering tassels from the firm tip of sweet corn, he fingered a single white kernel from its hollow and lifted it to her lips. "Here. Close your eyes and savor the first fruit of your land."

She hesitated. Donovan clearly saw the flicker of fear and uncertainty in her wide gaze.

"It's just a small taste. Perhaps once you try it, you'll want the rest."

He thought she would refuse. Then, with a sigh, her eyes fluttered closed. She parted her lips for his fingers. Donovan placed the sweet morsel on her tongue.

When she opened her eyes, they were glazed, the dark fringes around them dewy. Again her lips parted, pink, full, and she ran her tongue slowly over them relishing the taste.

His mouth ached to open hers, to take her, enter her, possess her. A breeze lifted the tendrils of hair clinging to her neck, blew the light cotton of her dress taut against the graceful curves of her breasts, her waist. She didn't move. Didn't speak.

He knew she mistrusted him, would be rid of him in

160

an instant if it were in her power to banish him from her life.

Yet he wanted her. And no matter what icy contempt her words might speak, buried deep was a hot need that echoed his.

A touch, a kiss, a stroke of her skin, provoking her passions, and he could seduce her to his will. The temptation nearly overcame any notion of honor he possessed.

No. Damn. He couldn't.

Long for her though he might, he realized that to push her to face her feelings for him now, when she thought him a murderer, would be a self-betrayal she would never forget. And she would never forgive him. It shouldn't matter. But it did.

Despite her brave front, she looked so young, so innocent, so vulnerable. He struggled for words, feeling awkward, as though he spoke to a child. "It's getting late."

The distance returned in her voice, her manner. "So. That's the way it's to be."

"For now."

"Never again."

"Don't be so certain. I'm afraid you're going to be cursed with my presence for a long time to come, pretty lady."

Donovan left her feeling he'd done the only thing he could. The thought did nothing to ease his frustrations, both in mind and body.

Maybe he should leave and never look back. His vagabond heart tempted him, reminding him he'd suffered nothing but trouble heaped upon trouble since the day he set foot in Treasure McGlavrin's kingdom. And with not so much as a single night with a warm, willing body for comfort.

How long had it been since he'd felt a woman's soft

thighs wrapped around him? "Too damned long," he muttered. As he stepped inside the cluttered room he pretended was home, the itch to bolt, to run to the bed of the first whore outside the state of Alabama, was stronger than he'd ever remembered.

"Why, Mr. River, a gentleman never curses in front of a lady," a sultry voice greeted him from the far side of the room. Camille was curled up on his bed, wearing a thin sheet.

Still afire from the heat of the desire Treasure aroused in him, Donovan's passion-darkened eyes met Camille's, and he found his desperate lust mirrored there.

He kicked the door closed behind him. "But we both know you're no lady," he said, his eyes sweeping the lush curves she so readily offered for his appraisal.

Camille gave a delicate shrug of her shoulders, dislodging the sheet from her full breasts. "Well, perhaps not. But it would appear, sugah, what you need you can't get from a *real* lady. I can give you anything you want, here and now, with no promises and no wedding rings as the price."

Donovan moved toward her until he stood but a breath away. Close enough to smell the heady honeysuckle scent of her perfume, to graze the white satin of her bared skin.

"You are lovely, Camille. I can't deny that."

It was the cue she needed, and he knew it. With the expertise of one well schooled in the art of seduction, she let the sheet slip to the floor. Every gesture was an invitation for him to sate his aching need as she bared herself completely to his hungry gaze.

Her fingers spread over him, inflaming, driving away reason. But when she reached for the buttons at his groin, Donovan shoved away, taking a few stumbling steps backward.

Turning from the bed, he rubbed a shaking hand over his jaw, struggling to retain the last vestiges of control.

162

"I don't mind a little teasin', sugah." The honey of Camille's voice was laced with bitter threads of temper. Donovan heard the soft rustle of sheets as she slipped off the bed, then felt her fingers splay over his back. "But you're takin' it a bit too far."

"No, I've taken it farther than I wanted." Escaping her touch, he faced her, the cold reality of what she was dousing his desire. "You'd better leave."

Camille let the sheet she'd loosely gathered around her fall to her waist. "I don't believe that's what you really want, honey." Knowing his eyes followed her, she walked back to the bed, each colubrine motion designed to entice. She lay back against the pillow, smiling. "Now is it?"

It was a.mistake. Treasure knew it and yet she couldn't stop herself from going to his cabin. Their encounter in the field left her with a restless, dissatisfied feeling. Donovan tempted her to abandon herself to her feelings for him, and then, when he could have pressed his advantage, he released her from his disturbing power, and left her alone.

Why. She had to know why.

Determination her only ally, she raised a hand and knocked firmly on the cabin door. The last thrust of her fist jarred it open. It flung wide on Donovan standing by his bed, a step away from Camille s reaching arms.

Her hand faltered against the door frame, groping for some support.

"Oh, my," Camille murmured, letting the sheet slip from one long, slender leg. "Why, Treasure, sugar,

Chapter Nine

Treasure's eyes memorized every cruel and painful detail of the shocking scene: the heated air redolent with an earthy, musk essence, the faint lingering of Camille's honeysuckle scent, hastily discarded clothing scattered across the floor in pools of perfumed silk and sweat-damp cotton. Camille wound in Donovan's sheets, her dark tousled hair thinly veiling a satisfied smirk.

And Donovan—

He had dared Treasure to risk an impulsive act, and she rashly let her heart accept the dare, nurturing the impossible hope they could come together on some common ground. And this was her reward—knowing Donovan and Camille shared the intimacies he had tempted her to taste only hours ago. Without thought or regret, how easily he had abandoned his supposed caring for her to satisfy his lust.

The same hands and mouth that had caressed the first tentative taste of passion from her heart had indulged in every tempting curve, every secret valley Camille's willing body could offer. Treasure's stomach lurched at the too-clear vision, humiliation and outrage rising red hot in her cheeks. It hurt. Hurt in a way she didn't know she could hurt, more than she believed possible.

164

Her hand faltered against the door frame, groping for some support.

"Oh, my," Camille murmured, letting the sheet slip from one long, slender leg. "Why, Treasure, sugah, you look so very pale. How terribly embarrassin' you happened to call just now. You must be truly mortified." Camille gave a light, flirting laugh that ended in a little cough when Donovan whipped around and slapped her with a hard stare.

Disheveled, half-dressed in rumpled trousers, he turned back to Treasure, rubbing a hand over his jaw. From the familiar gesture, Treasure knew he was struggling to invent something to say. She decided to save him the effort; his words would only compound her agony.

"I apologize for the interruption," she said flatly, her features set in stone. Refusing to look at either of them, Treasure turned and forced her legs to take her away from the cabin. She had taken less than a dozen steps away before Donovan caught her shoulder and pivoted her around to face him.

"Treasure . . ." he said, quickly pulling on his shirt, "wait . . ."

She jerked away from him, trembling with shame and indignation. "Don't touch me again. Ever again," she hissed. "Just go back to—to her."

"Give me a chance to explain—"

"How you came to bed my sister? I hardly need to hear the tawdry details to draw my own conclusions."

"Is that so?" He forestalled her ready answer, plunging ahead with a torrent of words as if he had waited as long as he could to say them. "I don't think you can begin to understand. You're still an infant at heart; a child in a woman's body who doesn't have the faintest clue what those guileless, green eyes and that sweet, soft mouth can do to a man."

"That's not true!"

"No?"

Donovan stared at her a long moment, then with an explosive sigh, turned away, raking an unsteady hand through his hair. "Maybe not. And maybe it doesn't matter anymore." He turned back to her. "I didn't bed Camille. She was here and she made it easy. I was tempted — hell, any man would be," he added with a rueful grimace. "But I couldn't. I kept thinking of you. I wanted you."

"You're lying," Treasure whispered. She blinked away the burning mist clouding her vision. "You're always lying to me. You have been from the first day you walked on my plantation. I let you — you . . . and now you expect me meekly to forgive your dalliance with Camille simply because you regret yet another of your impulses — an impulse that, by my estimation, nearly surpasses thievery and murder."

"I'm not asking you forgive me. I'm asking you, just once, to accept the truth. I didn't make love to Camille." He made no move to touch her, but Treasure sensed the struggle he waged to keep from reaching out to her. "I only wish you could remember what it feels like when we're not hurting each other. But I'm beginning to believe perhaps that's the one thing I *should* ask you to forget."

Treasure watched him turn sharply back to the cabin, pride and pain holding her transfixed, her heart's whisper a damning chant: *I can never forget. Never.*

Camille was still lounging on the narrow bed when Donovan slammed back into the cabin. She studied the tense set of his jaw and shoulders and then, with a little provocative shrug, let the sheet slide down her body in a sensual sweep. "Poor little Treasure isn't worth the effort, darlin'. Let me remind you that I am."

Donovan scooped up her rumpled silk dress and froth of crinolines from the floor and dropped them in her lap. "Get dressed, Camille. Then get out."

Her eyes narrowed, but her mouth curved in an indulgent smile. "Oooh, I just adore it when you act so manly, Mr. River." Pushing clothing and covers aside, Camille slowly rose to her feet. She stepped close to him and slid her hands up his chest, her nails biting into the taut muscle. "I know what you really want." She raked her fingertips down his skin, letting one hand toy with the buttons of his trousers. "And I'm more than willin' to supply it. Givin' and gettin' back, that's how I like it," she purred, running her thumbs up the center of his chest.

It would be so easy, Donovan told himself, so easy to accept the lush pleasures Camille so brashly offered, to slip back into his old ways of bed and forget. Simple, satisfying, with none of the heart-wringing and tortuous emotion to poison the fiery drought of desire. She was hot and willing; he was able and tempted.

But looking down into her face, he could see only the river green eyes of Treasure McGlavrin. Like the river, ever-changing. Cool and depthless in her proud moods; turbulent with fiery anger or newfound desire; clear and sparkling and inviting when he touched the vulnerable sweetness in her.

It was Camille's eyes, though, that gazed back at him. Camille's soft flesh pressed against him. Suddenly, he felt sick—with her, with himself. Grasping Camille's wandering hands at the wrists, Donovan guided her to the bed. She wet her lips, avid lust in her eyes.

Her face slacked in stunned shock when, instead of pushing her down on the rumpled bedclothes, Donovan plucked up her clothes and put them into her arms. "I meant what I said. This was a mistake. For both of us."

Camille didn't move for a long moment, staring at him as if he'd gone mad. Then rage suffused her face with an unlovely shade of red. "You're quite right," she snarled as she jerked her clothes on, fumbling with stays and buttons in her angry haste. "It was a mistake.

But the error was yours, Mr. River. And I'll make certain you sorely regret it. You and my darlin' sister."

Her eyes spitting venom, Camille flounced out of the cabin. The slam of the door echoed through the empty room and lingered, as if to remind Donovan he was alone.

Alone. *Maybe I am crazy.* Camille was the kind of woman he had expected—anticipated finding in Alabama. Treasure McGlavrin was the last thing he had wanted.

Yet the last thing on earth he ever wished for suddenly had become the thing he wanted most.

Treasure, struggling to tame her hair into a neat twist at her nape, longed to invent some polite lie to avoid dinner with the Johnsons. She could scarcely rescind the invitation now, but maintaining a gracious mien seemed the sorest of tasks.

At least she would not have to face Camille. Pleading one of her spells (Treasure guessed a fit of temper—what had Donovan said to her?), Camille had taken to bed and was driving Eura Mae to distraction, calling for trays of tea and soup, and mint leaf compresses.

If only Donovan River could be made to vanish so easily. If only he were gentleman enough to stay away.

His name in her thoughts sent a quickening through her veins, an anticipation compounded of dread and anger. Of course he wouldn't stay away. Donovan River was no gentleman.

Treasure desperately longed to erase the memory of him with Camille. Did he hope by bedding her stepsister he would gain an ally in his scheme to take over Rose of Heaven? Or was he motivated by lust alone?

I didn't make love to Camille.

She wanted to believe him. How could she? He had stolen her father's plantation—her plantation; cheated, then murdered a man to keep it. He tempted

168

her heart one moment, seduced her stepsister in the next. Most unnerving of all, she hadn't a hope of understanding Donovan's complete reliance on his feelings. He never acted sensibly. He just acted. She could never trust his motives.

She could never trust him.

Donovan River stood between her and her most beloved possession, Rose of Heaven. He threatened her determined goal to make the plantation succeed; to finally make her Papa proud.

But Donovan hadn't reckoned on her resolve.

Treasure took one last look in the mirror. The dark copper-brown silk she had rummaged from the depths of her wardrobe, with its high collar and austere lines, gave her a severe air, invited no nonsense. Inside, she might waver. From the outside, Donovan River would never know it.

Smiling grimly at her image in the long mirror, Treasure drew a breath and started downstairs to the parlor.

Sounds of murmured conversation filtered into the hallway as Treasure stepped into the room. She attempted to slip in unobtrusively, but the rustle of her skirts betrayed her and four pairs of eyes fixed on her. Treasure resisted an urge to tug at the suddenly tight neck of her dress.

Eliza rose and pressed her cheek to Treasure's in warm greeting. "Quite the mistress of the manor, honey," she said in a tart, teasing tone Treasure tolerated only from her.

Spring, seated near Donovan at the piano, wrinkled her nose at her sister. "You look dressed for winter. I surely would be boiling hot in all that silk. What do you think, Mr. River?"

Treasure reluctantly glanced at Donovan, disturbed to find him studying her. But she in turn found reason to stare back. Dressed in finely tailored black with a crisp white shirt, he was scarcely recognizable. He stood and bowed slightly her way, his air of refined elegance making him more a stranger than ever before. He looked as if soirees and opera houses, not gambling dens and taverns, were his natural habitats.

"Well?" Spring demanded, a spark of mischief in her eyes. "It's impolite not to answer a lady's question."

"Miss McGlavrin does appear rather warm," Donovan said with a faint smile. "But quite charming."

As the party stood to move to the next room, Spring smothered a giggle behind her hand and Rader and Eliza exchanged glances. It was then Treasure realized Emmaline was missing from the company. "Didn't you tell Emmy we were dining early tonight, Spring?"

"Of course, hours ago. Perhaps she's wrapped up in a drawing and has forgotten. I'll go and fetch her."

"Don't bother yourself, Missy Spring," a voice boomed behind them. "Missy Emmaline ain't in her room. She ain't nowhere to be found."

Eura Mae waited in the doorway, unmoved by the host of incredulous stares. Her foot rapped impatiently against the oak floor. "Well, heavenly days, ain't you all gonna do nothin' but stand 'round lookin' like hogs 'fo de butcher? De chile done gone and run off, I tell you."

Treasure, the first to recover her composure, stepped forward with brisk assurance, intending to put an end to Eura Mae's foolish notions. "Mammy Eura Mae, don't talk nonsense. Of course Emmaline isn't missing. Something has caught her fancy, and she's forgotten the time, that's all."

"Don't matter how forgetful dat chile be, she ain't never been out past dark." Slapping her hands to wide hips, Eura Mae threw a pointed glance at the twilight-darkened windows. "She run off, plain and simple," she said with a look that clearly told Treasure she ought to have known, too.

"It is simply ridiculous. Why should Emmaline run away?" The answer flashed across her thoughts as the question left her lips. A vision of Emmy defiantly defending her sketch of Jimmy Rae Stanton — surely Em-

170

maline had more sense than to let a schoolgirl infatuation persuade her into such rash action. Such foolish, puerile emotions couldn't mean anything — could they?

As if somehow divining her thoughts, Donovan spoke up behind her. "Emmaline was upset earlier when she overheard us arguing. She's sensitive to upheaval right now," he said, then added as an afterthought, "And Jimmy Rae's recent attentions haven't helped matters."

The soft note of empathy in his voice gave Treasure a sharp pang. She turned to look at him, momentarily forgetting their harsh words, her fears and doubts about him, and seeing only the unmasked feeling in his eyes. Sympathy, concern for Emmy, an innate empathy. How perceptive he was — how little she understood. Her own adolescence had died before it was born. She could find no echo within herself in Emmaline's growing pains. But he simply accepted them. . . .

"Bless my heart, I hope that child hasn't gone along with Jimmy Rae Stanton," Eliza said, sharing a worried glance with her husband. "If ever there was a blackguard in the making, that Stanton boy is he. I'm sorry, honey," she added as Treasure winced, "but if Donovan is right, we must find Emmaline as soon as possible."

"But we don't know for certain Emmy has run away. Mammie Eura Mae — "

"Missy Treasure — " Eura Mae fixed her with an intimidating glare Treasure knew well from her nursery days. "I'se been mammie to you chilin' for nigh on twenty years. I knows when one of you'se in trouble or upset in de heart." She paused, and Treasure, without knowing , suddenly felt six years old again; ashamed, ready to lower her eyes and scuff her feet in abasement. "Missy Emmy's sketchin' things, her two favorite dresses, and dat locket you done give her two birthdays ago is all missin'. Gone with Missy Emmy. Lord strike my heart dead if dat chile ain't up and left home."

As she tried to reason away the heart fear that sprung from Eura Mae's certainty, Treasure caught her lower lip in her teeth. Her fingers twisted over themselves. "She knows I cannot tolerate the Stantons. And Jimmy Rae — " Treasure shuddered, her skin crawling with the remembered rasp of Jimmy Rae's greedy hands groping over her.

Her senses blinded by the recollection, Treasure couldn't muster a protest when Donovan stepped between her and Eura Mae and sheltered both her hands in his. "Don't think about it," he ordered. "It will only make the situation worse."

Treasure felt small, uncertain. She suddenly, desperately needed reassurance — *his* reassurance. Her mind cruelly mocked her: *Foolish! Weak!* But her heart craved the soothing balm of his conviction that everything could be put right. When she spoke, her voice trembled, but she managed the words, compelled to speak them aloud. "Jimmy Rae takes pleasure in hurting things — people."

"He won't hurt Emmaline."

"How can you know that?"

"Because I'll kill the sonofabitch if he tries." The cocky lift of his brow told Treasure he couldn't resist the touch of dry irony. But his expression immediately softened and he gently squeezed her hands. "I promise to keep her safe."

Treasure searched his eyes. His strength became hers and Treasure's self-reliance reasserted itself.

It jolted her into realizing that, in front of several curious witnesses, she stood helplessly clinging to the hands of a man mere minutes ago she had condemned as a low, conniving cheat, a murderer. She held the same hands that had pleasured Camille's willing body so soon after caressing her own.

Embarrassment flushed her neck and face as she tugged her hands away. "I must apologize for my lapse," she murmured with stilted politeness. "Concern

172

for my sister has made me forget myself."

Donovan stepped back quickly, as if stricken with blows, not words. "It appears we both forgot, Miss McGlavrin. I assure you, it won't happen again."

Treasure flinched as he cut her from his attention with saber-keen swiftness. Hoping for relief, she felt instead a surprising stab of regret. What had she expected? What did she want?

Turning to Rader, Donovan said, "We've got about an hour before it's full dark. If we leave now . . ."

Rader nodded. "We'll pair up with Elijah and Bettis. Then if the patroller's about, there won't be trouble. If we don't have luck by nightfall, I'll ride back into town and fetch the sheriff."

Spring laid a trembling hand on Treasure's arm. She gave her sister a pale smile. "We'll see to the twins. They'll be done up over all the excitement."

Returning Spring's weak smile, Treasure slipped away from her sister's comfort. The two men were heading for the door when she stepped in their path. "I'm going with you."

"No." Donovan's steel gaze didn't tempt argument. "Stay. Emmy may come back. If so, you should be here."

Treasure refused to falter. "Spring and Camille and Miss Eliza and Eura Mae will stay . . ."

Donovan's dark gaze bore into her. "*You* should be here."

The insinuation hurt. "I am always here for Emmaline," she bit back.

"Treasure, honey, you're wasting good time," Eliza broke in. "Let the men do their work." She put a gentle hand on Treasure's arm and nodded at Donovan and her husband. "You two get along and find that child."

As the two men disappeared out the doorway, Treasure protested, "Miss Eliza —"

"Now honey, don't you fuss at me. I've had a tryin' day and I don't intend to let you make it worse. You

173

wouldn't be any help to them tripping over your crinolines in the dark. You and Mr. River would be sassing each other, Rader'd be frettin' over both of you, and not one good thing would come of it."

"I don't wear crinolines — "

"Well, you should. They work miracles on a nice full silk."

"And I've a mind to go out on my own. I can look out for myself, day or night."

"Oh, Treasure, honey," Eliza sighed, "I'm sure you can. But I dearly believe that stubborn pride of yours could stand for you to take a good cry on someone's shoulder once every harvest moon or so."

Treasure straightened her shoulders, chin firmly in the air. "That's the last remedy I need."

Eliza's lips parted and then, as if thinking better of it, she firmly closed them. Instead, she arched one brow, a faint smile playing at the corner of her mouth. With a rueful shake of her head, she settled herself on the settee, leaning one cheek against her hand to watch Treasure begin to pace the room.

Treasure envied Eliza's ability to carry herself so lightly, even in the most frustrating situations. As she walked back and forth, she tried to banish the heavy weight settling on her own shoulders, an ominous feeling Emmaline had become prey to a boy who would steal her virtue with no more caring than if it were a bottle of cheap whiskey. The clock on the fireplace mantel ticked seconds off into the silence, its rhythmic tempo rubbing her nerves raw.

"This is intolerable! I should have gone with them." She flung an accusing look at Eliza. "I should never have allowed you to bully me into staying."

"Bully you? I declare, Treasure, there's not a soul livin' who could bully you into doing a single thing you didn't want to. This is best, and you know it — although I surely won't live long enough to see the day you admit it."

174

Treasure paused by the piano. Her fingers drummed against the polished wood, keeping anxious pace with the mantel clock. "Why did she do it, Miss Eliza?"

"Emmaline?" Eliza smoothed a hand over her hair. Her shoulders lifted in a delicate shrug. "I daresay Mr. River was right. Emmaline was upset, and she decided to hide away from it all. A natural impulse in a girl her age."

"Is it?" Treasure said softly, not looking at her friend.

"Of course. Haven't you ever just wanted to run away and leave everything behind?"

"No—no, I haven't." Treasure struggled with an unaccustomed urge to explain her feelings. "I know I belong here. All I've ever wanted is here. Only by running Rose of Heaven could I ever hope to make Papa proud of me."

Eliza studied her a moment, then said, "Treasure, your papa is dead. It's past time you started writing your own pages of life, instead of the ones he penned for you. You can't live according to others' expectations, honey. You have to make some of your own."

"I've made Papa's my own. I just wish . . ." She looked out the windows at the darkening expanse of Rose of Heaven. "I just wish I knew how to raise a family. But there was no one to teach me. Mama . . . was gone. Lettia was more concerned about ensuring her social status—and Papa's money. The only other person that might have helped me learn about those matters, Mama's sister, Aunt Valene, well, she wasn't available."

"You did say she's plannin' a visit, though."

"Yes. I suppose the grudge that kept her from Rose of Heaven died along with Papa. And she raised my cousin alone after Mr. Ellis died. Surely she will be more adept at mothering than I," she said, unconsciously knotting and unknotting her fists at her sides. "I feel so terribly inept at dealing with them: Camille, the twins, Emmaline — except for Spring." Her face softened a little. "I can always depend on Spring."

Shaking off the moment of reverie, Treasure focused on the vista outside the window again, as if willing some trace of Emmy to appear in the melding lilac shadows. "There must be something I can do now."

"There is," Eliza said. She came up behind her and laid a comforting hand on Treasure's arm. "Wait — and pray."

Donovan, Elijah at his heels, shoved through the scrubby underbrush of the grove, wishing he'd had the sense to bring a lantern. The little forested hill behind Rose of Heaven made a nice walk during the day, but night bewitched the trail, and made it seem impossibly crooked and tangled.

"You sure we're headed in the right direction, Mastuh River? This doesn't seem like a place Miss Emmaline would go."

"There's a clearing at the top of this rise," Donovan said, trying to convince himself as much as Elijah. "Emmy sneaks off here sometimes to sketch the wildlife." In answer to Elijah's unspoken question he added, "I stumbled on her once when I was walking. It's a good place to get away from everyone."

"Or to meet someone," Elijah said, his voice toneless.

Donovan paused a moment, resting a hand against a tree. He saw only the shadow of Elijah's face in the moonlit darkness. But Donovan knew him well enough to imagine the faint probing in the depths of his unusual azure eyes. "True. Although I trust you won't be making that generally known."

"No. Was just a guess, that's all."

"The problem with you, Elijah, is that your guesses sound uncomfortably like the truth. But in this case, you can decide for yourself. We're almost there."

Pushing aside a snarl of blackberry bramble,

Donovan took the last yards of the hill in long strides. Ahead, through the charcoal outlines of the trees, he could see a shimmer of moonlight on the open stretch of meadow grass.

When they reached the edge of the clearing, Elijah made a sudden start forward. Donovan stopped him with a hand. "Let me. You come around the back, in case there's trouble."

"You expecting trouble?"

"I always expect trouble."

"Good thing. Let's hope this time you don't get it," Elijah whispered before creeping off through the trees.

Donovan waited to give him a few moments' lead. Then, moving slowly, he started across the clearing, keeping to the forested edge. He stopped a few yards from his goal, the pale light clearly illuminating what he had expected to find.

Emmaline in the arms of Jimmy Rae Stanton.

Absorbed in each other, neither had noticed his approach. Jimmy Rae was pressing Emmy close to him, kissing her with the fervor of adolescent passion. Emmaline clung to him, a sort of desperation in her clutching hands.

Donovan deliberately brought his foot down hard against a fallen branch. At the loud crack Emmaline and Jimmy leapt apart as if divided by lightning.

When she saw Donovan, Emmaline gasped, her hands flying to her mouth. "Oh! I—I . . ." Tears sprung into her eyes, and she looked away.

The surprise momentarily caught Jimmy Rae without his usual sneer. He stared at Donovan, his expression a mixture of defiance and distress. Abruptly realizing his lapse, the captious smirk slowly returned. He eyed Donovan from under the fall of hair on his brow. "Emmy swore no one'd ever find us here. Guess she was wrong."

"Obviously," Donovan said, his voice easy, eyes hard. "Let me offer you a piece of advice. There's a

177

search party under way of men not likely to be as accommodating as I, if they find you here. I suggest you get off Miss McGlavrin's land now, and forget how you found your way here."

Jimmy Rae snickered, as though ready to trip off some clever quip of refusal. He glanced at Emmaline, who refused to look at him. With a mocking shrug, he challenged Donovan, "I don't forget that easy."

"You're young enough to learn. Now get out before I forget you're only a kid."

Jimmy Rae's sassy smile turned sour. "Kid, huh?" he ground out between gritted teeth. "I'm as much a man as anybody . . ." Glaring hard at Donovan through slitted eyes he stood and added, "Just you wait and see if I don't prove it too." Behind him Elijah's sudden, imposing presence stilled any further argument. "Good night, Miss Emmaline," he called out as he started down the hill. "I certainly do thank you for such a pleasant evenin'. I'm lookin' forward to the next."

At a nod from Donovan, Elijah followed Jimmy Rae long enough to ensure he didn't decide to return. Donovan, left alone with Emmaline, waited for the trembling girl to break the silence between them.

"I suppose," she said at last, paying assiduous attention to the ground under her feet. "I suppose you think it's wrong, my running away — and everything."

"Do you think it was wrong?"

"Yes. No!" Defiance flared and then Emmy's shoulders sagged. "Treasure will be furious with me. But I — I just couldn't make her understand. She's so worried all the time, about everything, and she hates it when I go off sketching. I can't make her see that I *have* to. *You* understand — it's like your writing. And then Jimmy — he likes my pictures, you know, and he's kind of, kind of . . ."

"Exciting?" Emmaline gave him a shy glance and nodded. "Emmy," Donovan said softly, "there's nothing wrong with caring about someone. But caring for

178

the wrong person can be dangerous."

"I know Jimmy gets into a lot of trouble, but he can be nice — to me anyway."

"Maybe. He could also get you into a lot of trouble. Like tonight."

Emmaline's mouth quivered. "I am in trouble, aren't I? Are you mad at me too?"

"No, Emmy, I'm not." Donovan reached one finger under her chin and tipped her face to his. "I'll confess something to you, if you promise not to tell your sister. I'm running away from home, too. The difference is I can't go back. You can." When Emmaline winced in anxious distress, he smiled.

Emmaline's eyes searched his face. Then with a timid, trusting smile she put her hand in his.

Treasure waited at the front door as Donovan and Emmaline, followed by the rest of the search party, trudged up to the house.

She didn't say a word in response to Emmaline's timid glance, but waited until Rader and Eliza had slipped out and she was alone with Emmy and Donovan in the parlor. "Mr. River," she said stiffly, the words forced from her lips. "I am grateful you found Emmaline, but I intend to speak with my sister alone."

"No, Treasure!" Emmaline burst out. "I want Donovan to stay! Please," she added, turning beseeching eyes to her ally. "Don't go."

Donovan looked at Treasure, then bent to Emmaline, giving her shoulder a reassuring squeeze. "I think you can do this on your own, Emmy," he said.

"Will you at least stay in the house? For a little while?"

"Emmaline, I believe Mr. River has more important things to attend to," Treasure said. "You've caused him quite enough trouble this evening. And you've" — her voice trembled a little — "you've given us all an unnecessary fright."

"But Treasure, you promised he could stay! You said you would think about it —"

"Emmaline!"

Holding up both hands, Donovan stopped the burgeoning argument. "With your permission," he said to Treasure, "I'll borrow your study. I've some correspondence to attend to."

Treasure hesitated, then dismissed him with a reluctant nod. She had more pressing problems to deal with. The door clicked shut behind him, and she turned to her young sister, grappling with a mixture of giddy relief and rampant anger. "I'm glad you're back safely, Emmy," she said, struggling to contain her fury. "I was worried about you."

"Were you?"

"Of course I was! Especially when I feared you'd gone off with Jimmy Rae Stanton. I do hope you are able to give me some sort of explanation for this behavior."

Emmaline fidgeted with the buttons of her dress. "I've tried to explain to you, over and over. When I heard you arguing with Donovan, I just — I just couldn't stay here anymore. You don't care about us. All you care about is Rose of Heaven."

"Emmy, that's not true. I care about all of you."

"Donovan, too?"

Treasure couldn't answer for a moment. "Mr. River isn't family. And I don't care for the familiar way you've come to address him. It's impertinent."

"He's my friend," Emmaline said, a pout on her lips.

"He is dangerous," Treasure countered. "Just like Jimmy Rae Stanton. I cannot abide you associating with either of them. And I intend to make certain you don't. For the next month, you will not leave this house. I will ask Mammie Eura Mae and Aunt Orange Jane to keep you too busy with chores to be tempted to disobey me again. Between the work and the extra time you're going to spend studying the Scriptures, you'll learn your lesson. Do I make myself clear?"

Head bowed, Emmaline nodded.

Unwillingly touched by the dejected slump of Emmaline's small shoulders, Treasure felt moved to relinquish a little of her sternness. She recalled the reassurance and understanding Donovan had extended to her sister. Perhaps softness, a comforting word now, might reach Emmy where strictness and reason had failed.

Treasure walked over to where Emmaline stood and put gentle hands on her sister's shoulders. "Emmy, I — I want to understand, but I also want to do what is best for you. I don't want anyone to hurt you."

"You're the only one that's hurting me, Treasure," Emmy said, keeping her eyes fixed on the floor. "All I want is to have a friend. I want someone to listen to me."

"Oh, Emmy . . ." Briefly squeezing her eyes shut, Treasure fought a feeling of utter helplessness. "I want to be your friend, Emmy, but I still intend to do all I can to protect you. And if that means keeping you away from Jimmy Rae Stanton and Donovan River, I will do it. Do you understand?"

Emmy gave a shrug, not answering, refusing to look up at Treasure.

Treasure watched her a long moment, searching for any sign Emmaline accepted her decision. Finally, with a weary sigh, she said, "It's late. We can talk about this further tomorrow. I think you should get off to bed now."

Without a word, Emmaline turned and ran from the room, leaving the door gaping open behind her.

Treasure waited to collect herself before following Emmaline out of the parlor. She had one more confrontation tonight, and it was one she dreaded more than facing Emmaline. She paused at the study door.

181

Donovan had brought her sister safely home — and he had murdered a man. How could he be capable of such tenderness and such violence simultaneously? Which was the real Donovan River?

It was so quiet in the study that, as Treasure slipped inside, she wondered if Donovan had forgone his promise to Emmy and retired to his cabin. A single lamp burned at the large desk and a pen and inkwell lay abandoned on a scattering of papers where Donovan had given up on his correspondence. His boots propped on the desk, he leaned into the corner of one of the large leather chairs, eyes closed.

Treasure, with careful steps, crept close. The peaceful repose of his face and his slow, rhythmic breathing told her he had fallen asleep, apparently in the midst of his work.

With the house still around them, the study seemed an isolated universe of its own. Dusky shadow made secret nooks of familiar corners. Quiet embraced her like a living presence guarding her from the turmoil outside the door.

Emboldened by her fantasy, Treasure let herself watch Donovan as he slept. He looked rumpled, tired beyond the healing capacity of sleep, vulnerable almost. Absently, she reached down and brushed an errant lock from his brow.

The kiss of his skin against hers sparked a memory deep inside her, a rippling echo of the feelings and sensations he aroused when he touched her, held her against him, kissed her with the hungry abandon of a lover.

Refusing to let disturbing thoughts poison the fragile sweetness of remembrance, Treasure let her fingers linger on his face, whispering over each angle and curve. She traced the sensual line of his mouth, the stubble-rough line of his jaw. Temptation coaxed her hand to wander over his throat and lower, to the deep cleft in his shirt to tentatively caress the soft mat of hair. She

182

closed her eyes, her senses vibrantly alive with the feel, the vision, the warm, earthly scent of him. It was a delicious feeling, a wickedly delightful excitement. As if he were hers and she alone would have the pleasure forever of memorizing with her heart every hollow and plane of his body.

Her touch seemed to penetrate Donovan's dreams, and he shifted slightly, muttering something Treasure couldn't understand.

She snatched her hand back, her face burning with a shaming heat. Whatever could have prompted her to take such liberties? She detested and scorned the sly flirting airs women like Camille cultivated, yet she herself succumbed to Donovan River's sleeping charm like the loosest of creatures. And she did it knowing Camille's fingers had traveled the same paths with no hesitation, no need to steal secret pleasure.

Small wonder Papa had little hope for her. This was the very behavior he mocked in women, their fate. *Makin' their way with a simpering smile and a lift of the skirts.*

But Papa had never told her how to will away the crazy, tumultuous feelings a single admiring glance from hot, quicksilver eyes could incite.

Seeking some outlet for the tension inside her, she turned away from Donovan, pacing aimlessly about the room. She paused at the desk, automatically reaching down to straighten the chaos Donovan had left behind. As she did, the lines of an unfinished letter caught her eye. Treasure, recognizing Donovan in the bold strokes, nearly gathered up the pile of papers without satisfying her curiosity. But she knew so little about him. . . . The urge to uncover some key to his past overcame her sense of propriety. Holding the smudged paper close to the lamp light, she quickly scanned the hastily scrawled words, all the while darting fearful glances at Donovan.

183

Jared,

I will preclude the fistful of questions you must be anxious to throw at me by admitting you were correct in both your promises and threats about the fine state of Alabama and the nation of the South. I am beginning to understand your fears of some future violent division, for here, honor, justice, and freedom have quite different definitions. It seems often a country of its own, although for many reasons, I am compelled to stay.

You will no doubt accuse me of indulging my penchant for hopeless causes (although you, in no small measure, are indulging in one of your own), but I am relying on your acquaintance with Mr. Purvis to see me through my latest difficulty. It is agreeably dangerous, and I am kept company by innumerable apprehensions about success. Yet I have an ally who willingly shares the risk, and if we are able to gently distract the mistress of the house, then perhaps it can be done.

For that reason, I would stay. Although, I will confess to you alone, something wholly unexpected has occurred that gives me a new, stronger desire to remain—

Here the letter broke off, as if Donovan was suddenly beset by doubts about admitting his secrets. Forgetting her fear of being caught in the act of spying, Treasure carefully reread the missile. Again, its unfamiliar, tediously correct tone struck her. And yet, the letter was not of a business nature that might merit such formality. Rather, its content said he was on familiar terms with this Jared—to the extent he would employ his help in some illicit scheme.

She clutched at scant clues, culling them over in her mind. She had been right in guessing Donovan wasn't bred a Southerner. But if Alabama was so alien to him,

184

why had he come? And more importantly, why did he stay?

It was obvious he had reasons, and gaining control of her plantation was certainly one of them. Any others, though, Treasure couldn't fathom, except to infer he knew she wouldn't or couldn't abide them, so he had convinced someone else to help him deceive her while he accomplished his purpose.

All her doubts and fears slammed back with painful force. She itched to shake him awake and demand an explanation, to force him to give her the truth.

At the same time, she felt an unexpected sadness. Obviously, his attentions to her had been a lie. . . . *if we are able to gently distract the mistress of the house* . . .

Treasure closed her eyes for a moment, hands balled at her sides. Then, squaring her shoulders, she gathered her determination around her like a shield.

Working quickly, she rearranged the letter on the desk again to duplicate Donovan's disorder. Satisfied with the job, she gave one final glance around the room, letting her eyes settle briefly on him.

"If you think you're going to best me, Donovan River," she warned his sleeping form, "you're in for a sad disappointment. Rose of Heaven is mine, and nothing you or anyone can do will change that."

Chapter Ten

Treasure choked on the vermilion swirl of dust the hoe kicked up in her face. Hot, dry oppression stung her eyes in the tiny flecks of parched earth coating her face. Days had dragged into listless weeks until the whole of McGlavrin's Valley bowed beneath the burden of the heat.

Behind her, from the fields, the earth's desperate cry for water seemed to repeat itself in the mournful chants of the slaves. Their once uplifting songs had slowed, deepened, grown heavy with fatigue, drawn out into all-day, all-night pleas in a dialect uniquely their own. Ceaseless in their haunting sadness, they increased in number and frequency in proportion to the gradual lessening and final end to the rains.

This recent, eerie language differed from any Treasure had heard in hard times past. It struck her with a sense of foreboding and left her feeling strangely excluded. Since having to sell so many, she'd worked among the remainder of her people almost daily for months, gradually growing familiar with their ways.

Her life, once a world apart, had steadily melded closer to theirs. She learned to understand and appreciate their beautiful music and earthy, energetic dances. Although the distance between mistress and slave always dictated her every behavior, inwardly, secretly,

186

she'd grown to care deeply for each man and woman at Rose of Heaven.

She fretted for the future of their children just as she did for her own sisters'. They, too, were family—of a sort. And here, family meant everything. Especially in these desperate days.

Bending low, Treasure caressed the wilted leaf of a bean plant. How much longer could her garden outlast the drought? And worse, so much worse, how long could her cotton bear the dry spell without irreparable loss?

Scorching days frazzled shortened tempers and as a result in recent days Treasure's sisters and most of her people had taken to avoiding her. It was just as well. She fretted constantly, fearful for the fate of her plantation. Her cotton ruled her future. And her anxiety often sought release in berating the inevitable shortcomings of the slaves and her family. After a row with Spring over some insignificant failure on Spring's part to finish mending the twins' play clothes, Treasure decided she'd rather her family avoid her. The fewer human problems she had to contend with now, she considered, the better.

Except for one irritating glitch.

In lieu of turning to her for direction and with questions, the entire household took to seeking out Donovan in her stead. And he, of course, bore the new role with a mix of humor and insight that she envied.

"Damn him." Treasure kicked at the clumps of dirt crumbling beneath the blade of her hoe.

How easy for him to keep whistling his merry tune. It isn't his family at risk to drought and starvation if this spell hangs on. Of course, he can go about smiling, laughing. What does he really care for our plight when he can, on a whim, move on, none the worse for the time wasted?

Even as she cursed him for his dauntless good humor, she knew the real cause for her resentment lay with memories she could not banish. The most painfully clear vision, humiliating every time she recalled it, of Donovan and Camille together.

Although her heart wouldn't admit the reason, that betrayal of her trust hurt more than even his scheming to take Rose of Heaven. All his attentions to her, all his pretense of feeling, were nothing more than a deception. A deception designed to make her forget her Papa's wretched letter, naming Donovan the owner of her plantation.

Treasure yanked a weed from the rock-hard ground. Never, never could she excuse Donovan's actions. And never would she forgive him or forget he was responsible for this unwanted ache lodged in her heart.

Across the wide stretch of fields behind her, the object of Treasure's loathing leaned over the top of his hoe, chin on hands, listening. In the middle of the largest of the cotton fields, Donovan propped one boot on the hoe's blade, trying to distract himself from the dreary vista of withered and sun-browned plants. "Which do you think will last longer, Elijah? These melancholy songs or Treasure's bad temper?"

Elijah glanced up. "Hard to tell, Mastuh River. Both believe they have good reason to be angry."

Donovan closed his eyes and let himself drift into the songs, layered and interwoven in each other in uncanny harmony, dying away as soon as they were uttered in the deadly still afternoon air. "I don't understand the words," he said at last. "But the music is heartbreaking enough."

"It's a funeral song." Elijah offered the information without looking up. A quick tightening of muscle rippled his shoulders.

"Someone died? I hadn't heard."

"You won't."

"Someone you knew?"

188

"Not directly. It was Samuel, one of Orange Jane's brothers. Mastuh Stanton bought him when Miss Treasure had to sell off most of her people."

"What happened to him? Illness?"

"No." Elijah's big hand gripped the handle of his hoe. He stared at the horizon. "Mastuh Stanton had him beat for sneakin' off to be with his wife when she was birthing her first, then took the baby boy and sold him off before one day passed. Samuel went straight up to the big house and picked one ugly fight. Next day, his body turned up outside the door to his room, beat up so bad his woman barely recognized him."

"And Southerners say Yankees are barbarians," Donovan muttered. Avoiding Elijah's sudden questioning glance, he hastily asked, "What about Samuel's wife? What happens to her now?"

"She's a fine-looking woman and young. Mastuh Stanton took her for himself."

"Unfortunately, I'm not surprised."

"Neither is anyone at Gold Meadow. But they haven't forgotten either."

Donovan wondered at the edge of menace in Elijah's words. He waited a long moment, hoping Elijah might confide more. Pressing the matter was pointless. Elijah spoke his thoughts when and if he wanted, and no amount of prodding would budge him into telling more than he wanted. Still, instinct told him Elijah's shuttered azure eyes masked some private determined purpose he'd yet to reveal.

All he could do was watch, listen. And wait. Resigned, Donovan swiped a rivulet of sweat from his bare chest, shading his eyes with the brim of his hat as he glanced skyward.

Waiting. All the residents of Rose of Heaven and the whole of McGlavrin's Valley were waiting for rain. For hope. Toiling on each day, working to keep their minds off the threat of crop devastation that the dry spell held over their lives all around.

189

He knelt down and fingered the russet earth that sifted into dust with the mere touch of his hand. All around the crops — *his crops* — starved for the relief of a nourishing rain to revive them from their faltering slump.

In some odd way, he felt their anguish. Maybe this was what Treasure meant when she'd said Rose of Heaven lived inside her; every stalk of corn, every shrubby cotton plant, embedded in her soul as deeply as they were in her Alabama earth.

A strange sense of bonding to the dust in his palm tugged at his insides, pulling him closer than he'd ever been to becoming attached to a place. It was the sort of feeling that made him know he'd miss it everyday the rest of his life if he left; the sort of sentimental familiarity with a place he heard in other people's voices when they talked about "home."

Disconcerted by the notion his wanderlust might be slowly, silently succumbing to the lure of an alien land and a way of life he happened into by accident (a lark of good fortune he had intended to take advantage of, then be on his way), he suddenly had the urge to shake free of it all and bolt like a pole cat out of a snake's hole. Slapping the dirt from his hand he jerked to his feet.

He stepped back and pulled his journal from his hip pocket. Of late, distant from Treasure and bogged by the depression crushing Rose of Heaven, his battered book proved a perfect confidant; his private escape and satisfaction.

Jumbled thoughts and perceptions spilled out across the pages in disjointed fragments of frustration. *Hell! I can't leave now. Not with that whole brood of women depending on these wretched plants for a future. I want to see the harvest through. I have to.*

Why?

He almost wished he could say Treasure couldn't finish it without him. *Not likely, River.*

Then there was Elijah. Donovan wanted to help him;

that was a private cause that extended beyond his unlikely fascination with Treasure McGlavrin, beyond Rose of Heaven, beyond the borders separating North and South.

But the real reason—Donovan chopped short the thought. That reason was too disturbing to contemplate, too incredible to consider.

He glanced over to where Elijah was steadily working his way to the other side of the field. Even Elijah's seemingly boundless supply of energy seemed tapped. He moved lethargically, as if the relentless heat eroded his strength.

"This is insane," Donovan said low under his breath, scuffing a patch of arid soil with his boot. "You may be set on waiting for rain, Miss McGlavrin, but I'm either going to put some life back into this place or get the hell out." Motioning to Elijah, he called over, "Drop that for a minute."

Elijah lumbered up, rubbing at the perspiration dripping into his eyes. "Something the matter?"

"Damned right there is. We're wasting time. Treasure may thrive on sunup to sundown labor in this inferno, but I don't. And I don't think I'm the only one around here who could use a break."

Elijah cocked his head, visibly perplexed. "Meaning?"

Donovan slapped Elijah playfully on the shoulder. "Meaning we have work to do elsewhere."

Where was everyone? Treasure, drained from working outdoors from dawn till supper, possessed neither the inclination nor the energy to search the entire plantation for a family and slaves that seemed to have vanished. She tossed her red-stained work gloves on the foyer table and stood still for a moment, listening for the familiar signs of activity.

"Hello?" she called down the empty center hall corri-

191

dor, after searching the kitchen and parlors. No answer. Where on earth was Solomon, at least? Though he might not be the most adept at his job, he was always faithful to his post.

Treasure cast off the uneasy, empty feeling prickling up her spine. They all must be here somewhere. They wouldn't just up and mutiny in force. Would they? Where could her sisters go with no money, no one to care for them? *He* certainly had nothing to offer them . . . did he?

Good Lord in heaven, I've gone fool crazy! Papa always said too much sun caused delusions. It must be the heat going to my senses.

A thin wisp of laughter drifted down the long hall in front of her. Camille? And—? Her heart lurched. The laughter seemed to come from the ballroom. The ballroom? No. Impossible. They wouldn't dare. Not here. Of course not. Would they?

She'd had Elijah board up the once-elegant hall and bolt it securely after her papa left. Papa and Mama were the only ones who knew how to put on a real party. Oh, Lettia had thrown balls from time to time as social obligations dictated. But her balls, though shamelessly lavish and perfect in decorum, fell consistently flat. They lacked the sparkle, the rompish abandon, that was the magical gift Papa and Mama inspired. No one could ever recreate that magic.

After Mama died and Papa left, there was no reason to use the room ever again.

Again, laughter, louder this time, beckoned Treasure to the back of the house. She followed the sound straight to beneath the archway heralding the closed ballroom doors. Then stopped. What if she stumbled onto a repeat of the shocking scene in Donovan's cabin? But there seemed to be a bevy of voices behind the impassive wood. What in heaven . . . ?

With a quick twist, Treasure turned the handles and opened the doors. Amid the dust and cloth-draped fur-

192

niture, a roomful of sisters and slaves stared at her. Dead silence smothered their laughter. They wordlessly let her pass as Treasure strode through them, straight toward the man at center of their attention.

Donovan grinned raffishly, shrugging in response to her angry face.

"I knew this must be your doing," she snapped, her ire undisguised.

"Oh, Treasure," Spring burst in, her eyes glowing with pleasure and not a little mischief. "Isn't this just the perfect remedy for all the gloom and boredom?"

"Can we come, can we?" Abby cried, grabbing Erin's hands, then capturing Treasure between them. The twins skipped around Treasure, Erin tentatively joining in Abby's raucous chant. "We're going to have a party! We're going to have a party!"

Treasure's eyes narrowed at Donovan. "Of course you're responsible for this."

He nodded, challenge in his eyes, his smile. "After Bettis's spells and incantations didn't bring rain, I thought we might as well try and beat this cursed drought with a little fun."

Appalled at the silly cheers and squeals of her sisters and her slaves, Treasure waited, hands fidgeting nervously with her apron, for them to calm themselves. Even Camille had deigned to join them, lounging against the windowsill, watching the revelry and Treasure's annoyance with malicious pleasure.

"Such a darlin' idea, don't you agree, dear sistuh?" she drawled. "I can see you're simply thrilled. Donovan does think of the most interestin' ways to pass the time."

The jab pricked at Treasure's heart. "I'm quite sure he does. Interesting, though, is hardly the word I would apply to this particular notion of Mr. River's."

"But don't you understand?" Emmy tugged at her elbow. "A ball! We'll throw a ball and invite everyone in the valley! Donovan is even planning a party for all our

193

people." With that she spun away from Treasure only to be caught in Donovan's arms and whirled off her feet in a flurry of circles. The others joined in, in a mad fit of excitement, long faces vanishing in the glimmer of hope Donovan's impulsive idea sparked.

Treasure looked on, fuming, until finally she could stand it no longer. "Stop! Stop this ridiculous display at once!" Frozen faces swiveled her way. "You all have duties which you are sorely neglecting. Entertaining fanciful notions isn't going to bring in the harvest nor feed and clothe everyone. Now, get back to your work. This moment."

The reprimand had the effect of a lashing. With eyes lowered, mouths drawn visibly tight to keep from open defiance, her charges trudged out.

Treasure, with a searing glare at Donovan, whirled on her heel and, avoiding the condemning glances, stalked toward the study, her heart in her throat, her reason a cold companion.

When she'd gone, Emmy ran to Donovan, her self-control succumbing to miserable sobs. "I knew she'd ruin your idea. She doesn't care how bored or sad or lonely we are because she doesn't have any feelings."

Donovan patted her back. "Look at you, eyes all red and swollen. Why, you'd have a hard time catching a young gentleman's fancy if we did have a ball." He gently lifted her chin with his fingertip. "And we will have it. I promise," he said firmly, choosing to ignore the fact of Treasure's formidable opposition.

"It does sound just like a dream, Mr. River, but you know how stubborn Treasure can be," Spring said, shaking her head. "She's just so busy taking over Papa's and Mama's responsibilities all at once, the very idea of enjoying herself for even one evening is practically sinful."

"Miss Spring be right, Mastuh River." Eura Mae's

194

mouth pursed in a disapproving line. "Miss Treasure never did play like d'other chillen. Her heart done got hard early on." She paused and looked wistfully off to nowhere. "Had to, I s'pose. Ain't likely she'll change neither, now or never."

"Come on now. Have a little faith," Donovan countered, feeling a distinct lack of it. "Give me some time to help Treasure see how much this would improve everyone's spirits—and their motivation. Even hers."

Erin, who'd been hiding behind Eura Mae's skirts since Treasure left, peeked out. "Will we have a party, Mr. River? With cakes and gum drops? Like Papa used to give us?"

Donovan stooped and held his hands out to her in a coaxing gesture.

Erin hesitated to grasp his outstretched hand, glancing up to her mammie then over to Donovan. Eura Mae shot Donovan a sharp warning look then nodded to her charge. Reluctantly, clutching a swatch of Eura Mae's white apron, Erin inched toward him.

Before he'd landed smack in the middle of Treasure's brood, children rarely crossed his mind. They were simply short, demanding annoyances. Other people's burdens. But now, looking into the widest, most searching green eyes he'd ever seen, Donovan suddenly ached to be worthy of this child's innocent trust. "It's all right," he said softly.

Erin let go of Eura Mae's apron and padded to Donovan. He met her with his most charming smile and a bow. "You may have your gum balls and cake at our ball, but you must first promise me one thing."

"Must I?"

Donovan lifted her hand and rested it on his palm. He put on a solemn face. "Most assuredly. You must partner me for the first dance, or my evening will be ruined and I'll have nothing to do but sit out and eat all of the candy and cake myself."

Color flooded Erin's already pink cheeks. She covered her giggle with a hand. "Yessir, Mr. River," she squeaked out, her answer nearly smothered by her sister's outrage.

"Not fair! That's not fair! Mammie Eura Mae, do something!" Abby stamped her foot. "I want to be first. I'm the oldest."

Before Eura Mae had a chance to mediate, Donovan scooped both girls up, one in each arm. "I'll just have to dance with you both at the same time, then, won't I?" he said, twirling them at his sides until they begged him to stop.

Smiles back on their faces, Donovan set the twins carefully down. "Do you suppose Miss Treasure's temper has improved?" he asked Eura Mae, who answered with a doubtful shrug.

"Hard tellin'. She may not have no mercy for a man who she thinks don't want to grow up." Scooting the twins but in front of her, Eura Mae, followed by the others, went back to her duties.

On her way past Donovan, Camille cuddled Erin. "Don't you fret, precious," she cooed. "You're my special baby doll, and I'll see to it you and your sister have pretty new party dresses and candy, ball or no ball. Treasure won't spoil our fun" — she shot Donovan a spiteful glance — "even if she does spoil Mr. River's."

She sauntered out, leaving Donovan alone in the cobweb-laced ballroom with a sudden memory of his own childhood and a too-familiar lament.

When are you going to stop playing at life and grow up? You'll be in my shoes soon, boy. Show a little self-control, damn you!

He knocked at the study door, then braced himself. When a voice from within sent a curt permission to enter, the terrier hanging at his heels turned and trotted away. "Coward," he mumbled under his breath. Across the room, Treasure met him with a furious scowl, indignation blazing in her wide green eyes.

"No need to thank me," he ventured, his tone deliberately cocky.

Silence.

He strode in confidently, wearing his best gambler's smile. "You must admit, it's an intriguing idea."

"Intrigued hardly describes my feelings, Mr. River."

"Ah, the despised Mr. River again. We're regressing."

He saw Treasure's jaw tighten, but aside from that one concession to her inner turmoil, she didn't flinch. "Pray, do sit down," she said with a lift of her chin.

"Why thank you, Miss McGlavrin." The sight of her, so slender and small, yet regal in her proud bearing, ramrod straight in a chair she'd never grow to fill, inspired an odd mix of protectiveness and respect. At the same time, the glacial look in her eye was enough to thwart his altruism.

Treasure stayed silent a moment, fingering a scattering of papers in front of her. When she looked up at him, her face was set, rigid with determination. "You arrived on my doorstep, claimed to have won my home cheating at a hand of cards. You have moved onto my land, and endeared yourself to every human and beast in my care. You have even managed to murder a man and convince everyone you were wronged. Rose of Heaven used to be a place accustomed to order. But your erratic and appalling behavior has put that in a deep grave. Increasingly, I fear we shall never again see blessed peace reign here."

"At least you can't accuse me of being dull," Donovan said, unable to resist the dangerous temptation to provoke some hot, unbridled emotion to usurp her stony, reasoned control.

She ignored him. "I truly believed your last escapade, bedding my sister—you do recall, do you not?"

"No, I don't remember," Donovan broke into her tirade. "I didn't make love to her."

"—displayed the ultimate in your disregard for respectable behavior," Treasure went on, heedless of his

197

interruption. "But again, I have underestimated you. You have convinced my entire household there is to be a ball under my roof for people who can scarce grudge me a civil word, and without so much as a mention of it to me. I cannot decide whether to applaud your sheer audacity or see you quietly hung. All I do know is that I am at my utter wit's end with you, Donovan River."

Donovan waited a heartbeat then affected his best guileless expression. "By the way, Camille is your step-sister. There's no blood between you."

Treasure's stubborn restraint snapped. She lunged out of her chair and, grabbing the first thing that came to hand — a large, leather-bound book — flung it straight at his chest. "You bastard! I have never hated anyone more than I hate you!"

Ducking the missile, Donovan reached her in two strides and caught her wrists in his hands. "I do believe I asked for this."

"Let me go!" she cried, kicking out at his shins.

"Not until we talk."

"I have nothing to say to you. Now or ever again."

"Then I'll talk. Why are you so against this idea? The real reason." He watched with interest as the color flushed and waned in her face. "What are you afraid of?"

"Of letting a murderous, lying blackguard take hold of my family and my plantation." Her eyes didn't quite meet his.

"That's not it."

"Oh, do tell, Mr. River." She defended her feelings with a mocking facade. "What, in your wisdom, might the reason be?"

"I don't know. I — " Suddenly, Donovan glimpsed the frightened eyes of a fragile girl-woman behind the mask of self-reliant mistress. Vulnerable, sacrificing, alone. And afraid to expose herself to the prying eyes of the people who shunned her as too bold and peculiar. They knew, and Treasure knew, no true Southern lady

198

would so obstinately insist on controlling the destinies of a large family and an entire plantation on her own. His heart lurched. He knew he'd goaded her beyond fair play to break her stiff-necked pride. But all at once, he wanted more than anything to convince her she needed this reprieve more than anyone else.

He considered his words carefully for a change, knowing she wouldn't thank him for baring her fears. "Treasure, the whole valley needs a celebration. Your own family, your people, are desperate for a little hope."

"Leave my family to me," she warned, pulling away from him. She turned aside, her voice strangely muffled. "It isn't so much the notion, but the timing. Have you considered the expense of such a gala? I can barely feed my own. And I can't afford the time it would take to prepare for such an event. The entire household is consumed with excitement over something that cannot happen. Spring and Emmy and the twins will be crushed . . ." Her words died in throaty emotion and Donovan noticed the tell-tale clenching of her hands at her sides.

He experienced a longing to sweep her into his arms and comfort her. But that was a luxury neither of them could afford. "Look — I'll see to it the cost to Rose of Heaven, to you, is minimal in time and in dollars. Just let everyone have this."

"And how do you propose to afford it?"

"That's my business."

He nearly convinced himself she would refuse when she faced him, a bleak surrender in her eyes that gave his small victory a cutting edge. "Have your affair then, Donovan. Only arrange it for the earliest possible time. I want the least amount of disruption before harvest."

"You won't regret it, pretty lady."

"I already do. Now, please leave. I have work to attend to."

She turned away in dismissal and Donovan moved

toward the door. He stopped with his hand on the knob and looked back. "Thank you."

"Don't thank me. I still believe this whole idea is a shameless waste of effort and money."

"I realize that. I wasn't thanking you for the ball. I was thanking you for calling me by my first name again."

In the days following Donovan's victorious announcement, everyone seemed to have a tune to hum. The air buzzed with songs and activity until Treasure's head ached from her effort to concentrate in the noisy pandemonium. Each time she passed Donovan, his devil-may-care smile reminded her he was the one who'd turned her ordered household into utter chaos.

And they thrived on it. Walking faster, laughing louder, working harder than they'd done since Papa died. All because of him.

And because of Donovan and his impulsive plans, she had wrestled with a growing uneasiness. She couldn't understand his reasons for organizing the ball; she mistrusted his motives. And yet, he seemed genuinely to enjoy joining in the jovial mayhem he had invoked.

Treasure didn't understand, yet she admired him and envied his rapport with her family and people. He was like Papa in that way—made for good times. But would he walk away if Rose of Heaven turned sour, if the harvest failed?

Shading her eyes, she glanced up to the clear, azure sky for the hundred and tenth time since the dry spell had begun. The crops would die of thirst if the heavens continued to hoard their life's blood. And then, yes, Donovan River would pack up and leave them behind as if they had never existed.

Leave her behind. Why should it matter? Why should she grace the notion with a care?

She sipped the last bit of her midmorning lemonade and pulled herself out of her comfortable willow rocker. *Odd,* she thought, *they all work tirelessly, and I haven't an ounce of energy.* She started to force herself to return to the kitchen garden, when Emmy peeked around the edge of the door, a length of gold satin tangled in her fingers.

"Treasure? I'm sorry to bother you but I can't fix this bow right."

Treasure knew Spring, Orange Jane, and Eura Mae must be overwhelmed with work for Emmy to come to her for help. Camille, the other last resort for assistance, had left for town with Ira first thing this morning, making certain all present knew he was having a new gown measured for her just for the grand occasion.

Thanks to Donovan's charitable invitations, even the despicable Colonel Stanton was included in the long list of guests. Another of the unforgivable affronts he saw fit to inflict on her. As if facing hundreds of eyes in her own ballroom wouldn't be enough! Suppressing a shudder, she conjured a smile for Emmy.

"I'll help you. I saw Mama wrap those dozens of times when I was even younger than you." Treasure hoped her voice carried the sincerity she felt. She wanted so to heal the wounds between her and her sister. *Dear Lord, let me hold my tongue this time. Bring her close to me again.*

"Oh, thank you," Emmy said, looking relieved. "Here . . ." She put the swathe of gold in Treasure's hand. "I dug it out of my mama's chest of ribbons in the attic."

"Such a pretty shade of gold," Treasure said, winding and knotting the fabric with an old, familiar clumsiness of hand. "I — I never was too adept at this sort of thing," she added, struggling with the unyielding strip of cloth.

A firm tread drew her eyes from her task to an imposing shadow she knew too well.

She squinted into the sun. "Good morning."

"It certainly is, isn't it?" Donovan returned lightly, the greeting honey in his mouth. He stepped in front of her, blocking the bright golden light. His freshly bathed scent drifted to her nose, and she looked up again. His hair, still wet from a morning dip, was slicked back from his face, exposing the exquisite lines of his high forehead. And those mysterious smoky eyes. How often she lay awake wondering what he had secreted behind them. A simple game of taking advantage of fortuitous circumstances? Or some deeper treachery she couldn't guess at?

"Princess gold," he murmured.

He watched her with disturbing intensity that brought a warm rush of rose to her face. "Excuse me?"

Donovan reached out and captured the trailing end of the ribbon, idly winding the length around her wrist. He let the end slide between her fingers, then slipped the smooth satin out again. "I'd name that color princess gold for the princess who'll wear it on Friday," he said, tossing a charmer's smile at Emmy.

The glow of her sister's returning smile might well have been a searing iron to Treasure's heart. She stared blindly at the nest of gold in her lap.

"Would you like my help?"

Treasure's eyes flew to his laughing ones. "Do your talents include making bows?"

"You've yet to discover all my true talents," he said, an invitation to sin in the velvet inflection of his voice.

"Can you do it, Donovan?" Emmy piped up.

"Of course. I used to help my—my neighbor girl wrap them all the time."

"Well, by all means," Treasure said tartly, holding out her ribbon-bound hands. "You must show us."

"By all means." She gritted her teeth as he took his leisure disentangling her from the satin tumble. His fingers lingered over hers. Traitorous, her skin relished the barest touch from him. Their eyes met for a long, searching moment.

"Where did you live?" Emmy asked, breaking the silence.

Donovan shrugged, his attention fixed on the ribbon. "Everywhere and nowhere."

"Oh, Donovan, you never answer me directly."

"I guess that's why sooner or later everyone stops asking. Here you go, princess in gold." Donovan handed Emmy a beautiful confection, earning himself a delighted smile.

"Thank you. It's perfect," Emmy said. "I think it will look nice with my yellow dress, don't you, Treasure? It's not exactly the same shade . . ." She held the ribbon to the light, scrunching her nose at it. "But — "

"You know, Emmy," Treasure began, ignoring Donovan's interested glance. "I believe Miss Eliza has a bolt of satin in her shop that would match perfectly."

Emmy's eyes flew to Treasure's, wide with astonishment. "But — but, you said we didn't have the money to spend. And the ball *is* Friday. I mean we have chores and everything . . ."

"We have six days. I'm sure we can set aside a few chores until next week. And if we persuade Mammie Eura Mae to help us — "

She got no further. Emmy threw herself into Treasure's arms and hugged her tightly. "Oh, Treasure! I've never had a ball dress before. Wait until I tell everyone!" Giving Treasure another fierce squeeze, she whirled away, clutching her bow to her chest as she danced around the porch.

"I'm glad you're happy, Emmy." *So very glad.* Treasure basked in the warmth of her sister's joy, marveling at how a bolt of cloth could bring such happiness.

"So, pretty lady . . ." Donovan said. "What color will you be wearing to the grand ball?"

The tender teasing in his voice and obvious approval in his eyes evoked a different kind of heat in Treasure.

203

She avoided his gaze, feeling her face grow hot. "You are assuming I intend to go."

"You have to go," Emmy said, looking distressed. "You're mistress of Rose of Heaven."

"Why, Emmy. Do you really feel that way?"

"Of course. How silly. Who else could be mistress? And the mistress always goes to the balls. Dressed in the most beautiful gown."

"You wouldn't dare to break tradition now, would you, Miss McGlavrin?" Donovan asked. His tone was bantering, but Treasure's quick ear caught a challenging edge.

"No," she said, putting her chin in the air. "I suppose I wouldn't."

The next days flew by in a whirlwind of last-minute preparations, and Treasure found herself caught up in the midst of it all. Grudgingly at first, she fell into her place as hostess for the event the whole of McGlavrin's Valley now anticipated.

Perhaps Donovan was right after all. People did accomplish more when they were happy. She admitted to herself that seeing her sisters smile for days on end justified every delay in her schedule, every added expense.

"Missy Treasure?"

Treasure glanced up from the linens she was counting. Solomon, bobbing from foot to foot, peered through the half-open door of the parlor. "Yes? What is it?"

"A letter." He held out the crumpled envelope. "It jus' come for Mastuh River. But he done left for town."

"I'll take it then." When Solomon retreated, Treasure examined the weathered missive. It was peculiar in that there were no outward signs identifying the sender. No clues for her to follow. *Why had the sender taken such precautions?*

Idly, she traced the line beneath the envelope's closure with her fingernail and found it loosened by its journey, a lengthy one by the tattered looks of it. Curiosity burning at her fingertips, she gave the fragile seal a little flick. It yielded.

No. This sort of thing was beneath her. She couldn't stoop so low as to read his mail. Yet . . .

Why not? After the despicable acts he was guilty of? All the lies she suspected him of? What if this letter had something to do with Papa or Rose of Heaven? Why should she wait for him to catch her unawares as he had the first time with Papa's note? She had a right, no a duty, to try to uncover anything and everything she could about Donovan River.

Before her shaky logic failed her, Treasure broke the seal and pulled out the single page.

Donovan,

It has been so long since your last communication, I feared you were in greater difficulty than you were wont to tell me. There is so much I would say to you, but I know with your concern, time is precious.

Despite the difficulty in honoring your requests for secrecy, I can assure you your ally there is reliable and discreet and of the utmost importance to our cause. As to your mention of assistance from Mister Purvis, I cannot yet make you that promise. But, with time and patience (of which I know you have very little of either), I am confident it can be arranged.

I will restrain the questions I am anxious to ask, but will close with one personal note.

Father is ailing. We fear he will not live through winter. I can allow for your feelings in this matter, but hope you will reconsider. As always, even as she did the day you left us, Mother remains stoic.

I wish you Godspeed. May your infernal luck keep you safe to return to us when you have made your peace.

Yr devoted brother,
Jared

"Lord in heaven." Feeling suddenly guilty, Treasure hurriedly stuffed the letter back into the envelope, doing her best to reseal it.

Her thoughts careened off each other. So, he did have a family somewhere who obviously cared for him. Jared River. Treasure tried the name in her mind, unable to reconcile herself to such an unlikely combination. Why had he left them? What could be so terrible between them that he would ignore the appeal of an ill parent? And what of the ally his brother wrote of? Who and what was that person? What was the cause shared by the mysterious ally, Donovan, and a brother he had abandoned?

Who was Donovan River?

Myriad questions about him assaulted her mind at the same time details of the fast approaching evening of *his* ball competed to monopolize her attention. His ball . . . hadn't the whole idea seemed oddly timed from the start? Oh, he justified it eloquently, convincing her of its merit.

Yet did he have another motive? Her suspicions fed on each other. *Was* he scheming to arrange a clandestine meeting with his "ally" under the guise of a festive gala?

Treasure pressed fingers to her temples. Damn him. Questions, always questions. Just once, she dearly yearned to know one single facet of him that wasn't shadowed in confusing shades of gray.

"Miz Treasure. Miz Treasure!" Orange Jane burst into the room, disrupting Treasure's dark musings. "Miz Treasure, dat ole' churn done split straight down de middle! We ain't got near 'nough butter fer all de bakin we got ta do."

Treasure took a single glance at the cook and her own slew of troubles receded. Orange Jane looked as if she'd spent too many nights awake. Dark circles rimmed her eyes, and her tall, graceful figure drooped. Remembering the news she'd heard about Orange Jane's brother's death, she reached out and took the cook's hand, throwing aside decorum in favor of sympathy.

"Aunt Orange Jane—I'm so sorry about Samuel. Perhaps . . . this ball has been quite a lot of extra work for you. If you'd like a few days to yourself, I can easily arrange it. We'd miss your cooking, of course . . ." Treasure stopped, feeling awkward.

"It's all right, Miz Treasure," Orange Jane said, giving Treasure's hand a brief squeeze before pulling away. "Youse always been fair with me, and I does appreciate you offerin'. It's hard, about Samuel. But de work helps me to not remember so much."

Treasure gave Orange Jane a small smile. "I do understand that."

"I knows you do, Miz Treasure. Sometimes, workin' is easier dan feelin'." A brief expression of sadness crossed her face. Then, she squared her shoulders and straightened her bright yellow apron. "Well now. We's got work to do. Mastuh River ain't back with dem extra supplies. And Aunt Eura Mae done loosed dose two chillun in my kitchen again. Lawd, and de churn! A body cain't bake without no butter!"

"Of course. We'll tend to it right away." Treasure smiled and flung open the door. "Solomon!" When the houseboy scuttled in, she handed him Donovan's letter. "Take this to Mr. River's cabin and leave it lie somewhere."

As she followed Orange Jane out of the parlor, Treasure set aside the bevy of badgering queries in her mind. At least for now. "One crisis at a time," she muttered. "One crisis at a time."

Chapter Eleven

Treasure paused at the top of the staircase, her fingers taut around the oak railing. The damp imprint of her palm marred the new beeswax shine of it. In a waft of music and laughter, festive sounds drifted to her ears from the ballroom downstairs.

To Treasure, they rang out as invitingly as a funeral dirge.

People. A room full of them. A large room full of them. Waiting for her. They would be watching her. And worse yet, she would have to talk to them.

Why in all of heaven had she let Donovan River and her sisters bully and cajole her into agreeing to this affair?

Tackle a year's worth of knitting and sewing; sow and reap a crop; clean, and cook; tend to the sick; mother an entire plantation — Treasure willingly shouldered each and every task at Rose of Heaven. But the role of charming hostess? Dancing, chatting, lending wit to a thousand conversations?

"I can't do it."

"Of course you can, pretty lady."

Unaware she had voiced her feelings aloud, Treasure blushed with a hot rush of embarrassment. Donovan leaned against the railing at the bottom of the stairs, one hand behind his back, his lopsided grin teasing her.

"I shouldn't wager my last dollar on that, Mr. River,"

she said primly, secretly glad of his unexpected presence. Even at his worst, Donovan River was at least distracting.

And tonight — she tried, and failed, to hide her sweeping perusal — tonight he came fairly near to his best.

He answered her with a bold, admiring glance, prompting Treasure to give her off-the-shoulder drape of a sleeve a self-conscious tug. She wished the deep emerald silk didn't hug her waist so tightly, regretted letting Spring talk her into having the bosom tailored to cup her breasts in such a daring display above the curved décolletage.

Taking in the magnificent figure he cut in formal evening attire, she envied his effortless confidence. Sweaty and shirtless in a field, or cool and elegant in fine black broadcloth, he maintained his self-assurance. She constantly worked to sustain her control. But nothing it seemed — not the Stantons, the financial woes at Rose of Heaven, not even murder — daunted his spirit for long.

"See something you like?"

Treasure didn't flinch at the raffish amusement in his smile. "Not in the least."

"Hmmm . . . I do. I've been waiting for you." He started up the stairs, his steps slow and measured.

Uneasiness nuzzled her spine. She shivered, cold at heart, her skin hot. She felt inept at exchanging seductive banter with him, especially now. Certain she looked a fool, she stared, tongue-tied, aggravated to think he was undoubtedly reveling in her discomfort.

When he reached the landing, Donovan took his leisure studying her with a roaming appraisal, drinking in her eyes, her lips, the soft show of creamy skin at her low neckline. A naked hunger showed in his eyes. Treasure struggled for words to rid herself of him, to chill the disconcerting heat in his gaze. But he only made nonsense of her attempts by reaching out and embracing her fingers in his. Slowly, he raised her hand to his lips and brushed it with a lingering kiss. Treasure saw herself reflected in his eyes, her hair a flame in a silver and gold pool.

"The guests are waiting," she managed, saying the first thing she could think of. The last thing she cared about.

"Let them." He moved closer, his breath falling softly against her cheek. "This moment is ours."

Their gazes locked, suspending all but the magnetic force drawing them together.

Reluctantly, Treasure at last broke the spell, dragging her eyes from his. "I must go to them. It's most improper."

"Tonight, pretend you don't care what's proper, what's reasonable. I'll show you what it's like to forget. To trust only your feelings."

"It isn't that simple. I've never—I can't."

"You can. You've just never tried." He paused, rubbing his fingers over the smooth line of his jaw. The velvet timbre of his voice deepened with challenge. "Call it a dare. I'm willing to take a chance. Are you?"

"Mr. River—"

"Donovan." He held her with the dark caress of his voice. "I want to hear you say it."

Treasure ran the tip of her tongue over dry lips. She drew his eyes to the gesture—eyes suddenly tempest gray. Between each tremulous breath, she forgot how to draw the next.

He waited. A silent longing trembled in the air between them. Treasure wondered if it was hers or his or a poignant mingling. Restless, unsatisfied, she wanted, she needed—

"Donovan," she whispered. She tasted his name on her lips, bittersweet.

Her small surrender seemed to bring him as much pain as pleasure. For a moment, his hand tightened over hers. He searched her face, as if intent on discovering a path to her soul. Then, as swiftly as it came, his fleeting impression vanished.

Letting her fingers slide out of his, Donovan brought his other hand out of hiding. He held a single rose, a perfect dark silver-lavender bud, the color Treasure had always called twilight. With the barest of touches, he drew the whisper-soft petals down her cheek to her throat. The sweet elusive fragrance of the rose mingled with the earth and sun scent of his skin.

The petals grazed the swell of creamy flesh at her bodice. "You're beautiful, Treasure McGlavrin," he murmured.

Treasure held her breath, wanting to believe — not daring to believe. The feathery kiss of rose petals against her shoulder started a tremble in her heart.

"I hope you'll do me the honor of letting me escort you tonight," Donovan said, putting his gift into her hand. He guided her fingers around the stem, matching them with his own.

"I—"

"Say yes."

Unable to voice her feelings, Treasure glanced away from him to the flower in her hand. Beguiled by the sultry summer air, the tightly furled petals were beginning to open.

Donovan tipped her face to his, then curved her hand in the crook of his arm. "It'll be all right, I promise you. Just for tonight, let me make it all right."

Mesmerized by the tenderness in his voice, his palpable strength beneath her fingertips, Treasure let her panic slip away. Her eyes fired with determination. "Yes," she said. "I will."

Treasure's resolve stood firm until they reached the imposing double doorway to the ballroom. There, it faltered miserably, freezing her feet to the threshold.

"Come on, pretty lady," Donovan whispered against her ear. "This can't be any worse than, say, shoveling woodpile manure over black raspberry vines

211

on the hottest day of the year. And I should know."

"That is so reassuring."

"Just trust me."

Treasure arched a brow. "You are asking a considerable amount of me this evening, Mr. River."

"I can't let you win my dare too easily. It could prove fatal for my ego."

"Now you are asking me to believe the impossible."

"No — just the possible." Donovan drew her forward through the doors into the ballroom. "And tonight, Treasure McGlavrin, anything and everything is possible."

Treasure blinked. She looked away and looked again. The impossible was still there.

A thousand amber flames dazzled her eyes. The heady perfume of gardenias, sultry-sweet, seduced her with the scent of temptations promised. Her skin melted under the flirting warmth of a twilight breeze. The sudden surge of vibrant sensations gave truth to her absurd notion that Donovan had somehow managed to draw her into an enchantment of his creation.

Papa once boasted that Rose of Heaven's ballroom was the finest of any Alabama plantation house. Treasure now knew it was no idle brag, although she scarcely believed this was the same dusty, neglected room she'd seen barely a week past. Garlands of creamy gardenias festooned the high, ivory walls. Their attar mingled with the summer-warmed fragrances drifting in through windows open on the back gardens. Gold drapes were drawn back to frame panes of sable sky. A quintet of musicians grouped around the elegant piano, set like a dark jewel against one wall. Her guests were everywhere — on the dance floor, at the long buffet table, scattered on the window balconies for a taste of night air.

"It's beautiful," Treasure breathed.

"It's all for you, pretty lady."

She looked up at Donovan, feeling a shivery delight to see his pleasure, knowing her own had caused it. "I don't know how you managed it all. You are truly a sorcerer, Donovan River."

He shrugged away her compliment. "I thought it was time you had a debut."

"A debut?" Treasure plucked at the silk of her skirt, not quite able to meet his eyes. "Like a sixteen-year-old valley belle? I'm much older and hardly society darling material. I believe my time for 'coming out' has passed."

"Everyone comes out when they're ready. I think you're ready. I only wanted to make it memorable."

A treacherous tenderness found a vulnerable hollow in her heart and lodged there. It created a longing ache; it sowed a seed of joy. *How could a feeling hurt and exult at the same time?* "It is memorable," she said, wonderment and a soft catch in her voice. "Because of you."

Because of you. The words struck her as if she had made some awesome discovery with implications she'd yet to comprehend.

The inner revelation left her facing him, oblivious to everyone around her, searching his eyes for something she had no name for.

"Oh! You're here. At last!" Spring flew up to them, her gown a foaming sea blue silk. "I was beginning to think you wouldn't come, Treasure, and that I'd be left to make the most awful excuses! And then, of course, Mr. River would be sulking all evening and wouldn't be the least interested in dancing, and I'd probably be forced to waltz with that horrid Uless Clement. Maybe even twice!"

Spring paused to draw a breath and Treasure seized the momentary silence. "Uless Clement can hardly be the horror you paint him."

"Oh, Treasure, *really.*" Spring wrinkled her nose.

"Have you *seen* Uless Clement?" She darted a mischievous glance at Donovan, who did his best to smother an answering smile. Lowering her voice, Spring leaned close and said, "He has these little pig eyes, he sweats most profusely, and — he snorts!"

"Spring!" Treasure glared at her sister, then at Donovan, who was suddenly beset by an uncontrollable fit of coughing. "That is hardly a charitable or ladylike remark. He appears sober and well mannered. A quiet gentleman and quite respectable. I have also heard he is apt at running his family's plantation."

"Treasure McGlavrin's ideal — respectable, responsible, and perpetually dull," Donovan murmured.

Treasure pretended not to hear his mocking aside. She fixed stern eyes on Spring. "It's past time you began to consider those qualities in the young gentlemen who continually dangle after you, rather than picking at every slight fault you find. I can't fathom your complete disinterest in finding someone suitable."

"Suitable?" Spring's laughter bubbled over in a joyful tumble of sound. "You're right, Treasure, you haven't the first notion why I'm not the least bit interested in finding someone *suitable*."

"I think you omitted a few of the more important husbandly qualities," Donovan put in.

Treasure scowled at him. "And pray tell, what would those be? Good at a hand of cards? Skilled at eluding responsibility? Able to make rash decisions without a single thought?"

"You forgot able to drink any respectable man under the table," Donovan said with a grin.

"How careless of me." The devilish gleam in his eyes led Treasure to expect anything but a sincere response.

"Actually, I was thinking of somewhat different qualities — empathy, devotion, a sense of humor." He paused, the corner of his mouth curling in a wry smirk. "Skilled in the art of lovemaking."

"Mr. River!"

"Why Treasure, I don't think I've ever seen you that particular shade of pink. It so becomes you," Spring said, giggling. "I'll tell you what. I volunteer to rescue you from Mr. River's wickedness. Since you're so taken with Uless Clement, you dance with him. I'll be content to let Mr. River prove to me he can dance as well as he tends a field."

Spring put a hand on Donovan's arm as the last notes of a reel came to a high-spirited end. Donovan hesitated a moment. Treasure sensed his refusal. She quickly stepped away from him and her sister. "I am sure Mr. River will be happy to oblige you. If you will excuse me, I'll see to our guests."

Before either of them could protest, Treasure turned and left them, trying to feign a confidence she didn't possess. A sense of the security she'd felt moments earlier holding on to Donovan's arm crossed her thoughts. The lack of it now stung her.

Guests surged around her in a confusion of voices and color and Treasure felt asea, without a haven to shelter her. She managed, smiling stiffly, to find her way to a corner of the buffet table, and busied herself with the imaginary task of perusing the ballroom.

Near the open French doors, she caught sight of Camille. The soft amber light favored her creamy complexion and wisps of dark hair fanned her cheeks and neck in the evening breeze. She looked completely at ease, flirting and chatting with a group of admiring men. Here, Camille was in her element, while Treasure felt lost in an alien country.

A twinge of jealousy pricked at her as she watched her stepsister smile and laugh. Was it that smile, that coquettish trill of laughter, that attracted Donovan? And how did one learn those little feminine secrets that made a woman desirable?

"You can't frown, Treasure!" Emmy's voice startled her back to awareness. "This is a ball!" She pirouetted, her golden shirts whirling around her.

"Can we have one of everything?" Abby piped up, her pudgy fingers eagerly reaching for a dish on the buffet table.

Beside her, Erin toyed with the wide pink sash of her white, frilly dress, a frock identical to her twin's. "I'd like a chocolate," she whispered, putting a small hand on Treasure's skirt. "Please?"

"Tonight you can have anything you want," Treasure assured them. She brushed an errant curl from Erin's forehead. "Only remember tomorrow your tummies might not be too happy about it." She smiled indulgently at their identical delighted smiles and helped Emmy gather up plates and napkins for them.

"You look so pretty tonight, Treasure," Emmy said as she settled Erin on a chair. "I never realized . . ." She broke off, flushing.

"That I could *be* pretty?" Treasure laughed. "Well, it does feel nice to dress up, I must say. Are you enjoying your first ball?"

"Oh yes! Although . . ." Emmy ducked her head. "I haven't had much of a chance to dance with anyone. I've been looking after the twins and—"

"And it would be nice to have a little time without them? I'll tell you what, if you'll sit with them while they eat, I'll fetch Eura Mae and she can take charge of them. You can have the whole rest of the evening to dance."

"Really?" Emmy's expression wavered between disbelief and joy. "May I stay up until everyone leaves, then?"

"Every last guest."

"I can't believe it," Emmy said, her smile wide. "I do feel like a princess, just like Donovan said."

Treasure smiled as she watched Emmy rush to help Abby carry a plate laden with cakes, pies, and candy to a waiting chair.

The musicians struck up another song, and Treasure returned her attention to the dance floor. Trying to appear to sweep the room in a casual glance, Treasure dared to look back at Donovan and Spring. They danced, slowly, with the ease of friends. But Treasure sensed a tension in their animated conversation. Several times, Spring let go of Donovan's leading hand to make some punctuating gesture. Treasure forgot her pretense and watched as she tried to gauge her sister's mood. Spring seemed excited, but distracted somehow, as though only going through the motions of enjoying herself, while her mind wandered elsewhere.

The music crescendoed toward its finale and Donovan swung Spring into a wide turn, then pulled her close. Quickly, he bent and whispered something against her ear. Spring faltered a step.

Two thoughts simultaneously clashed in Treasure's mind: *She cares for him. He could easily seduce her.*

"I declare, honey, you look as if Satan himself decided to dance a jig on your buffet table."

Treasure nearly lost her balance as she whirled about. Dark blue eyes twinkled at her from behind a gaily painted fan. "Miss Eliza." She covered her confusion with a stiff demeanor. "You startled me."

"I daresay something has." Eliza looked pointedly at Spring and Donovan. The music ended, but they still stood close, intent in conversation.

"Spring merely asked for a dance, and Mr. River obliged her."

"I'm relieved you realize that. For a minute, the way you were scowlin' at them, why I imagined you were jealous. But it's perfectly obvious that man's just waitin' to catch your eye again."

"Miss Eliza, I have absolutely no desire — "

"Why, Sam Dereford!" Eliza snared the attention of a tall, fair-haired man passing by, carrying a cup of punch. Before Treasure could divine her friend's intention, Eliza had initiated a lively conversation, extracted the cup from his hand, and slyly maneuvered the young man into asking Treasure for a dance.

Treasure envisioned all forms of embarrassing consequences as she self-consciously allowed her newfound partner to lead her to the dance floor. She ached to draw back. Panicked, considering all and any excuses, she looked around the room, to find someone, anyone, to give her a reason to abandon her escort.

She caught Donovan staring at her.

He smiled. And in that simple gesture Treasure found encouragement enough to give her a spurt of confidence.

As a result, she was able to carry her part of a light conversation while her feet carried out graceful steps. The small triumph put pleasure's blush in her face, and by the time the dance ended, she began to admit the evening mightn't be so harrowing an experience after all.

A flurry of applause and encouraging murmurs fortuitously interrupted Treasure's awkward thank-you to her partner. Curious, she wove her way through the guests, to where an attentive group thronged around the piano.

Donovan looked up as she poised at the piano's edge. He sat on the tapestry-covered bench, readying to play.

The expression in his eyes swept away the gay noise of the celebration and held her spellbound in an intimate silence. The tenderness there evoked an ache in her heart nearly beyond bearing. Her knees weakened. She rested quivering hands on the piano's edge. In the polished ebony gloss of the wood, her fingertips brushed Donovan's reflection. Her abandoned rose lay on the piano top and she picked it up, cradling its bloom.

A random gathering of candles burned between them, flame shadows waltzing to the wind's song. The warm breeze from the open windows sent a scattering of gardenia petals wafting like moths' wings to the fire. Every sensation seemed surreal, as if she had conjured them in her dreams. She feared the merest breath would dispel them like star dust at dawn.

Donovan reminded her the dream was real by running a languid hand over the piano keys. He glanced at the haphazard sheets of music in front of him, then back to her. Pushing the sheets aside, he cleared his throat.

As he began to play, his husky tenor drew passion from the words and melody, and Treasure let his song weave new threads of flame and silver desire into the tapestry of her fantasy.

> *"O whisper in the twilight,*
> *Softly sweet and low;*
> *Tell me art thou mine, love?*
> *Tell me ere you go.*
> *While the stars are shining*
> *In the sky above,*
> *Answer little fairy,*
> *Wilt thou be my love?*
> *O whisper in the twilight,*
> *Softly, sweet and low,*
> *Tell me little fairy,*
> *Art thou mine or no?*
> *O whisper in the twilight*
> *Ere the birds have flown;*
> *Say in loving accents,*
> *Thou art mine alone.*
> *Whilst the spring flow'rs blossom,*
> *Smiling sweet and fair,*
> *Tell me little darling,*
> *Thou my love wilt share.*
> *O whisper in the twilight,*
> *Softly, sweet and low,*
> *Tell me little fairy,*
> *Art thou mine or no?"*

Treasure heard his voice, wedded to the sweet music, long after the last note faded, amid the clamor of clapping hands and loud praises. A flock of town belles

219

gathered around Donovan, fans fluttering, soft voices admiring as he stepped away from the piano. For a moment, as Treasure watched, the array of silks and lawns melted like a water-color rainbow. She blinked and found his eyes searching hers.

Treasure's heart compelled her to do something — something to acknowledge the question of his gaze. The question he had asked with the words of his song. She didn't know how to answer. How could she tell him about the burgeoning feelings inside when she couldn't explain them to herself?

"Look!"

An excited shout broke the tender spell and drew the guests to the open balcony where several people had already gathered. Grateful for the distraction, Treasure hurried to see the cause of the disturbance. As she stepped out among the darkened arbors, she felt it — the gentle touch of raindrops against her skin.

"So — it came at last."

She turned and found Donovan at her side. He smiled down at her and then looked up, letting the water play on his face. "I knew it would. I could never stop believing it would."

"I hoped," Treasure whispered. "But I was afraid to hope. I was afraid it might be too late."

Donovan brushed a finger down her cheek. "It's a new beginning. Isn't it?"

"I want it to be."

"It can be." He moved close and Treasure knew he intended to kiss her. Right here, in her garden, in the midst of a lively celebration of dancing and cheers, in full view of every citizen of McGlavrin's Valley. It was reckless, impulsive, the worst possible thing he could do for her reputation. In her South, a public kiss meant a proposal best soon follow. And yet, Treasure had no illusions he would give a care for a mere social mandate.

So typically Donovan River.

220

But at that moment his intentions couldn't have mattered less. And she couldn't have wanted him more.

The festivities, the long-needed rain, Donovan's tenderness, all fed her sudden, wild, unfettered joy. She was happy, happier than she ever had been, happier than she dreamed she had a right to be.

Drunk on pure, intoxicating pleasure, Treasure raised a hand to draw him near. He caught it against his heart. The unsteady pulse under her fingertips increased her giddiness. He was close, so close. Not near enough. She half closed her eyes, her lips parted, waiting for the first taste of his mouth on hers.

Waiting in vain.

Donovan's hand tightened on hers. Then he drew back, chastely brushing her fingers with a stranger's polite salute. Only his eyes told her what the restraint cost him. "You're getting wet, Miss McGlavrin," he murmured.

"And you surprise me, Mr. River," she said. Her disappointment was tempered by wonderment. "Making the respectable choice. So unlike you."

"And so unlike you to mind." He held her back as the rest of the guests began to spill out of the garden into the house, laughing at the quickening raindrops. "Would you have kissed me?"

"Yes."

He drew back, startled. "At the utter disregard of your reputation? Why, I wonder?"

Treasure twisted a handful of green silk between her fingers, heat burning her cheeks. "Because," she said. "I — I simply wanted to."

Without waiting for his reply, she turned and fled into the house. She left Donovan staring after her, alone in the warm summer shower, the petals of a twilight rose in his open palm. . . .

Donovan strolled back into the ballroom, rain pelting a strong, steady beat overhead. He lingered in the downpour long after the others had sought shelter in the house, foolishly mesmerized by a handful of rose petals. They had survived the endless burning sun, erratic summer showers, the buffeting of wind and storm. And still, they held their elusive, sweet fragrance, still felt silken to his touch. In them he saw Treasure, proud and beautiful, strong yet fragile, weathering every hardship with stoic grace. Admiration for her swelled inside him, furious and protective. She awed him, infuriated him, inflamed his desire for her until he feared the power of his burning need to possess her would one day overcome his flagging restraint.

A pleasant laugh drew his attention to the center of the ballroom. Treasure, in the midst of a small group of guests, smiled up to one of the young men beside her. Damp and slightly disarrayed, she looked even more exquisite, more alive, than the moment he had seen her perfect in all her pretty trappings.

Her hair, misted with jewels of rainwater, glowed like a morning sunrise. The green silk of her gown caught and clung, beguiling, each time she turned or raised a hand. Each time she flattered her companion with a smile or a laugh, her eyes sparkled with new discovery, her delicate features lit up, vibrant with life.

You wanted her to blossom. You wanted this to happen. No, not this. He wanted—hell, he didn't know anymore. But one thing was certain. He couldn't abide watching her gift someone else with the same soul-touching gaze she'd given him in the garden. He didn't want the untried passion in her heart taken by anyone else.

She was complimenting the man next to her on some clever anecdote when Donovan took her arm, startling her in the middle of a sentence. "Mr. River . . ."

"You promised me this dance, I believe."

"I don't think—"

"The music is about to begin." He gave her little

222

choice as he took her hand and led her to the floor.

"My, we are in a temper," Treasure murmured. "You might have simply asked."

Donovan relaxed a little at the teasing glint in her eyes. With a wicked grin, he stepped back and bowed over her hand. "I am sorry, ma'am. All those nights in gambling dens and bordellos seemed to have rusted my manners. Will you honor me with a dance, Miss McGlavrin?"

Giggling, Treasure curtsied in return. "Why, yes, Mr. River. How charmin' of you to ask." She put her hand on his arm, but hesitated at the first strains of the music. "Oh — a waltz."

"Yes, it is done, you know."

"It's just — I can't. I've never done it before. At home, we practiced reels, and the country steps, but Papa hated to waltz. So I've never — I mean, I just can't."

"You're not your papa. And I'll teach you. You'll enjoy it. It's like making love when you have all night to savor it."

Treasure gasped. "I haven't . . ." Her mouth set in a firm line, belied by the warm flush in her cheeks. "I have no intention of — "

"I should hope not. Right now would be rather inconvenient. To say nothing of the reaction of your guests."

"Donovan — Mr. River. *Please.*"

"One lesson at a time, pretty lady."

She had the slender fragility of a wood sprite. But as he took her into his arms, he wondered anew at the supple strength beneath her soft skin. Awkwardly at first, then more boldly, she moved with him, both learning and teaching, an equal partner in the sensual sway of an age-old dance that mocked the civilized steps of the waltz. The trusting way she curved her hand into his, letting him guide her through each step until the unfamiliar became a natural, smooth rhythm, aroused his banked desire. His own reckless teasing imagination

223

haunted him with visions of her. Slipping green silk from her shoulders. Letting it melt into a pool at her feet. Slowly, very slowly, untying each ribbon of her chemise. Diaphanous lace revealing sun-golden skin inch by inch in tortuous seduction. Her eyes beckoning, inviting him to—

"You missed a step."

Frowning, Donovan tried to shake off the too-real sensations his fantasies evoked. "Did I?"

"What were you thinking about?"

He tried to lie, to grasp at some vague reply to fob her off. The faint, vulnerable tremor in her voice robbed him of any reason he might have mustered. "You. In my bed."

Her eyes shied from his. She tried to look back, couldn't. Her face pressed against his shoulder, and on a sigh, he heard the whisper of his name.

For once, unable to seize on a single word, Donovan simply pulled her close. He lightly rested his cheek against her damp, red-gold curls. She let him hold her, even after the last strains of the music had drifted to silence.

He wanted to stay that way. Together, unconcerned with crops or sisters or the fate of Rose of Heaven. And he sensed an echo of his own longing in the way she leaned against him, trusting, at ease. Donovan nearly convinced himself the rest of the party would fade away and leave them undisturbed when a firm tap on his shoulder pulled them apart.

"Music's over," Rader said. "Case you hadn't noticed."

"Mr. Johnson is sorely disappointed with you, Treasure," Eliza chimed in. "Now don't frown so, darlin'," she said, rapping her husband's arm with her fan. "You know it's the truth. You've been waitin' for a dance with the hostess all night long. And don't *you*"—she stared hard at Donovan—"look like I'm the wicked chaperone, come to spoil your courtin'. You've already managed in one evening to give the gossips enough to wag about through next year's harvest."

"I'll take that as a subtle hint I should accept your husband's charming offer," Treasure said. Donovan took pleasure in the decided lift of her chin. Treasure McGlavrin would never be a wilting Alabama belle. "Shall we, Mr. Johnson? I do believe I can teach you a few things about the waltz."

"I declare," Eliza sighed as she watched Treasure and Rader move onto the dance floor. "Separating you two has been harder than pryin' honey from a bear's maw."

"I assume you went through all those difficulties for some reason other than to discuss my gossip-mongering activities."

"You can be quite stuffy when you try, Donovan. It must be an unfortunate result of your mysterious past. I must tell you, it's most unflattering."

Eliza's exaggerated pout eased his annoyance at her untimely interruption. The corner of his mouth lifted in a rueful smile. "Yes, ma'am, I do my poor best. *Was* there something you wanted?"

"Spring. She's not in the ballroom."

Donovan rubbed a hand over his jaw. "I see."

"I thought you might."

"You don't seem unduly disturbed."

Eliza glanced at her husband. "Not yet, honey. But I believe I'll leave the rescuin' to you. You seem to have a knack for it."

What I have a knack for is getting involved when I should be running the other way. The thought kept him company as he casually wove his way back into the garden.

The rain had diminished to a soft patter against the leaves and rose arbors. Ducking under widely spread branches for shelter, Donovan took a path leading away from the house. When he had walked far enough for the light and music to wane to the faintest of glow and sound, he stopped, intent on the sounds around him.

225

"This is wrong. It's too risky for both of us. If Miss Treasure found out —"

"She won't. And I don't care if she does!" Spring's voice rang out clear and defiant. "I've made my choice. Now you have to make yours."

"Miss Spring . . ."

"Stop calling me that!"

"This isn't an ordinary choice. The wrong one will ruin your life, and it will likely end mine. Miss Treasure's kinder than some, but she won't have any pity for you, and less for me. I have dreams, Miss — Spring, things I have to do. I have to think carefully, not just about how terribly bad I want you to be my woman."

"I know. And I want to be a part of those dreams. Oh, let me, Elijah. Forget about the others. Forget about laws. Besides, we'll have Donovan's support. He can't help himself."

Donovan winced. He nearly gave away his position in a niche of trees, but a feeling stopped him. He waited, picking out Spring and her companion among the shadows.

"We can't count on anyone, no matter how generous. I've got to make my own way. And — if I live to see it through — it sure as Hades won't be easy. You best be sure, real sure you're ready to give up everything for us."

Spring put a hand to Elijah's face. "I've never been more certain of anything."

Elijah reached for her, and Donovan turned away.

They were foolish and reckless, their perilous choices of the heart impetuous at best. The choices he would have made.

But the last decision Treasure would consider.

He could stop them. A word, a threat, and it would end out of fear and necessity. Instead he trusted his instinct. Yet reason said his impulse betrayed Treasure.

Without warning, her voice rang out in the darkness, startling them all.

"Spring?" She was searching, he knew. And near.

Very near. Spring and Elijah froze, hesitating between flight and confrontation.

He had to choose.

He had no choice.

"Looking for someone?"

Treasure found herself encircled by strong arms, staring up into the laughing eyes of Donovan River. "I would say that was obvious. Let me go."

He ignored her command. "Who's missing?"

"Spring. She's left the dance." Treasure didn't dare add she suspected her sister had left with Donovan. From the amused gleam in his eyes, she decided he'd already guessed. Shame washed over her as she tried to pull away from his disturbing nearness.

"You're jealous," he said with smug satisfaction.

"Don't flatter yourself. I'm worried about Spring."

"Worried about me kissing her in the rose arbor?"

"Were you?"

"What do you think?"

"I think you wouldn't tell me the truth if I offered you the deed to my plantation."

"You're wrong, pretty lady. About Spring. And there are some things I wouldn't tell you even if you did promise me *my* deed. Although . . ." He studied her with the appearance of careful consideration. "I could think of several interesting ways you could coax it from me."

Treasure opened her mouth to tell him exactly how she felt about coaxing anything from him, but a rustle of leaves distracted her. "Someone is there," she whispered, gesturing over Donovan's shoulder.

Donovan glanced back. "Among the lilac bushes? In the rain? Whatever could they be doing?"

She pretended not to notice the wicked challenge in his smile. "I don't have the faintest notion, Mr. River." Treasure wriggled against his hold. "But I intend to find out."

"Perhaps I don't want you to."

His tone was pleasant, yet it unsettled her. His implacable expression felt like a dare, a test in their clash of wills. "Should I consider that a threat?"

His arms fell away from her so abruptly Treasure swayed on unsteady legs. "I seem to have forgotten your low opinion of me. And I don't make threats, Miss McGlavrin." Donovan stepped aside and swept an arm toward the dense shrubbery behind them. "Please, explore at your leisure. I'll make your excuses for you at the house."

Pride kept her from stopping him from striding back toward the house. It held her until his tall figure melded with the blackness.

He was through the French doors of the balcony before she caught up to him. Treasure wanted to speak to him. Their confrontation in the garden had snapped the fragile twig of trust grown between them. She missed the warm comfort of it more than she dared admit to. Even if she had found the words and the courage to voice them, the opportunity was lost to her.

Lively debate had broken out among the guests. And at the center of it were Camille and her escort, Ira Stanton. As Treasure followed Donovan into the ballroom, she felt the icy stab of Camille's glare. As she drew closer, Camille's lilting voice became noticeably louder.

"Why, I just think it's the most marvelous notion, Colonel Stanton," she trilled. "I can't for all my days imagine why my dear sister wouldn't leap at the opportunity. And to think of all the good it would do for the valley, to say nothin' of my dress allowance!"

A scattering of Camille's admirers laughed obediently. And her stepsister's comments earned Treasure more than a few unfriendly glances. She didn't need to guess the topic of discussion.

"I'm afraid I haven't had the opportunity to hear Colonel Stanton's marvelous plan in detail," Donovan spoke up. Treasure, aching to kick him, darted him an evil-tempered glance. The look he returned told her he intended to best Ira Stanton.

"Of course, I'm quite willin' to oblige," the colonel boomed, his face set in a genial smile that didn't touch his eyes. "Especially seein' as you, Mr. River, have the decidin' vote in this matter."

"That is a matter of opinion, Colonel Stanton," Treasure boldly challenged. "Yours. Not mine."

"Well now, I wouldn't argue with a lady." He bowed, tossing an amused smirk at his audience. "But seein' as Mr. River is interested . . ." He launched into a spirited rendition of his plan to lumber the rich timberland that made up the northern quarter of Rose of Heaven.

Donovan, at first, stood with arms folded, his expression clearly doubting. But as the colonel's narrative went on, she saw with dismay, he began to relax his stance, listening with undisguised interest.

"You'd need some way to transport it," Donovan put in. "Now, a ferry, right at the southern corner of Rose of Heaven where the river bends in a little . . ."

"Not a bad scheme," Rader mused. When Eliza prodded him in the ribs, he turned an apologetic glance on Treasure. "If a person had the notion to try it."

"Of course, it would take a man who knew his business — "

"And a woman willing to give up the land. Which, Colonel Stanton, I am not."

"Seems it wouldn't hurt you to share the wealth. You got the best river bottom land and timber and river access besides." The complaint came from somewhere behind her.

All around a loud buzz of approval followed. Then another guest broke in with his opinion. "And what do the rest of us got? A stinkin' little town and a handful of farms barely gettin' by. This valley hasn't got a chance in hell of survivin' if we can't drum up some sort of commerce besides Miss Treasure's cotton. And that don't do *us* no good."

229

"Lumber," several voices answered the implied question simultaneously.

Treasure braved all the eyes that immediately swiveled in her direction. She knew she was a minority of one. People had stepped away from her, leaving her vulnerable, on display. Hands clenched at her side, she kept her gaze fixed on Ira Stanton. "My papa trusted me with Rose of Heaven, and I have no intention of ever letting you or anyone else take it away from me."

Murmurs rippled through the crowd. Treasure sensed a wave of ill will toward her. Inwardly, she cringed. But she was determined to maintain her outward composure.

"I don't think your papa wanted you to sacrifice your heart and soul for his plantation."

Treasure whirled on Donovan. "You would like me to believe that, wouldn't you. How much easier it would be!"

"Easier, hell! What I'd like is for you to realize there's a world outside your cotton fields and that other people live in it."

"Other people who want to steal what is mine!"

"Other people who might just have an idea that could benefit everyone—including you, Treasure McGlavrin."

"Forgive me, Mr. River, if I find it difficult to believe you have my best interests at heart."

"That's quite enough." Eliza stepped between them. Treasure abruptly became aware of the picture they made for the attentive gallery of guests—squared off against each other in the center of the ballroom, arguing loudly enough to be heard at the farthest corner of the house. "I do believe this discussion would be better carried out in private," Eliza said. "You two are making a frightful habit out of deciding your differences in the most public places."

Treasure looked at Donovan. She immediately regretted it. Their debate had provoked his capricious

230

temper into a fury. "It appears Miss McGlavrin and I have nothing more to discuss," he said, his voice strained with his effort to maintain a tenuous control. "She has obviously made up her mind already — on several matters. If you will excuse me . . ." Ignoring Eliza's outstretched hand, Donovan stalked past both women to the ballroom door and yanked it open.

Spring stood framed in the doorway.

Mud smudged her face and gown. Her hair tangled around her shoulders in a wild mass. Tears had drawn streaks in the dirt, marring her cheeks.

She swept the ballroom with a single wild look. Then, giving a little strangled cry, she threw herself into Donovan's arms.

Chapter Twelve

The guests flocked to encircle Spring and Donovan. Only Treasure, frozen in shock, hung back. All she could do was stare, and pray what she feared had not come to pass.

Elijah. Spring had flirted, goaded him on for months — beyond measure? God, no. Surely he valued his life too much to do this. Spring. Foolish, impetuous child.

Dear Lord, give me the courage to do what I must do.

Gathering all her will, Treasure pushed through the tight circle of guests whispering and gawking at her bedraggled little sister. "Let go of her, Mr. River. I will handle this," she said, prying Spring from Donovan's arms none too gently.

Donovan let Spring go with a soft frown of concern. When he turned to Treasure, his eyes hardened. "Don't you think we ought to allow her to explain before you jump to conclusions?"

"You know the conclusion," Treasure hissed. "And as far as I'm concerned, you have a share of the blame."

"Oh stop! Stop it, both of you!" Spring wailed. She pushed away from Treasure. "It's not me! It's Gold Meadow. There's a slave uprising. Oh, hurry! You have to hurry! The barns are on fire and they're starting to burn the fields. Elijah went back to Gold Meadow with the slave who came to tell him. I tried to follow" — she touched her soiled gown — "but he sent me back to tell all of you." "Hell and damnation!" Ira spat. "Jimmy's home alone. I left him there sleepin' off a bad drunk."

"Jimmy Rae was drinking?"

Treasure caught sight of Emmy agog with curiosity and now dismay. "Yes, Emmaline. And you can be certain it wasn't the first time — or the last."

"It's hardly the time for recriminations," Donovan interrupted brusquely. "I'll follow you over, Stanton."

Spring stopped him at the door, eyes pleading. "I'm going with you. I must. I left Elijah there. He insisted on going when he heard what was happening. It was terrible. Colonel Stanton's overseer had sent for the vigilantes and by the time Elijah and I got there, the — the killing had started." Spring gripped Donovan's sleeve. "Please, I have to go back."

Eliza moved to the foreground, near Donovan. Treasure noticed an odd, understanding look flit between them. "Now, honey, you know how foolish that would be."

"You aren't going anywhere," Treasure said firmly. "It's too dangerous. You will go right upstairs with Eura Mae and stay there until this is over."

"No! Please, no. I have to go back. Donovan, please, take me with you."

"Your sister is right. You'll be safer here." He lowered his voice. "I'll send word. I promise."

Spring was not consoled by his vow. Treasure stepped up and put an arm around her sister. "There's nothing you can do and I need you here to watch over Emmy and the twins. Please Spring," Treasure coaxed. "You're the only one I can trust."

"But Elijah — "

"I'll see he comes back to Rose of Heaven, I promise. Now go up with Mammie Eura Mae."

Tears coursing down her face, Spring allowed Eura Mae to turn and guide her up the stairs.

233

"I'll help." Emmy lifted the hoop of her skirt and hurried after them.

Ira had already slammed his way out of the house as Donovan strode out of the room, heading for the study. "Give me your keys," he commanded Treasure, who followed hot on his heels.

"Not on your life!" She pulled the keys from a pocket hidden in the folds of her gown. Always her pantry keys, the keys to Papa's gun case, and to her mama's jewelry box stayed on her person. Even when she slept.

"I need those damned keys. I don't have time to waste getting my pistol from the cabin. And I'm not going armed with a stick."

"Neither am I."

"You're not going."

"The hell I'm not! Elijah is mine and I intend to deal with him. Besides, I'll not have him waging war for the likes of Ira Stanton!"

"You are not going."

Treasure jammed the key in the gun case lock, and flung open the door. She jerked out a rifle.

Donovan took two.

Without a word, she locked the case, turned away from him, and stomped off toward the stables. In minutes she had Bettis rig the cart.

She made to climb in, but a strong arm caught her forcefully around the waist and pulled her off. "You weren't listening to me, as usual. You will not go and risk your life over this."

"And you will?"

"Yes."

"Because you are a man?"

"Because I know what I'm doing."

Outraged, she kicked him soundly in the shins. When he doubled over in pain, she deftly swung herself into the seat and grabbed the reins. "So do I, Mr. River." Slapping the reins against the horses' backs, she headed toward Gold Meadow.

"Goddamned woman. Bettis! Saddle Belial! Fast!"

"Already done, Mastuh River. When I saw de look on Miz Treasure's face, I know'd you'd be ridin' alone."

Donovan yanked off his coat as he flung himself into the saddle, catching the reins Bettis threw over the stallion's head. "You a good man, Mastuh River, best think hard 'bout who you turn your back to over t' Gold Meadow." He lowered his voice. "Yessuh. White or black."

"Thanks for the warning," Donovan said as he wheeled Belial about, "but I've been listening to my gut instinct so long, it's the only voice I hear."

"I jus hope you's listenin' good tonight," Bettis muttered into the wake of mud and mist Belial kicked up.

The stallion proved far faster than the cart, and Donovan tipped his hat as he flew past Treasure on the narrow, rutted road that led behind Rose of Heaven to Gold Meadow. His cavalier attitude, even in the face of imminent danger, confounded her. But she had no time to dwell on Donovan River.

Following her—all around her, it seemed—the eerie songs of the slaves rang out, their language becoming less and less discernible. Apprehension crept over her. Was it anxiety and fear of the violence at Gold Meadow? Or did her own people smell the lure of freedom in the orange-tinted clouds billowing above Gold Meadow? Had she been a fool to leave her family to their mercy?

Treasure banished the thought. She'd been fair, downright generous, with her people. They wouldn't chance escape or revolt. Where could they go? They'd be caught and whipped, or sent to the slave markets if they tried. Surely they knew that.

But even as she reassured herself, the noise and excitement around heightened to a frenzy. Treasure clamped down her fear as she spurred her team up the

235

drive of Gold Meadow. The horses, skittish from the scent of blood and smoke, pulled nervously at the leathers, nostrils flaring. Treasure peered through the haze. At least the big house didn't appear damaged — yet. She tied the horses in front of the Georgian home and jumped from her seat, sprinting toward the fields.

Like a storm from hell, fire swarmed over the entire back portion of the plantation, slaves' quarters, out-buildings, and fields. Bodies boiled out of cabins and the barns; others came running from every direction, forcing Treasure to duck and dodge to avoid being crushed in the chaos.

Already, the dead and wounded littered the grounds: some silent, others crying out in pain. Midnight dark against black soil, only the yellow and orange flame re-flections and their woeful moans told her where the un-fortunate victims of their own revolt had fallen.

She nearly stumbled over a boy, no older than Emmy, motionless at her feet. A vicious wound ripped his chest open over his heart. All that would never be — his future, his loves, his laughter, his sorrows — spilled out in a crimson pool that seeped into the ground and dis-appeared.

Her heart cried out as she fell to her knees beside him, groping for words of prayer. Instead, despair surged inside her. "Why? Why did you have to do this to yourselves?" she cried, slamming her fist into the ground near the boy's unresponsive face.

"Perhaps it was a fate preferable to the only other of-fered him."

Treasure jerked her head around. Donovan stared down at her, a rifle in his hand. His expression was masked in night. "Never, never will I believe that. Life, no matter how harsh, must be preferable to — this." She glanced at the boy.

"You were born a free woman, Treasure McGlavrin." His voice spat contempt. "How would you know?"

Treasure sprang to her feet. "I? Ask yourself that

236

question! These are my people! You—you're just an interloper, a Yankee. You will never understand our ways."

"I hope to God I never do. I don't want to understand what it means to buy and sell humans and keep them like animals to be used and disposed of on white men's orders and white women's whims."

"That's not fair. You know damned well I don't treat my people that way!"

"Open your eyes." Donovan gestured around them with the barrel of the rifle. "You can't go on living in your own narrow world. What do you think caused this nightmare? Fairness and kind treatment? Pretending the abuses don't exsist won't make them any less real."

"What did Stanton do?" She had to shout to be heard over the commotion. Gunfire echoed around them in rapid sharp retorts, mingling with the screams and yells.

"He killed Orange Jane's brother for wanting to be with his wife when she was birthing her first child."

"Dear Lord in heaven . . . she didn't tell me."

"You would have ignored it even if she had!"

"That's not true! But I can't mourn every wrong done. It is a way of life that is survival for us. I have no choice; Rose of Heaven has no choice." With the boy lying lifeless at her feet, Treasure's defense sounded suddenly hollow to her own ear. She stared at the child. Did she really believe there was no other way?

A woman's scream pierced the air nearby and Treasure whirled. A few feet behind Donovan, a thin figure swayed from side to side, wailing. In her arms, blood dripped from the small bundle she clutched to her chest.

Weak-kneed, Treasure reached out to Donovan.

He didn't budge. "Had enough?"

"I—I . . ." Treasure passed a trembling hand over her eyes.

"Go inside. Stay there. You aren't helping anyone,

least of all yourself. They'll need bandages and supplies when it's settled. You can have them ready."

"What about you?"

"If I thought you cared, I would—" He broke off, leaving Treasure baffled at the intent of his aborted confession. "Look—Rader's brought several men up from the valley."

"Maybe this will end quickly. And without more bloodshed."

"Don't count on it." He shouldered his rifle. "The bloodshed has just begun—unless I can convince them otherwise, that is."

Treasure stared in disbelief. "Do you actually think you can reason with them?"

"I'm sure as hell going to try."

He strode up to Rader, and Treasure quailed at the steely determination in Donovan's eyes. His foolhardy interference could cost him his life.

"The overseer rounded up most of the vigilantes. The patroller's bringing more who've gathered down at the guardhouse. We're ready to end this now," Rader was telling Donovan as she hurried up to them. "I don't like the notion, but there's no reasoning when it gets this bad."

"Stop yappin' and go shoot me some darkies." Ira stomped up, his face smudged with soot, his expression murderous. "The bastards are runnin' off in every direction while you're sittin' here enjoyin' the view!"

"No! Wait! All of you."

Over a dozen angry and shocked faces turned on Donovan. Treasure's breath caught in her throat. "If you kill them, they'll be of no use to you, Stanton. And after the damage done tonight to your barn and fields, you're going to need every hand you can get, and you won't have the money to replace the ones you lose."

"The man's a damned Yankee nigger lover," someone called out. "Don't listen to him, Ira."

"Yeah, he ain't one of us."

238

Despite herself, Treasure admired Donovan. To openly contradict a way of life she and the others had accepted since birth was to risk his own life. And yet he continued to argue, unflinching, before a group of men ready to kill opposition, whatever form it took.

"Don't be a fool, Stanton," he was saying. "Use the men to encircle the ground, bring them in alive. Killing them at random, what does it prove? It's pure waste, just like your burning crops. Useless."

"They'll sure as hell think twice before tryin' this again!"

With a startling jolt, Donovan turned on Treasure. She took at step back, fearful of the challenge in his eyes. "You own the biggest plantation. What do you think?"

Treasure could have slapped him. He wanted her to take sides in a very public debate, before men who resented her already. But with all eyes riveted on her, she couldn't back away. "I say," she began hesitantly. "I say they knew the consequences of their actions before they took them. But in the interest of salvaging Gold Meadow, if any crops can be saved, then it only seems prudent to bring them back alive. You cannot run a plantation this size without slaves."

Gratitude flickered briefly across Donovan's face. Some of the men began shuffling about, muttering among themselves.

"Miss Treasure makes a good argument, Stanton," Rader put in.

A smattering of curses rippled through the crowd. "You gonna let him tell you how to run your place, Ira?"

Donovan stared hard at the colonel, and Treasure shuddered. The steely gaze, the rigid set of his jaw — he wore the same expression the day he killed a man in cold blood. *Don't be a fool, Ira.*

Ira sized him up with a long look. Then, with an explosive sigh, he jerked out, "Oh hell, do as he says.

Once I have them back, they'll wish they were dead."

As Ira whipped about on his heel, ending the debate, Treasure wondered if anyone else noticed relief ease the tension on Donovan's face. *He's certainly made no friends this night,* she mused. But he had earned something unexpected: her heartfelt respect.

She turned to him, searching for a way to tell him. The words never came. Without warning, Donovan scooped her to his side and kissed her soundly, letting her feel the strength of his satisfaction. Then, before she could recover her wits, he was gone.

"You there, see to the cotton." Donovan shouted the order to one of the vigilante group. "The corn is gone, but some of the other crops might be saved."

Nearby, Ira slashed through the remaining slaves like a righteous avenger, whip in one hand, machete in the other. Some of them tried to flee the chaos; others fought the losing fight, as if determined to win freedom, even if the only freedom was death. "Don't let the bastards get my cotton," Ira snarled. "It's all I have left."

"It's still damp from the rain, Stanton. And Rader's taken a few of the men to guard it." Donovan slogged through the soot-dark mud, moving toward the slaves' quarters, leaving Ira to lament over his fields. He kept the rifle propped on his shoulder. He hadn't used it for any more than warning shots so far, and he fervently hoped he wouldn't have to use it to kill.

The slaves' cabins, ravaged by fire and the rampage of people, were little more than hollowed shells. The dirt paths between the rows of buildings were strewn with the slaves' meager belongings: pots and pans, clothing, even precious hunks of pork and vegetables lay trampled into the muddy ground. No light shone through the cracked and smashed windows. An eerie

The Publishers of Zebra Books Make This Special Offer to Zebra Romance Readers...

AFTER YOU HAVE READ THIS BOOK WE'D LIKE TO SEND YOU 4 MORE FOR *FREE* AN $18.00 VALUE

No Obligation!

MORE PASSION AND ADVENTURE AWAIT... YOUR TRIP TO A BIG ADVENTUROUS WORLD BEGINS WHEN YOU ACCEPT YOUR FIRST 4 NOVELS ABSOLUTELY *FREE*
(AN $18.00 VALUE)

Accept your Free gift and start to experience more of the passion and adventure you like in a historical romance novel. Each Zebra novel is filled with proud men, spirited women and tempestuous love that you'll remember long after you turn the last page.

Zebra Historical Romances are the finest novels of their kind. They are written by authors who really know how to weave tales of romance and adventure in the historical settings you love. You'll feel like you've actually gone back in time with the thrilling stories that each Zebra novel offers.

GET YOUR FREE GIFT WITH THE START OF YOUR HOME SUBSCRIPTION

Our readers tell us that these books sell out very fast in book stores and often they miss the newest titles. So Zebra has made arrangements for you to receive the four newest novels published each month.

You'll be guaranteed that you'll never miss a title, and home delivery is so convenient. And to show you just how easy it is to get Zebra Historical Romances, we'll send you your first 4 books absolutely FREE! Our gift to you just for trying our home subscription service.

BIG SAVINGS AND FREE HOME DELIVERY

Each month, you'll receive the four newest titles as soon as they are published. You'll probably receive them even before the bookstores do. What's more, you may preview these exciting novels free for 10 days. If you like them as much as we think you will, just pay the low preferred subscriber's price of just $3.75 each. *You'll save $3.00 each month off the publisher's price.* AND, your savings are even greater because there are never any shipping, handling or other hidden charges—FREE Home Delivery. Of course you can return any shipment within 10 days for full credit, no questions asked. There is no minimum number of books you must buy.

4 FREE BOOKS

TO GET YOUR 4 FREE BOOKS WORTH $18.00 — MAIL IN THE FREE BOOK CERTIFICATE T O D A Y

Fill in the Free Book Certificate below, and we'll send your FREE BOOKS to you as soon as we receive it.

If the certificate is missing below, write to: Zebra Home Subscription Service, Inc., P.O. Box 5214, 120 Brighton Road, Clifton, New Jersey 07015-5214.

FREE BOOK CERTIFICATE

4 FREE BOOKS

ZEBRA HOME SUBSCRIPTION SERVICE, INC.

YES! Please start my subscription to Zebra Historical Romances and send me my first 4 books absolutely FREE. I understand that each month I may preview four new Zebra Historical Romances free for 10 days. If I'm not satisfied with them, I may return the four books within 10 days and owe nothing. Otherwise, I will pay the low preferred subscriber's price of just $3.75 each; a total of $15.00, *a savings off the publisher's price of $3.00.* I may return any shipment and I may cancel this subscription at any time. There is no obligation to buy any ship-ment and there are no shipping, handling or other hidden charges. Regardless of what I decide, the four free books are mine to keep.

NAME

ADDRESS   APT

CITY   STATE   ZIP

(   )
TELEPHONE

SIGNATURE   (If under 18, parent or guardian must sign)

Terms, offer and prices subject to change without notice. Subscription subject to acceptance by Zebra Books. Zebra Books reserves the right to reject any order or cancel any subscription.

stillness, unsettling in its contrast to the raging upheaval behind them in the fields, blanketed the whole area.

Donovan intended to check every cabin for wounded and any abandoned children. But foremost, he needed to locate Elijah. He'd seen no sign of him since he'd set foot on Gold Meadow.

Starting at one end, he worked his way down the row of cabins. The first three doors he pushed aside opened to empty rooms. The fourth refused to budge. He knocked against it with the butt of his rifle. No response.

"I don't mean any harm. I want to help. Are there any wounded inside?"

When no answer came, Donovan decided to move on. Obviously someone had decided to stay safe, locked behind his or her cabin door.

Then a moan, a woman's deep, painful moan, filtered out through the open window at the cabin's side. Donovan trotted back, peering inside, trying to make out more than shadow in the darkened room. "Is anyone there? Can I help?"

He paused before forcing his way in, but another, weaker noise convinced him someone's need outweighed the folly of breaking in. The window proved too small. Returning to the front, he slammed his shoulder against the door until it crashed to the ground at his feet.

A thin gasp greeted him. At the back of the one-room cabin, a huddled figure cringed away. Donovan propped his gun against a wall and, moving slowly, held out his hands in front of him to soothe the figure's obvious fear.

Intent on his task, he never sensed the danger behind him until it struck him a staggering blow.

Pain, raw and deep, surged through him, numbing his senses, and in its wake, he felt a warm flow on his back. He lurched forward, vaguely aware of a scuffle

241

and the hard thud of a body falling to the dirt floor at his back.

Fighting a wave of dizziness, Donovan whirled. Elijah stood behind him. In his palm lay a knife wet with blood.

Chapter Thirteen

Before the scene registered full with Donovan, Elijah flung aside the knife and grabbed a rag to swaddle the gash on his back.

"It's not as deep as it feels, Mastuh River. Rest next to Mama a minute. You'll know it when the bleedin' stops."

"Mama?" With Elijah's help, Donovan eased down next to the sparrow of a woman cowering among a pile of clothing and quilts in the corner. "This woman is your mother?"

"I didn't know she was here until I came down to try to put a stop to this tonight."

Donovan winced as Elijah tied off the makeshift bandage, for the first time noticing the man who lay slumped on the floor behind Elijah. "Who's he? Is he dead?"

"Seems he's part my brother." Elijah's face registered the blankness Donovan recognized as a mask for any emotion. "And he's not dead. Just knocked out good. He didn't take kindly to a white man comin' near his mama tonight."

"After seeing the welcoming party outside, I can't blame him." Donovan let a silence slip between them, then he held Elijah's gaze steady with his. "You saved my life. I won't forget it."

"I hope not," Elijah said, a wry twist to his mouth. "We best get moving. Can you walk?"

"No problem. How about your mother? Is she ill?"

"In a manner of speakin'." Elijah paused, then said in a low voice, "She's sick in her mind."

"Bring her to Rose of Heaven."

"But Miss Treasure — "

"I'll deal with Treasure." Donovan hoisted himself to his feet. "Let's get moving. You can tell me on the way how it is you can be living next door to your mother and not know it."

Elijah lifted the woman as though she were weightless, protecting her in his arms. "What about him?" Donovan nodded at the man still senseless on the floor.

"I'll try to get back for him. Though I don't think he'll be too likely to want to leave. I think his spirit's broken. Hardly talks. Just goes about his chores, day after day, stayin' clean away from trouble. He must have been crazy with worry for her to do what he did to you."

"Forget it." Donovan led the way out of the cabin. The men walked side by side, Donovan tapping on doors as they moved slowly through the narrow alley between the slaves' cabins, now deadly silent in the waning of rebellion.

Donovan stepped around a pile of rotting vegetables. "So, what happened?" Donovan pursued the question when Elijah volunteered nothing.

In the darkness, Donovan sensed Elijah's inner debate over whether to trust him or not. Finally, he sighed. "My papa was a planter. Mastuh Matthew Thomas. Lived not far north of here. He took to Mama when she was barely more than a child herself. Only he didn't just want to bed her, like some. He wanted to take her into the big house and keep her in the rooms next to his. Wasn't too long, she was carrying his baby. I'll give him his due, he took good care of me, almost as good as his own children."

"And his wife? What did she say?"

"Nothing much until I got a bit older. Then I heard told she swore she'd have us both killed unless he sent us to the auction block. Seems she didn't much like me always being mistaken for her own."

"So your father — sold you?"

"He hid us in our own place way behind the other slaves' quarters. Mama convinced him to let me keep up the reading and writing I learned from bein' companion to his children."

Intrigued by the unfolding story, Donovan had to remember to keep moving forward, keep checking behind doors. "Isn't that against the law?"

Elijah shrugged. "Mama told him after living in the big house, her boy would never be a regular slave. She told Mastuh Thomas she would take me and run. Said she'd rather we both die than me not have a chance for a better life."

"Quite a woman. But why would the master of a plantation take the risk?"

"He said he couldn't live without her lovin'. He gave her just about anything she wanted. Some women have that power over a man. Mama said times even the impossible can't keep two people apart." There was a long silence. Donovan wondered if Elijah's words were truths of the present instead of echoes of the past. "It went that way until Mastuh Thomas's boy found out. He ran straight to his mama. After that, Mastuh Thomas sent me to his brother. That's where I learned the lumbering business and to keep books. I never knew where Mama was sent."

Donovan looked at the woman curled against Elijah. He tried to imagine a strong, determined beauty, fighting for her son's future in the pitifully thin figure, staring blankly as she hummed disjointed phrases of some half-forgotten song. "What about your brother?"

"I don't know much about him. I only found out he and Mama were here a few days past. I heard from

245

Samuel—before Mastuh Stanton killed him." Elijah's face hardened for a moment, then cleared as he went on with his story. "My brother told me some other white man took to Mama. Only this one did her real bad then sent her off with a baby in her belly. Two more masters sold her off because she wasn't any good at earning her way after they were done with her. My brother says she's spent her life looking for me, trying to get us back together."

"I'm sorry," Donovan said, feeling the simple words were more than inadequate. Did Stanton put her in this condition?"

"Don't know. She hasn't been a beauty for some time, I'd guess. Stanton bought my brother because he's worth three men. I suppose Mama must be able to work at something, or Mastuh Stanton wouldn't have wasted his money."

"How long has she been—"

"With half her wits?" Elijah shook his head. "My brother says it's been happenin' since the day she was sent away from my papa. He says she still talks about him."

"She'll be safe at Rose of Heaven."

"She'll be dead soon, Mastuh River. I know it. But I have to do what she wanted." Elijah stopped walking and stared straight at Donovan. There was no indecision, no question in his voice. "I have to take the learnin' she gave me and make a better life. Just like she wanted me to."

He was asking for help, daring everything. Donovan didn't draw back. Even though the silent request might cost them both their futures. Their lives. "I understand. I'll help. You have my word."

A sudden confusion of voices and people around them interrupted whatever reply Elijah might have intended. A woman tugging along three small boys scurried out from behind a huge, black cauldron in one of the fire pits. With a little urging from Donovan, they

246

trudged along behind up to the back lawn of the big house. Most of the household slaves had gathered there, milling about, talking among themselves.

Donovan left the woman and children in the care of them and was turning to Elijah when he caught a glimpse of Treasure.

She stood on an upstairs balcony. Through the sooty haze, by the amber light of the candelabrum she held, he saw her smile.

He was safe.

Thank God. It had been hours since she'd seen him. No one she talked to knew where he was. He looked dirty and exhausted. But alive. Alive. She wondered over the word, at the relief and tender feeling it evoked. He smiled back at her, that lopsided, take-on-the-devil grin she knew too well, and her heart gave a queer lurch. Unable to assimilate the emotions washing over her, Treasure retreated back inside, the candle flames wavering with her trembling hand.

The house was fairly quiet now. She had helped to tend to the wounded brought here, sent many down to the slaves' hospital for safety and to rest; some she watched carried away to be buried. Treasure had found the best vantage point was, ironically, here in Colonel Stanton's bedroom. She'd hesitated to enter the room, until she discovered it was the only unlocked door on the second floor facing the front lawns.

Below, she watched Ira and the townsmen round up the remainder of the slaves like wild horses. They'd surrounded the grounds and corralled them, then bound them, one by one, hand and foot. Those who escaped would be tracked down with dogs and vigilantes and brought back to face whatever punishment Ira Stanton saw fit to dole out.

Part of Treasure pitied them with all her heart. But with another part she damned them for the foolishness of their actions. Hadn't they only made life worse for themselves?

An unwilling vision of a dying boy and an echo of Donovan's words visited her. *Perhaps it was a fate preferable to the only other offered.* Was it? The traditions and necessities of a lifetime warred with Donovan River's argument. Treasure put a hand over her eyes, briefly blocking out the chaos below. Donovan somehow had a talent for showing her an unexpected perspective on situations and ideas never before questioned. And in seeing them differently, a seed of change was planted, often so subtly that Treasure did not immediately notice it. She thought of Rose of Heaven and the new hope blooming with the ball and the rain. And she thought of herself, discovering her own heart for the first time. She uncovered her eyes.

It was over and done now, and by morning order would be restored. But something inside her had shifted. She set it aside now, too exhausted and shaken to deal with it.

With a sigh, Treasure smoothed her soiled ball gown, fingering the tattered green silk. The remembered pleasure of Donovan's holding her, whirling her in his arms, sent a warm rush of sensation through her. She wrapped her arms around her waist where he had gently held her to him. "At least we had one dance," she murmured.

"And I figure, the way you look in that dress, he wanted a hell of a lot more than that."

Whipping around, Treasure met the leering eyes of Jimmy Rae Stanton. He stood in the entrance to the small parlor that adjoined the master suite, a near-empty bottle dangling from his hand.

Treasure glanced to the door. Too far. He was closer. The balcony. She had a chance. "So that's where you've been hiding, while your brother and half the valley risk their lives for you," she spat. "You little coward!" Defending Ira Stanton was the last thing she ever thought

248

she'd hear herself do, but she had to gain the upper hand.

Jimmy sauntered up to her, breathing sour whiskey into her face. "I ain't a little anything, *Missy* Treasure." He flung the bottle against the wall, spattering whiskey and splinters of glass. "Everyone's gonna see that. You'll see it," he snarled, roughly grabbing her waist and crushing her hard against his groin. "Feel that and tell me I'm a kid."

More revolted and angry than afraid, Treasure shoved at his shoulders. "Your juvenile behavior is ridiculous and insulting! Take your grimy fingers off me before you regret this any more than you're going to once you get your wits back."

"I got all the wits I need. And you're gonna see what a *real* man is." Jimmy Rae threw his weight against her, snatching a handful of hair. He slapped his mouth against hers, letting his weight and the momentum knock her backward.

Treasure lost her balance and fell. She landed gainfully in a graceless heap, Jimmy Rae atop her. His mouth continued to assault hers as she kicked and struggled against his weight. Though he was no match for a grown man, she was too slight to knock him away. "Get off me!" she managed when he took a breath. "You damned fool boy!"

"Damned fool boy, is it? I'll show you!" Straddling her body, he ripped her dress from the shoulder, exposing one breast barely covered by her lacy chemise. His mouth groped at the thin material while he struggled to shove a hand under her petticoats.

Treasure took full advantage of the awkward moment to shove her knee between his legs. The impact sent him reeling off her onto his back, whimpering. Struggling to her feet, Treasure shot out of the room and down the staircase, not stopping until she was out the front door and on the lawn.

Donovan stood there, talking to Ira. He looked up as

Treasure came running up to them. Both men stared blankly at her furious face.

"That low-down, scurvy brother of yours just tried to rape me, Ira Stanton!"

"Looks like he didn't get away with it," Ira observed, his tone flat.

Donovan stabbed him with a dark look, then whipped about to Treasure. Tension clenched every muscle, tightened the line of his jaw. Steeled anger flared swift and hot in his eyes. "Are you hurt?" He gripped her chin in his hand. "Tell me."

His sudden temper frightened Treasure as Jimmy Rae's fumbling attack hadn't. After everything tonight, she didn't want to see him start a new battle with the Stantons. "No. I managed to get away. He's drunk."

"Again." Ira spat at the ground, shaking his head in disgust. "I'm gonna wallop that boy alongside all those darkies first thing tomorrow."

"I'll spare you the trouble," Donovan growled. Pushing past Treasure, he strode toward the front door of the big house.

"Donovan, no—"

"Goddamn you, River." Ira shouldered his rifle, pointing it at Donovan's back. "You've gone one too far tonight."

"You can't!" Treasure grabbed at his arm, looking wildly at an oblivious Donovan.

Ira shoved her away. "Get out of my way or I'll finish what my little brother started." His gaze roved her torn dress. "But first I'm gonna have the pleasure of killin' that interferin' bastard." He raised the rifle again. Ira's finger closed on the trigger.

Treasure, half-turned in Donovan's wake, reacted without thought. Rushing straight at Ira, she flung both hands hard against the rifle barrel. The retort of the gun exploded close to her ear.

The shot went wildly astray, shattering the glass of a second-story window. Ira cursed her soundly.

Donovan, already up the front steps, didn't pause.

"I should have let him shoot you," Treasure muttered, hiking her skirts and racing after him. She'd nearly made it to the top of the long staircase when she heard a loud crash and the splintering of wood, followed by another resounding smash of wood and glass.

The door to Ira's bedroom had been wrenched nearly off its hinges. Treasure arrived in the entryway just in time to see Donovan haul Jimmy Rae off his feet by his shirt front and slam him hard against the wall.

Dodging around the remains of a table and whiskey bottle, she snatched at Donovan's wrist before he could strike Jimmy. "Donovan—stop it! You'll kill him!"

His hand tightened on Jimmy's shirt. He jerked his wrist free. "That was my intention," he said in a voice tainted with menace. Jimmy Rae was white to the bone, shaking, his mouth moving but unable to make a sound.

"He's just a stupid boy. Let it go. I'm asking you."

Donovan stared at her, a cold, merciless stranger looking out of his eyes. She'd seen that stranger once before: the day he shot Slade Gunter.

"Please," she whispered, suddenly afraid.

For a harrowing moment, Treasure believed he would refuse. She saw his rage nearly win over her plea. Finally, he dropped Jimmy in a heap and turned away. He lowered his fists, clenching and unclenching, to his sides, working to release the fury.

Treasure let her own breath out slowly. She realized she was quivering all over.

"What in the hell—" Ira burst into the room, his face convulsing in fury as he saw Jimmy curled in a ball on the floor, looking distinctly sick. "You sonofabitch—" He launched himself at Donovan.

It was over before it began. In one quick, powerful motion, Donovan slammed a fist against Ira's jaw, sending him sprawling. He kicked his way through the debris to the door, stopping to glare daggers at Treasure. "I've had all I can stomach of the Stanton brothers for one night. You stay if you want to."

Treasure caught up to him on the road back to Rose of Heaven. He was walking fast, one hand gripping the rifle at his side.

Panting a little, she fell into step beside him. His long strides forced her to take two steps to his one. "Elijah went ahead with the cart," she ventured after they walked in stony silence for several minutes. "You could have spared yourself a long walk."

"You should have taken your own advice," he snapped, not looking at her.

"I suppose I should have," she fired back. "Perhaps you could have found someone else to hit along the way."

"And perhaps I should have let you settle with the Stantons on your own."

"I don't want you to commit murder for me!"

Donovan stopped dead in the center of the road. He glared at her, and Treasure stared back, meeting his anger and frustration measure for measure. Abruptly, as quickly as it came, his temper waned. Shoving a hand through his hair, he offered her a small rueful smile. "I haven't thanked you for saving my life."

"Think nothing of it, Mr. River." Treasure turned on her heel and stalked away from him.

"Hell." Donovan suddenly felt bone-tired. His back throbbed and he could feel the bleeding had started again, probably due to his tangle with the Stantons. He'd managed in one night to make enemies out of just about everyone in the valley. Including, once again, Treasure McGlavrin. All because he couldn't stand the notion of someone else, even a drunken boy, touching her. "Damn," he muttered. "Treasure!"

She didn't pause a step.

Jogging after her, he reached her side in a few paces. "Treasure—aren't you tired?"

She scowled at him. "Exhausted."

"Then for both our sakes, let it lie for tonight. We've got all of tomorrow to argue it out."

"It nearly is tomorrow."

"I'll ignore that."

"I suppose it is useless tonight." She fell silent for a moment, then burst out, "But you have considerably more to answer for, Donovan River. You were crazy, rushing into the middle of the fray! And what about Elijah? And Spring? I know you have something to do with —"

Donovan threw up his hands in a mock gesture of protection. "Have mercy, pretty lady. I promise, tomorrow you can ask any question you like. Right now . . ." He cautiously moved his shoulder, regretting it as pain shot through him. "I need to sit down."

Treasure slowed at the suggestion. "Now?"

"Now."

She sighed. "If you must. Surely someone will be along soon to fetch us." Selecting a spot against the fat trunk of an oak, Treasure spread her skirts over the damp grass beside the road, curling her legs underneath her.

Donovan eased himself to the ground with a great deal more difficulty, laying his rifle carefully beside him. His back was stiff now, besides the pain.

"Why are you moving so awkwardly?" Treasure peered closely at him. "Are you injured?"

Deciding a little sympathy might improve matters, he nodded. "Let's just say someone with a quick blade caught me off guard."

"You were stabbed? You didn't tell me!"

"We were debating more interesting matters."

"How bad is it?" She laid a hand against his chest in guileless action as she leaned forward to trace Elijah's makeshift bandage.

How bad do I want it to be? Bad enough to keep her

253

there, close against me, tender concern in her touch?
"Not bad. Elijah did a fine job dressing it. Oh — I met
his mother. She's coming to Rose of Heaven. I told Elijah you wouldn't mind."

"What?" Treasure, momentarily outraged, pulled
away from him. In the next instant, though, she relented, shaking her head. "Never mind that now. Come
here." She put gentle hands on his shoulders, thinking
only of his hurt, forgetting the danger of letting him so
intimately close. "You can lean against me and rest
while we wait. I'll watch for the cart."

"No, really. It's fine." Donovan didn't care to explain
that a slashed shoulder and exhaustion weren't antidote
enough against her artless allure.

"Don't be tiresome. In that position you look like
Bonnie when she's begging for scraps: uncomfortable
and downright pathetic."

Not quite meeting his eyes, she tugged his arm in her
direction, and Donovan surrendered before he could
convince himself it wasn't the best of ideas. Treasure
twisted to allow him to recline across her chest, his head
resting more on her soft breasts than her shoulder.
"There," she said briskly. "Isn't that more comfortable?"

Discovering he could easily, contentedly spend the
rest of his life right there, he nudged closer, breathing
the honeysuckle scent of her that still lingered.
"Much," he murmured. Beneath his cheek, her breasts
rose and fell in a rapid rhythm, the motion arousing his
body despite the temptation to sleep.

He lay still against her, eyes closed, and gradually the
tenseness in her eased. Tentatively, one hand moved to
cradle his head against her; the fingers of her free hand
began stroking through his hair. She brushed every
strand from his forehead, her fingertips sliding over his
skin in a slow, sensuous pattern. It was so strange, she
mused, how he angered her one instant and instilled an
odd need to comfort in the next. For this moment she

254

refused to understand it; she wanted only to revel in the feeling.

Donovan willed himself not to respond to the growing desire to sweep her into his arms. He knew she had no idea how her whispering touch could drive a man wild with desire.

This was a side of Treasure McGlavrin Donovan suspected she kept carefully hidden from all but those sisters closest to her. What inspired her to reveal it now? The way she was touching him, he couldn't much care. She began to hum softly, phrases of the same sweet, mesmerizing song he'd sung for her at the ball.

Drifting somewhere between sleep and wakeful bliss, part of him yielded wholly to the cherished moment; the other part fought to rouse him enough to take advantage of it.

But he sensed how fragile their intimacy was. He had to control himself, no matter how the feel of her supple body melded to his made his body ache with need of her.

"Donovan? Are you awake?" she whispered, her light breath warming his ear.

Am I? "Hmmm? Did you say something?" he mumbled, adding a yawn for effect.

"I want to tell you something."

"What? Is something wrong?" He struggled to sit up.

"No, no. Be still or you'll hurt yourself." When he lay back, she sighed, her fingers teasing the strands at his nape. There was a long silence then she quietly said, "I simply want you to know that . . . well, although I will never abide your Yankee behaviors, I realize what you did tonight. You risked your life to stop that uprising. You could easily have stayed at Rose of Heaven. This wasn't your battle. But you cared."

"I can't stand back while lives are wasted."

"Yes, well . . ." She stopped, and Donovan knew without seeing it in her eyes she thought of Slade Gunter. And her father. "Whether or not I agree with your reasoning, I must thank you for helping us. And Donovan . . ."

He waited.

She drew an unsteady breath. "I am proud of you for the way you stood up to the men. You took control and made order out of mayhem. Even Colonel Stanton listened. Although I fear you haven't made yourself excessively popular."

"I'm becoming accustomed to being despised," he returned lightly, determined not to let her know how her unexpected praise touched him. "And I'm going to make sure Stanton got the message. I intend to call on him tomorrow."

"He's likely to shoot you as soon as you turn your back. And I won't be there to rescue you this time."

"Then I won't turn my back."

"I'm quite serious."

"So am I," he said, twisting to look up at her, his head in her lap.

"I rather doubt it." With a hesitating smile, she glanced her fingers over his arm. "You've put yourself in a vulnerable position, Mr. River."

Donovan gave up the fight against his desire. He thrust a hand into the thick waves of red-gold at her neck and pulled her mouth to his. "So have you, Miss McGlavrin," he murmured against her lips. Her hands moved to his chest to repel his caress, but he quickly captured her mouth in a slow, probing kiss.

As if she were melting into his embrace, she slid her hands to his shoulders. He tasted, searched, plunged into her sweetness. Her innocent response, tentative but fervent, dashed everything from his mind except his body's aching need for everything promised in her kiss.

Treasure felt as if she were caught in a maelstrom of hot, blinding sensation. Her emotions conspired against her reason to push her closer to him, to be nearer than the confines of conscience and clothing would allow. The thought shocked and excited her all at once.

How could she feel like this, want to be with him like this, when in a heartbeat he could change into the menacing stranger who kept secrets and frightened her with his rages?

In a swift motion, Donovan rolled to his side, carrying her with him, guiding her downward. She found herself lying half-beneath him, the hard length of his body matched against the softness of hers. The sudden shift left her hands trapped awkwardly. One pressed against the cleft in his shirt, the other flat on his thigh. The cold metal of Donovan's rifle pressed against her back. But the heated feel of his flesh against her hands consumed her attention.

He freed her mouth long enough to trace a line of hungry, nibbling kisses from her face down her throat and up to the tender point behind her ear, strong arms wrapping her close. Unnerved by the insidious weakness he evoked with his tormenting caresses, Treasure tried to loose one of her hands by slipping it up his leg. His sharp intake of breath stilled her fingers on his abdomen.

Donovan had to call on all his fast-fading will to keep from taking her there, in the wet grass, alongside a public road. He had never felt so out of control. Of all the women who had tempted and pleasured his body, none had ever induced this kind of primal madness in him. He pulled her to him, almost roughly, hugging her tightly, stroking her back and hair, unable to break from her warmth, yet needing to soothe away the hot, crazy turmoil inside.

Bewildered by his abrupt withdrawal, Treasure allowed herself to rest against him, cradled to his muscled chest. She listened to the feverish beat of his heart and wondered at how she could be responsible for it. When at last he drew away a little, looking down into her eyes, Treasure gazed steadily back.

257

Donovan felt helpless to answer the questions in her eyes. Instead he countered with one of his own. "Did that bastard brat really touch you?"

"Jimmy Rae?" She shifted her gaze downward. "He did his best. But . . ." Her eyes flitted up, sparkling with mischief. "My knee touched him first."

"I should have guessed. The lady knows how to take care of herself." There was no humor in his voice. He pulled her into a sitting position. He kept her close and Treasure felt the quickening tension grip his body. She turned a little to look at him. His eyes were fixed on his clenched hand, the skin stretched tight over his knuckles. He slowly turned his wrist to look at his palm and then turned it back again, the muscles of his forearm flexing with the measured motion.

A shiver raced over her. "Donovan . . ."

"Come on." Standing, he pulled her to her feet. "Let's go see if we can find that ride back to Heaven."

Treasure let him take her hand and lead her to the road. But she couldn't settle the sudden disquiet in her heart.

They'd gone only a short way when out of nowhere something flew at Treasure from behind, thrusting her face first into the rock and mud. She opened her mouth to scream but the impact stole her breath. A harsh yank on her arm jerked her to her feet. She wiped her free hand against her mouth, the bitter, metallic taste of blood on her lips.

"Donovan!" Someone large and strong clutched her to his body. She couldn't see his face. He smelled of sweat and fear. Not Donovan. Through the fog blurring her vision she found Donovan's tall figure, struggling to reach out to her. His hands were empty. Where was his rifle?

"Right here. Are you hurt?"

Treasure licked her lips. "No." She struggled to make

the shapes around her come into focus. In the black-ness she picked out Donovan, held in the grip of two dark men. Another stood near, pointing the rifle at Donovan. Runaways. Ira's people, rough and bent on revenge for every humiliation, every whipping and beating, every man and woman Ira let die at the hands of the vigilantes and dogs. Treasure's heart struck wildly against her chest.

"Shut yo' mouth, both o' yous," the man holding her demanded, giving Treasure a painful shake. "You gonna get us outa here, safe. You heah?"

"This isn't the way," Donovan said as the two men dragged him forward. "The vigilantes will keep search-ing until every one of you is found. They'll bring slave hunters—"

"Shut up," growled the man holding the rifle. He shoved the point of the gun in Donovan's throat. "Dey find us and dey find you—dead."

Donovan persisted. "How far do you think you can get? Dead or alive we won't be of any use to you once you leave the valley. If you kill us, you'll hang for cer-tain. There are better ways. I can help."

Help? Treasure stared at him. *Was he truly insane?*

"You!" The rifle-toting slave spat at Donovan's feet. "Youse ready t' help 'em, ain't ya? Youse ready t' help 'em put a rope 'round our necks. And Mastuh Stan-ton'd be mighty happy t' whup me bloody first and leave de rest to de dogs if he catch us."

"I don' wanna hang," said one of the men holding Donovan, younger, from the sound of his quivering voice.

"Shut up, boy!" The man with the rifle sounded wild. He pushed the gun harder against Donovan's throat. "He jus' talkin' t' save his own neck. Maybe I oughta kill him now 'long side you. We got dis here white missy and—"

"Listen!" the boy cried out.

Treasure' eyes flew wide. "Elijah!"

Donovan silenced her with a sharp glance.

"Git off de road." The slave holding Treasure hauled her, kicking and clawing, into a covering of brush. He pinned her wrists tightly in one hand and clamped a hand over her mouth with the other. "One sound and I snap dat skinny neck like a chicken. Heah?"

Treasure nodded. Somewhere near, she heard a grunt and then a frantic scuffling. Donovan. Where was he?

The rumble of wheels on loose gravel, sloshing through puddles, grew louder. How could she signal Elijah? The slave's arms were iron bars around her. Dared she risk screaming? His huge hand smothered her mouth, but she might be able to bite . . .

The cart neared. In a moment, it would go past, leaving them at the mercy of desperate runaways. She knew, if he could, Donovan would try to catch Elijah's attention. But what if he couldn't? What if he were already — Treasure refused to think the word.

The mule cart was directly in front of them now, mere feet away, its wooden wheels so close she felt a spattering of mud and gravel against her face. She could almost reach out and grab one. She wriggled against the slave's hold. He yanked her wrists upward, bruising the tender flesh.

Suddenly, a rifle shot rang out. Then another. *Donovan!*

The hands around her slacked for a moment at the sound. Treasure seized the advantage. With a painful twist, she pulled her wrists free and lurched away from her captor. He lunged after her, ripping away at a section of her skirt. Scrabbling frantically at the ground, Treasure grabbed a handful of rock and dirt, and turned, flinging it into his face. He cursed and clawed at his eyes, still groping for her with his free hand.

Treasure tried to get to her feet, but the brush next to her erupted in chaos, sending her sprawling. She heard a man's startled yelp. Elijah shouting. And then she was tossed into a furious tangle of humanity, thorny bushes, and scraping branches. Arms and legs pummeled her as she desperately tried to fight free of the mayhem.

All at once, a welcome rush of air hit her face, and she found herself roughly caught up against Donovan's heaving chest. He held her against him with one arm. Her head hung low, gasping for air, she saw him shove the blade of a small, razor-edged knife back into a slot in his boot.

"You had a knife?" She looked up at him, dazed.

"A swamp rat's always ready to skin a gator." His hands moved over her body urgently, as if he were trying to reassure himself she was safe. "Are you all right?"

Treasure pressed herself close to him, unable to stop trembling. "I thought you were dead."

"You couldn't be that lucky, pretty lady." He pulled himself to his feet. "Wait here a minute."

Feeling drained with reaction, sore and scraped all over from the scuffle, Treasure obeyed. He walked up to Elijah, who was climbing down from the cart, and murmured something. The two men then began to drag all four runaways to the cart. Two were wounded, enough to thwart any further escapes; the others they tied, wrists behind them, to the slats on the side of the cart.

Treasure climbed up onto the front bench. Donovan helped Elijah up beside her, then hoisted himself up the other side to take the harness leathers himself. Elijah, strangely silent, swayed against her as the cart jerked into motion. She looked at him closely, then reached up to touch his face. "You're bleeding. How badly?"

"Just a graze. Bullet came too close to my head."

Donovan brought the horses to a halt. "Take the reins," he told Treasure. "I'll take a look." He jumped down from the seat and climbed up next to Elijah, deft fingers probing a gash at his temple. "Damn. I need a bandage of sorts. Do you . . . ?" He looked at Treasure.

She ripped a wide swathe from the shreds of her petticoats and handed it to him. "I'm glad you got here, Elijah," she said. "We feared you would never come."

"I should have done something earlier," Elijah muttered.

"What do you mean?"

Donovan frowned at her. "Let it go."

"No," she countered, glaring at him. "Did you know this would happen, Elijah?"

"Not exactly, Miss Treasure," he said, looking miserable. "I just heard how Mastuh Stanton's people were plannin' a revenge on him."

"How could you know that?"

Elijah flinched as Donovan tightened the makeshift bandage around his head. "The songs."

"Songs? What songs? Elijah?"

"Don't waste your breath," Donovan said as Elijah slumped against him. "He's passed out." With difficulty, he managed to get Elijah down from the seat and laid him out in the back of the cart.

"What was he talking about?" Treasure asked when Donovan climbed up next to her again, taking the reins.

Donovan clucked to the horses. "The slaves. They pass messages in their songs."

"Messages?" Treasure thought about the past weeks, the eerie, heart-wrenching melodies. "I thought it was the drought that made the songs so sad."

"No. It was another death at Gold Meadow."

For the first time in her life, Treasure couldn't claim innocence in the brutality that ran, unchecked, beneath the surface of the refined planters who were demigods in their own kingdoms. Donovan's simple truths left her no room to rationalize a way of life that could strip dignity, pride and the most basic of human rights: freedom.

And she played a part in that life. She did not use cruelty herself. But in admitting her livelihood depended on slavery, she often turned a blind eye to its atrocities.

"Why did you come here, why do you stay, if you hate

262

slavery so much?" she asked, tracing his strong, set features in the moonlight.

"I stay because I want to. I didn't know how strong
my convictions were until I lived them. Sometimes you
have to experience something to learn the depth of your
feelings. Whether it's hate — or love."

Treasure didn't reply. She had no answers.

"Lord a-mercy! Bring that poor chile on in here,"
Eura Mae clucked when Donovan carried Treasure inside. Treasure had attempted to protest his scooping
her up, but he easily overrode her halfhearted effort.

Eura Mae furiously called out orders to Solomon,
sending him for water, as Donovan set her gently on a
settee in the front parlor. Spring and Emmy, still in
their rumpled ball dresses, hovered over her. Darting
and weaving her way through the sea of legs, Bonnie
yapped wildly, the scent of blood sending her to a near
frenzy.

"Stay with her," Donovan told them. He bent to
brush soothing strokes over the dog's back. "I'll get Elijah. He's been injured. Bettis, we'll need your help with
the wounds. And we'll have to get someone to take care
of those runaways. We'll put them in the south barn
until I can decide what to do about them." On his way
out, he slapped his thigh. "Come on, girl." Reassured,
Bonnie fell quietly in step after him.

Spring paled. Treasure saw a look pass between her
sister and Donovan. "I'll help," Spring said at last, her
voice firm.

"It's plenty clear where your loyalty lies, little
Spring," Camille drawled from the doorway. "So like
dear Treasure."

Treasure struggled to her feet. "We'll all help," she
said, looking straight at Camille. She pushed past her
stepsister to follow Donovan, smiling grimly as Camille
drew back in distaste. "Afraid you'll soil your gown?"

Ignoring Camille's hiss of fury, Treasure stepped into the foyer where Spring and Emmy watched Donovan help Elijah into the house. Elijah's arm was draped around Donovan's shoulder and he looked drained, the bandage around his head already soaked with blood.

"Will he be all right?" Spring moved close enough to touch him but, glancing at Treasure, dropped her half-raised hand.

Treasure brushed her fingers against Spring's arm, holding her sister's gaze with her own. Remembering her own heartfear for Donovan enabled her to set aside her misgivings about Spring's obvious concern for Elijah. "Bettis can take care of him, I'm sure."

"I don't think it's bad," Donovan put in. He was about to move Elijah toward the back rooms when a startled gasp drew everyone's attention to the open front door.

"Heavenly days!"

A fair woman, dressed in a tailored navy blue suit and traveling cloak, looked back at them all, eyes wide with horror. She clapped a gloved hand to her mouth.

At last, she managed a small titter. "I must say, this surely is a frightful welcome home for your dear old aunt."

Chapter Fourteen

Through her exhaustion, Treasure struggled to place the familiarity in the woman's delicate cheekbones and tiny, straight nose. Had they met somewhere, sometime long ago? She watched her new guest's sharp, cobalt eyes scan every face in the curious crowd, belying her beneficent smile. They lingered on Donovan, his arm still supporting a wobbly Elijah, and the smile flickered. It brightened as quickly, and with a musical trill of laughter, she waved a hand at the circle of blank faces.

"Well, my dears. I must give you due credit for a most excitin' welcome. McGlavrin's Valley has certainly become an interestin' place."

Treasure managed to shake off her surprised inertia and her befuddled mind at last gave a name to her visitor. "Aunt Valene! I—I can scarce believe it. We didn't expect you, especially at this hour." She gave a glance toward the square of predawn sky framed by the doorway. "If we had known you were coming we would have—"

"Why, don't you dare make a fuss, now." Valene Ellis, ignoring the dirty smudges that sullied her ivory gloves, took Treasure's hand in hers, bestowing a kiss on her niece's cheek. "When you wrote me about your awful dilemma, I did so want to lend my support. But I simply had no funds to spare. Then dear Ransom"—

she beamed at the man waiting in the doorway — "insisted we come and do what we could for you. But it's simply been the most awful trip. We've had all manner of delay, and then, when dear Ransom thought we could make up time travelin' into the evening, our wretched carriage became hopelessly stuck in this horrid mud. Well, of course, it delayed us further and I insisted we just come ahead. I'm a patient woman but one simply cannot wait forever." Valene stopped and drew a breath. "I do hope you aren't cross with me, my dear. I should have written again, but I didn't want you to worry over preparin' for our little visit."

"Of course. You are family. You're always welcome."

"I do hope your kind invitation also extends to me," an elegant voice drawled behind Valene.

In the confusion, Treasure had barely spared a glance for her aunt's traveling companion. He was the sort of man, she decided in a look, she would walk straight past without a glance. Not because of any unusual or unsightly quality, but because he seemed to meld with the scenery. Of average build, with thin, blond hair, and a neat, unpretentious traveling suit, only the green eyes peering from behind his gold pince-nez suggested any personality. He spoke to Treasure, but looked past her in the same manner Aunt Valene had, scrutinizing every face in the room. Ransom, her aunt called him? A memory suddenly sparked. "You must be —"

"Your cousin." Favoring her with a stiff little bow, he stepped forward and lifted her fingers to his lips. "It is a pleasure to meet you at last. We've lost so many years. . . . It's long past time we were as close as family ought to be. Don't you agree?"

Flustered by the keen intensity of his eyes on her face, Treasure murmured a vague reply. An artificial cough interrupted her.

"With your permission, Miss McGlavrin . . ."

Treasure turned to Donovan. He glared at her, his expression a mix of irritation and exhaustion. "I hate to disrupt a family reunion, but Elijah needs tending."

"Oh!" A guilty flush stained her face. Donovan slumped under Elijah's weight, the gash in his back splitting more beneath the extra burden. Spring stared at her with accusing eyes, and Eura Mae, the twins clinging to her skirts, eyed her with grim disapproval. Emmaline ignored her, her worry for Donovan evident. "I can help."

"Now, Treasure dear, you let your overseer do his work," Valene broke in, patting Treasure's arm. "I'm sure he is quite capable of lookin' after a slave."

The dark look on Donovan's face told Treasure his small store of patience had expired. Her aunt backed away from him as if he were some wild and dangerous animal that ought to be caged. "I am capable," he said, leveling Valene a hard stare. "Even if I'm not Treasure dear's overseer. Now if you'll excuse me, I'm sure you'll agree it's rude to stand here dripping blood on the mistress's floor."

Ransom bristled. His long fingers fidgeted with his eyeglasses.

Valene sniffed in affront. "Why, the very idea—"

"You chillun' come along with me," Eura Mae said, quickly shooing the twins and Emmy upstairs as Donovan half supported, half carried Elijah toward the back rooms. "You, too, Miss Spring," Eura Mae called over her shoulder. Spring, glancing once at Treasure, shook her head and darted after Donovan.

"Treasure, I am quite astonished." Valene put a hand to her cheek. "That ruffian in your home—and allowin' your sister to traipse after him in that manner . . . my dear, it's quite appallin'. I am so glad Ransom and I are here. You certainly are in need of a firm hand to assist you."

"I am sorry. It has been a most trying evening." Hearing her own silly understatement, Treasure pushed

back the onslaught of hysteria that threatened to overcome her precarious hold on civilized conversation.

"Pray tell, whatever *is* goin' on here?"

Treasure sighed. "Aunt Valene, we are all exhausted
and you must have had a tiring journey. Tomorrow, I
can explain. Tonight . . ." Tonight, she didn't have any
answers. Worry for Elijah and Donovan nagged at her.
She should have gone with Donovan. Instead, she left
him, wounded himself, to tend to a sick man, with only
her sister as help, while she stood about exchanging
niceties with relations she hadn't laid eyes on in nearly
as many years as she had been alive.

Valene regarded her with pity. "Oh, my dear, of
course." She laid a hand against Treasure's lank hair, a
wistful smile playing at her lips. "You do so remind
me of your mother. Darlin' Claire, why I do declare, I
never could fathom what she saw in a man like
Seamus McGlavrin. It was the cause of our final
quarrel, I'm afraid, and I do deeply regret it. Poor
Claire."

Treasure, her strongest remembrances of her mother
formed through her Papa's eyes, said nothing. Instead,
she led her guests upstairs and, with Eura Mae's help,
settled her aunt and cousin in what had been Papa and
Lettia's rooms. She felt a pang of sorrow as she rearranged some of her papa's things to make room for
Ransom's. The room looked the same as the day Papa
left, as if the household expected him to return any
evening. *As if I, fool that I am, expect him to return,*
Treasure thought, then brusquely swept aside her feelings. She didn't have time or energy to indulge in useless sentiment.

Nearly an hour later, she trudged down the staircase,
relieved quiet had at last settled over the second-floor
bedrooms. But silence seemed somehow unnatural
after the excitement of the ball and the chaos at Gold
Meadow. As she walked past the empty ballroom, Treasure paused in the doorway. It was darkened now, the

flower garlands gray specters dancing to the breeze that blew through the still-open windows.

She neared the back rooms of the house, which were formerly quarters for a staff of house slaves. Now, only Orange Jane and Solomon used the rooms. From behind the closest door, hushed murmurs floated into the hallway. Spring's lilting voice, Bettis's rumble, Orange Jane's throaty alto. Treasure rapped softly and the voices quieted. She eased open the door and they all turned to look at her.

"I came to check on Elijah — and Mr. River," she said haltingly. Spring's eyes reproached her, and Treasure felt compelled to offer a defense for an unnamed sin. "I had to get Aunt Valene and Cousin Ransom settled in first. They are family — "

"Oh, do stop going on about it, Treasure," Spring snapped, startling Treasure with an uncharacteristic sharpness. "She was never there when we needed her! I don't believe she cares one bit for us." She waved a hand toward the others. "They are our family. Our people, and Mr. River."

Spring's condemnation whipped against raw nerves. Treasure gripped her tattered skirts, but kept her face composed. "That is enough, Spring!" Breathing deeply, she calmed her voice. "How is Elijah?" she asked, nodding to his sleeping figure stretched out on a narrow bed behind her sister. Bettis bent over him, administering a poultice to the gash on his forehead.

"He's a strong buck, Miz Treasure. Few days' rest all he need," Bettis said, straightening. "I be lookin' after him. It won't be no trouble."

"Your property — safe and sound," Spring muttered. Turning away, she took a basin of water and a cloth from Orange Jane's arms and knelt beside the bed. Wringing the cloth in the basin, she gently soothed it over Elijah's face.

Watching her sister, Treasure tried to quell an irrational panic. Spring's tender heart led her to care for any-

269

thing in trouble. No need to worry, she reminded herself. Elijah would never allow himself to consider Spring's actions to be anything but kindness. Treasure relaxed. She understood Elijah. Like herself, he was sensible, rational. She'd grown to respect him after a fashion, for he'd always maintained cool control, never falling prey to foolish impulses or fleeting emotions.

"I'm sorry I snapped, Spring," she said, offering a tentative smile. "I'm worried about Elijah, too. And I think it's very kind of you to be so concerned."

"Kind?" Spring opened her mouth to say something, and then shut it. "Yes," she finally said, her voice soft. "I'm concerned, Treasure. Just as you must be about Donovan."

Donovan . . . "Where is Mr. River?" she asked suddenly, looking to Bettis.

Bettis and Orange Jane exchanged a glance. Finally, Bettis, looking down at his feet, answered, "He be down at de cabin, Miz Treasure."

"Alone? He's hurt. He needs attention."

Bettis's shoulders shifted and he looked distinctly uncomfortable. "He say he be back soon."

"I'll make certain of that."

"Miz Treasure, if you jus' wait a few minutes . . ."

Bettis's protest followed her as she slipped out into the early morning darkness. The rain had returned, this time only a fine silvery mist, making the air warm and wet against her skin. It was daybreak, the hour that was the stillest time of morning, when everything seemed poised for the first tentative light; the hour that decided the fate of the day.

Just as she, at the door to Donovan's cabin, felt poised, ready to confront him, to comfort him — which did she want? What would be the outcome of this night? The beginning of tomorrow?

A single lamp burned in the back room window of the cabin. Treasure, gathering militant courage around her, knocked firmly on the door. Silence answered her.

Gritting her teeth, she knocked again, insistently. "You might as well let me in," she called out. "I won't leave."

She heard nothing. As she raised her hand to pound the wood again, the door flung open. Donovan, his hands braced against the frame, was etched in shades of gray against the darkened room. He glowered at her. "Well?"

"I wanted to see you," she said, refusing to let him unnerve her.

"Shouldn't you be looking after your guests? They are *family* after all."

Treasure let the jibe pass. "I was worried about you."

Donovan arched a mocking brow. But his fierce scowl eased. "You were?"

"Yes, of course."

"Of course," he echoed softly.

He turned slightly to look back into the cabin and Treasure glimpsed a large patch, black in the darkness, staining his shirt, a reminder of his night's adventures. Treasure felt his pain as sharply as a dagger against her own skin. She reached out a hand. He caught her wrist. "Please." His voice was a harsh whisper. "Don't."

She tried to feign a detached concern. The tremor in her voice betrayed her. "I want to help."

"You can't. Not now. Not yet."

"I can." She fumbled for words she had never before used, never before believed. "You tell me to trust my heart. Trust yours now. Let me help."

His hands clenched against the wood. "God in heaven, I want to."

Emotion welled up inside Treasure, hot and crazy, all the tumultuous, muddled feelings she had tried to fight since the moment she saw him rush headlong into the fray at Gold Meadow. She'd never met a man willing to sacrifice himself for people who weren't kin, weren't even equals. He cared enough for men and women who were no more than another man's property to risk his

271

own life to help them. And at that moment, she cared, too. Cared for him, respected him more deeply than she ever wanted to. More than she imagined possible.

"Treasure . . ."

She took a step away from him, then spun around to face him. A wildness in his eyes, he shoved an unsteady hand through his hair. Treasure found no voice for the riot of emotion she felt. The strained lines of his brow echoed her frustration.

Caught in an eternity, their gazes locked.

She moved toward him and suddenly she was in his arms. Donovan tangled a handful of her hair in his fingers and bent her head back. She gripped his shoulders, pulling him closer as his mouth frantically kissed a path from her throat to her lips.

It was fire. Pure and raging. Fed by all her worry and fear, all the feelings she didn't want, yet yearned to have. She let her heart speak with her kiss. She needed him to touch her, needed to be near him, to feel him, whole and alive against her.

His hands moved urgently, as if he too needed that assurance. Every touch burned through the silk of her dress, leaving her restless, longing for the feel of his hand against her bare skin.

She moved her fingers from around his neck to the gape in his shirt. He groaned her name as, brazen with a racing excitement, she slipped her hands inside and slid them against his hot flesh. His tongue flicked against her throat and she shivered, her nails clenching into his skin, eliciting an answering tremor.

They had the power to do this to each other, she marveled, exulted by the discovery. A magic conjured between them from the fire of passion and the silver sweetness of love.

. . . of love.

Donovan flinched as she unknowingly gripped the gash on his arm.

"Oh!" She looked up at him, awe-struck. The word

had crept into her thoughts. Or had it been there all along, patiently waiting for her to recognize it?

Mistaking her stunned expression for consternation at accidentally hurting him, Donovan gently pulled her head against his heart, as tender as he had been passionate. "It's all right. I won't break apart."

"You're very warm," she murmured, her thoughts elsewhere. But as she said the words, she realized they were true. Suddenly concerned, she laid a hand against his face. "You're feverish. Damn you, Donovan, why didn't you stay at the house?"

"Mmm . . ." He pressed her to him. "Why didn't you?"

Treasure wriggled out of his arms. "Come on," she said, taking his hand. "You are going straight to bed."

"An interesting proposition, Miss McGlavrin, but I don't think I have the strength."

Scowling at him, Treasure slipped his arm over her shoulder and managed to guide him a few steps into the cabin before he balked. "Look, I can do this myself."

"Why, Mr. River, I never suspected you to be shy."

"Hardly that."

"You haven't much reputation to worry over," she teased. "Are you worried I'll uncover your secrets?"

"No, darlin'," a voice spoke up behind them. "I do think Donovan's afraid you'll uncover mine."

If Donovan's arm hadn't supported her waist, Treasure knew her knees would have buckled with the force of the shock. "Miss Eliza!"

Eliza stepped out from the shadow, wiping her hands on a cloth. The front of her dress was spattered with grime and blood. "I think you'd best sit down, Treasure," she said, lighting one of the wall lamps. "I declare you look paler than Donovan."

Stunned, Treasure gaped at her friend. "Miss Eliza . . ." She pulled away from Donovan, looked up at him. His expression told her nothing. Surely he and Eliza . . . No, even she couldn't believe that of Donovan; and less of Eliza. "I don't understand . . ."

"No, honey, it's obvious you don't." Eliza turned to Donovan. "I think you should explain."

"Eliza very kindly came by to make certain I hadn't gotten myself killed leaping before I looked. She—"

"Donovan River, you tell her the truth!" Eliza burst in. "I won't have Treasure thinking—"

"Stop it! Both of you! I don't think anything of the sort. I just don't want to hear any more lies." She looked at Eliza. "Obviously, you are aiding Donovan in some way. Why are you here?"

"Because . . ."

"Because she wanted to help me," Donovan finished. "Trust me, it's the only reason."

His eyes asked her for understanding. Part of Treasure wanted to believe him; her reason despised his power to make her believe. *I wanted to help you, too.*

"Every time I start to trust you, Mr. River, you give me another reason to question you. Both of you." She looked at Eliza, one last plea in her eyes. *Tell me. Please tell me.* Eliza bit her lower lip, distress plain on her face.

Treasure, gathering strength from the painful chill settling over her, walked to the door. Before she stepped out into the gray dawn, she turned back. "I meant what I said about helping you," she said to Donovan. "I only wish you felt you could trust me. I wish we could trust each other."

"You should have told her." Eliza finished redressing the gash on Donovan's back. He winced as she tied off the bandage with a little more force than necessary.

"I couldn't," he said, gingerly rubbing the sore spot. "She doesn't feel the same way you do. I would have forced her to make a choice she isn't ready to make. A lot of lives are at stake." He paused. "Including yours."

Eliza sighed, shaking her head. "You know something, Donovan River? You underestimate that child. She's prickly and hard-headed, and sometimes downright annoyin' with that stiff attitude of hers. But underneath she's got a tender heart. And I don't intend to let you break it."

"Yes, ma'am, I'll consider myself warned."

"Spare me your cheek. I know full well you're tryin' your level best to run from your feelings for her. But it isn't so easy this time, is it?"

Donovan rubbed a hand over his jaw, examining her with thoughtful eyes. "You know, Miss Eliza, I wonder how a woman so plain-spoken at times manages such discretion at others. You amaze even me."

Eliza answered with an indulgent smile. "Treasure is right — you are feverish." She scooped up the bag she'd brought along and pulled a dark cloak over her shoulders. "Take her advice, honey. Go to bed. I'll finish what has to be done."

"Be careful."

Eliza tossed a smile over her shoulder, winking. "That, darlin', is one thing I always am."

"Is something botherin' you, dear? You look troubled."

Treasure glanced up from her untouched breakfast and smiled wanly. "It's nothing, Aunt Valene. I was just thinking about the work I've neglected."

"I see. I sympathize, darlin', but I am also relieved. I worried myself you might be upset over that slave and that horrid man you have livin' under your roof. For what reason you allow him here — "

"Elijah and Mr. River are both recovered, Aunt Valene," Treasure interrupted. "I have no reason to spare either of them a thought." The lie caused Treasure a twinge of guilt.

But she could hardly confess her thoughts centered on an impossible, frustrating, enigmatic scoundrel and his baffling alliance with her closest friend.

During the past week, she'd wasted precious hours

trying to reason it out. Most bothersome was the re-membered line of Donovan's letter to his brother telling of an ally, at Rose of Heaven. Eliza must be Donovan's ally, yet an ally in what scheme?

Eliza would never aid Donovan in taking control of Rose of Heaven. And Eliza would never keep secrets unless she felt the cause was critical enough to merit it.

Donovan obviously felt deeply enough about their shared cause to risk his relationship with his parents, and to stay in a place where he and his convictions were as welcome as a six-month drought.

She knew he cared for anyone in trouble; he had risked his life to protect Ira Stanton's slaves. She admired his courage, was intrigued by the strength of his passions.

Had she misjudged his motives?

Still, how could she trust him? His claim to Rose of Heaven stood between them. He was her rival for the thing she cared about most. He had cheated, possibly murdered, to get her plantation. And she couldn't forget his impulsive tryst with Camille. How could she trust a man whose emotions ruled his actions?

"It's too fine a morning for two lovely ladies to be frowning." Her cousin's voice brought Treasure out of her intent reverie. Ransom smiled as she blushed under his amused eyes, aware she had been insufferably rude in ignoring her aunt.

"I'm sorry. I'm afraid I haven't been good company."

Valene waved the apology away with her painted fan. "Never mind, my dear. Ransom, do sit down," she said, patting the seat of the chair next to her. "You've nearly missed breakfast."

Treasure noticed her aunt's frown as Ransom settled in a chair next to her, ignoring Valene's invitation. But her cousin seemed oblivious. "I hope you will forgive me, Treasure, but I took the liberty of examining your account books."

The forkful of egg stopped midway between Trea-

276

sure's plate and her mouth. She struggled to contain her irritation. "My books?"

"My Ransom is a brilliant mathematician," Valene said. She stirred her coffee with unnecessary vigor. "But it's his legal expertise you may most benefit from. Bein' an attorney, and bein' family and all, he'll have you free of this messy business with that odious Mr. River in short time."

Ransom smiled affably. "For now, Mama, I think I can best assist cousin Treasure by counseling her on necessary business transactions before harvest."

Unwillingly at first, and then with growing interest, Treasure listened as he outlined a plan to increase her net profits from both her corn and cotton crops. "I am impressed," she said when he had finished. "I will admit, this first harvest has me more than a little concerned. Its success is vital if Rose of Heaven is to survive."

Her compliment seemed to fluster Ransom's usual calm. He took off his pince-nez and polished them several times with his handkerchief. "I would be pleased to advise you in any matter. I know it must be difficult for you since your father . . ." He broke off when Treasure glanced down at her plate again. "I didn't intend to distress you."

"You didn't," she said, his sympathetic expression lending warmth to her smile. "You are right. Things have been — difficult. And I am grateful for your help. Both of you," she added quickly, looking at her aunt.

The pinched line of Valene's mouth softened a little. "Of course, my dear. We're family."

"If you will excuse me" — Ransom pushed back his chair — "I have some business to attend to." He hesitated. "Treasure, if it is not inconvenient, I wonder if you might care to accompany me into the valley this afternoon. I should like to acquaint myself with some of the local people."

"Of course," Treasure said, smiling over the proper little bow he made before leaving.

The smile faded as she turned back to her aunt. Valene stared at the closed door of the dining room, scowling. "Aunt Valene, is something wrong?"

"Wrong?" Valene seemed to consider the question as if it were a matter of critical importance. At last, she said slowly, still smiling at the door, "No — my dear — not in the least. In fact" — she beamed at her niece — "when I decided to come and lend you assistance, I didn't know how we might best serve you. But it's becoming perfectly clear to me now, dear." She patted her niece's hand. "Oh, I am delighted to be back where I belong again. Simply delighted."

"And we are fortunate to have you both here." Treasure looked at her, puzzled. "Do you have something specific in mind?" she asked, feeling somewhat apprehensive of the answer and not knowing why.

Valene leaned over and clasped Treasure's hand. "Ransom is taken with you, my dear. How nice it would be if you and he should make a match. You told me yourself you felt a great need for approval from the valley. Ransom is well bred, respectable, and certainly successful. Why, I declare, it's an ideal arrangement."

Two nights past, Treasure had confided some of her fears and desires to her aunt. She hadn't spoken to Eliza since the night she discovered her in Donovan's cabin and felt bereft without Eliza's comfort and support. Now, she sorely regretted her admissions. Her aunt obviously misinterpreted a little loneliness as a hint her niece desired permanent companionship in the form of a husband. Lord in heaven, the last thing she wanted was to be the pawn in a matchmaking scheme. It would sour her tentative friendship with Ransom and, if her sisters discovered it, force her to cope with a chaos of questions, advice, and opinions.

"Aunt Valene," she began, searching for a way to gently dissuade her aunt of her new notion.

"Tsh, tsh, my dear. Right now you think I'm simply an interferin' busybody. But I've a notion this will prove the best course of action for all of us."

Treasure cat-footed up the stairs of the darkened house as quietly as possible, not wanting to chance awakening either her sisters or her aunt. The afternoon in town with Ransom had lasted hours longer than she had expected. Her cousin had insisted on taking her to dinner, and then suggested an evening ride along the riverside. His quiet manners and elegant attentions were soothing after the dramas of the past weeks, and Treasure found herself glad she had accepted. She admired his business acumen, and was pleased to find they shared some tastes and ideas. It should, as Aunt Valene predicted, have been perfect.

Except each time he took her hand, or lightly kissed her fingers, she found herself waiting for the fierce excitement she felt when Donovan touched her. Ransom epitomized the man she called her ideal; Donovan the essence of all she should despise. Yet one look, one brush of his lips to hers, sent her senses reeling, while her cousin's most gentlemanly efforts failed to rouse anything but mild revulsion.

It made no sense, she decided, softly closing her bedroom door behind her. Tonight she was too exhausted to try to sort it out. Tonight, she wanted only to savor the peace and quiet of solitude.

"Enjoy your evening, pretty lady?"

Treasure spun around, nearly knocking over the lamp she had lit. But she didn't need the light to recognize the man stretched out on her bed.

"What are you doing here? Get out this moment!"

"Should I answer the question first?" Lazily, he swung his feet off the bed and stood up, propping himself against the four poster. "You and Cousin Ransom must have had quite an evening. Tell me, has he already proposed?"

"That is not your concern. How did you get in my bedroom?"

He waved at hand at the open window. "If I said I'd shinnied up the trellis, risking life and limb to sneak into your room for a midnight rendezvous, would you be impressed?"

Treasure glared.

"I thought not, so, I simply took the back stairs when no one was watching."

"Well, you smell like you've drunk enough to have the nerve," Treasure mocked, taking in his disheveled appearance and the smell of bourbon. She glanced to the window then the door. "Choose your exit."

"Not yet." He reached out and, before she could elude him, snagged her arm in his hand. "I want to talk to you."

"About Ransom? Why? Are you jealous?" Treasure regretted the words the moment they left her lips.

"Hell!" Donovan dropped her arm and almost pushed her away from him. "Go ahead and marry the ass, if you've convinced yourself that's what you want. Why the hell should I be jealous. I don't have any intention of sticking around here forever, tying myself to a piece of land and a brood of women with more problems already than I'll have in a lifetime. I don't need that kind of trouble, do I?"

Stung, Treasure flung a hand to the window. "Apparently not. So the sooner you leave, the better for us all."

"Don't worry, I don't intend to let you suffer my company much longer."

"Oh, is Camille waiting?"

"She'll be waiting forever if she is." The prompt, blunt reply and his straightforward gaze gave Treasure no room to doubt him.

"You were with her," she said, feeling the pain of the memory of seeing Donovan and Camille together. "Camille was in your bed."

"Alone. I came back to the cabin and found her

there. I was tempted, I told you. But nothing more." He paused. "Do you believe me?"

Treasure answered with her heart. "Yes."

Surprise flickered in Donovan's eyes, but he showed no sign of pleasure at her answer. "Thank you."

"You're welcome," she said, matching his cool tone. "Is there anything else you wanted, Mr. River?"

"Quite a bit. But I'll settle for passing along one little piece of advice. Cousin Ransom may be the perfect Southern gentleman, but I'd watch my back when he and your aunt are in the room."

"And what, pray tell, are you trying to insinuate?"

Donovan shrugged. "Just that I don't think they're here for a friendly visit."

"You have no right to say that! They are—"

"Family. Yes, I know. Forgive me if I don't find that reassuring."

"Then you don't know the meaning of family."

He turned and slammed a hand into the bedpost. It snapped where his palm hit, giving way with a loud crack that sent Treasure back with a jump. "I know what it means to be ousted from one."

Treasure remembered his brother's letter mentioning Donovan's alienation from his parents, and it sparked a glimmer of understanding. Tentatively, she stepped near and touched his shoulder. "Donovan . . ."

She felt him stiffen, set a clamp on his aggression. When he turned, Treasure sensed she had drawn too near some truth, and he had pulled a shield around him to keep her out. "I apologize for the dramatics. I only want you to be careful."

How can I be? she wanted to ask him. *When you are this close, when I allow myself to touch you, it's more a danger than any you could warn me against.*

"I had better go," he said, not moving.

"Yes. It is best if you do."

Donovan freed a strand of her hair from its confin-

281

ing chignon and stroked it between his fingers. "You're right, pretty lady, it is."

"Now. You should leave at once." Her voice sounded wrong — soft and hushed. It was an invitation instead of a rejection.

"Yes, I know." His quickened breath brushed her face.

"You're so irresponsible; you never stop to think." She couldn't think with him so near. When he slid behind her and pressed a lingering kiss to the nape of her neck, she couldn't remember why he shouldn't be so close.

He wrapped his arms around her beneath her breasts. "And you've been a self-appointed mistress of Heaven so long, you've never taken time to be a woman," he whispered into her hair.

"I have no use for mysterious scoundrels." The room suddenly seemed overheated. Donovan's mouth wandered down the curve of her neck to her throat. "Stop that. I don't like it."

"Mmm . . ." He turned her to face him. "What do you like? This?" His lips teased at her temple. "Or this?" A kiss traced the line of her jaw, taunted the corner of her mouth. "Tell me," he murmured, a breath away from touching her lips.

Every argument failed to compete with the anticipation of his warm mouth searching the sweetness of hers. She had no defenses. No words. Instead, she brought their lips together. He kissed her, slowly, deeply, letting her savor all the fire and longing of his passion. He tasted of bourbon and sin, his mouth velvet, his body steel to her softness. She drowned in the sensations, weak with need, strong with desire.

His leg wrapped around hers, pressing her intimately against him, while his hands traced a path over her spine. The first hard crush of his body against hers shocked her. Would he become violent like Papa had been with Lettia? Surely that wasn't the only way.

She felt his fingers against the bare skin of her back and realized with a sharp stab of alarm he had unfastened her gown. She shivered, drawing a little away, suddenly uncertain.

He searched her eyes for a long moment. Then, kissing her gently, he slowly drew the dress from her shoulders, letting it slide to her waist, his hands following the glide of the material.

Eyes tightly closed, Treasure waited, afraid to move. She couldn't watch. What did he expect her to do? Was this wrong? Would it be pain or pleasure?

The minutes dragged on like hours, and finally, she dared to look at him.

The expression on his face made nonsense of her fears.

Donovan watched her with an almost reverent awe, his fingers brushing her skin with a faltering touch as if she were something rare and fragile instead of flesh and blood. He cupped her face between his hands, then slipped his fingers to her nape, spilling her hair onto his hands like red-gold rain. "You're so beautiful," he whispered. "There aren't any words powerful enough to speak for me, to tell you how I feel just looking at you. I'm afraid to realize how much I need you. How much I want to love you."

His image shimmered before her. "I need you, too. I don't understand it. I — I don't know if it's right. But I need you."

When he gathered her in his arms again, each gentle caress eased her fears. His hand learned every curve of her body, finding a match for it with his own. Treasure let her doubts sear to ashes under the heat of his embrace. Her mind warned her away, but her resolve tottered and collapsed beneath his tender assault. Yet he never abandoned the care that gently seduced her into savoring each new sensation, and anticipating every passionate discovery.

Her dress pooled around her feet as he eased away

283

her stays and petticoats, leaving her clad in nothing but the diaphanous cotton of her shift. In the hot room it clung to her moist skin like a soft silken web. Whispering her name, Donovan lifted her into his arms, kissing the shy blush in her face. He carried her to the bed and gently laid her down.

She watched, fascinated, as he took long minutes to unbutton his shirt and pull it away from his chest. Each sinuous motion quickened the pace of her heartbeat until Treasure moved restlessly against the bedclothes. She felt feverish, her blood trembling, her body aching. She wanted to beg him to assuage her tormenting need.

As he lay down beside her, she whispered his name. His skin was hot against hers. He bent over her and slid his hand up her thigh, under the edge of her shift and higher, until his fingers splayed over the curve of her hip. She gasped, and he captured her parted lips in a deep, ardent kiss, his hand moving to cover the taut peak of her breast. A fiery excitement showered over her like falling stars.

She longed to capture each new feeling and hold it in her heart's memory. But the combination of them was too overwhelming. She could only be swept along by them, to whatever journey's end Donovan would lead her.

She no longer feared that end, no longer compared the moment to her childhood nightmare. This was different: pure, giving, sharing.

"Sissy! Please let me come in!" A tiny but furious tap at the door froze Treasure and Donovan in each other's arms. Donovan, his expression bemused, stared at her as if suddenly awakened from a depthless sleep.

"It's Erin," she murmured. "Since Papa left, she's had nightmares. I — I sometimes let her sleep with me when it happens. It's often the only way to calm her."

"You can't soothe her back into her own bed?" Donovan's voice sounded low and husky. He nuzzled the curve of her neck, still caught up in their passion.

Treasure shook her head, wriggling away, feeling ill at ease as the seductive haze dissipated with Erin's pathetic pleas. "Just a minute, sweetheart," she called.

She slipped out of bed. Her reflection, surprising her in her dressing table mirror, gave her pause despite her urgency. She stared in wonder at the stranger there. Tousled hair rioted around her flushed face, and her lips were pink and slightly swollen from Donovan's kisses.

Is it me? she thought, hesitantly touching the cool glass.

Donovan's reflection smiled at her before he turned her to face him. He took her hand and led her to the open window.

"You can't get down this way. Have you seen the size of the thorns on those roses? Besides, you'll break your Yankee neck."

"Not with my devil's luck," Donovan quipped, playing the rogue. "Don't forget me, pretty lady. I intend to make sure you finish what we started." Stealing a last lingering kiss, he tipped her a jaunty salute and climbed over the window ledge. "Hell. Romeo I'm not." Then, "Ouch! Dammit," she heard him swear as he clambered far enough to drop with a thud to the ground. Letting go her breath, she returned his wave.

Wrapped in a warm haze of pleasure, Treasure hurried to the door to scoop Erin into her arms. "Did you have another nightmare, honey?" Erin nodded, burying her little face in Treasure's shoulder. "It's all right. Come here and lie down with me for a little while."

She carried her little sister to the bed and snuggled her under the quilt. Lying down beside Erin, Treasure held her close, humming a soft, soothing melody, the same sweet song Donovan had played for her at the ball.

Gradually, Erin relaxed against her. Treasure touched her sister's bright curls, reassured by Erin's peaceful repose.

When she was certain Erin had fallen soundly asleep, Treasure slipped from the bed and padded back to the window, looking out toward Donovan's cabin. She could see a single pinpoint of light still burning in one window.

Her doubts, fears, questions, would awake with her tomorrow, and she knew one day she would have to resolve them. But tonight — tonight she would think only of him.

Valene gripped the fragile teacup so tightly the handle snapped. A tiny rivulet of blood ran down her forefinger. She flung the cup at the balcony window.

So. Her prim and proper niece was bedding the ruffian she'd so foolishly let lay claim to Rose of Heaven.

She had watched until Treasure and Ransom returned. Shortly after, she'd spied Donovan sneaking up the back stairs. It took little imagination to realize their relationship was considerably more than her niece had confided.

It had been too simple. Treasure, overburdened and alone, dependent on her aunt and cousin. Ransom's unexpected infatuation. But she hadn't counted on her niece's fascination with some down-at-the-heels drifter. Valene found it only too easy to hate them both.

Oh yes, little Treasure certainly was like her mother. *Deceitful little bitch.*

There was a portrait of Seamus and Claire on the mantel and Valene walked up to it and took it in her hands. She hadn't come back to Rose of Heaven to fail, she mused. Smiling, she pulled the picture from its silver frame and held it over the flame of a lamp. As she made a silent vow, it caught fire. This time she would be the winner. Even if she had to destroy Claire's wretched child to claim her victory.

Tossing the picture in the fireplace, she watched it slowly shrivel to ashes.

Chapter Fifteen

It wasn't pale early morning sunlight filtering through her open window or the bustle of activity below that woke Treasure the next day. It was Donovan River. All night she'd tossed and turned, alternating between remembered pleasure and a vague, frustrated sense of being unfulfilled.

Still drowsy, she smiled and brushed her fingertips over her lips. The warmth from his lingered there. Sweet sensations awoke with her, vividly alive. She lazed back against her pillows and trailed a languorous hand down her arm, her waist, her bare thigh, feeling a delicious wickedness. Her skin reacted with a shivering tingle to the fantasy of Donovan, there with her, his hands exploring the same path.

She missed him. Ached for him. Was he still sleeping? What did he wear to bed? Anything? Or nothing? Her mind raced, wondering, imagining his exquisitely sculpted body in bed beside her, wanting her in ways she only guessed at.

She knew now that what she'd seen all those years ago, the raw, base act Lettia and Papa committed, was not the only kind of intimacy between a man and a woman. What she had accidentally seen lacked the gentle seduction of Donovan's touch, the tender emotion he had evoked inside her.

But what exactly did she feel for him? And he for her?

How frustrating that she knew so little about the relations between men and women. She had nothing to compare. And to ask someone . . . Blushing, she thrust the thought away.

I have to find my own answers, she thought, tossing back the quilt. On the far side of the bed, Erin slept curled up like a kitten. She'd scarcely moved all night, and Treasure hesitated to disturb her now. Carefully, she tucked the quilt around her small sister, anxious she sleep as long as possible after her uneasy night.

Not bothering to call Eura Mae for fear of waking Erin, Treasure moved to her wardrobe, riffling through her dresses for a flattering color. She needed to see Donovan this morning. He had elicited something inside her, frightening in its driving power; something that compelled her to be near him again.

Sorting through the frocks, she finally selected a simple jade calico. Yes, that would do perfectly against her hair. She held up the crisp cotton under her chin and stared at her face in the long glass. A stranger stared back. Heavy, red-gold tresses tumbled over warm apricot cheeks, her river green eyes sparkling with secret joy. She laughed at her reflection. How silly to care for clothes and colors. It only mattered that they be functional. Until now.

This morning her appearance mattered very much. She wanted him to look at her with the passion and longing of last night. Brushing her streaming locks of hair until they flowed in a glistening river down her back, she tied a loose bow at her nape. She reveled in this new feeling, this girlish delight in knowing a smile or a becoming gown could keep his eyes on her alone.

A light tap sounded at her door and Treasure, with one last glance in the mirror, hurried to answer it.

"Lawdy, chile!" Eura Mae gaped, looking Treasure up and down. "You look fit to go to a party, not to be tendin' fields."

Treasure put a quick finger to her lips, motioning to the bed. "Erin had a nightmare. I want to let her sleep. I

288

thought you might look in on her later, and make certain Abby doesn't disturb her. Promise Abby an extra biscuit and jam at breakfast. She loves that."

"And what 'bout dis little one? I knows how you hate it when deys late for meals."

"Oh, it doesn't matter. Aunt Orange Jane won't mind fixing Erin a late breakfast."

"I'se sure she can." Eura Mae eyed her with a calculating look. Then she smiled broadly. "Well, you get along now. You don't want to keep Mastuh River waitin'."

"I didn't say—"

"I knows you didn't," Eura Mae said, giving her a slight prod toward the hallway. "Go along now."

Feeling foolish and free, Treasure gave her mammie a quick kiss and darted from the room.

Deciding the impending harvest and all its details were true enough reasons to visit Donovan at so early an hour, Treasure slipped down the hall to the slaves' stairs and out into the new morning. Silvery dew clung to the grass and late-summer leaves, renewing their hues in misty watercolor greens and browns. The recent rains had rediscovered the heart of Rose of Heaven. Their gentle coaxing and tempestuous downpours had coaxed the buried life from the once-arid fields and gardens.

Treasure paused to pluck a long-stemmed rose of heaven from a sturdy clump. She fondled the shimmery lilac-rose bloom as she continued down the pebbled path to Donovan's cabin. It was odd to find the flowers so late in summer. The rains, it seemed, inspired blossoms despite the chances against it.

Distracted by her private musings, Treasure nearly careened into Bettis outside the cabin. "You won't be findin' Mastuh River in daire, Miz Treasure," he said, glancing to the blossom entwined in her fingers.

Treasure twisted her hands behind her, attempting a casual interest. "Do you know where he is?"

Bettis shrugged. "Can't say. Ain't seen him yet dis mornin'."

"Oh." She looked around her. "Did you need something?"

Bettis grinned. "I come down t' tell Mastuh River somethin' fo' Miz Orange Jane. She done fixed his favorite honey buns fo' breakfast, and she sent me t' fetch Mastuh River fo' Mastuh Ellis and his mama done 'et 'em all up."

Treasure laughed. "Well, if I see Mr. River, I'll certainly pass along the warning. How do the bolls look today?"

"Prime, prime, Miz Treasure. And I do think we'll have us plenty o' time 'fo de first frost."

"Oh? Why do you say that?"

" 'Cause a rabbit done run right out across my path. But he ain't runned to de left; he run to de right. Means dey be good luck a-commin'." He winked and nodded to the side. " 'Sides, we got us new blooms on Heaven's flowers."

"Let's just hope these afternoon showers continue."

"Amen t' dat." With a wide smile, Bettis tipped his straw hat to Treasure before stumping off toward the barn and his morning chores.

Feeling foolish, Treasure watched until Bettis disappeared up the path then tried knocking. No answer. Disappointment welled up in her. She found herself clinging to the doorknob, though reason told her to give up. Ignoring good sense, she tried the knob. It turned easily in her hand.

"Hello—" Silence. On impulse, with a quick glance to both sides, she opened the door and hurriedly stepped inside, shutting the door fast behind her. Leaning her back to it, as breathless as a naughty child, she reveled in a wicked rush of excitement. *No wonder he lives by his whims instead of his intellect.*

Delighting in her own impetuous deed, Treasure decided to indulge her curiosity and look about. She had only been inside his cabin twice. Both instances had been disastrous. This time, emboldened by her illicit entry, she wanted to come away knowing something more about Donovan River and how he spent his days — and nights.

The room pulsed with his scent, earthy, male, mingling with the faint smell of whiskey. It evoked memories so strong, Treasure felt his presence, following her every move.

One thing was certain. The man was no housekeeper. The little table was piled so high with newspapers and books, its spindled legs bowed under the weight. Beside his chair, on the floor, everywhere it seemed, more books lay strewn about, some opened, facedown, others stacked in haphazard piles with scraps of paper sticking out in every direction. Treasure frowned over the expensive leather covers, the extensive number of titles. He kept a virtual library on his floor!

And he seemed intent on reading each one. Beside one particularly imposing volume of history, three bourbon bottles, all empty, stood next to a shot glass. Candle stubs littered the floor and every table nook. "At least he drinks from a glass," she murmured.

Treasure stepped around the piles, drawn to the rumpled bed. She felt positively sinful now. She let her hand touch his pillow, smooth over the tangle of linen sheets. Had his body lain bare on this spot? She imagined she still felt his warmth from the night's sleep.

Suddenly, she jerked her hand back. What a fool she must look, letting herself be carried away by such wanton notions. She smoothed her hands over her skirts, glancing around. She should leave. Before he discovered her trespass. But —

But now was a perfect chance to answer some questions, to learn things about him he refused to reveal. It seemed wrong to pry into his private affairs, yet, she justified, he asked for it, worming his way onto her plantation, keeping so many secrets. Still, her conscience rebelled against the potent combination of defiance and curiosity.

A low doorway beyond the bed led to another small room. From where she stood, Treasure could see a desk, darkened lamp, and a huge stack of papers. Her fingers idly trailing the bed from head to foot, she wandered closer.

Eliza had come from this room the night of the slave revolt and had wanted to tell her something. But Donovan stopped her. What was he intent on hiding? Did Eliza know something about his mysterious past? Resentment stabbed sharply. She considered Eliza her closest friend. Yet Eliza obviously harbored a secret for a man she scarcely knew. A secret so deep, Eliza couldn't confide in Treasure.

"Fine," Treasure said aloud, "I'll just have to figure it out for myself." She held on to her determination as she began sifting through some of the stack atop the desk. Actually, there was one particular stack among the clutter, she discovered. She glanced over the first few pages. Her eyes widened. It was the start of a novel, a story beginning with a man on a journey to Louisiana. She wanted to read more, but decided Donovan's unexpected pastime wasn't the clue she needed.

Suddenly, it caught her eye. One ragged corner of Donovan's leather-bound journal just visible beneath a pile of papers. He and the book were inseparable. He'd told her it was how he kept track of the multitudes of details involved in planting and tending crops and managing an entire plantation.

Well, I'll just see how much you've learned, Mr. River.

Eyes black and depthless, mystic as obsidian. Bullish-strong, a temper to match. The secrets of the earth in a pouch.

"What nonsense is this?" Treasure flipped forward

292

through page after page of evocative descriptions of people, some extremely detailed, others just a word here and there. A few he'd given names and scratched out the beginnings of stories about. Treasure recognized a few of the worded pictures. *A strong silent giant in heart and body.* Others left her bemused.

At dawn, when the fields awake, they are as alive as any human or beast. Hundreds of strands of living emeralds in soldiers' ranks. Like a woman; sometimes willful, sometimes pure pleasure.

Treasure found herself caught up again in images, obviously inspired by the land, the crops, the people of Rose of Heaven. But she didn't find one hint of the actual business of planting amid them. *Why, he could care less about the plantation! He obviously has no intention of working the land, he just wants to write about it.*

Thumbing backward through the pages, near the beginning of the journal, she finally came across something that seemed to be more of a rambling personal dialogue.

Why have I allowed this cursed penchant I seem to have for lost causes to trap me here with this cursed household of women. I'll bet you're laughing in hell, Seamus my friend,

If you weren't already rotting in a Louisiana swamp, I'd put you in the ground with my own hands for not telling me about the firebrand you left to guard your pretty piece of land. She's the coldest, most stubborn, waspish scrap of a girl I've ever had the misfortune to have to handle. Little wonder you jumped ship.

Treasure slammed the book shut. "Cold! Waspish!

293

Stubborn! You haven't learned the meaning of the words, Donovan River, but you're about to."

Anger flaring, she stomped out of the cabin, determined to find him and set him straight on a number of points. *Handle me! Is that what you think you've been doing with your velvet tongue and your attentions to me?* "You'll soon learn, Donovan River, no one handles me — especially you."

By the time she'd searched the back grounds, several barns, and the blacksmith's shed and had aroused the curiosity of the two slave girls tending a steaming vat of laundry in the wash house, Treasure's sense had cooled her ire. She'd wasted enough time, and for no reason other than to indulge a fit of temper. She often chided her sisters for the same. And above all, why give Donovan the satisfaction of knowing he annoyed her?

Making up for lost time, Treasure took a shortcut back to the house. The path cut through an overgrown garden, one her mama had planted but Lettia had let languish. Treasure promised herself she'd revive it one day, but never seemed to find time or energy to spare.

At the center of the garden was the beginning of a fountain, a tall water spigot, that was to have been the core of a beautiful sculpture surrounded by a circular lily pond. When Mama died, the project died with her.

As Treasure wound her way through periwinkle run amok over a once charming brick path, she lifted drooping wisteria branches and dodged a rhododendron so overgrown it looked more like a tree than a shrub. Above her a feisty sparrow chirped down an objection to her invasion. The intimate solitude wove an enchantment around the neglected garden. It could be the perfect place to steal away from responsibility and care.

The unexpected sound of water splashing against stone startled her. Had one of the girls sneaked in here, turned the spigot on, then abandoned it? It seemed unlikely. Treasure doubted the rusted metal contraption even worked.

Curious, Treasure moved toward the sound. It came clearly, water burbling and singing, from behind an imposing mass of neglected azaleas. Crouching low, Treasure pushed open a hole through the scraggly branches and leaves for a clear view of —

— a man's bronzed, sinewed back and bare, white bottom. His long, muscular thighs and calves were as sun-browned as his back, slickly wet from the fountain of droplets cascading over his body from the spigot facing him. He stood in a patch of sunlight and the golden glow turned the water to sparkling gems in an amber prism.

Treasure sucked in a breath and stared shamelessly. Donovan knelt down, the muscles in his arms and legs flexing, and scooped up a bar of soap. His movements were slow and lazy as he worked the creamy lather over his shoulders and back, stretching as his hand eased downward over his hard, molded buttocks. Then, with a quick turn, he twisted to let the water play against his back, facing her fully.

"Oh — " Treasure barely smothered a shocked gasp. She snapped her eyes shut, her fingers tightening on handfuls of branches as a hot prickling sensation flushed her skin. He was naked as the day he was born. And she crouched there like a curious little girl, watching. Even taking salacious enjoyment in her furtive action.

A sinful, secret, spine-tingling enjoyment. It spread through her, as insidious as a siren's call, tempting her to all manner of indiscretions. Coaxing her to toss aside decorum and responsible behavior. To, just once, do as dared. Almost of their own volition, her eyes opened.

Her gaze followed his hands as he rubbed foamy water over his wet skin. As his hands slid over the muscles of his chest and arms, she remembered what it was like to be held against that body, to feel its hardness urgent against hers. She stared, mesmerized, as water and soap trailed down over the dark mat of hair on his chest, to his flat abdomen and over his hips and loins.

Treasure thought she should turn from so intimate a gesture when his hands followed the water's flow. But he made the action seem so natural, that it held her attention captive, just as every other inch of his body did.

She allowed herself to wonder how it would have felt if last evening he had brought what they had began to its conclusion. If he had lain like this beside her and touched her body with his, flesh moving against flesh, and then slid the length of his desire against her, inside her . . .

Treasure snatched her mind away from the too-real fantasy. She closed her eyes against the potent vision of his body and sucked in a breath, trying to calm away the strange tightness quivering low in her belly. He upset every order and rhythm of her life, turning even her own body traitor against her. Yet she wanted things from him she had never imagined wanting or needing from a man.

It made no sense. She hated it. She was excited by it. She couldn't explain her topsy-turvy feelings, and she desperately longed to.

When she opened her eyes again, Donovan was bending to finish his shower. He straightened, then threw his head back under the water and gurgled beneath its flow like a playful child. Treasure smiled a little at the contradiction of his sensuality and this boyish display.

Quietly, she crept away from the azaleas and out of the garden.

"Why, good morning, cousin dear. My, you are quite flushed. Have you been out taking a bit of morning exercise?" Ransom lifted his pince-nez to sharpen his vision of Treasure.

"I — I was attending to a few chores. You slept well, I

296

trust?"

"Truthfully, I did not."

"I am sorry. Were you too warm? I will—"

"No, no." Ransom waved a thin hand. "My rooms are perfectly adequate." He lowered his pince-nez, polishing them with a white handkerchief. A faint tinge of color came into his sallow face. "I hope you will not consider me insolent, but thoughts stole my sleep, Treasure dear—thoughts of you."

Treasure swallowed hard. In a way she'd been expecting a confession of this sort. Ransom had appeared smitten with her since he and her aunt arrived. Everyone noticed it, much to Treasure's dismay. "I see," she said, not certain how to respond. "Perhaps we should sit in the morning parlor where we can talk privately."

"Yes, I should like to talk with you alone," Ransom said with a courtly bow. He proffered an elbow to escort her.

Treasure nearly walked past him and had to recall herself. She laughed up at him. "My, I had almost forgotten what gentlemanly manners are."

As soon as she'd uttered the words, she regretted them. Ransom disliked Donovan, and the last thing she wanted to do was give her cousin a forum for criticizing him. Her affairs with Donovan River were personal. And giving Ransom any hint of them was tantamount to telling Aunt Valene, who cared even less for Donovan's brash manner.

Ransom, however, seemed intent on a comparison. Once they were seated in the parlor, he launched his campaign. "I do hope the improvement in your bookkeeping we devised has been a help to you. I know how terribly overburdened you are. My only hope is to lighten the weight of your many responsibilities."

"Yes, you have certainly done that already, in many ways. I shall always owe you my sincere gratitude for your assistance."

"That is certainly not what I care for, darling Treasure."

Oh dear! Treasure smiled gently, trying to lighten the suddenly intent expression on Ransom's face. "The very least I can do is thank you."

"Very well. Please, do not take offense to what I have to say, but I feel it is my duty."

"Please, feel free to speak your mind, Cousin Ransom." Treasure was fast becoming weary of having to guard her speech with too-polite niceties. She never had this constraint with Donovan.

"That is very kind of you." Ransom cleared his throat. "It seems to me, my dear, that an interloper has not only bullied his way onto your land, but has seriously hindered the progress of Rose of Heaven. Donovan River, though he claims to rightfully own this plantation, has yet to make one productive improvement."

Treasure just managed to maintain her reserve. "He has assisted Elijah in making numerous repairs. And he is useful in managing the slaves and horses."

Ransom reached over and took her hand in his. He patted it. "A true gentleman is an efficient overseer who keeps a sacred distance between himself and the common laborer."

She looked up into his pale eyes, and thought of the mysterious fire in Donovan's piercing gaze. Something in the memory compelled her to speak in his defense, even though she herself often harbored the same qualms about Donovan River. "Mr. River has worked since he came, demanding little, learning our ways. He's been keeping notes on planting methods." The lie came easily.

Yet it was a wishful lie. Why hadn't he taken a real interest in farming? Why hadn't he taken to responsibility? A quiet voice answered her from somewhere deep within. *Because he simply can't. He's a wanderer, an adventurer. He'll never settle down, put down roots. He'll leave you. Just like Papa.*

Solomon brought in a tea tray and set it on the table in front of the settee they shared. Treasure dismissed him and began to reach for the china pot.

"No. I insist." Ransom offered her a kind smile.

The gesture, like her cousin, elicited a feeling of gratitude, warm appreciation, a gentle affection. But nothing else. When Donovan flashed her that crooked, mischievous grin of his, she felt a riotous rush of emotions and illicit sensations. He made her skin quiver, her blood hot, her thoughts turn wanton. Simultaneously, she wanted to throttle him and throw her arms around him and kiss him wildly.

Yet Ransom epitomized everything she professed to admire: responsibility, security, and safe, peaceful, ordered action.

"Cream and honey?" Ransom was asking. He watched her with a questioning expression.

Treasure avoided his eyes. "Just cream, please."

"Ah! You see, there we have it. Just the way I drink my tea."

"I beg your pardon?"

"Admit it, my dear. We are two of a kind. We come from the same background, share the same goals. We have like minds. We are not given over to the whims of foolish emotions and our lower natures as others are."

Treasure wriggled a little in her seat, thinking of the garden. "Yes, I suppose you are right. But then, that is the role we must assume to ensure our families are cared for." She sipped at her tea. Finding the drink oddly bland, she decided to spoon in a dollop of honey.

"Yes, that is so," Ransom went on, something approaching eagerness in his face. "You and I are kindred spirits. I knew it from the first, when you admired my suggestions over the ledgers. Business and profit. That is what a plantation is about. The fact that you, a woman, can comprehend such a concept has set me in awe of you."

"How kind of you, Cousin Ransom," Treasure murmured. She prayed the unexpected disappointment surging in her didn't sound in her voice. Ransom admired her business acumen and her sense. A calm, contained woman attracted him. She supposed she should be flattered. His unspoken offer—she sensed it as clearly as if he had said it—should be most enticing to her.

A vision of Donovan bathing in the morning sunlight crept wickedly into her thoughts. *As enticing as this?* Donovan's deep, velvet voice whispered from nowhere.

Treasure felt her cheeks grow warm.

"You are flushed again. Are you sure you're quite well?"

Treasure fidgeted with her saucer. "It is a bit warm, that's all." Setting her cup down, she rose quickly to her feet. "You will excuse me, Cousin Ransom, but I must attend to my chores. Perhaps we could finish our discussion this evening."

"Certainly. I understand." He stepped close. "You are as overwhelmed by your feelings as I have been. Being the modest woman you are, you must have time to recover yourself. I am flattered, darling Treasure, most flattered." Ransom took her hand in his and bent down.

She knew he was about to kiss her. And she wanted him to. She needed to know if his kiss could weaken her knees, make her heart throb the way Donovan's did. Obliging him, she lifted her chin slightly as he placed his long, thin fingers around her shoulders.

He lowered himself to touch not her lips but her cheek. At the same time she heard a familiar tread in the hallway.

She swung around in time to see Donovan in the doorway, his face drawn into a dark scowl. Instead of leaving them in private, he stood and watched, long legs splayed, black boots heavy against the oak planks, arms crossed like some barbarian conqueror come to claim his conquest.

Ransom, visibly shaken by Donovan's imperious stance, backed away from Treasure with alacrity. He pulled off his pince-nez and scrubbed them with his handkerchief. "G-good morning, Mr. River. I was just about to take my leave."

Beneath the low brim of his hat, Donovan's smoky eyes were inscrutable. He said nothing.

"Yes — well, good day, Cousin Treasure." Ransom stepped toward the door.

"Yes, we will finish our talk when we can be alone," Treasure said. Though she spoke to Ransom, she stared straight at Donovan.

Donovan stayed in the doorway, unmoving, as Ransom came past, squirming to the side to avoid him. When her cousin had left, Donovan slammed the double doors closed behind him. He leaned against the hard wood, insolently raking her body with a stare that left Treasure feeling as naked as if he'd undressed her slowly, piece by piece. "Quite a touching little display," he sneered.

Despite her anger, Treasure felt an equal rush of raw desire. She could see every hard line of his body under the thin white cotton shirt and snug black trousers. And he knew it. She met his sardonic gaze, struggling to maintain a cool demeanor. "Why, Mr. River, are you jealous?"

"Of that?" Donovan jerked a thumb at the closed door. "He's got as much life in him as a bowl of grits without maple syrup." He straightened, taking a few prowling steps toward her. "And you, pretty lady, well know it."

She held her ground. He wanted to touch her. She could see it in his eyes, the hot, crazy look he got when his passion overran any reason he had. That look inflamed her, flicked against her nerves with a bittersweet sting. But she would not surrender, not when the game was this intriguing, the stakes so desirable.

301

"What do you know about grits? You refuse to eat them."

"I like them now." Donovan circled around behind her. His breath brushed her ear. "Very hot, with lots of maple syrup. And I like to eat them slowly. One taste at a time."

"Why did you come here?" Her skin screamed for the release of his caress. Yet she didn't dare move.

"To talk to you."

"About what?"

He moved slightly, enough to taunt her body with a fleeting touch of his. "How you like your grits, perhaps."

Treasure twisted to look at him. He paused, a heartbeat from her. "Very sweet," she brazenly returned. "But I'm beginning to consider the merits of other ways."

"Like this?" Donovan captured her wrists between his hands and pulled her mouth to his. He kissed her long and hard, not with his usual slow tenderness, but with a raw, feral hunger. Images of him in the garden welled up, making Treasure forget everything but his taste of honey and temptation, the eager probing of his tongue, the strength in the arms that moved to encircle her.

Breathless, ravaged with longing, she matched his kiss with a fire of her own. Her fingers tangled in the hair at his nape and urged him closer, demanding he satisfy the agonized ache he kindled in the depths of her body and soul.

"Miss me?" he whispered, scattering hot, frenzied kisses on her face and neck.

"All night. I couldn't stop thinking about you."

Abruptly he pulled back and snarled her hair in his fist, forcing her to look at him. She saw anger, dangerous and threatening, darken his face. "Then why in the hell were you kissing your cousin?"

Treasure tried to twist away, but his grasp tightened

302

almost painfully. "What I do and whom I see in my own parlor are my business. You certainly have no claim on me."

"I could argue that, pretty lady." His free hand moved to appreciate her waist, then slid upward to cup the curve of her breast. "Your body begs me to touch you. And I can't deny I want you, I need you, like I've never needed anyone."

She hated the treacherous tremble his brazen caress elicited. Yet she craved the feeling, yearned for more than a mere touch. "You need me for a night, a week of nights, and then what?" she managed. "Then you pack up and walk away, thinking of me only as a fond memory. That's what you want, Mr. River. A present, not a future."

Donovan abruptly released her. He stared at her with an almost bewildered gaze. "Is that what you want? A vow I'll be here to take care of you?"

"Take care of me? Not hardly, Mr. River. I am quite capable of taking care of myself and my family. I don't need you — any man — to take care of me!"

"There's more to caring for someone than just providing food and shelter." Donovan flung up a hand. "There's love, and trust and understanding. Have you learned to provide that?"

"Far more than you ever will." Treasure whipped around and strode to the doors, her shaking hands gripping the handles. Pulling open the doors, she slammed them closed behind her, collapsing against them, shaking. She would die before she let him see how deeply hurtful his blow had been. And it did hurt, oh how it hurt. Because he was right. He had exposed her loathsome weakness and forced her to face it.

She wanted to despise him. But knowing he spoke the truth stole the sting from her anger.

How many times had she answered her sisters' need for love, comfort, and understanding with discipline or lectures? She kept them fed and clothed, struggled to

303

build a plantation they could take pride in. Yet in her diligent determination to be responsible, she had, time and again, ignored their more important emotional needs.

For the first time, she realized how utterly she had failed them. In her ignorance — and her avoidance — of their feelings and her own, she had created emptiness and loneliness.

She understood now how devastating those feelings could be.

For Donovan had made her discover her heart. And then shown her it could be broken.

Off the master suite, lounging in what was once Treasure's mother's refuge, her private parlor, Valene Ellis glared at her son. Ransom, she thought, was scarcely worth the aggravation at times. "Did you propose to her? I am waitin' for an answer and my breakfast is growin' quite cold while I do."

Ransom sat rod straight opposite his mother. He stared at the carpet under his feet. "Almost, Mama."

"Almost? Ransom, are you tellin' me you lost your nerve?" Valene crumbled a blackberry muffin between her manicured fingers. Ransom might be a brilliant lawyer, but the boy had no skill when it came to courting the ladies. Such a sad trial he proved at times.

"Not quite. She . . ." Ransom removed his spectacles, fiddling with the lenses. "I believe Miss Treasure knew what I was leading to and she wanted to delay the question to give herself time to consider, as any lady would. Then *he* had the audacity to burst in."

"He being Donovan River, no doubt. Oh, Ransom." Valene sighed. *"He,* my dear son, is quite the reason you must propose without delay. That odious man wants Rose of Heaven and he will use his dubious charm to beguile poor Treasure into giving it to him. From what I have seen, he has nearly succeeded in seducin' her to his side."

"I'm to meet with her after dinner this evening. I will ask her then." Ransom paused as if carefully choosing his next words. "She does care for me, I am certain. And we do have so very much in common."

"Yes, yes." Valene waved a languid hand, bored with Ransom's fulsome avowals of regard for her niece. "I am sure you will be very happy, *if* you don't ruin your chance." She pushed aside her plate and sat up against the cushions of the plush couch. "You have only one chance to win her as your wife. Then, Rose of Heaven will rightfully be mine." She looked beyond the man in front of her as though he did not exist, seeing a world of her own creation.

"Sometimes, my son, sometimes destiny is thwarted by an unfortunate twist of fate. But with patience — oh yes it has taken a great deal of patience — and the knowledge of one's rightful place, destiny can be restored."

"Mama . . ."

Valene brought herself back with a charming smile for Ransom. "Don't mind my prattle, my dear. You know I simply get carried away with my own little musings from time to time. Now you stop worrin' about me and start concentrating on what you are going to say to put a ring on Treasure's finger. When that's done . . ." She smiled again, a secret, satisfied gesture. "When that's done, I shall have everything I want."

Treasure paced the parlor waiting for Ransom, dreading the scene to come. She'd scarcely touched a bite of her supper and noticed Ransom ate little more. Donovan hadn't bothered to show, despite the fact he usually took great pleasure in chafing her cousin and aunt by disrupting proper supper decorum with a series of stories or jokes that set her sisters giggling.

And poor Orange Jane. She went to so much work to

make the most of the limited selection of foodstuffs in the depleted pantry to accommodate the house guests. Tonight, she practically begged Treasure to let her have the last of the peaches for her famed peach cobbler. But only Camille, her aunt, and the twins enjoyed it. Emmy excused herself early (to take a plate to Donovan, Treasure suspected, unable to find the will to refuse her). And Spring, usually the first to take dessert and a bottomless source of conversation, had been apathetic to both food and company.

A hesitant rap on the door drew her from her musings. "I do apologize for keeping you waiting," Ransom said. "I had a few items to attend to."

"I have enjoyed a moment's quiet," Treasure said. She sat in the center of a narrow settee, hoping to dissuade Ransom from taking the seat next to her.

"May I?" he asked, motioning to the spot on her left.

"Of course." She complied by moving as far to the right as the short couch would allow.

He lifted her left hand in his palm and brushed his lips over it "I won't waste words, cousin. We are both practical people. It's only one of our many similarities, I'm happy to say." He paused to smile.

"Ransom—"

"Please, I beg of you, allow me to finish. Treasure, there is nothing I want more than to see your pride when your home is returned to its former glory. The only thing I would ask is that I be at your side to share that moment, and every moment after." Ransom slipped to the floor on one knee. "I am asking you to do me the honor of becoming my wife."

Treasure looked down into her cousin's pale eyes, watery with emotion, and tried to think of a suitable reply. One that satisfied both her reason and her contrary heart. "I—I don't know what to say. It is so sudden. And we are related."

"Cousins marry every day." He patted her hand. "That is how we in the South keep our fortunes in the family. I have no doubt you are acquainted with many girls who have married cousins. It is our tradition and it makes perfect sense."

"Yes—but we scarcely know one another." Treasure knew her objections sounded weak, and Ransom would likely interpret them as a modest fear of marriage. But she desperately wanted time to think. Her heart and mind were jumbled and nothing seemed clear. If he had asked her just months ago, before Donovan River . . .

"I will be a good husband to you, you need not fear. I will naturally assume the management of Rose of Heaven to leave you free to concentrate on a proper lady's pursuits. I am certain you sadly miss the opportunity of using your needle, and planning parties and afternoon teas." His voice gathered assurance from her silence. "I will also quiet your mind by making certain your sisters never want for anything again. They will marry well. I know many families here and in Atlanta."

"I am certain you do." Treasure rose and walked to the piano, rubbing her hand back and forth over its polished wood. On the surface, Ransom's proposal seemed the answer to her prayers. Especially where her sisters were concerned. Yet at what cost? She would lose Rose of Heaven. With Ransom as her husband, she would become Treasure Ellis, not herself, but Ransom's wife. After all her work to make her plantation succeed, could she hand it to him simply for the promise of security and peace? What would be left of her? Tatting and tea parties?

Drawing a deep breath, she turned to Ransom. "I am sorry, but I cannot answer you tonight." She took pity on his fallen face and managed a smile. "It is an attractive prospect, and I am honored, but I must give it the serious consideration due it."

Ransom climbed to his feet. "I quite understand. And as I am certain of your eventual answer, I will wait."

"Thank you. I am leaving in a few days to attend an agricultural convention in Savannah —"

"You did not tell me!"

Because I did not know myself. She had received the invitation several weeks ago and tossed it aside, never expecting to leave Rose of Heaven. Now, it seemed a godsend, an opportunity to gain the time she so needed to sort out her emotions and regain control of her life. She waved aside Ransom's protest. "Papa always attended, and now I must represent our interests. Eura Mae will be accompanying me, so there is no need to inconvenience you. I understand how busy you are," she said firmly. "But when I return . . ." She pushed aside the dead feeling in her heart. "When I return, you will have your answer."

"Damnation, woman, do you have to use my skin to sharpen your claws?" Ira Stanton rolled over on his back, gingerly tracing the thin red welts on his bare chest.

"Why, you told me you liked my wild ways," Camille purred. "I do recall more than one occasion when you've begged for it. Are you turnin' soft, old man?" She raked her nails over his belly, laughing when he winced.

Ira watched as Camille took her leisure stretching each milk-white limb before sliding out of bed and draping a red silk wrap over her cat's body. She was enough in a day to keep a man satisfied for a week, and that alone was worth the price he paid to keep her returning to Gold Meadow. He didn't flatter himself into believing his charm talked her into his bed. Camille was a greedy bitch. The moment he couldn't buy her with fancy baubles and prestige, she would be spreading her thighs for someone who could.

And that moment might be soon enough unless he found a way to salvage something from the ruined mess

308

of Gold Meadow.

"Too much thinking spoils the fun, darlin'." Camille, deliberately exaggerating each motion, sidled up to him. She mussed his hair with her fingertips. "Still brooding?"

Ira smacked her hand away and got up, not bothering with a robe as he poured himself out a stiff shot of whiskey. He tossed it back with a grimace. The liquor slid down his throat in a hot rush, rekindling his banked anger. "If you could've used your talents to soften up Donovan River, then I wouldn't be worryin' over anything those black bastards did to this sorry excuse for a plantation."

"I don't believe 'softening up' Mr. River was what you had in mind." Camille's tone was intended to annoy. She smiled as if she'd accomplished something clever. One shoulder of her wrap slipped to her elbow. "And trust me, honey, my efforts weren't in vain. If Treasure hadn't walked in — "

"I'd be no further along than I am this minute. Mistuh River's tastes obviously run to innocents. And you, my deah, hardly qualify."

Her eyes narrowed dangerously. "Insults? My, we are havin' us a fit."

Ira grunted his reply, splashing more whiskey in his glass. "I don't like waitin'. Maybe it's time I stop bein' so civilized over this."

A frown shaded Camille's face. She wandered around the bedroom, idly fingering various items, not looking at him. "You know I don't want trouble."

"Honey, you were born makin' trouble. You eat it for supper and sleep with it at night."

"Not your kind of trouble, Mr. Stanton," she said, flicking a finger at the whiskey bottle. "I said I'd do whatever I could to help toss my stepsister off her throne, but mind you, Ira, keep your hands off my full-blooded kin. The twins are the only goodness I know in this disgusting excuse of a life I'm living. I warn you, if any of your trouble making brings them to harm" — she splayed her long fingers in the air, curling her razor-edge nails at him — "these nails *will* draw blood."

Ira snatched a handful of dark hair and pulled her head back, forcing her eyes to his. "What's the matter? You goin' soft on me? Or maybe you've just gotten used to livin' like a slave? Maybe that's what you want."

"I know what I want," Camille hissed. "And I intend to get it. With or without the likes of you."

"You can't get it without me, sugah. Your mama ruined you for everything but making a fine picture between the sheets."

"My mama taught me how to use a man. Use him until he can't give any more and then find someone else who's willing. Don't think I won't either, old man. I'll have every pretty thing I want. And I don't much care who I take from. The only thing different from one man to the next is the size of his" — she arched a brow and stared brazenly below Ira's fleshy belly — "his pocketbook."

Ira shot her a scornful glare. "Willin', maybe. Willin' to bed you for a night." With his free hand, he split open her wrapper, and yanked it to the floor. "Or two. Hell, you could probably coax him into a week if you were real nice. But I do doubt you'll have too many respectable suitors linin' up at your doorstep when I describe the things I've done to this body. And trust me." He smoothed a hand from breast to thigh. "I remember them all."

He took pleasure in seeing the color wash from her face. "You bastard," she spat through gritted teeth. "You wouldn't have the liver to do it."

"Yes, my deah, I would. And then you'd lose the last remnant of your questionable reputation, and you'd have to mess those pretty hands with work, beggin' your stepsister for a roof over your head and —"

"Stop it!" Camille's nails slashed at his face. She wriggled like an angry snake as he snared her wrist in his

310

hand.

"That is what you're most afraid of, now, isn't it?"

A cunning crept into Camille's eyes, and for a moment she stilled under his hands. "Since we're trading secrets, let me remind you I know of few of yours, *Colonel* Stanton."

Ira didn't pretend to misunderstand her. But how had she found out — Jimmy Rae? Or did he talk in his sleep? Pushing her away from him, he shot another whiskey down his throat. Damnation, another complication was all he needed.

It didn't matter how she'd found out. She knew he'd bought his title just like he bought everything else in his life. Respectability. Power. A woman in his bed.

His daddy had been a colonel, and when he died, no one much noticed when Ira assumed the rank. There'd always been a Colonel Stanton at Gold Meadow. He was as good as any. The few people who knew otherwise were either dead and dust or paid well not to remember.

It was a shortcut to stature in the valley. Just like buying the mayoral election. And he thought he could as easily buy the gold mine of Rose of Heaven for a few lucky pennies.

He wanted it now so badly it was a gnawing ache in his gut. The lumber mill he'd made plans for would satisfy a few annoying debts and make him a king in the valley.

But he could see now courting Camille's aid had been a mistake.

"Now don't you worry," she said, rousing him from his black reverie. "I surely don't intend to tell a soul. Just as long as you keep my little secret."

"A whore would have a hard time convincin' respectable valley society of anythin'. Just who do you think they'd believe, sugah?" Setting down his drink, Ira reached for her body again, aroused by her furious struggles. Jerking her head to his, he pushed his tongue through her clenched teeth, forcing her body to his, until at last, she capitulated to his demanding hands.

"You win this time, old man. But if you ever again remind me of why I stay with you," she said, "I'll kill you."

Ira laughed as he lowered her to the bed. "You know, I do believe you would," he taunted. As soon as he said the words, he was paid a visit by the disturbing suspicion they might be true.

Camille, suddenly the seductress again, smiled up at him through slanted eyes. "Oh yes, darlin'. Do believe it. I would."

Chapter Sixteen

Treasure hurried to answer the tap at her hotel room door, knowing it would be Donovan come to escort her to supper. She quickly smoothed a hand over the full skirts of the new gown she'd indulged in, hoping the deep gold flattered her half as much as the shopkeeper insisted. "I'll be right there," she called.

After her rattling day as the only female planter at the convention, she was looking forward to an evening in his company. At least *he* wasn't hostile. No, she mused, far from hostile, Donovan's reassuring presence at her side today had proved invaluable. Though she'd never admit it, she was secretly delighted he'd shirked her orders to remain at Rose of Heaven and caught up with her in Savannah in time to accompany her to the planters' meeting.

Despite her vow to spend the time alone, to think about Ransom's proposal, Rose of Heaven, her future, she couldn't deny the trip would have been dismal without him.

Eura Mae looked up from her sewing as Treasure swept into the sitting room they shared. "Well now, seems you ain't fumin' no more 'bout Mastuh River followin' you down here." She clucked her tongue and shook a finger at Treasure. "Catch your breath, chile. Ain't right a lady should show how anxious she is to see her man."

Treasure bristled and turned away from her mammie's knowing eyes. "I am not anxious. And he is not *my* man. He's made it perfectly clear he belongs to no one and no place and never will."

"I heared what he said. And I know he's still sayin' it, but he ain't gone nowhere, is he?" She tied off the thread at her fingertips. " 'Cept chasin' down here after you."

Treasure laughed, her heart full of excitement for the evening ahead and a strange sense of freedom from all the cares she left behind in Aunt Valene's willing hands. "Oh, Mammie Eura Mae, I don't know what to make of him. He scares me. What if he's just like Papa? What if I trusted him and he up and left me forever?"

Eura Mae set aside her sewing and opened her arms to her charge. Treasure eagerly nestled into the comfort of her mammie's bosom. "Chile, only thing 'bout dat man like your papa is he can't see he already got what he been searchin' for."

Treasure backed away to face her. "What do you mean?"

"Your papa was so busy wishin' for a son, chile, he done looked right past you. Lord knows, you got more good sense 'n harder workin' hands than any spoilt rotten planter's son I ever seen. And you got just what dat wanderin' man needs t' make him settle down happy as a sapling pine on the sunny side of the hill."

Treasure kissed Eura Mae on the cheek. "If only I could believe that."

The knock sounded again, more insistent. "Go on now. Let him in fo' he break down dat door."

Treasure's smile was welcoming as she opened the door. But it quickly faded to surprise. The man standing outside, cap between his hands, wasn't Donovan.

"Miz McGlavrin?"

She nodded, bewildered.

"I've come to fetch you. My rig's in front." He stepped aside to let her pass.

Treasure glanced back to Eura Mae, who shrugged,

paying assiduous attention to her sewing. "Who sent you?"

"Gentleman, said to give you this." From behind his cap, the man produced a single, twilight-hued rose.

With trembling fingers, Treasure accepted the bloom, her mind buzzing with a thousand questions. She turned again to Eura Mae. "Come with me."

"No, chile. You be on your own tonight." Eura Mae grinned at Treasure's wide-eyed apprehension. "You's all growd up now. You don't need your mammie no more."

Minutes later, seated in the hackney, on a road leading away from the city, Treasure wondered, for the hundredth time, what Donovan had planned. That, she decided, was useless speculation. After his surprise appearance along the road just outside Savannah — when she'd given him strict orders to stay at Rose of Heaven — she should have guessed the rest of the trip would be utterly unpredictable.

The thought that he had come after her at once thrilled her, frightened her, angered her, and pricked at her guilt where Ransom was concerned. She had hesitated to give him an answer to his unexpected proposal (*Coward!* her mind taunted), and in the end had placated him by promising a reply upon her return. He tolerated that, she assumed, only because he seemed assured of her answer.

Lost in her imaginings, Treasure had no idea how much time had passed, and failed to notice when the carriage slowed. A sharp, briny tang of wind wafted through the open window, and in the distance she could hear a low rhythmic roar.

Where am I?

She leaned out the window gaping, feeling like a foreigner in her own country. Yet since she'd never been outside of Alabama before, she brushed aside the trepidation and anticipation she felt, determined to enjoy her surroundings.

The carriage rumbled down a narrow street lined with

clusters of white-wood shops tinted pale blue with the last brush of daylight. A fine, salty mist kissed her face. The carriage turned a corner and Treasure found herself facing a gently sloping sandy rise scattered with outcroppings of spiky grasses and thin trees. Puzzled, she turned to the opposite window. Her breath caught in wonderment.

The road hugged along the coast, a startling vista of rocky shoreline and beach and foam-edged waves. A full, ivory moon wrapped the panorama in a silvery glow. Rocks, shells, and sand shimmered a thousand shades of blacks, grays, and whites.

Absorbed in the view, Treasure started nervously when the carriage jerked to a stop. Journey's end.

She swallowed hard. *Now what?*

The temptation to beg the driver to take her back to Savannah rose in her, strong and urgent. Back to safety where she wouldn't have to confront Donovan or any of the disturbing feelings he aroused.

The door opened. Her one chance.

Donovan. He was there, holding out his hand to her. He wore sleek black trousers and a tailored gray coat that matched the hue of his smoldering eyes.

"Supper's a little late tonight, pretty lady. I hope you won't mind."

"Supper?" Treasure stared, incredulous. "You brought me all this way for supper?" Her voice quivered.

There was temptation in his slow smile. "Come and find out," he invited softly.

She hesitated. He was asking so much: that she follow her heart — that enemy of all reason, the dangerous part of her she never dared trust.

"You'll only find what you want to find," he said. "Nothing more. And I promise, never less."

The gentle understanding in his voice, the seduction in his eyes, made her choice.

She placed her hand in his.

* * *

He had brought her to a quaint inn, set atop a small rise overlooking the sea, where he'd taken a secluded suite of rooms facing the beach. The Savannah Rose nestled under the massive spread of a miniature grove of live oaks all hung with lacy drapes of Spanish moss. In a fragrant twining of leaves and blossoms, the brick walls and wrought iron fence and balconies were massed with yellow jessamine vines and roses in shades of purest white to deepest scarlet.

Smiling away her questions, Donovan led her up a winding staircase to their rooms. When he closed the door behind them, for the first time, Treasure felt they were truly alone, in intimate isolation from her problems, her sisters, Rose of Heaven. It was a strange and welcome release.

Donovan's body brushed hers from behind as his hands slipped the mantle from her shoulders. His breath kissed the bared skin of her shoulders. She shivered as a feathery warmth skated up her spine. "Treasure," he whispered against her neck, "you're so beautiful."

"I — I don't know what to say."

Donovan smiled as he took her hand. "Come. I want to show you something."

The flames flickering in the fireplace and a single candelabrum lighted the room, casting a warm golden glow over the cozy parlor. Picking up the candelabrum, he led her through a gossamer veil of drapes onto a small terrace. A rush of delight swept Treasure's uneasiness away. She flew to the iron railing to relish the moonlit sky and sea spread before her. Donovan placed the candles on a small table set for supper.

"I'm glad you came to Savannah," she said, feeling oddly compelled to tell him the very thing she'd vowed never to admit.

"Why? Because you don't have to worry that I'm back in Alabama filching the cotton crop from your unsuspecting sisters?"

She knew the teasing tone well, and turned to match it. "No," she said with a laugh. "I shouldn't worry about that. You'd have to harvest it first."

Donovan took the jibe with a smile.

"It helped to have you beside me today."

"You took them on all by yourself, Treasure. You are right, you know, no matter how vehemently they disagree. Perhaps I can't harvest a crop, but I can read. I've kept up on those stacks of agricultural periodicals you have scattered all over the house."

"You read them? I never — and you agree soil exhaustion is our greatest threat to crop yields?"

"Of course. The states' surveys tell the story. Planters are going to have to change their ways. Rotate crops, plant legumes, and so forth."

"You saw them, though. They don't want to talk agricultural reform, they only want to brag about who owns the finest bottle of bourbon."

"Speaking of libation, I've ordered up a fair bottle of Chardonnay for us." He motioned to the table. "Just the thing to take your mind from legumes and crop rotation."

The tang of wind and sea mingled with the savory aroma wafting above covered dishes. Two dozen silver-lavender roses overflowed the edges of a crystal vase at the center.

"Supper awaits," Donovan said, moving to seat her.

"It smells delicious," she murmured, sweeping her skirts to the side to take her place opposite him. She studied the supple motion of his hands as he poured white wine and offered her plump, pink shrimp and buttery asparagus. His slow, refined gestures fascinated her, as if if she were seeing him for the first time.

"Are you happy?"

"What?" She realized he had been talking, but she had not been listening to the words, only hearing the dark, sweet sound of his voice.

"You look happy."

"I am." *Every other happiness seems like a poor dream compared with this.* She couldn't place a time or a day he'd become lodged in her heart, but now she despaired of ever ousting him.

"I want that — for you. I never imagined . . ." He stopped, toying with the stem of his wineglass. When he looked up at her again, Treasure caught her breath at the bared emotion in his eyes. "I never imagined it would be so important to me."

Treasure's thoughts scattered like whispers in the wind. For a single moment, she felt they shared a perfect communion, beyond words, beyond understanding.

Then, as if at all costs he had to move, Donovan pushed back his chair and paced to the railing. He leaned strong arms against it and looked out at the sea. Treasure watched a moment before slipping out of her own chair and stepping to his side. In front of them, the sea moved in an unhurried pulse and ebb against the shore, moving in, sliding away, always returning, suddenly crashing against the sand and rocks in a spray of fury and release.

"I had almost forgotten how much I love the sea," Donovan murmured.

"This is the first time I've seen the ocean, but I can certainly understand how men write and speak of it like a woman they love. The constant motion, waves breathing in and out; it seems alive."

"When I was a boy, I could see the ocean from my bedroom window. I used to try to bring it closer to me, recreate its soothing songs, its mystery and beauty in my own room with paper and pen." He laughed and looked out over the railing, and Treasure knew he saw a shore she could never see. With a start, he recalled himself and suddenly he was her rogue again. "Come on," he said, pulling off his coat and tossing it aside. "Let's go."

Startled at his quicksilver change of mood, Treasure shook her head. "Where? It must be nearly midnight."

"Perfect."

319

"What are you doing?" She faltered a step backward, feeling something near panic as he began to unbutton his shirt.

Rolling his sleeves up over his sinewed forearm to his elbow, he pulled off his black boots and flung them after his coat. "Going for a walk, in the surf. It's a perfect night for it. Come with me. You can't learn about the sea just by looking at it from the balcony."

"I . . ." Part of her wildly rebelled against her reason and urged her to toss caution and decorum aside. "I can't. I — my dress will be ruined."

"Then leave it behind."

Color flushed her cheeks. "What! I — I can't do that sort of thing. No proper lady — if anyone saw me — "

"To hell with being proper. Besides, not another soul will see you." He paused, letting his eyes wander over her with very improper appraisal. "Do you think I'd risk allowing another man's eyes to see you?"

"Donovan — Mr. River — "

"Donovan. I left Mr. River in McGlavrin's Valley." He stepped forward. Treasure slid a pace back.

She groped behind her for the support of the rail, moving away from him. He matched her, motion for motion. The hard iron of the rail prodded her back, foiling her halfhearted attempt to elude him.

He put a hand to either side of her and leaned toward her. Treasure waited, unable to breathe. To her surprise, he began to laugh, a sound so full of life and joy, her uneasiness faded like fog in sunshine. "Listen to your heart, pretty lady. You'll hear it begging to take control. You'll never have a safer chance. For once, be impulsive. Feel the excitement."

"Yes." Treasure's heart raced madly. Her breath matched the rapid pace of his. "It is exciting. But I — I shouldn't . . ."

Disappointment flickered in his eyes, but he smiled, gently drawing a finger down her cheek. "All right," he said finally, stepping back. "I won't choose for you. I'll let you decide what you want. But I intend to take that walk. If you change your mind . . ."

He let the words trail away with a suggestive half smile. Treasure watched as he walked down the winding stairs that led to the beach. Without a backward glance he meandered down to the water and along the shoreline, hands shoved in his pockets, kicking up the surf as he went along. By moonlight she saw a light breeze ruffle his dark hair and pull his shirt taut against his broad chest and shoulders.

All at once, a wicked impulse took command of her. Who would ever know? Home was an eternity away; responsibility something she had left far behind. With fumbling fingers, quickly, fearful she would lose her wanton courage, Treasure unfastened her dress, corset, and petticoats, leaving them draped over a chair. She kicked off her slippers and pulled her hair loose from its confining ribbons. Barefoot, clad only in her knee-length shift, she drew a deep breath then plunged down the staircase, running to ease the wild, tumultuous thrill rampaging inside her.

She stopped at the sea's edge, gasping as the first rush of warm water foamed around her legs. It felt freeing, as if she'd been granted the key to a cage that had long imprisoned her emotions and now they bounded out in joyful chaos.

Throwing back her head, she looked up at the stars, dizzied by the vastness of the black and diamond canopy. *Is this what he feels? So intoxicated by the simple feeling of being alive? So—*

—consumed by the feelings between us? Is that what she feels?

Donovan watched her, bewitched by the silver and flame creature that seemed to have sprung from a coupling of moon and sea. She was unaware of her own innocent beauty, of the artless seduction she wielded with one glance, and that made her all the more beguiling. He had known, it seemed forever, that the temptress at the sea's edge lay hidden beneath the proud plantation mistress's stoic facade. Yet seeing his fantasy released by the force of her own passion left him no escape from desires too strong to fight.

How long have you held my heart in your hands?

She paused at the water's edge, the sea licking at her bare legs. As if hearing his heart's whisper, she slowly turned.

How many nights have I known we belong to each other?

The huge mother-of-pearl sphere above her illuminated her skin with an ethereal silver sheen. She began walking toward him.

He could see her soul in the depths of her eyes, looking for his.

How many days have you been mine?

She stood before him, a heartbeat away.

How long have I known I love you?

He touched her.

His fingertips swanned her face, her throat, explored lower to her shoulder and the tender curve of her breast. Her skin glided warm and wet beneath his hand. Passion burst inside him like a madness. With a strong will, he buried it deep, but the echo of it was a hunger, begging to be sated.

Reaching out, feeling powerful, yet uncertain, he brushed the damp hair at her temple. "I realized long ago if I were blind . . ." He slid his fingertips to the fine line of her cheekbones, caressed the curve of her mouth, the stubborn lift of her chin. ". . . if I were blind, I would still know you."

She thought his voice as warm as the night air. "Would you?"

"Always."

Always.

Donovan cupped her face between his hands, savoring every nuance of her expression as he softly kissed her parted lips. Her eyes fluttered closed, and her breath escaped on a sigh. He kissed her again, deeper, hotter, longer, kindling her desires until they were a match for his own.

Then, sweeping her into his arms, he carried her back to the balcony, no longer hearing the siren serenade of the sea.

Treasure's recklessness wavered as Donovan carefully set her back on her feet. He took her hand and stepped toward the sitting room. Her own steps faltered.

She couldn't fearlessly walk with him into that bedroom, to — to do what his kisses suggested. It felt too strange, too bold. She couldn't even name it. The revulsion evoked by her childhood visions of Papa and Lettia stalked her, relentlessly cruel in their ugly torment. The sea air was suddenly cold against her skin. Hugging her arms around her body, she rubbed her hands against her shoulders.

Donovan studied her for a moment. "Come inside," he said. "I'll start a fire."

Treasure nodded wordlessly. After a moment, he followed her into the sitting room, his arm full of twilight roses.

Her eyes opened wide and questioning. He offered no answer. Instead, he moved to the fireplace and, after stirring the embers into a tentative flame, dropped onto the sofa, the roses in his lap. "It's warmer here." He nodded to the place next to him.

After a moment's pause, Treasure sat down, curling her legs under her, admitting he was right. It was warmer. Sinfully so. The heat poured over her like a honey balm. It uncoiled some of the tension inside her.

Donovan appeared content to let her bask in the fire light. His fingers idled the petals of the roses, then pulled away a single petal and let it drift to the thick rug that lay in front of the hearth.

Almost aimlessly, he separated another, and then another, letting them fall to the floor. His fingers' caress and the fire's warmth released their sweet, elusive attar.

Treasure found her eyes drawn to Donovan's languid pastime as he rubbed the blooms in his hand until they opened and parted. Watching the petals drift silently through his splayed fingers to the rug lured her with a hypnotic seduction.

When he had finished, and had put aside the bare stems, a silver-twilight carpet had been strewn at their feet.

Donovan turned to her. Slowly, so slowly Treasure feared she would die from the wait, his hand slid across the space between them and touched hers. Unhurried, he drew his fingertips up her arm, to her shoulder and the hollow of her throat. Looking into her eyes, he slipped one finger under the neck of her shift, tracing a path from shoulder to shoulder.

Frightened by the lightning jolt of raw desire his touch provoked, Treasure reached up to stop his meandering hand. Donovan caught her fingers in his. Instead of pushing them aside, he drew her hand between both of his. Opening her curled fingers, he pressed his lips to her palm. The simple caress affected her more than any bolder touch. Every fiber of every nerve quivered. She sucked in a sudden breath, recapturing Donovan's gaze in a flash of fever.

His hands tightened over hers. Dropping one knee to the floor, he slowly eased her down with him until they both knelt on the rose-strewn rug. Treasure waited for him to push her down, to force her to bend to his will, knowing she was too weak, wanted him too much to deny him.

Instead, he simply looked at her with the same knowing gaze he had had the night in her room at Rose of Heaven. *How long ago that seems.*

She didn't realize she'd spoken the words aloud until he smiled. "Tonight is how it begins." Gathering up a handful of rose petals, he smoothed them over her neck

324

and shoulder, letting them fall in a silken shower down her arm. "Forever is where it ends."

The fire-warmed perfume of roses and the heady mingle of sea and wind embraced her as Donovan bent close and parted her lips under his. His kiss overpowered her with its sweetness. As she melted into his arms, she moaned quietly. His hard chest muscles crushed into the softness of her breast. A shivery, tingling sensation, hot and flickering like the firelight, shot straight to her loins. Blindly, willingly, she slid her arms around him to bring him closer. She drowned in his embrace, lost herself to her intimate exploration as her fingertips found smooth ripples of flesh beneath his shirt.

I'm giving myself completely to him.

Was this any different, in the end, from what she would be to Ransom? Becoming something to him, for him, with nothing left of herself. Treasure tried to bring order to her thoughts. It was hard, so hard, with Donovan's mouth at her throat, teasing the soft skin with warm, wet kisses. This was what Papa meant. But was this all she was made for?

She didn't want it to be. Yet she wanted nothing else. She longed for it, ached for it, more with each look, each caress.

"You're thinking again," Donovan's dark voice whispered in her ear. He drew back a little, his hands lingering on her shoulders. "Did you know that sometimes, when you forget, I can see your feelings in your eyes? You think you've locked them safely away, but they're there. All the laughter and the tears. The passion." Drawing in a steadying breath, he coaxed a red-gold curl around his forefinger, then slowly drew it out again. "I've known for a long time, maybe from the beginning, that you could take me to the heights of heaven or the depths of hell. And right now, I don't care which. You decide. I want us to be lovers tonight, but I want to make love with you, not to you. So, pretty lady . . ." His touch released her. "Which is it to be?"

Treasure searched his eyes, but found no guile. Feeling as if she were leaping headlong from the highest peak into the hottest fire, she let her heart and soul make her answer. "Heaven," she whispered. "Show me heaven."

"For you, nothing less," Donovan murmured against her mouth. She yielded her lips to him, encouraging him to kiss her deeply, in the slow, sensual way that seemed to drain the very life from her body then pour it back in.

Donovan deliberately held back his raging need for release. She was an innocent, and he wanted nothing more than for her to cherish this night for an eternity, to burn his memory in her heart. He took his leisure, inviting her to savor each kiss, the provocative invasion of his tongue, the taste of his mouth in hers, fanning the flames of her burgeoning desire until her body heaved against him, pleading for his touch. His breath was a hot rasp against her throat when at last he dragged his mouth from hers and slid his hands up her bared thighs, slipping up the thin cotton of her shift.

In a faraway crevice of Treasure's mind a tiny fear tried to surface. But the roughened slide of his hands against her flesh was too delicious a sensation to ignore. She craved to know each contour of his body, to feel each band of muscles tense beneath her hands. Following his lead, she unbuttoned his shirt, teasing him with his own tormenting slowness as she pushed the soft linen off his shoulders. She stared, thinking him beautiful beyond imagination. His dark chest was a luminous copper shield awaiting her passionate assault. A small smile softened the angular lines of his face as he focused on her, his eyes intense, beckoning her to discover the secret pleasures he could offer.

He moved to pull her back into his arms, but Treasure stopped him with a hand against his chest. She hesitated, then ran both hands over his shoulders and arms, searching the body her eyes had memorized. In the near dark, he was her man of twilight: romantic, mysterious, dangerous, exciting.

Her hand brushed over his heart and she felt his unsteady pulse. His breathing deepened, quickened. Treasure caught her breath, amazed at her newfound power. He could arouse her with a touch, but she too could make him tremble with her caress.

Sensing her discovery, Donovan answered with his touch. He slipped her shift higher, to her waist, and then gently drew it over her head and tossed it aside. Behind her, firelight shaped and shadowed the round swell of her breasts, the delicate recess of her waist, the gentle slope of her hips. "My God, you are perfect," he rasped.

"Am I?" It was a question to herself as much to him. This first time, having her body and heart completely bared to him, felt both strange and exciting. Wonderful and frightening.

"I thought I knew how beautiful you were. I was wrong. So wrong." He slid his hands over her hips to her waist, and then covered her breasts with strong hands. "I want you. All of you."

She gave way to him, letting her head fall back. Her eyes closed and she felt a bead of sweat trickle down between her breasts where he lightly rubbed his palms against the dusky peaks of her aching nipples. When his tongue flicked against the sensitive buds, she arched back further. He buried his head between her breasts and she sank her fingers into his hair, pressing his face to her. Tension coiled low in her belly, begging for a release she couldn't name. "I've never—I can't name the way I feel," she gasped. "I can't seem to have enough of you."

"There can never be enough." His lips moved to her breasts, suckling her taut nipples, as his hands danced over her thighs, her arms, to the base of her spine.

She wanted to isolate each new sensation and draw it out, savor the taste, the scent, the touch. But it was like trying to separate a single raindrop from a deluge. Donovan's hands eased her backward, floating her into a velvet crush of rose petals. They cradled her bared skin cool and satiny as she lay beside him, mesmerized by the wanton image of herself in the silver pool of his eyes. His chest brushed her breasts as he leaned close and kissed her, long and hot, his tongue flirting against hers. At the same time, his hands coaxed a restless desire from a thousand sensitive places on her skin.

She felt she had drifted to a world somewhere far away, where only the frantic pleasure of his flesh meeting her flesh, his soul meeting her soul, mattered. His fingers sought the supple insides of her thighs like hot, licking flames, creating a feverish, aching need there. But when she felt his touch slip between them, she stiffened, unnerved by the intimacy of his exploration.

"It's all right, pretty lady," Donovan rasped against her ear. His voice sounded oddly disjointed. "I'll never hurt you." He continued to murmur breathless phrases in her ear while his hand gently plundered her most tender spot.

Treasure forgot why she didn't want him to touch her as her body awoke to an unexpected bolt of pure, primal fire. His coaxing touch found places she had never known. Her scant resistance burned to ashes. Desire was a searing, tightening coil of agony and ecstasy that rocked her hips to the tormenting rhythm of his fingers.

Something inside was building, building. Bringing her closer to . . . closer. And she couldn't stop it. Not for anything, for anyone. Not if it cost her life to assuage it.

A cool waft of air suddenly separated them. Treasure, her thoughts lost in a whirl, gazed up at him, confused by his sudden withdrawal. Donovan, on his knees beside her, looked at her, his expression dazed. His fingers fumbled at the waist of his trousers. Treasure, letting her instinct act where reason failed, moved his hands aside.

His fist tangled in her hair as she slid the material away. Her breath caught at the remembered perfection of his body. This intimacy was infinitely more powerful than the morning she had watched him, unseen. She stopped, unable to finish, to let her hands touch him.

328

Impatient, Donovan kicked free of the last of his clothing and lay back beside her, pulling her into his arms. Her flesh burned into his. He guided her hand down his hip, over the mat of dark curls below his belly to grasp him. At once her hand yielded to his, and she took control, stroking him, caressing his hot, hard shaft, spurring him on to an unbearable edge. He groaned her name. "I want you," he gasped. "But I have to be sure this is your choice. Say it, Treasure. Tell me you want this."

Treasure sensed the pause in him, the fight he waged with his desires. She took his face in her hands and looked deeply into his eyes. "Yes." Then she wasn't sure whether she spoke the words or he heard her heart: "Love me. Please love me."

Slowly, he moved his body over hers. Gazing into her eyes, he parted her legs with his knee, then lowered himself carefully, probing slowly at first between her thighs. Watching her, he hesitated a moment longer. Then, pressing a confusion of kisses over her eyes, her cheeks, her mouth, her chin, he thrust into her, burying himself inside her silken essence.

Treasure flinched at the unexpected twinge of pain. He held her against him, not moving, waiting until she learned the feel of his body joined with hers. When he began to plunge and rotate his hips against hers, a sweet invasion, Treasure felt the demanding tension in her loins renew, stronger and bolder.

Her body, of its own will, soon matched his motion. Their fusion inspired a more frantic pace. Each rapid slap of his sweat-slicked skin against hers fed her hunger for the next. She was soaring upward with him, spiraling to dizzying heights. Upward. Higher. Farther from reality; nearer to paradise. She clutched at him, pulling him deeper inside, a savage craving possessing her senses.

All at once, it burst over her. She was dying, coming alive. Falling and soaring. Spine-shattering sensation shot along every nerve. In that moment she surrendered her heart to him. He had promised her heaven and then delivered it, body and soul.

From somewhere far away she felt Donovan shudder against her and was struck by the wonder that he, too, must share this utter fulfillment. She felt herself melt into his arms, trembling with the echo of what they had created together. Something so perfect, so pure, she knew nothing that had happened or would ever happen could shake the foundation of it. She might deny it, or lock it in a place in her soul where no one would find it. But it would always find her. Always.

Donovan took her face between his hands and tasted the sweet nectar of her lips. "You belong to me," he whispered. "Always."

He touched her tenderly, and the emotion in her heart was almost unbearable. Treasure reached up and brushed her fingers against his face, caressing each familiar and beloved line and angle. Her heart gave a queer lurch and suddenly she felt a warm wetness on her cheek. For the first time since the devastating moment she had lost her childhood, tears released the tide of feelings in her heart. They spilled down her face onto Donovan's fingers.

He opened his mouth to speak and then stopped, his gift for words abruptly abandoning him. Instead, he pressed a dozen kisses over her damp face and gathered her close.

They lay together, among the rose petals and the scattering of their clothing, warmed by the fire, sated by each other.

And between them, Treasure felt her tears form the last silver link of a bond neither heaven nor hell could ever break.

Chapter Seventeen

A draft, moist and cool, wafted over Treasure's arms. Eyes closed, her mind foggy with sleep, she yawned and stretched. Bare fingertips brushed bare skin. Drawing her hand back up the side of her nude body to rub her eyes awake, confusion roused her from her drowsy haze.

Something was terribly wrong.

Forcing herself to wake up, she found she was lying amid a crushed bed of rose petals, half-draped with a satin quilt, Donovan's warm body curved intimately against hers. She sat bolt upright, a confusing flood of memories overwhelming her. Beside her, Donovan lay still, deep in dreams.

Donovan. Her lover.

What have I done?

What am I going to do?

Fumbling in the pre-dawn shadows, Treasure struggled to her feet, only to discover she ached where she didn't even realize she had muscles. She blushed, recalling the pleasures that provoked the pain. Pleasures she'd practically begged for.

Panic welled up inside her. She'd given herself to him. Wholly. Irrevocably. She'd acted every bit as wanton as Camille, whom she'd condemned countless times; as wanton as Papa had accused every woman of being. For all her protests of independence, her insistence on relying only on her reason, on guarding her heart, she had abandoned herself to a man, depended on him to teach her joy.

She had loved him knowing he could give her nothing but a timeless night. Had given her heart to a man who would walk away. Again.

Tears stung her eyes. She furiously blinked them away. She would not cry. She would go home, home to her family, her beloved Rose of Heaven. A wave of homesickness washed over her. Suddenly, she realized how much she missed her sisters, and the familiar faces and voices of her home. She needed to be close to her family, to return to security and the daily routine of the plantation. Once home, she could devote herself to her family. She would open her heart and pray it wasn't too late to right her past wrongs.

And she would try and forget Donovan River.

Groping for her clothes, Treasure dressed as noiselessly as possible. Before she fled, she paused, looking down at him, peaceful in sleep. Then, unable to stop herself, she knelt and gently touched her lips to his.

"Goodbye, Donovan," she whispered.

Eura Mae said nothing when Treasure burst into the hotel room, announcing her intention to depart immediately. It wasn't until they were loaded into the carriage bound for Atlanta that she turned thoughtful eyes to her mistress.

"You's runnin' away, chile. Ain't you?"

Treasure kept her eyes fixed on the passing morning-lit landscape, her hands gripped together in her lap. "I'm going home."

"You's runnin'. Jus' like you been runnin' since de first day dat man showed up on your doorstep."

"Mr. River decided to stay behind—"

"No, chile," Eura Mae said, shaking her head. "Ever since you was a little girl, you been scared o' yo' own heart. Same as you is now."

"It doesn't matter."

332

"It sho' 'nough matter t' Mastuh River! And Mastuh Ellis. Only one man be de man you love. And dat one better be de one you marry, or you gonna heap mo' trouble on yo' head 'en you ever seen!"

Treasure opened her mouth to contradict her mammie, then closed it. What was the use? "I don't wish to discuss this any further. It's pointless."

"Maybe so. But you best think 'bout one thing. Mastuh Ellis be expectin' a virgin bride. Whatchu gonna do if Mastuh River put a chile in yo' belly?" Eura Mae bundled her cloak about her. "Dat man's in yo' blood, girl. One way or 'nother, he gonna catch up wit' you."

Treasure turned from Eura Mae's scrutiny. She watched the verdant green of the Georgia countryside slide by in a blur of mixed impressions: the landscape changing before her like the erratic beat of her heart. How she wished she could reason with her heart, make it see the impossibility of caring for an impulsive rover like Donovan River. What about Ransom? Perhaps she needed his stability to tame her newfound impetuous tendencies. And her sisters. She had to consider their future.

After all her self-righteous lectures to them about propriety, after judging Camille for her promiscuous behavior, she—cool, controlled Treasure—had succumbed to her own desires. She'd failed. Failed herself and her family. Ransom seemed her only hope of rescuing the family's reputation—if it wasn't already too late.

Yet though she berated herself for her lack of discretion, she could not, Lord help her, regret making love with Donovan. Already, she had secreted the memories in her heart to cherish. For one timeless night, she had felt adored, loved passionately by the only man she ever wanted to be loved by.

Though she knew it would be best never to see his face again, she ached to feel his strong arms around her.

It's impossible. It has to be impossible.

Each jolt from the ruts in the road, aggravated further by the side-to-side sway of the carriage, tightened the knot in her stomach. Eura Mae began to hum low and Treasure let herself yield to the soothing, lullaby melody, her tormented thoughts giving way to a restless sleep. But before she drifted into a numbing haze, her mind put haunting words to the familiar tune.

> *Shall I come to dance, to sing,*
> *my heart relearn to live?*
> *Or have I left with you, my love,*
> *more than I dared to give.*

Oblivious to the midmorning sun filtering through the filmy balcony curtains, Donovan awoke to a stirring of desire evoked by the memory of the night's passion. Eyes still closed, he reached out a hand to pull her near, avid for the warmth of her body, to recreate the enchantment she wove around him. It had never been like this for him. He had never felt desire so intense, longing so strong. He wanted her now, tonight, and every tomorrow. . . .

The empty feel of withered rose petals slapped his eyes open. He sat up and, with a quick glance, knew as certain as a cold, quick blade to the heart that she had left him.

She was gone.

Anger, laced with a blinding pain, spread slowly from the center of his gut outward, tensing every muscle. He crushed a handful of rose petals in his fist. Damn the woman. How could she leave without any explanation, without so much as goodbye?

Spurred by the necessity to do something, to *move,* Donovan threw back the quilt and hurried into his clothes. She must have gone back to the hotel for Eura Mae. There was a chance he could intercept her there.

But as he yanked on his boots, a disturbing thought stopped him cold.

Why the hell am I chasing after her? If she has regrets, then leave her to them. Why should I run after her and apologize for something we've both wanted for months?

He was still trying to answer the question as he stood in front of the port office ticket window, his eyes wandering over the available passages. Treasure McGlavrin had left him without a backward glance. It was though she'd erased him from her life. Feeling enraged and achingly empty at the same time, he decided there was no reason he couldn't return the favor.

That woman has caused me nothing but grief since the day I set foot on her cursed land.

Hadn't he regretted the damned poker game that landed him in that godforsaken valley? Hadn't he longed to escape the weight of responsibility — dreamed of adventure, fast women, and hot cards?

Run, you fool. Run while you still have the chance, What do you have to go back to?

"Next!" the ticket officer bellowed, looking expectantly at Donovan. Behind him, a restless line of customers shuffled their feet and peered around the shoulders of the persons in front. Donovan hesitated, then let the man behind him move ahead.

He slapped his slouch hat against his hand, wondering why he suddenly found it so hard to make up his mind. The impulse to pick up and go had always come easily before. What *did* he have to go back for?

The ticket collector finished with his customer and stared hard at Donovan. "Next?"

Donovan felt the agony of making the choice as keenly as if he were being drawn and quartered over it. He looked at the passage list and back at the office door. Then, tugging his hat low over his brow, he stepped up to the window.

Treasure had pushed the driver hard to make good time on the return to Rose of Heaven. As they passed the huge magnolia marking the plantation's entrance, and came to a jerking halt in front of the big house, she frowned to recognize the Johnsons' cart and three unfamiliar horses tied near.

Solomon hurried down the front steps toward Treasure as she helped Eura Mae lower her stiff limbs from the carriage.

"Lordy, I ain't never gonna walk right again."

"You'll be up and right after a few nights in a real bed," Treasure told her. "And Bettis can —"

"Missy Treasure, Missy Treasure!" Solomon rushed up, hands flailing. "I's right happy to see you!"

Solomon sounded more panicked than happy. Turning from Eura Mae, Treasure's heart sank at the sight of his wide-eyed fear. "Dey burned de barn! De sheep barn. Right to de ground. Last night dey come. A whole group!"

"Lord in Heaven!" Treasure's heart constricted with sudden fear. "Emmy, Spring, and the twins? And Camille? Where are they? Are they all right?"

"Dey was in de big house," Solomon said. "No one got hurt. Just de barn burned."

"Thank the Lord," Treasure breathed. "But they must be frightened out of their wits. I must go —"

"Treasure!"

Treasure whirled quickly as Emmy, followed closely by the twins and Spring, came bounding down the stairs. Treasure caught up Emmy in a fierce hug, widening her arms to include the twins and Spring. They clung together in a laughing, crying group, all talking at once.

"I'm so glad you're home, Treasure. No one's been to meals on time since you left," Spring teased.

"The fire was awful!" Emmy said. "We were so afraid the big house would burn, too."

"And Bonnie's tail got burned," Abby piped up, Erin nodding in wide-eyed agreement. "Bettis fixed her up, though."

Emmy gave Treasure another hug. "I wish you had been here, Treasure. You always know what to do."

The warm pleasure of being home, of knowing she had been missed, flooded through Treasure. "I wish I had been here, too. But I'll take care of things now."

"The barn is pretty bad," Spring said quietly. "And we lost a dozen of the sheep."

"It doesn't matter," Treasure said, realizing how true it was as she looked at all her sisters. "We can build a new barn and buy new stock. What matters is that all of you are safe. Camille is safe, isn't she?"

Spring wrinkled her nose in annoyance. "Oh, yes. She took to her bed after the fire saying it had all been too, too much for her to bear. I think it's an excuse to avoid helping with the cleanup."

Treasure smiled in shared amusement. "Probably. I suppose I should go look at it."

"I'll go with you," Spring offered.

"No, you stay here and look after the twins. There's no need in both of us getting covered in soot and mud." With one last smile for her sisters, Treasure lifted her skirts and started off across the yard.

She thought she had prepared herself for the sight, but when she saw the mass of blackened boards and ashes, her heart skipped a beat.

All this lost. Her knees weakened for a dizzying moment. The journey to and from Savannah, her worry for her sisters, had left her physically and emotionally bereft. Now this. She longed to weep, but the strength in her was determined never to allow her that simple release again.

Lost in her grief, she didn't see Rader and Eliza until Eliza wrapped a comforting arm around her shoulders. "We came as soon as we heard. It's not nearly as bad as it looks, honey."

337

"Liza's right," Rader said. "Your people put out the fire before it spread."

"My people?" Treasure stared at him. "They didn't do this?"

Rader glanced away. "Seems not."

"Then who? Why?" Even as she asked the question, the answer became apparent. Three men, men from the valley she recognized as avid supporters of Ira's lumbering scheme, hung in a group a few feet away, watching her.

Rage surged through Treasure like wildfire. Twisting away from Eliza, she stomped up to them. "I see I don't need to ask further. How dare you try and terrorize me and my family into giving up Rose of Heaven! I should have known Colonel Stanton would be low enough to try something of this sort."

"Whoa! Regular wildcat, like they says, ain't you? We only come up to see what happened, just like everyone else."

Treasure recognized the scrawny, weasel-faced man from the night of the slave revolt at Gold Meadow. "I know you work for Ira Stanton. What did you come back for—to check your handiwork? Forgive me for saying, but you did a rather shabby job of it."

The man's face went beet purple and he lunged out at Treasure. His companions grabbed at his arms. "She's just a skinny excuse for a woman, Joe. We don't need trouble with the sheriff," one warned. "Bitch ain't worth it."

Rader stepped up and pulled Treasure away from the trio. "I suggest you boys get back to where you came from."

"Yeah, we'll go," the weasel-faced man snarled. "But you take some advice, little Miss McGlavrin. If the colonel is sendin' you a warning—and I ain't sayin' he is—you damn well best pay attention. Stanton ain't a man to take no for an answer."

"Then perhaps he'd better learn," Treasure said,

refusing to be intimidated. She only prayed her skirts hid her trembling knees. "You can tell Colonel Stanton his warning is as impotent as the man who issued it." She twitched her skirts into place and whipped around, pausing to toss a hard glance over her shoulder. "And one more thing, gentlemen. If I ever see you on my land again, I'll shoot you myself."

As they sat down on the verandah with plates of Orange Jane's cinnamon cakes and lemonade, Rader asked Treasure the question she'd dreaded since she'd set foot back on the plantation. "Where is Mr. River? We could have used him here this afternoon."

Treasure glanced to Eliza and found her looking back. They stared at each other in silence.

She's wondering if we are lovers.

Eliza kept watching her, head cocked to one side, puzzling, eyes narrowing, gauging Treasure's response to her husband's question. Her expression soon changed from questioning to one of resolution. She smiled reassuringly.

Treasure felt Eliza's maternal understanding and would have been grateful except for the nagging knowledge that Eliza and Donovan harbored a secret. As a result she instead felt embarrassed and alone. Once, she could have confided all to Eliza. But the long-held trust between them had been breached by a chasm of suspicion that seemed too wide to bridge. Suddenly, she missed having a mother to talk with. Perhaps Aunt Valene . . .

"Where is my cousin?" she asked abruptly, avoiding Rader's query. "I would have expected him to be here to help."

Eliza's mouth pulled into a disapproving line. "Your aunt said he was called away on business. He left before all the trouble started."

"And a good thing my Ransom did." Valene swayed

339

out onto the verandah, waving a lace fan against the stifling late-summer air. "I trust it's safe for the ladies now? Treasure my dear, I'm so terribly appalled you had to return to such difficulties." Valene reached down and patted her niece's hand.

"It's quite all right, Aunt Valene. I should have guessed it would come to a confrontation sooner or later. Ira Stanton must be desperate after the rebellion at Gold Meadow to try such a thing, though."

"Stanton isn't the only one feelin' desperate." Rader shifted uncomfortably in his chair. "Most of the valley agrees with him about the lumbering project. They had a meeting about it while you were in Savannah."

"Don't fret over it, Treasure," Eliza put in. "Donovan won't allow anyone to force you away from Rose of Heaven."

Valene waved her fan with vigor. "Treasure doesn't need that man to do anything for her. My Ransom, when he returns, will settle this whole matter in a civilized fashion."

"I'm quite capable of fighting my own battles, Aunt Valene," Treasure said firmly. "I shouldn't think of troubling Ransom."

"It will be no trouble at all, my dear. My Ransom is a brilliant attorney. Why, he'll take care of Colonel Stanton and find a way to make nonsense of Mr. River's ludicrous claims to Rose of Heaven in short time. He is workin' on it this very minute."

"I don't recall asking for Ransom's assistance where Mr. River is concerned." The edge in Treasure's voice betrayed her tiredness and sense of despair.

"I asked him to use his expertise to help you rid yourself of that intruder. My Ransom is sharp as a tack, especially with matters pertainin' to contracts and such." Valene smiled indulgently. "You just get used to bein' taken care of by Ransom. Once you're married, he'll resolve all these annoyin' details and free you from the burdensome responsibility of runnin' a plantation."

Treasure flushed under the astonished stares of Rader and Eliza. "Aunt Valene—I haven't agreed to marry Ransom. And even if we were to wed, I don't intend to allow him, or any man, to take over Rose of Heaven. It is my plantation. I will stay its mistress."

"You don't know what you're sayin', my dear. You're naturally overwrought." Valene's smile dimmed. "The whole valley is against you. Why, to stay here would be madness. There's no tellin' what those heathens will subject you to next. The best thing you can do for your sisters and yourself is marry my Ransom and let him and me—"

"I'm sure you're quite tired, honey," Eliza interrupted. "Why don't you let me help you to bed?"

"Thank you, Miss Eliza," Treasure said, relieved at the respite. "I am tired. But I can manage alone. If you will all excuse me."

Eliza stood with her. "I insist. You shouldn't have to manage alone after such a long journey."

The slight emphasis Eliza put to her last word unearthed Treasure's uneasiness. But aware of the scrutiny of her aunt and Rader, she decided there was no way gracefully to avoid a confrontation with Eliza. With a curt nod and a weary heart, she strode into the house.

Halfway up the staircase, Eliza stopped Treasure with a hand on her arm. "When is he coming back?"

"Why does it matter to you?"

They faced off in a silent duel of wills.

At last Eliza broke the quiet with a sigh. "I'll tell you what I can. First, no matter what you may believe, Donovan is worthy of your trust—and your love. And secondly—" She bit uncertainly at her lower lip, then plunged ahead. "Treasure, everyone has to follow the dictates of their conscience, no matter what the cost. I've done nothin' to be ashamed of and certainly nothin' to betray our friendship. Donovan and I . . . we share a common interest. Nothing more."

Treasure clenched her hands in frustration. "You haven't told me a thing!"

"I can't!" Eliza burst out. "I have my reasons, honey. I just wish you could understand." She smiled ruefully. "As much as I love you, Treasure, you must realize you're not always the easiest person to confide in."

Flinching inwardly, Treasure kept her voice level. "Yes, I'm beginning to realize that. But it doesn't change the fact that you've sided with Donovan from the beginning, even though he was a stranger and you knew he was trying to take Rose of Heaven. And you're still defending him. If you would only tell me why . . ." Her words trailed off on a plea.

Eliza looked agonized. "I—I can't. I promised Donovan I would—"

"Help him betray me?"

"Treasure!"

"I'm sorry, Eliza." Treasure closed her eyes, rubbing her fingers against her temples. "I know you think you're doing what is best, but I'm so tired of questions without answers. Now, if you will excuse me, I do thank you and Rader for coming, but I'm exhausted." She started up the stairs again, alone.

"Treasure, wait." Eliza followed a few steps. "Do you intend to marry Ransom Ellis?"

"That's my business."

"Don't be forced into making a mistake like that. Ransom Ellis isn't your man and you know it. You're in love with Donovan. It's as plain as mornin' to everyone around, even if your stubborn heart won't admit it."

"Then everyone is wrong, Mrs. Johnson." With that, Treasure practically ran up the rest of the stairs to her room, slamming the door closed on the hurtful truth.

Late that afternoon, after uneasy fits of waking and

sleep filled with dreams of Donovan holding her, loving her, Treasure gave up trying to rest.

She dressed and headed straight to the barn to survey the damage. Elijah, his arms and legs covered in soot, was busy sorting through the charred rubbish. Several other slaves were shoveling up blackened refuse and piling it on the cart to be hauled away.

"Is there anything left worth saving?" Treasure asked him.

"Precious little, Miss Treasure. We did manage to save 'bout half the stock. The rest . . ." Elijah shook his head.

"Who did this? You and I both know it was not an accident."

Before he answered, Elijah glanced around to the other slaves nearby. Treasure noticed they'd stopped working and were staring hard at Elijah.

"Elijah?"

"I heard Mastuh Stanton had a hand in it. But maybe that's just talk."

"I rather doubt it," Treasure said with a scowl. She noticed the slaves still slanting her sidelong glances as they started poking at the remains of the barn again. "What is wrong?"

"They're afraid," Elijah answered, his eyes fixed on the darkening horizon.

"Of what?"

"I was told some of the men last night took a whip to a few of them and said they best get used to the taste of it 'cause they'd soon be workin' for the colonel." Elijah scuffed at the rubble under his feet, glancing to the sunset again. "I wouldn't pay it too much mind, Miss Treasure. Things will be back to usual here in a few days. If you'll excuse me, miss, I need to get this finished 'fore evening sets in."

Thinking Elijah seemed uncharacteristically hurried, Treasure sent him off with a nod. Yet it wasn't just Elijah. She'd been gone for weeks, but it seemed a lifetime. Something subtle had invaded, changed Rose of Heaven, made everything different.

Or is it me? Am I different?

She realized with a mix of pain and trepidation the answer might be yes.

Treasure sat on a fallen beam and surveyed the ruins long after Elijah and the rest of the slaves had returned to the compound for supper. Lost in thought, she idly tossed bits of wood into the ashes, her eyes fixed on the swirls of ebony dust they stirred to life. She didn't hear the footsteps stalking closer until a cloud blocked the last waning glow of the sun.

She glanced up and started. Donovan, dressed in black, his hat pulled low, towered over her. Twilight shadow masked his face.

Treasure shot to her feet. Her first glad impulse was to throw her arms around his neck and confess the sudden warm happiness in her heart. But something about the tense stance of his body, the implied menace of his silence, kept her quiet.

"A slap in the face would have been a kinder farewell," he said at last, his voice steel.

"I — I was giving you the chance you've surely been waiting for," Treasure faltered, hating her own weakness. Yet she couldn't quell the apprehension snaking up her spine.

"Were you? And what golden opportunity did you have in mind for me when you left my bed before sunrise?"

"Don't pretend you haven't wanted to leave all this behind," she said, waving a hand to the ashes around them. "Why did you come back?"

"I nearly didn't. But I don't remember your signing ownership papers for me. I'm free to leave whenever I wish."

"Then why haven't you? In Savannah . . ." She swallowed hard. "In Savannah you had the perfect opportunity."

"Who told you I wanted to leave Rose of Heaven?"

Treasure stumbled for a moment, not sure how to answer. "You've made it clear you don't care for duty and responsibility. I've sensed your restlessness."

"How perceptive of you." His mocking tone taunted her. "Tell me, Miss McGlavrin, what did you *sense* when we made love? What did I feel when I learned every inch of your body, when we—"

"Stop it!" Treasure scraped the tatters of her composure around her. "I don't wish to discuss that. It was a mistake. An error in judgment."

Donovan roughly caught her shoulders in his hands. "An error in judgment? Is that how you've rationalized what happened between us?" He gave her a shake. "You aren't dealing with the cold figures in a ledger now. This is the way we feel—the way you feel."

Trembling, Treasure tried to pull away. "You're hurting me. Let me go."

"Not until you stop lying to yourself and to me. You know what we shared was real. It mattered as much to you as it did to me and I'm not letting you go until you admit it!" Donovan's fingers tightened on her soft flesh. "Say it, Treasure. Say you want me, say you care."

"It doesn't matter if I do!" Treasure cried. Donovan suddenly stood very still, his eyes boring into hers. Treasure sucked in a breath. "What we did was wrong. We're wrong for each other. What we—what I feel has nothing to do with what is reasonable."

Donovan released her shoulders and jerked her against his chest. "Who the hell cares whether it's reasonable, pretty lady?"

Treasure leaned into him, relishing the feel of his powerful arms supporting her. "I care. I should care," she murmured.

"Care about this," he said, teasing his tongue over her ear. "Care about the way we feel when we're together. When I touch you . . ." His mouth sought hers in a long, rapacious kiss.

Treasure matched his hunger, letting all her agony at their separation, all her loneliness, pour away under his passionate assault. "We're still a lost cause, you know," she said when they parted.

"Lost causes are my passion," he said, moving to cup her face gently in his palms. "That's why you, Treasure McGlavrin, are my passion. Now and always." With that he swept her off her feet into his arms and captured her mouth in a kiss so slow, so tender, that for a timeless moment nothing else mattered but the precious exchange of emotion: kiss for kiss, touch for touch, need for need.

"What are you doing?" she managed when he swung around and began carrying her away from the ruined barn.

"Going to the cabin. You owe me an apology, remember?" he teased, nuzzling her neck. "I have a few suggestions on how you can persuade me to forgive you."

"I . . . I can't. The family will be expecting me for dinner," she said in lame argument.

"I'll make sure you don't stay hungry."

"Donovan—please." Treasure wasn't certain if she was asking him to set her down or take her to his cabin and do everything his eyes promised.

Donovan sighed. "Still hiding from me, aren't you, pretty lady? All right, all right." He stilled her fresh protests by gently lowering her to her feet. "I'll strike a bargain with you. I'll let you hurry off and appease your family if you tell me you'll have dinner with me later—alone."

The warmth in his gaze and his roguish smile crumbled her resistance. "You win, Mr. River," she said, laughing. "I have to stop off at the compound and check with Elijah about finishing this cleanup and then . . ."

346

"I'll do that for you," Donovan said quickly. He gave an offhand shrug at her questioning look. "I need to talk to him anyway. It'll save you the trouble."

Treasure's eyes narrowed with suspicion. "If you were the kind of man to keep secrets, I would think you were trying to get rid of me, Donovan River."

"Of course I'm not. So what the hell happened here?" he asked, slipping her hand in his as they walked toward the slaves' quarters.

Momentarily baffled, Treasure dismissed the previous line of conversation as swiftly as Donovan had. She had no desire to spoil the fragile peace between them. Not now.

When they reached Elijah's cabin at the far end of the second row of slave quarters, Donovan turned to her and said loudly, "Look, Elijah's probably in the slaves' kitchen, helping with supper. Let's try there first."

"Why are you practically shouting?"

"Me? I wasn't sure you could hear me over all the clanging and singing. Suppertime can get pretty noisy."

"Really?" Treasure arched a brow.

"What other reason could there be?"

Panic surged through Treasure's veins like water from melted snow, so cold it burned. "I have no idea." Her hand reached for the handle of Elijah's door. "Do I?"

"Treasure . . ."

She grabbed the doorknob and flung it wide. The scene before her, the culmination of her worst nightmares, shot through her heart as sure and painful as a bullet.

Clutching her unbuttoned dress to bare breasts, Spring stared at her in stunned shock. "Oh, no . . ."

Beside her Elijah yanked on a pair of breeches to cover his nakedness and flew to his feet. Protectively, he pulled Spring to him, sheltering her in his arms.

Donovan reached out a hand to Treasure to comfort,

to restrain — she didn't know which. "Don't touch me," she jerked out, shoving his hand aside. "You knew. All along. You knew." She whirled to Elijah. "And you. I trusted you. I thought we understood each other." Treasure curled her nails into her palm so hard they drew blood. "Spring, come with me. Now."

"No, Treasure. This is where I belong." Spring pulled up her dress, standing tall, her small hand in Elijah's. "I'm sorry you had to find out like this."

"We love each other, Miss Treasure," Elijah said.

"That's impossible!"

"Of course it's not," Spring said. "Treasure, try to understand. I've loved Elijah for months, almost since he came to Rose of Heaven. And now — now I'm carrying his child. We're going to be married."

"God in heaven." Treasure put a shaking hand to her face. "How could this happen? How could you do this, either of you?"

Donovan's dark voice answered her. "Perhaps it just happened to them. Sometimes love is unexpected."

Treasure whirled on him. "You knew. You encouraged this from the start, didn't you?"

"No, but when I did find out, I knew I didn't have a right to stop it. And neither do you."

"You and your damned Yankee notions. Don't you realize how impossible this situation is?"

"Donovan had nothing to do with it," Spring said. She was calm now, resolute. Treasure hardly knew the woman before her. "And it only seems impossible to you."

"Come home with me, Spring. Please."

"So you can send Elijah to the auction block and me to one of those butchers who'll kill our child? No. I've made my choices already. Elijah is the only man I'll ever love. We're staying together no matter what."

"You're still a child, Spring," Treasure said, her voice shaking. "How can you know about love?"

"Oh, Treasure. Once you find the only man for you,

all of the other questions don't matter. Love is worth any price. I just hope you realize it before you lose your chance to understand it."

"I want to understand, but what you're doing breaks every law, every tradition we've lived by." Treasure held out her hands to her sister. "It's not only impossible, it's dangerous. No one will accept you, or your child. Surely you can see that. I don't want you hurt because you've made an impulsive choice."

Spring hesitated for a moment, her mouth trembling, eyes bright with unshed tears. She looked at Elijah. Then, straightening her shoulders, she faced Treasure with firm determination. "I chose Elijah. There was nothing impulsive about it. If you can't accept it, the choice is yours."

Treasure looked at her, her heart torn.

"I'm sorry, Treasure. I love you. I wish . . . I wish you could know how we feel."

"I love you too, Spring. So much that I want to spare you all the grief and pain this decision will surely bring." She forced back the anguish bringing hot tears to her eyes and swallowed hard. "What will you do?"

Spring glanced at Elijah. "We can't stay in the valley. We'll leave, go north, as soon as — as soon as we can. Until then . . ."

"You can stay at my cabin," Donovan said. He stared hard at Treasure. "I'm sure your sister won't object."

"No." Treasure's voice was barely above a whisper. "I can't just turn you out. You're still my sister. Oh, Spring . . ." Tears trembled on her lashes, threatening to spill over.

As a single teardrop slid down her face, Treasure turned and fled the cabin. Alone in the concealing darkness, she hugged her arms around her trembling body, a single prayer in her heart. *Please, Lord, keep them safe. If you can't bring Spring home, then keep them safe.*

Chapter Eighteen

"I need your help."

Treasure started and her fingers let go of the fork she held. Silver clanked against china, the only sound in the suddenly silent dining room.

Donovan stood in the doorway, sweat dripping from his brow, rasping for air. His fingers rapped impatiently against the frame. "I don't have time for your usual spell of contemplation." At his heels, Bonnie echoed his volatile mood, panting and pacing beside him.

Valene set her wineglass down with a snap. "Mr. River, you cannot just come burstin' in here—"

"This is important." Donovan, ignoring Valene, stared directly at Treasure.

Treasure gauged the expression in his eyes. Glancing about the table, she met grim disapproval from Valene, lively interest on the faces of Emmy and the twins. Camille yawned.

"Maybe Spring has come home," Emmy piped up, her eyes alight with hope. She, of all her sisters, most missed Spring's cheering presence, Treasure thought with a pang.

"She wouldn't dare," Valene began.

Treasure warded off Emmy's indignant defense of Spring by pushing back her chair. "I will only be a moment," she said, offering her aunt an apologetic smile.

"Good. Then we shall hold supper until you return," Valene called after her.

Donovan was already striding toward the front foyer when she stepped into the hallway. "You might at least tell me what is so important you must interrupt supper," she said, a little breathless from having to fairly run to catch up to him. "If you think I am just going to follow you blindly without any sort of explanation . . ."

Donovan whirled on her so quickly Treasure stumbled back a step. The steel in his eyes quelled any sharp retort she might have mustered. "Eliza is ill. And your sister is in trouble. If you have any feeling for them hidden in the lock box you keep around your heart, then I suggest you keep your questions for later and come with me."

Without waiting for her answer, he turned and walked out the door.

"Eliza? And Spring? But . . ." Treasure grasped for answers as she hurried to keep stride with him. But she couldn't purge a nervous ripple of fear. She'd only seen Spring and Elijah twice since the day she discovered their secret, and the meetings had been strained.

Treasure tried to console herself by reaffirming that she had done the right and reasonable thing in not accepting her sister's decision. Hadn't she?

Then why does my heart torment me at every turn? Why do my instincts side with them, prodding me to accept their love for each other?

Spring met them at the door to Donovan's cabin. Ghostly pale, her dark eyes dulled, she glanced once at Treasure before turning to Donovan. "Are you sure this is safe? If anyone should find us . . ." She whispered the words into the night, as if afraid of being overheard.

351

"No one will." Donovan rubbed his knuckles against her cheek. "I'm an incurable romantic. I insist on a happy ending."

The small smile he provoked quickly vanished. "Miss Eliza is very ill." For the first time, she looked fully at her sister and Treasure read the plea in her eyes. "I know you can't help Elijah and me, but we'll be gone soon and Miss Eliza is your friend. For her sake, could you stay?"

"Gone?" Treasure looked from Spring to Donovan. "Where?"

"Oh, what does it matter!" Spring cried. "You can't care. It's what you want."

"I do care. All I ever wanted was for you to have a secure, respectable life," Treasure said, trying to put her feelings into words. "But I couldn't give that to you."

"Because it was what you wanted, not what I wanted! I don't want to be safe and respectable! I don't want to be like you. You're so afraid of love. But I want to love. And I love Elijah. You can't change that, Treasure, no matter how hard you want to reason it away. Nothing will ever change it. Ever."

Swiping at an overflow of tears, Spring turned and ran into the cabin. Helpless, Treasure watched her go. She took a step in her sister's wake, but Donovan's hand stopped her. "Before you go in, I must tell you something." He paused, shoving a hand through his hair, then blurted out the explanation as if saying it quickly would make it more acceptable to her. "Spring and Elijah are leaving for Boston tonight. Eliza arranged it. She planned to see them safely away, until the swelling in her legs started. You know she's not a young woman, and this baby means everything to her."

"Baby!" Treasure gaped at him. "Eliza is expecting?"

352

"Yes, she is. Even so, it was no easy task to get her off her feet. Now, I'm taking her place. I need you to stay with her. And"—he drew a deep breath—"I realize you won't give them your blessing, but I need your promise you will at least give them a fighting chance to escape. All I'm asking for is your silence. You could see me hang for this, and Elijah too. But Spring is your sister. I'm gambling you will try at least to protect her."

Treasure put a trembling hand to her forehead, reeling from the shock of his admissions, not fully able to comprehend what he was telling her. "Boston . . . Miss Eliza is helping them . . ." She rallied her thoughts. "They aren't the first, are they? And you've been helping her. The night of the revolt at Gold Meadow when I found you two—"

"Eliza was hiding several of Stanton's runaways here. It wasn't the first time. She knows my brother. When I arrived in the valley and she discovered I shared her feelings about slavery, she bullied me into abetting her. We were meeting—here, in the clearing."

"Does Rader know?"

"No." Donovan shoved a hand through his hair. "Or maybe he's guessed and loves Eliza too much to betray her. I don't know."

"Why couldn't you tell me? Were you so certain I would betray you, both of you?"

"I was certain of nothing. So I said nothing."

Treasure couldn't meet his incisive gaze. "I don't know." *Give them the chance you may never have, to love, to be free—stop them! It's all wrong. It's dangerous. This union can't be. Donovan, Eliza, all of them lied.* "The letters, from your brother . . ." Treasure glared at Donovan with accusing eyes.

"You read them?"

Lifting her chin, Treasure set aside a twinge of guilt. "Yes. You wouldn't tell me the truth."

353

"I couldn't. Not then."

"It doesn't matter. Spring is all that matters to me now. Will your brother help ensure she and Elijah find a safe haven?"

Donovan nodded. "Jared lives in Boston. He'll find a place for Spring and Elijah. And he is acquainted with Robert Purvis, the president of the underground railroad. My brother is one of Eliza's Northern contacts. When he enlightened her as to my presence here, she made it a point to recruit me."

"The underground railroad . . ." Treasure closed her eyes. "Eliza's cause that is worth keeping secrets for. Does she—do you?—realize what will happen if you are discovered?"

"I'd rather not dwell on it," Donovan said with a faint echo of his usual humor.

"You're risking your life for Spring, for Elijah, for people you don't even know, for a cause even many Northerners doubt. Why? Why would you do it?"

"Because I have to. Because I feel it's right. Because it's dangerous and damned near impossible and I can't resist the odds." He put his hands on her shoulders, compelling her to meet his steady gaze. "Because I'm like Spring, I believe in love."

Treasure shook her head. She wanted to believe he and Miss Eliza were on Satan's errand. But again, Donovan's courage and passionate dedication moved her to unwilling admiration. And seeing Spring again, her heart began to rebel in earnest. All her beliefs, the acceptances of a lifetime—could they be wrong?

Everything I've trusted to help me make the right choices. Am I wrong?

Donovan's hands tightened. "I have to know. Will you keep your silence? It's the only thing I'm asking. For Miss Eliza, for Spring."

"For you." The words were a vow she hadn't intended to make. She stepped away from him, knowing from the expression on his face that it was too late to draw back. "All of you. You have my promise."

"Treasure . . ."

"Where is Miss Eliza?"

He didn't answer at once. Instead, he raised a hand and gently tipped her face to his. "You know, sometimes we both make it harder than it is." Treasure's slight frown questioned him, but Donovan shook his head, his only reply a small rueful smile. Holding her with his touch, he kissed her mouth, a tender, lingering caress. She felt a sadness in him, maybe a regret, that aroused an answering softness in her heart. When he released her, it was reluctantly, as if the effort cost him. "Thank you," he said, and turned to lead her into the cabin before she could think of anything to say.

In the dimly lit back room of the cabin, Spring and Elijah were hovering near Eliza, who was lying on Donovan's bed, propped against several pillows. When she spied Treasure hesitating in the doorway, she managed a wan smile. "I knew you would come," she said. "I told Donovan he should have trusted you from the beginning."

"I'm sure I would spare myself endless grief if I let you make all my decisions for me," Donovan said.

Behind him, Elijah made a restless movement. "Mastuh River, we don't have the night to waste. Are you sure—No disrespect, Miss Treasure, but are you set on lettin' us leave here?"

Treasure met his steady gaze without flinching. "I won't stop you. I don't agree with your decision, but I won't force Spring into a life she can't abide."

Joyous gratitude leaped into Spring's eyes. Treasure held her sister's gaze for a long moment.

"Thank you," Spring whispered.

Not trusting her voice to stay steady, Treasure nodded. To hide the turmoil of emotion in her heart, she

355

turned to Eliza. The older woman was ghostly pale, a damp sheen on her brow.

Treasure knelt down by the bed. "I'm very happy about the baby. But I'm sorry you're so ill. If there's anything I can do. . . . You must go home and rest."

"Don't fuss, now. The swelling will pass. It has to. I surely don't have time to spare. The wagon will be here for Spring and Elijah soon." Eliza reached down to rub her legs.

"I'll have Bettis bring the carriage around for you as soon as you feel up to moving," Treasure said firmly.

"You'll have to trust me to see it through," Donovan told her, giving her a smile intended to reassure. "I do believe I can manage this once without you."

"I've no doubt you can, honey. You're an apt pupil."

Spring, in the midst of gathering up a small carpetbag and pulling on her mantle, paused and turned to Treasure. Her teeth worried her lower lip. "Treasure — if you'll allow it, I'd like to say goodbye. To Emmy, and the twins. And Camille. It may be a long time . . ." She stopped and looked at Elijah, tears suddenly welling in her eyes.

Aware they all turned to her in expectation, Treasure stood, willing herself not to flinch away. "If Emmy and the twins discovered why you are leaving . . ." She couldn't finish. How could she tell Spring, all of them, she didn't dare risk letting her younger sisters foster the notion Spring's decision was in any way right, or even romantic. She had failed to keep Spring safe. She couldn't bear to lose Emmy or the twins, even Camille, in the same manner.

"Please." Spring's features twitched with her effort to control her tears. "I won't tell them anything. I just need a few moments."

"I don't think anyone could deny you that,"

356

Donovan answered for Treasure. His eyes locked with hers and Treasure felt the struggle of wills between them. She wanted to stand strong against him, but her heart turned traitor, abandoning her with cold reason as her only ally. And a poor ally it was.

"I can't." She turned to Spring. "Of course you can see them. I will go with you. And I'll have Bettis send some of his willowbark tea to Eliza."

Treasure turned and strode out the door. After a pause, she heard Spring's light tread behind her. They walked in silence up to the front door of the big house. Treasure wasn't surprised to see Emmy, flanked by Eura Mae and the twins, on the doorstep. Camille stood behind them, strangely subdued. Valene, thankfully, had apparently refused to join the waiting vigil.

Seeing her sister, Emmy flung herself at Spring, hugging her tightly. "She's sending you away. Oh, I know she is. Please don't go! I don't want you to go."

Spring stroked Emmy's hair, her face tender. "No one is sending me away. But I have to leave. For a little while. Just for a little while." She softly crooned the words, as if they were said as much to comfort her own anguish as Emmy's.

Her throat tight, Treasure stood a little aside. *If they are wrong, if I'm right—Dear Lord, I pray their foolhardy notions of love will protect them and carry them to safety.*

Gently disengaging herself from Emmy, Spring kissed her sister, then gathered the tearful twins in her arms. She squeezed both of them. When she let them go, Erin hung back a moment longer than Abby. "Here." She stuck out her chubby palm and offered Spring a chip of rose-colored quartz, slightly sticky with chocolate residue. "It's the best one I ever found. It's lucky."

Spring nodded, looking as if she didn't trust herself

to speak. She touched a hand to Erin's copper curls, then kissed her forehead before turning to Camille. Erin crawled into Camille's arms.

"You best take care of yourself, you little idiot," Camille said. "I surely don't intend to come to your rescue."

"Nor I to yours," Spring said, hugging her close.

At last, she pulled away and drew a deep breath before turning to Treasure. "I'm ready."

From out of the thick, pitch gloom, Donovan suddenly materialized at her side before Treasure could muster the voice to speak. "The wagon is waiting."

Spring nodded. With a final glance and wave for her sisters, she followed him down the long drive, Treasure shadowing them behind.

She watched Spring put her carpetbag into the back where Elijah waited. When Spring looked back at her, Treasure tried to find the words to send her sister away. "I wish I could understand," she said finally. Even to her own ears, she sounded lost. "You're giving up everything: your home, your family, your future. How will you bear it? How can you survive the hardships?"

A tiny smile lifted Spring's mouth. She shook her head and took Treasure's hands in hers. "That's what love is for." For a brief moment, she pressed her cheek to her sister's.

The warm sweetness of Spring's tears dampened her own face before Spring broke their embrace. She climbed onto the front seat of the wagon beside Donovan and glanced back at Treasure. "I think you're the hardest to leave," Spring said. "Because I'm just beginning to believe you care the most."

Spring's face was the last she saw melting into the darkness as Donovan set the wagon in motion. Long after the three of them disappeared down the road, Treasure stood looking after them.

And alone in the emptiness of the night, she let the tears come. Not in a gentle release, but in great, wrenching sobs until she sank to her knees in the dew-damp grass. Sorrow engulfed her, drowning every voice but one—the conviction of her heart telling her that everything she believed about right and wrong ceased to matter when it came to love.

"This is really the most dreadful weather." Valene fanned herself vigorously. The air in the parlor was still and hung heavy as if the waning summer days were determined to last until the first hour of fall. "I do not know how you can tolerate walking the fields all day, Treasure. It seems to me a most unsuitable task for someone of your station."

Treasure stepped into the parlor and tossed her straw hat on a chair. In the past week, since Spring and Elijah's departure and Donovan's revelations, she had pushed herself harder than ever, working her fingers, her body, past exhaustion to a state of numbness where she had no energy left to worry, to regret, to cry.

She'd seen nothing of Donovan, knew only that he'd returned two days ago. Without him, an oppressive silence seemed to enclose Rose of Heaven, worsened by the relentless heat. Spring's leaving, Donovan's conspicuous absence, left a lifeless void. The unnatural quiet of it plagued her nerves like an omen of still before the fire storm.

Realizing her aunt impatiently awaited a response, Treasure pulled her thoughts back to the present. "This should be the last hot spell," she said, taking one of the bolls she had just picked out of the pocket of her soil-spattered dress to examine it. She plucked a small white bunch of cotton from the open capsule and pulled and twisted it between her fingertips.

"You're positively ruinin' your hands, Treasure. Let the buyers take care of that."

"I need to see how far I can push my price," Treasure said absently. When she'd lined the fibers, smooth and even between her fingers, she smiled. "At least an inch and snowy white. Papa was right to switch from blackseed to Mexican. These bolls spread open so wide, my best pickers ought to pull in two hundred pounds a day. We'll tag the healthiest, most top-heavy stalks for the next seeding."

"Really, my dear, that is not woman's work. Come, sit a spell. Help me with the knittin' instead."

"Honestly, Aunt Valene, I appreciate the concern. But we're ready to take in the first picking on the crop Papa and I planted before . . . that is, the one we planted last season. I have to watch constantly to be sure they harvest the right bolls. And then there's the ginning—"

"But it will take most all your profit just to settle the rest of Seamus's horrid debts, or so my Ransom tells me," Valene interrupted, her tone suddenly impatient. "I surely do not mean to pry into your affairs, Treasure dear, but is this awful struggle really worth your continued effort?"

Treasure clenched the sides of her dirty skirts, but kept her face impassive. "Rose of Heaven is my life."

"My dear." Valene slowly shook her head. "McGlavrin's Valley is languishin' before your very eyes. The people in town are hardly your fondest admirers. They'd like nothin' better than to drive you away. Your sisters are unhappy, indulging in the most unsuitable behavior. And Rose of Heaven is hardly the plantation your papa left behind. Why continue to carry this burden? You cannot possibly be content living in hardship."

"I am content doing what Papa would have wanted me to do," Treasure said. Her aunt's words scraped tender nerves because she recognized the truth in them. At the same time, a militant fire kindled her pride in what she'd accomplished. She drew a breath, intending to explain to Valene, but the plod of hooves against the drive drew her aunt's attention to the open windows.

"It's my Ransom," Valene said, her smile brilliant. "My, he looks quite grim. I do hope his business went well."

Quickly gathering up the tufts of cotton she'd scattered, Treasure tried to stem the panic suddenly threatening her calm assurance. She and Ransom hadn't spoken since she'd left on the journey to Savannah. Now that he was returning, she knew he would expect an answer to his proposal. A pang of guilt accompanied the realization that she had effortlessly dismissed the question of marriage from her mind. Donovan elicited the most disturbing and unforgettable longings in her; all at once it mattered terribly that Ransom could never do the same.

He came into the parlor, shedding hat and stick, greeting them with polite affection. When he had appeased his mother's demand for details about his travels and business successes, he turned to Treasure. "If Mama will excuse us for a time, I should like to discuss a matter of importance with you, cousin."

"Why, of course, Ransom dear." Valene beamed at them, and Treasure felt slightly sick with embarrassment and disquiet. "I shouldn't think of intruding."

Ransom saw Valene to the door. Closing it behind her, he came and sat next to Treasure on the settee. "It is not my intention to distress you in any way, Treasure."

Treasure frowned. Distress her? Had he guessed there was more to her hesitation over his proposal than she had confided? "I would never think that of you."

"You may," he said, "once I tell you the nature of my business in New Orleans."

"New Orleans?" Confusion overtook her. "I thought you were going to Atlanta on business."

Ransom took off his pince-nez and polished them vigorously with his handkerchief. "So I said. But my true intention was to go to New Orleans."

"Whatever for?"

"To look into the background of Mr. Donovan River."

"Donovan . . ." Treasure stared at him. "Perhaps you had better explain this business. I don't see Mr. River's background is any concern of yours."

"I made it my concern because you are concerned with him."

Treasure's mouth drew into a tight line. "I see."

"No, you do not. I suppose you will term it interfering, but I did it because I care ever so much for you, and I cannot abide your association with that man."

"My association with Mr. River is my affair," Treasure said shortly.

"I am afraid, cousin, any association you have with him is a lie." Ransom's small green eyes looked hard at her from behind his spectacles. "Because, my dear, Donovan River does not exist."

Treasure shoved open the door to Donovan's cabin, not bothering to knock, not caring what or who she found inside this time.

Donovan sat at his desk, propped back in a chair. Bare-chested, long legs wrapped in snug black trousers, heavy black boots crossed at the ankles atop his table: he looked every inch the low-life river rat Ransom had so aptly described. And when he looked up, his eyes bore the glazed dispassion of a man without conscience.

362

He raised a brow. "Do come in, Miss McGlavrin. Care for a drink?" He held up the near-empty bottle of bourbon.

Treasure swallowed her fear. "I'd care for the truth." She marched up to him, her anger matching his lazy impertinence. "I want to know about New Orleans. I want to know who you are. I want to know what you're doing here and what happened to my papa."

"Cousin Ransom must be home," Donovan drawled, rocking his chair back on two legs to glance out the window. "And making a fantastic guess, I'd say he brought you home a few tidbits of unsavory news about me and my black past. How thorough your legal advisor is."

"Is he telling the truth?"

"Probably." He dropped a hand to scratch Bonnie's ears. Beneath him, the dog looked up and wagged her scraggly tail.

Treasure stared at him, frustration tying her hands into knots at her side. She wanted to scream and shake him, to force him to tell her the truth she so desperately needed to hear. When Ransom told her what he'd learned in Louisiana, she didn't want to believe it, even though she chided herself for not guessing before now. But she had to hear Donovan say it. Something compelled her to run to him; something small inside hoped he would deny it.

Her whole body trembled with the force of the battle raging inside her: reason against emotion. She lowered herself to a seat opposite him. "He said . . ." Drawing a deep breath, she started again. "He said a man named Donovan River showed up in New Orleans nearly two years ago, a man with no past, nothing to prove he ever existed. He said you—he—made a life of gambling and frequenting the brothels, and that you spent a month's time in prison for assaulting a man. He said . . ." She closed her eyes. "He said

363

witnesses told him you pushed Papa off a hotel balcony to make sure you got Rose of Heaven."

Donovan kicked away from the table and walked over to the window. His face, half in shadow, was unreadable. "An interesting tale."

"And?"

"And what?"

"Is it true?"

Donovan raked a hand through his hair. "I never claimed to be a saint."

"But—but . . ."

"But what? Did I get myself thrown in jail? Yes. And I'd do it again. I tossed some bastard over the railing of a riverboat because he was literally beating the life out of a fancy girl who had ceased to give him pleasure. And no, I didn't kill your papa. You want the truth? Seamus fell off that damned balcony because he was too sick and too drunk to know what the hell he was doing."

Treasure felt the blood drain from her face and rush to her feet so quickly she nearly swooned. "It's not true."

"It is."

"Who are you?" she whispered.

He spoke slowly, as if every admission were forced from him at great cost. "I left my name behind in Boston. Along with a lot of other things. River seemed Southern enough for Louisiana."

"Louisiana. And now here. Where else? How many hotels, and brothels, and gambling dens? And how many more?"

"I can't answer that. I don't know. Maybe there won't be any more. Treasure . . ." He turned to her and stretched out a tentative hand.

"Don't." Treasure managed to get to her feet. There's something I have to tell you."

Donovan was suddenly still, his face frozen.

"I'm going to marry Ransom."

The fleeting expression in his eyes seared her. She would never forget it: pain, despondency, the look of the damned.

And then it was gone and he was lost to her, a stranger treating her with stiff politeness. "Congratulations. You're finally getting what you've said you've always wanted." His gaze sharpened along with his tone. "I only hope it satisfies you."

"Donovan, I . . ." She didn't know what she intended to say. What she wanted him to tell her. "I must go."

"Of course." He turned his back to her.

She let herself take one long look at him before leaving, quietly closing the door behind her.

She had made the only decision she could, for Rose of Heaven, for her sisters, for the future. Ransom would be a respectable husband, a willing and able partner. That she had made the choice in anger and hurt didn't alter the fact it was a responsible and proper choice. Donovan River was as she had always feared, a dangerous rover who only saw Rose of Heaven as the stake in another gamble. They had no future. Nothing that could last.

Only a past she couldn't forget. Only feelings between them she couldn't erase. Only the heart she had left behind when she walked away from him.

She had thought the decision would bring her peace, if not happiness. Instead, her insides went numb. Something cold and insidious crept up her veins, sapping her energy as it traversed her body. She felt doors slam shut in the attic of her mind, locking up the memories of all they had shared. Like sandstone in the rain, her heart melted away.

A wind whipped up as she neared the big house, pushing her back. Weakly, she paced against it until she reached the back porch. She stood there, gazing back toward Donovan's cabin, her eyes searching for the familiar light in his window.

But the golden flicker in his window, like the light in her heart, had faded to black.

Curled in the willow rocker, Treasure awoke realizing she must have taken refuge in the still dead of night. Her legs were stiff. Nothing but an erratic breeze moved in or outside the house. It was as if everyone had vanished, abandoning her to contemplate her aloneness. And behind the warm, black veil she found a certain melancholy comfort. It held her in secrecy, hid her from the pain she couldn't escape in the light. Here, no one could hurt her.

And she could hurt no one in return.

Treasure shifted a little in her chair, unable to completely banish a nagging disquiet that kicked up inside her at the same time the breeze began to gust to a fitful wind. It scattered specters of violet-gray clouds across the sliver of cold alabaster moon. A screech owl hooted, the shrill sound so eerie it shattered the silence like granite to glass.

Wrapping her arms around her knees, Treasure let her head droop against the back of the chair, deliberately forcing her taut limbs to relax. If only she could sleep more, for hours, for days. And then, tomorrow, or the tomorrow after, or in a hundred tomorrows, awake and find all the answers awaiting her. All the answers locked in her heart . . .

. . . she was having a nightmare.

In it, Ransom paced to and fro, berating her for betraying him. He carried a law book and shook it at her, lecturing on responsibility and loyalty.

She tried to explain, but it was hot, so hot his image

melted away into a smoky fog. The more she searched for him in the thickening mist, the farther away he seemed. Flames seemed to dance up around her, and through the fire, she saw Donovan, walking toward her, undaunted by the inferno. He offered his hand, but she was afraid to move. The fog grew denser. It was becoming hard even to draw a breath . . .

Treasure awoke with a snap, sitting straight up. The smell of smoke filled her nostrils. Scrambling off the rocker, she swept the area around her in a glance. It wasn't coming from the kitchen. "Oh, my Lord, not the house!" In the distance, a red hot glow in several downstairs windows confirmed her fear.

She darted across the yard to the back door. As she plunged inside, a searing blast of air slapped her face. Thick ashen smoke blinded her eyes. Her lungs rebelled against the onslaught, spewing it out in gasps and chokes. Shouting, peppered with the screams of her loved ones, tugged her deeper inside. Crazed with fear, she rushed down the hallway, nearly cannoning into Orange Jane. Bettis and Solomon flanked her, supporting her.

Bettis pushed a dazed Orange Jane toward the open doorway. "You best be gettin' outta de house. Mr. River's been near crazy tryin' to find you."

Treasure stared at him in disbelief. "I can't . . ." Stunned, she made an effort to shake off a paralyzing heart-fear. "The others—"

"Your cousin and his mama done took off fo' de valley." She followed him and helped the men set Orange Jane on the dew-misted lawn a safe distance from the house. "De smoke nearly done in Miz Eura Mae. She be lucky Solomon found her fainted on de stairs and drug her out. As fo' de rest, Mr. River gone back inside . . ."

For the first time, Treasure dared to turn and look back at Rose of Heaven. The scene before her dealt a blow so vicious, she felt it physically. It was as if she'd been brutally, mercilessly, struck down.

Flames licked up the southern wing of the house, eating away at the wood with a voracious appetite. Behind the big house, one of the barns was ablaze and farther still . . . A cry broke from Treasure's throat.

The fields, her precious crops, so long labored over, her only promise of a future, were now a vision of hell.

The fire crawled over her papa's two ripe cotton fields and now snaked its way into the biggest of the corn plots. The air wavered with intense heat. Scorching flames cast a nightmarish red glow, lighting the terror on the faces beside her.

"Look!"

Bettis's shout drew Treasure's attention to the front door. Donovan sprinted down the steps, half carrying, half dragging a sooty, bedraggled Camille. He left her near Orange Jane and, without a word, yanked Treasure into his arms. His hands moved roughly over her, as if he were assuring himself she was whole and unharmed.

Treasure threw her arms around him. He smelled of smoke and sweat. His frenzied breathing rose and fell in great heaves beneath her cheek. "Everyone is all right," she murmured. "Everyone—"

Cold fear shot over her. She jerked up, gripping his arms. "The twins. Emmy? Where are they?"

Donovan stared at her in confusion. "I thought they were here. I saw Eura Mae—God in heaven." He looked back at the house in sudden horror.

From somewhere inside the house, Abigail screamed.

Chapter Nineteen

Donovan and Treasure exchanged a horror-stricken glance. Treasure swung around, swiping furiously at her wet, stinging eyes.

"Emmy?" she screamed, "are you out there?"

"Over here. Safe, with Solomon," Emmy called back, her voice clear, her person obscured by smoke and the dark of night.

"I'm going back in," Donovan said.

"So am I. It's all my fault. My cursed determination to hold on to Rose of Heaven . . ."

For once her words were not a demand, but a desperate plea, and Donovan could not argue. "Stay close, then." He grabbed cloths Betis had doused in water and handed one to Treasure to cover her mouth.

They raced back into the inferno through a charred doorway. The black remnant of a door her papa had once called the perfect finish to his dream home, a door carved by his hand, hung askew on a single hinge. Quickly, cautiously, Treasure tried to match Donovan's step as they climbed over a smoldering fallen beam circumventing flaming tables and chairs. Donovan took one glance at the blazing stairway then shouted to her to head to the servants' stairs at the rear of the house.

At the base of the narrow stairwell he called back, "The heat is unbearable. Wait here."

The cloth clamped to her face, Treasure shook her head wildly and kept stumbling determinedly forward. A few steps behind him, she inched her way through the hallway partially blocked by a fallen portrait of her parents, its edges flaming and flaring out in all directions. Treasure jerked her eyes from the destruction. Later she would feel the pain. Now she must concentrate on finding the twins.

When she reached him, Donovan grabbed her hand and pulled her up the sweltering passageway two steps at a time to the second floor. Looking over his shoulder at her, he didn't see a silver sconce lying in the hallway. He tripped, ramming his hand against the wall to avert a fall. It felt like a branding iron searing his palm. He yelped and yanked his hand back, shaking it.

At once Treasure took the cloth from her face and wrapped his hand. Donovan pulled her close beneath the shelter of his arm, questioning, not for the first time, the madness of letting her come along. If anything happened to her—he shoved the thought away.

As they ran to the nursery door, Donovan shouted for the twins. Using both cloths as protection, he grabbed the door handle, jiggling it in vain. "They've locked the damn thing! Abby! Erin!" There was no answer. The smoke nearly blinded him. He couldn't be sure whether or not the room behind the door was ablaze. Glancing to Treasure's terrified face, he prayed the fire hadn't breached the wooden barrier. Donovan stepped back and rammed the door with his shoulder. Once. Twice. It took three times and all his weight to finally knock it off its sturdy hinges. A blast of heated smoke hit him in the face as he and Treasure dashed into the room.

Both girls sat huddled atop their toy chest at the

foot of the bed. "You're safe now," Donovan soothed as he swept Abby, coughing and choking on her tears, into his arms.

Erin reached out her hands toward Treasure, falling to the floor before Treasure could reach her. Her favorite doll rolled from her arms.

Fear shot through Treasure. "No, Erin!" She knelt beside the still child. "It's all right, sweetheart. I'm here," she crooned, her words choked by a fit of coughing. Treasure struggled to lift the limp little body in her arms.

"Give her to me," Donovan commanded.

"No—no, I have her." Treasure hugged her sister close. She stared at the doll a long moment, then gathered her wits and ran back out into the hallway.

Behind her, Donovan shifted Abby to one arm and bent to sweep up the homemade toy. In the hall, he met Treasure's eyes as they realized the full fury of the fire blazing toward them from the main stairs. Donovan made a quick decision. "The back stairs! Hurry!"

Halfway down, Donovan turned back and saw Treasure stagger against the railing. "Come on, pretty lady, we're almost out." Backtracking to her, he bent and caught an arm around her waist. The doll slipped through his fingers, catching fire instantly as it hit the live sparks strewn about the stairwell.

He supported her the rest of the way, cursing himself for ever letting her back inside this hell. When they at last reached the downstairs, one look told him that to retrace their steps to the front meant certain death. Instead he swung Treasure around toward the servants' door.

Treasure felt her strength faltering, but she kept a grip on Erin, determined to see her sister to safety. She no longer looked where they were headed or saw the raging flames around them. Her vision focused on

371

Donovan, on following him, step by step, out of the inferno. Inside, a part of her put all her trust in their escape on his resourcefulness and courage.

Donovan saw the blank expression in Treasure's eyes. "Just a little longer, pretty lady. A little longer." They rounded a corner, a few feet from the haven of the back lawn. Donovan's heart fell.

Fire ate at the door and most of the wall. Their only chance, slim at best, was through a window. Flames licked around the frames and shattered glass of each possible exit. Donovan herded Treasure and the twins toward the opening least consumed by the fire.

Frantically searching for something to break off the blazing remains of wood that had held the panes, he found only charred, red-hot scraps of wood and metal. Where was his damned gambler's luck when he most needed it? "Abby, hold on to my neck. Tight," he said, looking into the little girl's frightened face. He gripped her close against his chest and shoved his boot into the flames.

"Donovan, I—I can't breathe," Treasure rasped behind him. "And Erin . . ."

"Hold on, it's moving. One more—" Donovan kicked out hard and jolted the frame free. He grabbed Treasure and hoisted her and Erin through the still-smoldering opening, away from the flames.

Donovan plunged through after her, gulping air. He dragged Treasure and the twins away from the burning house. At last, surrounded by cool night breeze, free of the flames, Donovan collapsed on the ground beside Treasure, setting Abby gently down near him.

"They're safe," she whispered. "My babies are safe." She looked at him with an expression of wild relief and then fainted into his arms, carrying the motionless form of Erin with her.

Drenched in cold sweat, Treasure awoke in the pitch black of night. She sprung upright, awash in terror and confusion. "Help! Someone! Where are the babies? The twins?"

"Shhhh . . ." a deep voice soothed, "the fire is over." Treasure stared, still caught up in her nightmare, as Donovan jerked out of the chair near her bedside. He looked ravaged. He hadn't bothered to change and the white of his shirt was charred black in places. His right hand was swaddled in gauze to the wrist. His face was lined with exhaustion—and something she couldn't define. Something that frightened her.

She clutched his shoulders as he sat down next to her. "Where are my sisters? Tell me. Tell me they're safe."

Donovan shoved an unsteady hand through his hair. "Camille was distraught, hysterical. She insisted on getting away. Someone, Eura Mae I think, told me she went to Mobile to stay with her cousin—Patricia."

"Patricia?" Treasure stared blankly. "We don't have a cousin Patricia. Anywhere."

"I don't know. I've probably got it wrong. We'll straighten it out later."

"And the others?" She persisted, still uneasy over the look in his eyes. His voice faltered every now and then, and he seemed uncharacteristically shaken.

"They're in the valley staying with some people from the church."

"The valley! How could you! The valley did this. They wanted my land, my home. You, Ira Stanton, all of them."

"Treasure, listen to me." Donovan took her hands in his. "Stanton wanted to frighten you, but even he wouldn't be so stupid as to set this kind of fire. His tactic has been to turn the valley against you. And he was winning. Why would he jeopardize that?"

She put a hand to her whirling head. "I — I don't know. It doesn't matter now." Treasure felt dazed, beaten. "Ashes. It's all ashes now. I should have realized from the start it was an impossible dream."

It was over. The only thing that had ever given her a reason to be, given her worth. Nothing mattered now.

Treasure roused herself enough to ask, "The twins? Did you make certain the doctor tended to them? Were they frightened too badly?"

Sorrow welled in Donovan's eyes and he looked away.

"They are safe. They must be." Panic surged upward in a terrifying wave. "We took them out. My babies have to be safe. Donovan, tell me," she gripped his hands, pleading. "Tell me they're safe."

"Abby is safe. Erin . . ." Donovan's hands felt cold, shaking.

"No." Treasure shook her head back and forth as if she could ward away the truth. "No. Not Erin."

"The smoke. It was too late."

The words drifted to her ears on a slow, haunting wave of surreality. She felt her will to live dwindle. "Then it is over." Erin's death was cruel evidence, the fatal consummation of a lifetime of failures. "Dear God, why innocent little Erin? Oh, why didn't you take me instead?" she cried, burying her face on their clasped hands.

Donovan pulled her into his arms, rocking her, his body trembling with the storm of his own grief, with hers. But Treasure felt nothing. No pain. No anger. No comfort.

No hope.

"She's no better." Valene responded to Eliza's concern for Treasure the same way she'd answered every other friend and neighbor for the past three weeks.

She wished the girl would stop wallowing in self-pity. What was done was done. The fire ended in tragedy, but one couldn't dwell on that. It was all a mistake. And mistakes could always be rectified.

Valene delicately sniffed the bar of soap she'd stopped in the Johnsons' store for. The soap the Monroe family had given her was simply scathing to her skin.

"The worst of it is," she said, more to herself than Eliza, "that odious man has appointed himself guardian to dear Treasure. My Ransom has tried to visit her and left more than once for fear of his very life."

Eliza arched a brow. "Rader tells me Mr. River has coordinated the slaves and the volunteers from the valley so efficiently, the house should be ready for you to move back into by Christmas."

"Well, all I know is that Treasure has scarce set foot outside that filthy little cabin of his in a month. Shockin'. Quite shockin'. Livin' alone with such an uncivilized blackguard."

"They're hardly alone," Eliza pointed out. "The slaves are nearby. And there are people there every day helping with the rebuilding. I only wish my condition permitted me to visit as often." She glanced to her gently rounded belly.

"Yes, well, I'm certain a woman of your—maturity must take extra caution during pregnancy."

"Unfortunately that is true. We've waited a long time for this baby." Eliza smiled sweetly. "As far as the impropriety of the living arrangements at Rose of Heaven, I honestly think it's a minor concern by comparison to the fire. Besides, Donovan moved into the slaves' compound after the fire. Everyone knows the situation is as proper as it can be under the distressed circumstances," Eliza finished, wrapping the soap and handing it to Valene.

How dare the woman defend that man. Valene

375

fumed, counting out each penny with deliberate delay only because she knew Eliza wished to be rid of her. "Well, when my Ransom does speak to our Treasure, things are goin' to change and quickly, I dare say!"

Eliza had stooped to search for something beneath the counter. "I beg your pardon?"

"Oh, never mind." Valene marched out of the store, glad to get away from the vexing woman. How dare she be so arrogant. She a mere shopkeeper speaking with such a bold tongue to a proper lady. Things *were* about to be righted at Rose of Heaven. Ransom would easily dispense with Donovan River and surely the fire had convinced Treasure that managing Rose of Heaven was best left to one who knew how to behave as a proper mistress. Yes, soon, very soon. She hadn't come all this way, waited all this time, sacrificed so much, for nothing.

And soon, everyone in this wretched valley would know it.

"On your feet, pretty lady. Suppertime."

Treasure didn't look at Donovan. She stayed seated in the same chair she sat in each day gazing out the cabin window. "I'm not hungry."

"Oh, no, not that today. I have plans."

"Leave me be. Do us both a favor and just go away."

"Let's see now, you've said those exact words an average of three times a day for nearly a month, that's nearly one hundred rejections. But here I am, braving your wrath, courageously back again. Now what does that tell you?"

"That I need a gun."

"A joke? Yes, indeed, I knew we were making progress. Come on now." He stepped over to her and held out his hand. "I want to show you something."

"No."

"Let me put it another way. Either you can come with me peacefully, or I can throw you over my shoulder, screaming and kicking, and carry you out."

Treasure glared at him. His roguish smile told her he'd relish doing just that. Avoiding his outstretched hand, she reluctantly got to her feet. "Ten minutes. That's all. I don't like to go outside, and you know it."

"The whole valley knows it. But perhaps what I have to show you will change that."

As he led her out and up the path to the back lawns, from the corner of her eye Treasure noticed another wall of the big house had been completed. Donovan must have somehow coerced half the men and women in the valley to join the slaves in his rebuilding project.

Plans for the harvest of the cotton and corn not destroyed by the fire went on, too, arranged by Donovan and Bettis. Although she pretended not to listen, Donovan kept her abreast of the harvest, assuring her that the profits would carry Rose of Heaven through to the spring planting.

He'd bothered her endlessly about details, where she wanted this, and how big did she want that, and would she like a window here or there? How much corn should be set aside for wintering the stock, and was it time for the hog killing?

Making copious notes in his journal, he'd demanded she repeat every delicate step in the ginning process until he knew each one by memory. With Bettis at his side to advise and caution, he was certain they could soon ship clean, unstained bales downriver to market.

But he didn't fool her with his tales of neighborly concern. She knew full well he must have promised something in return to those who came up from the valley to help. A lumber mill might be incentive enough.

And as far as the house itself went, hadn't he maintained from the moment he set foot on Rose of Heaven that it belonged to him? It was in his interest to have a new structure under roof before winter.

"This way," Donovan said, taking a jog in the path leading to the once-overgrown area of her mama's garden. They walked through it easily now, the thorny roses and vines and scraggly hedgerow having been trimmed away and shaped.

"You have about two minutes to get this over with," Treasure warned him, already tiring of his subterfuge. "I want to go back to the cabin."

"Why? It's such a nice day."

His disgustingly cheerful tone annoyed her. "Where are you taking me?"

"Away from that window you've been sitting at every day for weeks. You need a change of scenery."

"I've had one. Thanks to your stories, I've visited Boston, Tennessee, Virginia, and Louisiana. You really have missed your calling, you know. Your writing is utterly engrossing."

"Do you think so?" Donovan said, although she knew he was only making a polite rejoinder. "Jared says my letters are entirely boring."

The sound of rushing water staved off another of Treasure's attempts to prod Donovan into sending off his writing for publication. She stared and listened, mystified. Ahead of her, he brushed back the bough of a low-hanging willow branch and she saw the source of the water. Her eyes flew wide.

A perfect stone and mortar rendition of what Mama had drawn to show her when she was four years old came to life before her, shooting liquid crystals of water up from the center to fall in radiant streams to the pool below.

"But—but how?" She gaped, stunned by the fountain's beauty, cascades of rainbow light, dancing as though each spray held a personality of its own. The fountain indeed seemed to exude life, blissfully oblivious to the fact that death and neglect surrounded it.

"When I was rummaging through the ruins, I found a strongbox hidden beneath the floor. In it was a drawing and plan for a garden, written in a woman's hand. Your mama's, I presume." He drew Treasure to his side. "Does it please you?"

Treasure looked up and searched his smiling eyes for guile, for a trace of deceit, something to justify her suspicions.

Donovan gently grasped her shoulders and bent to brush his lips over her forehead. "Come back to me, pretty lady. Live again. God in heaven, I need you, Treasure." Before she could protest, he lifted her face to his and kissed her with a desperation she felt in his tense hands, his searching mouth. Never had he consumed her lips with such agonizing need, as though his mouth melded to hers would infuse his determination to survive into her numbed, deadened soul.

He lifted her off her feet and crushed her against him, letting her feel his strength. "Whatever it takes, I'll do it. Just tell me how I can help you."

"Oh Donovan . . ." Treasure felt torn between the fire in his eyes and the coldness in her heart. "Please, I—I don't want to care again, I can't care again. Not for this land, this house. Not for anyone."

Donovan gently set her down and forced her to look straight at him. "You're grieving, we all are. A part of us always will mourn Erin. I understand you've needed time to think, to pray, to heal. But you can't go on like this. I need your help. The harvest is nearly ready and I sure as hell don't want the task of trying to market it. That's your talent." He bent and scooped up a handful of soil, holding it out to her. "This earth is in your blood. You can't ignore it. And you can't ignore me."

379

As if her hand moved of its own volition, Treasure hesitantly touched the soft, red dirt. She rubbed it beneath her fingertips and savored the smooth glide with a pleasure she'd hadn't felt in weeks. "You're right. You're no planter, Mr. River," she said, a small smile lifting the corner of her mouth. "But you are a hell of a pest."

Donovan threw his head back and laughed, a rich, deep sound vibrating through the still, hot air. Tossing the dirt aside, he whisked Treasure into his arms as though she were weightless and whirled her around. "Woman, you have the sassiest tongue on this good earth." Lowering his face over hers, he brushed a feathery kiss to her lips. "And I wouldn't have you any other way."

Treasure ran her fingers through his hair, her skin tingling at the sensation. It had been so long, so long since she had allowed herself to feel. "I know I should try to put things back together for the sake of my family. But I just can't help feeling Rose of Heaven is cursed under my hand."

"We'll see about that." Donovan rubbed his knuckles over her cheek. "Come and eat supper. You'll need your energy. We have work to do."

Slowly at first, days of rebuilding turned into busy weeks as autumn tumbled headlong toward winter. Reluctantly, at Donovan's firm insistence, Treasure managed the clearing of charred rubbish from the fields, while Donovan supervised the new big house. She marveled that he still never failed to consult her on any detail no matter how small, from the shelves in the pantry to the design of the master suite.

They worked together as friends and partners, memories of their shared passion ever-present. Yet it remained unspoken and untasted, subdued by the new opal betrothal ring on Treasure's finger. The fire and its aftermath had nearly driven away Treasure's memory of accepting Ransom's proposal. How long ago it seemed. But on one of his rare visits to the valley he presented her with the ring, reminding her of her promise they would wed.

Confused, her emotions too raw and new to think clearly, Treasure let him put the gem on her finger. All the while she thought how unreal it seemed, how little it meant.

Donovan said nothing and Treasure was glad for the constant deluge of people from the valley who came to help so the house would be ready for the rest of the family to return by Christmas. It provided a distraction she desperately needed. Through it all, they were able to talk naturally enough together, though she noticed Donovan scrupulously avoided any topic remotely intimate.

"And what will you do when the house is finished? You've already admitted you're no planter," Treasure had asked him one day while they drew out the plan for the back kitchen.

"I suppose I'll figure that out when the time comes."

"I have a suggestion," she ventured.

"Thought you might." He answered without looking up, chewing thoughtfully at the end of his pen.

"Take those stories you have scattered all over your cabin and send them to a publisher. It's what you should be doing."

"Hmm . . ." He glanced at her. "Well, if I should, I suppose I come by it honestly."

"How so?"

"My father runs a newspaper."

Shocked that Donovan had actually shared a bit of his past with her, Treasure tried to feign a casual interest, hoping he might volunteer something more. "My, how interesting."

Donovan shrugged and fixed his attention back on the scattering of papers on the table, as always leaving her with more questions than when she had begun.

November marked the end of fall harvests, and the restocking of storehouses and pantries. The reprieve brought Treasure into the valley to dine with her sisters and several of the people who had faithfully come to Rose of Heaven to lend a hand. It pained her that Donovan, at Aunt Valene's request, was omitted from the guest list.

"You look pleased, my dear. I'm glad," Ransom said, politely handing her a dish of stewed peaches.

Startled out of her reverie, Treasure let the spoon rattle against the china bowl. "Everything is wonderful," she said quickly, smiling to cover her momentary lapse.

"Yes, and soon, I intend to make it even more so." Ransom adjusted his pince-nez. "I should like to discuss our wedding plans this evening, my dear."

"Yes, you and my Ransom should be makin' plans," Valene put in. "You've been sadly neglectin' to do so, Treasure."

"December is not too soon for me," Ransom began.

"Please, Ransom." Treasure glanced around the table. "Perhaps later." In truth, she yearned to avoid the entire topic. More and more, the idea of becoming Ransom's wife unnerved her. He talked endlessly of taking over Rose of Heaven, relieving her of responsibilities, seeing to it she settled into a calm domestic order. And Aunt Valene loudly and persistently echoed him until Treasure longed to scream at them both to let her be.

At one time, the idea of marrying security would have been welcome. Now, Treasure rebelled against it and for no reason she wanted to give a name to.

"I'm not hungry," Abby interrupted Treasure's musings. "Can I go to my room?"

"The meal is not over, child," Valene said tartly. "It's most impolite to leave before dessert."

Abby's mouth pulled into a pout. "Treasure!"

Treasure looked down to her small sister, seated next to her at the end of the long table. Abby had lost so much weight since Erin's death. At times Treasure scarcely recognized her. Worse yet, Abby had withdrawn into herself. She had lost that mischievous, assertive spirit that, while at times exasperating, was Abigail's charm.

Ignoring her aunt's frown, Treasure pulled Abby into her lap. "One bite, sweetie. Here, won't you just eat a bite or two of my peaches? I know they're one of your favorites."

Abby vigorously shook her copper curls. Turning from the table, she buried her face in Treasure's shoulder, a gesture so reminiscent of Erin, Treasure felt tears sting her eyes.

"If you'll excuse me, Treasure," Emmy said softly from her place across the table. "I'll take Abby to her room and play with her awhile. I'm not really hungry either."

"No, I'll do it, Emmy." Treasure stood up with Abby in her arms. "Surely you'll want to stay for the apple cobbler. I told Aunt Orange Jane to give you extra cream, just the way you like it."

Emmy's face lit up for a moment. "Well . . ." She hesitated, then said, smiling, "It does sound good."

"Treasure, let the mammie take care of that child," Valene said. "You don't need to be runnin' around with her in your arms. You'll spoil her in no time."

"I certainly hope so, Aunt Valene," Treasure said, carrying Abby from the dining room. Happy to spend a few minutes alone with her young sister—and a few moments away from Ransom and Valene—Treasure hugged Abby close.

She took Abby to her new bedroom. After the fire, Treasure insisted on Abby having a new room to spare her the constant reminder of her lost twin. It wasn't quite finished, but it was beginning to resemble more a little girl's room than a hollow shell. Sitting cross-legged with her sister on the floor, Treasure leaned over and whispered in Abby's ear. "I have a new thimble."

"New?" Abby's eyes brightened.

Treasure nodded. "Yes, and if you play find the thimble with me, and you find my new thimble, it's yours."

"Really? All mine?"

"All yours."

"Then I'll play!" Abby scrambled to her feet.

"I've already hidden it," Treasure told her. "In a very hard place." She smiled as Abby began to hunt around the room, turning over cushions and checking under furniture for her prize.

She will heal, Treasure thought, watching Abby's determined search. *With time, we'll all heal.*

A half-moon hung over the horizon like a cut orange on a blue china plate when Ransom chastely kissed Treasure good night on the stoop of the cabin. He didn't bother to hide his displeasure at her refusal to talk about a wedding until after the big house was finished. Treasure couldn't find it in herself to care.

She tolerated the cold touch of his lips and his sulky farewell, then shut the door to Donovan's cabin against the crisp night air. Drawing her wrap from her shoulders, she sighed deeply, and unexpectedly caught the scent of bourbon and musk. *Donovan? Has he been here?*

The answer came languidly from a far corner. "Is your beloved safely away?"

Groping in the darkness, Treasure lighted a lamp and held it up enough to find his tall figure ranging against the wall, a smirk on his lips. "I don't recall giving you permission to enter my cabin."

Donovan straightened. The motion drew Treasure's eyes to his open shirt. "It's still my cabin, pretty lady," he said, stretching his arms behind his neck. "I'm lending it to you out of the charity of my heart, remember?"

"It will be yours again soon enough." She wanted to look away, but her greedy eyes fixed on the smooth ripple of muscle casually draped by the soft linen. She set the lamp on a table to disguise the quiver in her hand. "What are you doing here? I thought you were dining with the Johnsons."

As quiet and graceful as a predator, Donovan moved to the table and doused the tiny flame between his fingertips. "Eliza was tired. I left early. You wouldn't want to arouse unwanted interest with two shadows and a midnight light, now would you?" he countered smoothly when Treasure opened her mouth to protest the intimate darkness. "I thought not. An affianced woman has her reputation to guard, doesn't she?"

"How kind of you to care about my engagement."

"I don't."

The shadow of him melded into the blackness. Treasure heard his footsteps, slow, measured; the soft, quick whisper of her breath; his breathing, hard and fast.

She felt the heat of Donovan's body before he slid behind her, just letting his length brush against hers.

"Would you like to gamble, pretty lady?" His velvet voice stroked her ear.

Treasure grasped at her wits in a losing effort. She

should walk away. She should remind him she planned to marry her cousin. She should tell him the passion between them was impossible. But suddenly none of it mattered; the only thing that did matter was the instinct of her heart.

"I don't know the game," she said. "And I don't have anything to wager, Mr. River."

"Oh yes"—with a single motion, he slipped free the top button of her gown—"you do. And the game is truth. Tell me a lie . . ." He slowly undid another button.

"And you?" Treasure asked, her voice a stranger's. "What will you wager?"

Donovan turned her to face him and glided his hand in a languorous downward sweep over her shoulder. Covering her hand with his, he guided her fingers to the top button of his trousers. The danger of her touch was more menacing than any he'd ever dared. Donovan steeled himself against it, but knew from the moment her hand hesitantly moved against him, he had lost. "The odds are in your favor," he said, hearing the effort of control in his own voice. "But I'll risk it."

The hard heat of him lay beneath her palm. Treasure's mind cried out against the invasion of her senses. But it was a poor ally. Sensation—pure, sweet feeling so long suppressed—burst inside her. It flooded her with a desire so strong she reeled.

"My game," Donovan murmured. "I get the first question. Do you love him?"

Treasure abandoned herself to the danger of needing, of wanting Donovan River. "Yes," she whispered.

He slipped a button free. "Your turn."

"What do you wear to bed?"

"As much as possible."

Her hand trembled, but Treasure boldly unfastened his first button. "Your turn."

"Do you want him, more than you want to sleep, to eat, to draw your next breath?"

"Yes." His hand undid the next button, and then another. "Oh, yes."

"And you? Do you think about me, about us, together?" she asked. "Do you ever remember . . . ?"

"Never. Not once. Not ever."

Treasure matched a button with a lie. Her fingers touched his heated flesh and she caught her breath, barely able to form words—to think at all. "You're out of buttons," she managed.

"So are you." Donovan forgot any intention to torment her with the sensual game. He wanted her, with a need so profound, so deep-reaching, he couldn't test its limits, didn't know where it might lead, how it would change him. He was blind. And at the same time, visionary, knowing whatever the cost or the reward, they belonged to each other, always, forever.

With a jerk, he snapped open the back of her gown, scattering pearl studs over the wooden planks. Turning her between his hands, Donovan pushed silk and petticoats to her feet and pulled her into his embrace.

Treasure reached for him at the same time. Her mouth met his and she shuddered. She had thought other kisses they had shared had evoked the heights of her emotions. But this time it was like souls meeting— so deep, so intense, she felt a trembling weakness spread over her body in a powerful wave.

How could he know how to touch her in that way, so easily, so passionately, as to completely shatter every defense, every barrier she'd so carefully protected her heart with. She groped for a reason and found only a feeling.

Unable to stop the surge of desire they had unleashed, Donovan swept Treasure up and into his arms and carried her to the narrow bed. The moonlight illuminated the white tumble of sheets. She looked up at him, her hair splayed over his pillow, her lips half-parted, a wanton hunger in her depthless eyes.

Donovan bent one knee on the bed beside her and untied the ribbons of her camisole, slipping the diaphanous shift over her head. For a moment, he could only stare at her, completely overwhelmed by the beauty of her slender body. He stretched out a hand and slowly let it trace the curve of her neck, the hollow of her throat, and then brush the taut peak of her breast. Treasure sucked in a breath, arching her body to meet his touch.

His mouth followed the path of his hands, tasting, suckling, bringing alive a frenzied excitement that burned in her blood. She wanted him inside her, deep and strong. Driven by his tormenting caresses, she slid her hands over the corded muscles of his shoulders and chest to the flat plane of his abdomen. Desire emboldened her, and her fingers danced lower, stroking against his hardness. Donovan groaned low in his throat as her touch became surer. His hands tightened against her flesh.

She glimpsed the molten silver in his eyes as he moved away long enough to pull off his clothing. Treasure reached to draw him over her body, but he held back. Instead, starting at the delicate curve of her ankles, he scattered soft, hot kisses up her legs, following the path of his hands to the inside of her thighs. She opened to his coaxing hands. His tongue flicked against the tender skin and then flirted with the sensitive nub of her desire.

Treasure gasped and clutched his hair. The pounding of her heart became a thundering rhythm; lightning shot along her nerves.

When she feared she would explode from the tension coiled in her belly, Donovan moved over her and joined their bodies in a single thrust.

If a man could die from pleasure, Donovan knew he would spend his last night on earth in her arms. The feeling was towering, spine-shattering. For so long, forever it seemed, he'd been running away from commitment, from belonging anywhere, to anything—to anyone. Now he couldn't remember why. His heart knew this was what he had been looking for. This ecstasy, this feeling. This woman.

As their passion brought them to the highest heights, Donovan whispered the words he had so long feared to say, to admit even to himself.

I love you.

Had she heard the sweet confession or dreamed it in the fever peak of her desire? Treasure tried to remember, but utter fulfillment wrapped her in a contented drowsy haze, and she gave herself up to it, sated and warm in Donovan's embrace.

As she lay curled to his chest, his arms holding her close, she could only promise herself one thing. She had to find out who he was, what he was, before the last remnant of her prized reason surrendered to the demands of her heart.

389

Chapter Twenty

Treasure leaned back, letting the steady back and forth motion of the hackney rock her body into relaxing with the sway. Her breath escaped in a whispered sigh as she rested her cheek against the firm velvet seat. Her reflection, a shadow in the glass, studied her in return as if another part of herself sought answers from the woman seated in the dimly lighted coach.

Answers. The answers were here in New Orleans.

The night she had surrendered again to Donovan's passionate magic, she knew this journey must be made. Alone. She had to know the truth. About her papa, Donovan, Rose of Heaven. Only then could she choose between the man reason dictated she marry and the man her heart couldn't forget.

Ransom had sorely objected to her decision to make the journey, even to the extent that he refused to escort her to Gunter's Landing to board the steam packet. He considered it a personal insult that she should determine to pursue for herself questions he had already answered.

But Treasure defied him nonetheless, leaving him behind without regret. She could never be at peace until she saw and spoke to Donovan's accusers. Then, and only then, would she be equipped to draw her own conclusions.

She wished leaving Donovan behind had been as

easy. Even to the moment she boarded the river packet, she yearned to toss aside her pride and her reason and beg him to come along.

"Why am I left with the feeling I've let you talk me into something I'm going to regret?" Donovan had asked as he stood beside her on the dock waiting to board the *Uriah*. He took her hand, peeling off her glove to touch her skin to his. "I don't like to see you go off alone. Especially now."

His hand rubbed against hers in slow motion. It reminded Treasure too clearly of the way his fingers danced over her body the night they spent together in his cabin. He played her senses until they sang in harmony with a burning need nothing could assuage but the rhythm of his body melded to hers.

The fever began to flush her skin. Treasure sternly banked it, knowing she needed every ounce of reason she could muster. "I am not alone. I borrowed Sweetie, Mammie Eura Mae's helper, and I am perfectly—"

"Capable of taking care of yourself," he finished for her. "I know."

Her resolve weakened as the roughened hand continued caressing hers. Treasure gently disengaged her fingers and pulled her glove back on. "Besides, you'll be entirely too busy to spare a worry for me. I am confident organizing the lumbering operation will keep you out of trouble for at least a week."

Donovan grinned. "Maybe two." His teasing faded. "I know that decision wasn't easy. I'll make sure you don't regret it."

"It is a little late for that." She sighed. "At least I shouldn't have to worry about returning to a burned barn this time."

"No. The mill will mean as much to the valley as it will to Rose of Heaven. With the profits, we'll be able to finish the house and the barns."

We. Treasure's heart quivered at his automatic choice of words. One small word had suddenly transformed

391

the mill project into theirs, instead of his. She had been reluctant to give her permission and had submitted because it seemed the only way she could keep him in Alabama while she made the trek to New Orleans. And, she admitted it now, she felt compelled to do something for the valley after so many hands had helped with the rebuilding. The mill was the one act that could truly express her gratitude.

"You just best remember to keep out of my fields," she said with mock severity. "I don't want to come home to find you've built a new main street down the center of the south cotton field. You did promise — only the unused pasture will be cleared for roads. Nothing more."

"Don't worry, pretty lady. I'm a man of my word."

"I would like to believe that."

The words meant more than a glib reply to his teasing, and they both knew it. Her conscience jabbed at her. She had convinced him she needed to go to make peace with her papa's memory. It wasn't a lie, but it was little enough truth to make her uncomfortable. Now, looking at him, Treasure wondered if he had guessed the real reason she was traveling to New Orleans.

A thunderous warning, the steamer's whistle blasted, announcing the impending departure down the Black Warrior-Tombigbee to the Bay of Mobile. Donovan took both her hands in his. Looking into her eyes, he kissed her, savoring her mouth with his. "I hope you find what you're looking for," he said. "And that you can come home and finally lay your father to rest."

"There are many things I want to lay to rest," she said. "And I will."

He smiled at the defiant determination in her eyes. "I've no doubt of that." The whistle blew again and the stacks belched out black smoke. Donovan gave her hands a lingering squeeze before stepping back down the gangplank. "Take care of yourself, pretty lady. Don't forget me."

Don't forget me.

How silly a request, Treasure thought as she turned away from the darkened view. *I might as easily forget to breathe or command my heart to stop beating. After this journey, I may not choose to remember, but I can never forget you, Donovan River.*

"Dis be de place, ma'am." The hackney driver shrugged at Treasure's doubtful expression. "Maison de Rois. Dat what you say, dat where you is."

"Lordy!" Sweetie, Eura Mae's hand-chosen companion, stayed glued to her seat in the carriage, her round eyes fixed on the building in front of them. "Mis Treasure, why, you mama be a turnin' in her grave, and Aunt Eura Mae'd have herself a fit to end all if she found out we goed here. We oughta be turnin' back now 'fo, somethin' evil happen."

"I am not leaving until I talk to the proprietor," Treasure said firmly, although, casting a glance at the boardinghouse, she was inclined to share Sweetie's misgivings. But she hadn't come this far to be put off by one disreputable-looking building. Instructing the driver and Sweetie to wait, she straightened her hat, tugged at her gloves, and let blind stubbornness carry her to the door.

With the scant information she'd coerced out of Ransom, it had taken her two days after the steamer docked in New Orleans to settle into a hotel and then to locate this establishment. The very idea her papa and Donovan actually lived in such a filthy hovel sent a shiver of revulsion through her.

Maison des Rois was in the French Quarter, at the end of a narrow, gritty, cobbled street, and looked as if the owners neglected it more to encourage its sleazy character than out of apathy. Scuffs and chips patterned the sooty brick, and several spokes in the wrought iron listed precariously. At odd intervals, there was a touch of bawdy color—violent pink curtains in one window, scarlet and orange pantaloons hung to dry on a makeshift line on one balcony, a blaze of green carpet at the front doorstep. From somewhere above, the pungent smell of fried fish clashed with a strong waft of cloying perfume.

Treasure hesitantly tapped at the door, unable to hazard a guess as to who or what might answer.

After her third rap, she heard stomping, followed by a low, grumbling voice. The door jerked open several inches and a bloodshot eye glared at her. "We ain't got no rooms." The eye sized her up from head to toe. "Yo' customers won't set foot on this street nohow."

The door started to close. "Wait." Treasure stuck a foot in the opening. "I don't want a room. I want to speak with the proprietor."

"The what?" This time the door opened all the way and a fat woman clad in a deep purple robe eyed her suspiciously. "I own the place. What yo' business?"

Treasure decided bluntness would serve her best. "Two men who stayed here, several months ago." She briefly described her papa and Donovan.

"I remember 'em," the woman said through broken teeth. "The young one was a handsome devil, gamblin' and carousin' at all hours. And the other—" She shook her head. "Drunk. Mean drunk. Ah, but now and then his jokes 'n' stories did give us a laugh. He liked braggin', tellin' tall tales. Liked a hand of cards most nights, too."

Treasure's stomach contracted painfully, but she worked to keep her expression impassive. "He died here."

The woman shrugged. "Some do. He made hisself a few enemies. Many 'round here wouldn't spit at him if he was on fire. The young rascal saved his hide on more 'n one long night, I do recall."

Swallowing hard, Treasure asked, "How did he die?"

The woman stared at Treasure's purse, her eyes hot

with greed. "Couldn't say, exactly." Treasure took the hint and dropped a few coins in her fleshy palm. They disappeared at once into the folds of her robe. "Heard he fell off his balcony." She paused. "Also heard some-one pushed him off. I didn't see nothin'. But Judy Rouge did. She was the young one's favorite." She leaned forward and poked Treasure in the side with a thick, rubbery elbow. "He was most of the girls' favor-ite."

The swish of air the movement generated hit Treasure with the stench of stale whiskey, days-old sweat, and cheap perfume gone sour. Treasure stopped breathing until the woman receded. "And where might I find her?" she asked, trying not to gasp.

The woman backed away and pointed up a flight of rickety stairs. "Third door on the left. Though I best warn you, Judy Rouge is a witch this time of mornin'." She turned away then turned back. "Don't you cause me no trouble, hear?"

Thanking her, Treasure hitched up her skirts and climbed the narrow stairs, trying to calm herself with slow, steadying breaths. She padded down the plank floor of the stifling hallway. At the third door on the left, she stopped, steadied herself, tapped gloved knuckles against yellow wood.

A tall girl, draped in a loose, tangerine satin wrapper cracked the door. "I don't take women," she snapped. "I don't take no one before noon. Although" — puffy am-ber eyes, ringed with smutty circles, appraised Trea-sure, "for you, I could almost be tempted to make an exception."

Treasure shoved aside her revulsion. "N-no." She paused to still her trembling voice, then plunged ahead. "I want to talk to you about two men who once stayed here. Donovan — "

"Donovan River?" the girl shot back, before Trea-sure could finish. A flash of something sparked her lifeless eyes. "Is he back? After what happened with

Slade Gunter and the old man I was afraid—" She stopped abruptly, obviously feeling she'd said too much.

"That is what I want to ask you about. The—other man. How he died."

The girl cast a suspicious glance. "Why?"

"Donovan is a—my brother," Treasure lied sensing she'd be more likely to hear the truth if she professed a kinship with Donovan. "He's in trouble and I want to help."

"I see." Judy Rouge hesitated, as if weighing Treasure's words, then jerked a hand to the room behind her. "Come in, then." She waved Treasure to a shabby, crimson settee in one corner of the sitting room, sweeping aside a rumpled silk negligee and dropping in a chair opposite her. "Like I told that lawyer. There's not much say."

"Lawyer?"

"Yeah, the one that came a while back. Said he needed information about the old man's death for Donovan's defense."

Ransom. He'd go to any length to discredit Donovan. "Go on."

"Well,"—she rubbed her temples—"the old man liked his whiskey. He let Slade Gunter cheat him at cards again, lost that piece of land he was always going on about. Donovan saved his neck by cheatin' Slade. Slade didn't take too kindly to it and threatened to kill them both. Donovan got the old man back here, and my, was he in a temper. He argued for a good hour with the old man over some will or deed or—no! It was a note namin' Donovan his heir. Not that I believe the old man had anythin' to leave behind, mind you."

Treasure hid her pain. "Then what happened?"

"I poured Donovan a drink to calm him. Well, about that time, the old man got real good into one of his moods. He was hangin' off the balcony, wavin' and callin' to the girls in the street. Donovan ran out to get

396

him down, but he lost his balance and fell before Donovan reached him." The girl waited for Treasure's comment. After a silent moment, she added, "If you came to hear somethin' else, there ain't nothin' else to tell."

"No. Thank you." Treasure's body moved stiffly as she stood up. She managed a wan smile. "I came to hear the truth."

The girl threw up a hand. "You have. I hope it helps Donovan. Will it?"

"I don't know," Treasure answered truthfully. Her head throbbed. She had to get out of the horrible place.

"Look . . ." the girl curled long fingers around Treasure's arm. "When you see Donovan, tell him . . . Tell him Judy Rouge says thanks." She looked down, twisting the belt of her wrapper. "He helped me through some bad weeks, payin' the bills when I was sick and couldn't work. I never got the chance to pay back my debt. And I'll tell you, *chérie,* that is one I would have enjoyed repaying with interest."

"I'll relay the message," Treasure said coolly.

"Oh! I almost forgot. Did he ever finish that book of his?"

"Book? Yes — almost, I believe. Why do you ask?"

"Something he promised. Said I'd find myself in it someday, somewhere between the pages." She smiled slyly. "I told him I'd rather be between his sheets."

Treasure couldn't stop the rush of blood to her cheeks. "I'll see to it you receive a copy when it's published," she promised, inching herself free.

Treasure ignored Sweetie's curious glances as she climbed back into the carriage. She said nothing during the ride to the hotel and went straight into her bedroom as soon as they returned, telling Sweetie she was nursing a headache.

397

She sat in the room, curtains drawn, staring at nothing, more alone than she ever remembered, forced to confront the truth and her own feelings.

Papa . . . the dream of him she had kept alive in her heart for so long suddenly became a clear vision of a man. A flawed man who chose to escape rather than to admit his defeats with grace, his limitations with courage.

Sometime during the long, lonely hours that followed the realization, Treasure's childlike perception gave way to a woman's sight. In her memory, Papa would always be the gay, laughing man who had built his beloved plantation and town on the strength of his dreams. But from now on, her remembrances would also be an acceptance, both sad and happy, of what he was. Not what she wanted him to be.

And with a gradual dawning, as gentle and clear as the birth of a new day, she realized she could accept herself as Papa had not been able to. As Donovan did. Whether or not Papa felt her worthy of his love and trust, whether she won or lost Rose of Heaven, she needed and deserved love.

To give love.

To receive it.

Springing to her feet, Treasure began jamming her few unpacked articles, a hairbrush, an extra gown, into her bag. She called a timid Sweetie out from the adjoining room.

"Miz Treasure . . ." The girl's eyes widened. "Is you goin' somewhere else, Miz Treasure?"

"Yes. Yes I am." Treasure flung open the drapes. Bright noonday sun gushed into the room, chasing away the cold, morbid gray. Treasure laughed. "I'm going home. Home to my heart."

Chapter Twenty-one

She was home.

Incredulous, Donovan saw the emotion in her green eyes, at once timid and bold, deep as the heart of the river. She reached for him, and he caught her against him. Her kiss warmed his lips like the first breath of spring. Winter snow melted away by the new fire of passion. She whispered to him. He watched her mouth move. The sweetness of her words lingered in his heart.

I love you. It's what I've always wanted to say.

I love you.

"Donovan."

A hand, gentle but insistent, nudged his shoulder. Donovan heard the soft voice and somewhere through the half-daze of sleep knew it wasn't one of his dreams. The voice that had haunted him since he'd let the flesh and blood woman walk away from him. "Eliza." He dragged himself up, rubbing a hand against the stiff ache in his neck. "I thought you went to lie down."

"I didn't want to wake you. Lord knows you need the rest. But Mr. Johnson is back with the wagon. There's a family of five." Eliza swept her hair back from her brow with the back of her wrist. "We've run out of room in the house and the slaves' cabins. I suppose we'll have to put them in one of the barns . . ."

She broke off, her breath catching on a ragged sigh.

Donovan pulled out of the chair he'd dozed off in and curled a comforting arm around her shoulders. "We'll think of something. Anything is better than leaving them in the valley. The damned disease seems to be spreading faster every day."

"I've never seen the fever before. Only heard tell. It's odd, though, seems it usually strikes earlier, August or September. That's why Seamus used to take the girls and summer down at Pass Christian with the other planters and their families. Seems there's no end to the fevers and ills on their plantations that time of year."

"It still feels like summer. We haven't even had the first frost yet."

"True enough." Eliza fanned herself with her open palm. "The valley must be near deserted by now. Lord help us," she said, her eyes pleading. "If even one person takes ill here at Rose of Heaven . . ." She put a protective hand to the bulge in her belly.

"We're safe," Donovan said firmly, with more hope than he felt. "It's nearly midnight. Go on and get some rest. I'll help Rader get everyone settled."

Eliza eyed him critically. "You should take your own advice, Mr. River. You haven't slept more than a day's worth in two weeks."

"I'm only sleeping for one."

"Your impertinence isn't going to help if you turn up ailing. You and my husband are the only ones fool enough to keep riding into the valley after the doctor told you to stay away."

"They need whatever we can spare at the hospital he's set up, whether the good doctor cares to admit it or not." He didn't add that once he'd seen the suffering inside the makeshift sick ward at the valley courthouse, he'd been determined to do anything to see it end. Yellow fever was particularly swift and cruel to children and the elderly, the vile black purging draining their lives. The townspeople who'd come to Rose of Heaven supported his and Rader's decision—they would not close the door to Rose of Heaven on anyone, despite the danger.

Eliza, so far advanced with her pregnancy, hardly needed the added strain of knowing that. She'd labored as tirelessly as he and Rader, providing food and shelter for the families who'd fled the valley for the sanctuary of Rose of Heaven.

Valene Ellis and her proper son had vehemently objected to Donovan's decision to offer the house and grounds as a haven for the healthy. And he could have cared less. He wished they'd leave, and suspected they would have at the outset if not for fear of contracting the disease while it raged through the valley.

Donovan caught Eliza studying him and he made an effort to smile as he steered her out of the parlor and toward the staircase.

"Well, look at that," she said, bending close to the railing. Donovan followed her eyes. "A butterfly. So strange to see one now. Carefully, she reached for it. A copper and blue wing fell into her hand. "Hmmm."

"Hmmm what?"

"Oh, it's silly. I was just going to tell you that when you see a butterfly it means you'll see someone wearing that color the same day. . . . But I don't know what it means if the butterfly is dead."

"It means you're so exhausted your mind is playing tricks on you. That's what."

"All right. All right. I know when my insights aren't appreciated." She hesitated before starting upstairs. "You know, Donovan River, you're quite a man." She flashed an echo of her old mischievous smile. "I don't care what anyone says."

The last hour to Rose of Heaven stretched Treasure's anxiety to the screaming point. The packet had docked with less than three weeks to Christmas, greeted by the news of the yellow fever epidemic in the valley. She'd had to pay dearly to hire a carriage to take her the few miles home from Gunter's Landing.

The driver stopped at the edge of the long drive, underneath the huge, old magnolia that marked the plantation's entrance, obviously reluctant to go farther. Treasure left Sweetie to fetch someone for their bags. Hitching up her skirts, she ran up the drive, rows of longleaf pines on either side shading her. When she saw the nearly finished big house, her heart caught in her throat at the new, white beauty of it. But she had no time to admire it.

Eliza met her on the doorstep. Without a word, she looked at Treasure for a long moment then enveloped her in a shared embrace.

"I've been so worried," Treasure said, hugging her friend. "How is everyone? Abby and Emmy? They haven't taken sick, have they? Where are they staying?"

"One question at a time, honey." Eliza gave Treasure's arm a reassuring squeeze. "Abby and Emmy are fine. I've had them staying in Donovan's cabin. Donovan agreed we couldn't risk sending them away from Rose of Heaven. They've missed you something fierce. We all have, especially Donovan."

"I've missed all of you, too," Treasure said, ignoring Eliza's knowing smile. "Tell me, has there been any word of Camille? I was hoping while I was away . . ."

Eliza's smile slipped away. "Nothing, I'm afraid. It's as if she's up and vanished. I' m sorry, honey."

"No," Treasure said, tears pricking her eyes. "I'm sorry. For not listening with my heart. And for everything between us. I shouldn't have —"

"And neither should I. Let's not talk about it now, honey. It's past."

"My, how you've — blossomed."

"Fat as a smokehouse ham, aren't I?"

"You're lovely. In a way, I'm envious." Embarrassed at the disclosure, Treasure hastily changed the subject.

"How bad is it?" she asked as they walked arm in arm into the house.

Treasure sent Solomon out to tend to the carriage, then followed Eliza into the barely furnished parlor. "Bad enough. It's just so fast. In days it reduces strong men to helplessness, then they either recover or . . . So many have died, and I fear there'll be many more before it's ended." She closed her eyes, rubbing her temples. "I'm worried to death over Donovan and Mr. Johnson. They're simply determined to go into the valley several times every day. I'm afraid they're both going to turn up sick."

Treasure put an arm around her friend's shoulders, mutely offering her comfort. She knew Eliza's heart-fear matched her own. And she fought a sense of outrage. To finally discover her feelings, and then to come home to the possibility of losing the man who had taught her to trust them seemed cruelly unfair. She sighed, resigned. "I'd expect nothing less of either of them."

"I've become quite a wilting Southern belle, haven't I," Eliza said, mustering a smile.

"Expectant mothers are supposed to be weepy," Treasure teased.

"You wait, honey. One day—is that the wagon?" She turned to the window at the sound of horses' hooves pounding in a frenzied rhythm.

Treasure went to the windows to look. "It's Donovan. He's in a terrible rush."

"Something is wrong." Eliza paled. "Lord in heaven."

"You stay. I'll go and see."

She met Donovan as he yanked the horses to a stop at the circular drive in front of the house. Jumping down from the seat, he glanced once at her, and then back. "Treasure . . ." For a moment, his voice took on the soft caressing tone she knew too well. "You're wearing blue." Her senses responded to him in a dizzying rush.

The scent of him, the remembered taste and feel of his body, the tender expression in his eyes when he kissed her, the sound of his velvet voice against her ear. She yearned to rush into his arms and spill out everything — New Orleans, her discoveries, the awakening of her heart . . . "What did you say?"

The sudden tense set of his expression held her back. "Nothing. Later. Right now I need your help. Rader is ill. I couldn't leave him in the valley."

Treasure rushed to the back of the wagon. Rader lay there, doubled up in pain. She put a hand to his forehead. His skin burned into her palm.

"We need to take him inside and get the cupping glass." Donovan said shortly. "When he wakes up his temples will be throbbing."

Between the two of them, they supported Rader into the house. Eliza, white to the bone, followed them up the stairs and helped them put her husband into one of the beds. Treasure had turned to fetch the water Donovan asked for when Valene stepped into the doorway.

"Treasure! A fine welcome home they've mustered for you, I see." She whirled on Donovan. "And now it appears you have taken the liberty of puttin' me out of my rooms! My dear, I'm so glad you are back to restore order. This ruffian ignores my authority as blatantly as he does my Ransom's."

"This was the only available bed," Treasure said, stepping around her aunt. Valene followed her down the stairs. Treasure knew her aunt's temper was building, but she couldn't find a reason to care.

"Treasure, my dear, I realize you are distraught from your journey, but — "

"I'm distraught because my friends are ill and dying."

"Of course. But there is nothing you can do here. My Ransom and I have discussed it, and we agree the only sensible thing to do is somehow remove ourselves until this crisis has passed."

"That is your privilege, Aunt Valene. I intend to stay."

"You are my fiancée, and I forbid you to risk your life needlessly," Ransom announced as he joined them. "He is putting you, the entire family, in the worst possible danger allowing those people to invade our property. We have no choice but to leave."

Treasure faced him, chin in the air. "I have a choice, Ransom. And I have made it."

"Don't be a fool, my dear. These people set fire to your barn, then nearly succeeded in burning your whole plantation. Why ever would you stay and risk dying for them?"

"Ransom . . ." Treasure tried to soften her voice. "They need help. I will not turn and walk away."

"No! I forbid you to remain. I have the right. You are going to be my wife."

"I think not." Treasure took the ring he had given her from the pocket of her dress and put it into his hand. "It's obvious we aren't suited. You could never accept the fact that I make my own decisions."

Ransom stared blankly at the ring in his hand then at her. "You cannot be serious. Treasure — "

"I'm sorry, but I am."

Valene stepped between them. "Now, Treasure dear, you surely don't mean to let this little spat ruin your chance to be my Ransom's bride. You're overwrought. You don't realize what you are sayin'."

Treasure refused to be intimidated by her aunt's cajoling or Ransom's impotent anger. "I know exactly what I am saying."

"You are going to find you are mistaken," Ransom said tightly. "I cannot risk Mama's life by staying here. We're leaving now, but we will return. We are not finished with this."

"You will always be welcome as family here,"

Treasure told him. "But yes, we are finished, Ransom."

Bettis bent over the still form on the bed, muttering to himself. Treasure and Eliza anxiously watched him pull a pinch of blue vervain powder from his belt pouch and shake it into a jar of water.

"Dis help his achin' back, but you got t' git it down him," he told Eliza. He solemnly shook his head. "Ain't gonna be easy."

Murmuring her thanks to Bettis as he slipped out the door, Treasure turned to Eliza. Her friend knelt by Rader's bedside. She stood near Eliza, wishing Bettis's potion were a magic restorative. From two days of retching and fever, Rader's skin waxed sallow and lax. The whites of his eyes had taken on a peculiar yellow tinge that Donovan said would spread over his body. But the worst of it, Treasure thought, was the defeated dullness of his expression, as if he awaited the end with apathy.

Donovan tried to assure Treasure that people could and did recover. But seeing Rader so physically devastated and Eliza in such distress proved almost too much for her to bear. Not wanting to disturb Eliza, she gave her friend's shoulder a quick squeeze, and hurried from the room. She nearly collided with Donovan at the door.

He took her arm and guided her a little down the hallway. "Is Rader worse?"

Treasure shook her head, not quite trusting her voice. "No. At least, I don't think so. It's just so hard, seeing him and thinking about all the others . . ."

"I know."

The utter weariness in his voice made Treasure notice the shadows and lines of exhaustion on his face. "You should get some rest," she admonished.

"Not now. I have another run to make into town. Dr.

406

Grigsby is counting on having the extra food and water this evening."

"Let me help you."

"No."

The terse refusal didn't daunt her. "I want to do something more than sit about waiting for you to tell me who is sick and who has died. I'm healthy. I can drive a wagon as well—better than you. And with Rader ill, you need the help, even if you won't admit it."

"I don't need your help." His steel-hard defense against her tenacity weakened a little. He said more softly, "Going to the valley will only increase your chances catching the fever. I won't let you take that risk."

His possessiveness unwittingly echoed Ransom's earlier assertions, and it sparked Treasure's annoyance. "You're hardly in a position to allow me to do one thing or another. I don't belong to you, Donovan River."

"You're wrong." Gently, he brushed his fingers over her face. "We belong to each other. I know it and I think you do, too."

"If I do—" She caught her breath at the flare of hope and tenderness in his eyes. That look had the power to deliver her heart to him without question. "If I do, it doesn't mean I want you to think and act for me."

"I don't want to. But in this case, I can't think clearly." He raked a hand through his hair, turned away then back. "All I can think about is that I could lose you to this goddamned fever."

"Is that supposed to make it easier for me?" she cried. "Watching you take the risk day after day? No." Determination stiffened her spine. "We're together in everything. Or nothing at all. You taught me to trust my heart, no matter what the danger. My heart tells me those people need help and I can give it. I am going to the valley. You can do as you like."

She turned on her heel and strode quickly to the staircase, hearing his heavier tread behind her a heartbeat later. "You are the stubbornest, most exasperating woman I've ever known," he grumbled, following her out to where wagons were tied.

"I do believe that's a case of the kettle calling the pot black, Mr. River. Besides, you've told me numerous times, I recall, how submissiveness bores you."

"I take it back."

"Too late," she said, climbing onto the driver's seat and taking up the lines. Snapping them against the team's backs, she set the horses in motion, calling over her shoulder, "I'd better not tarry. You said Dr. Grigsby needs these supplies right away."

She couldn't catch his dark retort as she turned the horses toward the road and, with a secret smile to herself, guessed it likely wasn't anything near the sweet nonsense he liked to whisper in her ear.

Treasure rushed through two urgent treks into the valley, then hurried back to visit Emmaline and Abigail, whom she'd kept isolated with Eura Mae in Donovan's cabin away from the sick.

By that time, she'd learned to cope with the agony and horror she felt at the suffering she witnessed in the makeshift hospital. She spent as much time as she could spare helping to bathe the fevered, change beds, and clean chamber pots.

Treatment was woefully inadequate. Dr. Grigsby did his best, issuing drafts of calomel to cleanse his patients' stomachs. For the cramps and convulsions, he gave them laudanum; for the fever, grains of blue pill. quantities of each were severely limited, and many suffered without medication. Bettis sent herbal concoctions Dr. Grigsby ordinarily would have rejected. But desperation led him to administer them along with his own prescriptions.

As she padded hastily across the back yard to Donovan's cabin Treasure reflected she'd never felt quite as weary as she did now, nor as beaten. The plague was almost as devastating as Erin's death, as Spring's departure. Because the fever, like the fire, like Spring's love for Elijah, raged out of her control. *Perhaps my loved ones' lives are not meant to be mine to order and direct. Perhaps their choices, their fates, are not my doing, not my fault.*

Abigail met her at the door and threw herself into Treasure's arms. "Oh, I'm so happy to see you," she said, her little face wet with tears. "Please say we can go home now. I don't want to be here anymore. I miss everyone. Spring, and Donovan and Aunt Orange Jane, and Soloman and Bettis, and just everyone! And especially Erin," she added, mumbling into Treasure's shoulder.

Treasure felt her own tears sting her eyes. "We all miss Erin. And everyone misses you, too," she said. "But you can't move back to the house just yet. Maybe in a few days."

Abby clung to her, not consoled by anything she said, any promises she thought to make. Treasure wished Donovan had come with her. Somehow he always knew the right words to soothe sore hearts. She felt woefully inadequate to provide even meager comfort to her small sister.

She nearly surrendered and gathered Abby up to go and find Donovan when Abby flung her arms around her neck and squeezed hard. "I'm happy you came back. I know you'll take care of me now. I love you, Treasure."

"I love you too, Abby," Treasure whispered, choked by the overflowing feeling in her heart.

She hugged her close for a long time, before gently disengaging the embrace and coaxing a smile from Abby with the bag of licorice Donovan had sent along. Following Abby into the cabin, Treasure fervently wished a hug and a bag of sweets could make things as easy between her and Emmaline.

Emmy was sitting at the table, hands twisting in her lap. She didn't look up as Treasure came into the room and sat down beside her. "Emmy." Treasure touched her hands. "Emmy, I came to see how you are."

"Why? You were gone so long I didn't think you'd ever come back. It's almost Christmas. Everyone is sick. Maybe you should have stayed away."

"I'm home now. And I'm not going to leave again."

As she looked up for the first time, Treasure saw Emmy's eyes were wet with tears. "Everyone says that. Mama. Papa. Spring. Camille. Everyone is gone. No one is there when you need them."

Treasure nearly admonished her sister but Donovan's spirit seemed close, whispering to her. *Listen to your heart.* She studied Emmy, sensing a deeper turmoil. "Emmy, what is bothering you? Is it — Jimmy Rae?"

Emmy's eyes widened and then she burst into tears. "He's sick. Mrs. Johnson wouldn't let me go to see him because she knows you don't like him and Colonel Stanton. But I'm so worried. I just wish you would understand."

"Oh, Emmy." Treasure put an arm around Emmy's thin shoulders, sheltering her against her body. She wanted to keep Emmy safe in the haven of her arms, protecting her from the pain of caring.

Yet as strong as that impulse was, another now challenged it, telling her she couldn't control Emmy's heart any more than she could have Spring's. Neither could she lock Emmy's heart away as she had her own, denying her the joy and pain — the laughter and the tears — of love.

Drawing a deep breath, she put her hands on Emmy's shoulders, forcing Emmy to sit up and look at her. "Let's go. Now. We'll find out how Jimmy Rae is."

"Really?" Elation warred with disbelief on Emmy's face. "Do you mean it?"

"Of course."

"But — you don't like Jimmy Rae."

"No, and Emmy, honestly I don't know if I ever will. But I love you. And I know you won't be satisfied until you've seen him yourself. I will allow you to see him, if I am at your side. Agreed?"

Emmy's enthusiastic hug was her answer.

The door to Gold Meadow jerked open, releasing a blast of sour whiskey in Treasure's face. Ira tottered in the doorway looking pale and drawn, as if he'd aged a decade in just a few months' time.

Treasure curtly explained their visit, and for a moment she thought he would refuse Emmy's request. But after a long pause, he finally stepped aside to let them in.

"Jimmy Rae hasn't been much in his right mind these past days," he said as he led them up the staircase to the second-floor bedroom. "Damned kid nipped the bottle once too often, and now this fever." Ira passed a hand over his head and Treasure noticed the slight tremble. "Doctor can't do a goddamned thing for him either."

The close, acrid smell in Jimmy Rae's bedroom reminded Treasure of the makeshift hospital in the valley. Jimmy lay on the bed, limp and apathetic. Emmy crept near the bed, perching on the edge of a chair next to it, looking down at him with anxious eyes.

Treasure watched her for a moment, then touched her shoulder. Propped up against the door frame, Ira looked on, awkwardly squaring off against Treasure. She felt she should say something in sympathy, but the words were so hard to say with their past standing between them. "I am sorry about Jimmy Rae," she said finally. "No one deserves to suffer like this."

"Even a Stanton?" Ira sneered.

Treasure stiffened. "As you like." Turning her back to him, she paced to the far side of the room and stared out the window. When she glanced back over her shoulder, he'd disappeared.

After several minutes of quiet murmuring between Emmy and Jimmy Rae, Emmy announced she was ready to leave. She walked out into the hall.

Treasure followed. "Emmy?" The girl looked white to the bone, her dark eyes distant.

Emmaline stared at her. Her lips worked, but no sound came out.

"Emmy, what's wrong? Is he worse? What was he saying you?" Treasure began to feel the first touches of alarm lick her spine.

"He . . ." Emmy's eyes dropped to the floor. "Nothing. I just want to go." She took Treasure's hand and gripped it as they walked down the stairs together and out to the waiting wagon.

Treasure wrestled with a growing sense of foreboding on the journey back home. The feeling intensified when Emmy refused to talk on the way. When Treasure let her off at the door of Donovan's cabin, Emmy hugged her tightly, her face buried against Treasure as snugly as Abby's had, as if she sought comfort and reassurance.

She tried once more to draw Emmy out, certain Jimmy Rae had somehow upset her terribly. "If you like, I can stay for a while and we can talk," she offered tentatively.

Emmy pulled away from her and for a moment Treasure saw the struggle in her face. "No," she said at last. "No. Not now."

And before Treasure found word or gesture to stop her, Emmaline turned and ran into the sanctuary of the cabin.

Orange Jane waited with her large wooden tray while Treasure took out her keys and unlocked the storeroom. The honey and heat of Orange Jane's voice sparked the first bit of Christmas spirit she'd felt. The cook's throaty singing, like a soothing liniment, helped ease the strain of the last days' ministrations to the ill.

"I can't fix a proper Christmas dinner fo' all dose folks, Miz Treasure. Dey's too many mouths t' feed."

Treasure led the way downstairs. "No one knows that better than I. We'll just have to make do." She opened a tub of pickled pork. "With what's left here, and those hams hanging over there, everyone will have some meat at least."

"Sho 'nough. Bettis done slaughtered dem hogs while you was in New Orleans."

"I know. He did a fine job, too. I saw he put up the shoulders and the bacon flanks to corn too. Did he finish the lard? You'll need plenty for crusts."

"Yessum, I helped him."

"And I'll bet you minded that task terribly," Treasure teased. "Oh, there's the nutmeg. Bring your tray. Now then"—she pointed to her right—"there's plenty of flour yet in that barrel."

On an upper shelf, where she kept her prized supplies, behind a few boxes of raisins and a small stash of precious nuts, she'd hidden the last of her currants. Sighing, she pulled up a step ladder. "Perhaps your delicious currant buns will help bring Christmas cheer." She took down the currants and one box of nuts and laid them on Orange Jane's tray.

"Yessum, might help," Orange Jane mused, then resumed her humming.

"I'd like to do something special for Emmy and Abby and the other children here. But it's so late. I can't believe it's Christmas Eve morning."

"Bettis done give me my present already. See." She lifted her delicate wrist, newly adorned with a bracelet of intricately woven leather strips strung with bright orange and red beads.

"I'd say you have a devoted admirer." Treasure's gentle teasing was cut short by the sound of feet pounding overhead. Wondering at the commotion, she climbed up out of the storeroom.

"Treasure!" Two auburn-haired whirlwinds flung

413

themselves at her. "We're home!" Abby cried.

"Mr. River said we'll have Christmas here," Emmy added, her smile brilliant. "Can we stay this time? Please?"

"We don't like staying at the cabin all day. I had to eat lima beans and I ran out of licorice two whole days ago."

Her two sisters danced around her, both chattering at once. "Oh, I've missed you so," Treasure blurted out. Hearing their contagious excitement, Treasure felt having her little family home again would make it a real Christmas. Meager portions, even the horrors of the plague, could not quell her joy now. She gathered them in her arms.

"I see those two ruffians found you already," Donovan's voice drawled from the doorway. He smiled and held out his hands in mock innocence. "They forced their way onto the wagon and made me deliver them here. What's a poor man to do with two such determined women?"

"I could make several suggestions," she said, returning his grin with an attempt at severity. Unfortunately, the effect was ruined by her own smile. "I suppose I'll just have to keep them."

Emmy and Abby squealed their delight, and the three sisters hugged each other, content in their reunion. And as she held tight to them, Treasure brought Donovan into their circle, the glow in her eyes silently thanking him for showing her the way back to her family.

"Oooff." Treasure dropped down on the parlor settee, the next afternoon. "Well, from the looks of this room, I'd say our little Christmas celebration was a success." She managed an exhausted laugh. "I don't imagine I've ever seen so many children in one place before."

"A little different from your last soiree," Donovan

said, sitting down beside her. With a smile, he used his thumb to rub away a smudge of coconut cake streaked on her cheek. "I'm beginning to think you deliberately smudge your face just to invite me to touch your skin."

Aware of the flush rising in her cheeks, Treasure averted her eyes. "The treats, the gifts; they all helped. The children enjoyed them and I think everyone else did, too. I feel" — his eyes gently encouraged her as she struggled for words — "I feel like we have hope again. These past months, Erin's death," she paused, fighting the welling of grief. "The fever, it seemed as if we kept losing reason to hope. But today you've reminded me — all of us — we do have reasons. Thank you." Feeling shy, she leaned over and kissed his mouth with butterfly softness.

"If you'll thank me that way every time, I'll organize a party every day."

Treasure shook her head at his impudent grin and took a last look around the room. They'd managed, in just over a day, to put together a Christmas party for all the families staying at Rose of Heaven. Orange Jane, along with two cooks sent up from the valley, had baked special custards and cakes. With Eliza's blessing, Donovan raided the Johnsons' store for striped peppermint sticks and precious fresh oranges and apples. The healthy pitched in with donations of food, toys, and handmade decorations.

The children's joy, unblemished by the disease, and the message of hope in the morning church service, seemed to lighten the despair hanging over McGlavrin's Valley. Even Dr. Grigsby's grim expression relented a little, and he cautiously pronounced the epidemic to be waning. With so few people left in the valley, the number of new cases had decreased to only a handful. Those who would recover had begun to rest peacefully, their bodies mending.

Weariness permeated Treasure's every limb. She attributed it to overexertion and lack of sleep during the rush of activity in the past weeks. But she wished her arms and legs didn't weigh like lead.

"I hope you have just a little energy left, pretty lady." Donovan suddenly stood and held out his hand to her. "I have a present for you."

"A present?" Treasure questioned him with her eyes, but he only smiled. "I didn't expect . . . I mean —"

"No one expects a surprise. That's the best part about it."

Intrigued, Treasure took his hand and let him lead her out of the parlor and down the hallway to a closed door. With a smile and a flourish, Donovan swung open the door and invited her into the newly finished ballroom.

"It's beautiful," Treasure said, a little perplexed since she had seen the room nearly complete only days ago. "But I don't — oh, my! It can't be!"

In the center of the room, near the tall windows, was her mother's cherished piano, as beautiful as the day Treasure first remembered seeing it. She rushed to it, laying her hands against the cool ebony wood to reassure herself it was real.

She turned to Donovan, tears in her eyes. "I thought it was destroyed in the fire."

"I had some help rescuing it and I've been having it restored these past months. I knew what it meant to you."

One tear, an amber gem in the dim lamplight, slid down her cheek. "It seems I'm destined to be thanking you today." She went into his arms, holding him close, her head against his heart.

"I can only hope I'm destined to keep on making you happy," he murmured in her ear. Pulling a little away, he kissed her damp face. "I do believe a christening is in order." He drew her down on the bench beside him and took her face between his hands, his fingers threaded in her loosened hair, kissing her slowly as if he had forever. "You're most beautiful like this, I think,"

416

Donovan whispered when he finally released her. "In the barest of light, trembling from my touching you." He spilled her hair over his hand, trailed a finger down her face. "The tides of night and day. Moonlight and flame. I hold these in my hands when I hold you."

Treasure let her tears spill unheeded. "I wish this once I had your gift of words. I have no way to tell you the way I feel. I only know I've been waiting all my life to feel like this. And now that I've discovered my heart, I want to give it to you." She realized with a jolt she now could give him that and more. A gift she owed him—her soul.

Rose of Heaven.

Since her return, there had been no time to talk about New Orleans and her discoveries. Now his gesture to her forced her to accept the truth. Her beloved Rose of Heaven belonged to him. There was no denying it, no pretending Papa had intended anything else. And she wanted, she needed, to set this right between her and Donovan, once and for all. She drew a shaky breath. "Donovan . . ."

He stopped her words with a kiss. "I've found a new song for you. I think it fits the occasion."

As he tested the trueness of the sound from the ebony and ivory keys, he also played her senses, lulling her to set aside everything but him as he began the sweet, bewitching melody.

"From thy lattice look up at a star,
At the first tender star of the night,
I will gaze at it too, so, afar,
Shall our hearts in its bosom unite.
Or but whisper thy vow to the rose,
(Just as nightly I whisper of mine),
In its petals the message 'twill close,
And will bear me the words that were thine.
So when the night winds steal softly to thy bow'r
Think, they come from my home o'er the sea,

And thou'lt know in that magical hour,
Ev'ning bringeth my heart back to thee."

The lingering echo of the music left its magic behind. They were silent for a shared eternity, and Treasure thought nothing said as much as the touch of their hands, the emotion in each glance, each mingled breath.

She lay resting her head against his chest, wrapped in shared enchantment. From nowhere, a shrill shot of cold shook through Treasure, disrupting their sweet tranquillity. Donovan rubbed his hands over her arms. "Are you chilled?"

"Just a little." She pressed a hand to her forehead, feeling a sudden dizziness wash over her. "It's nothing. I—I think I've had too much excitement this evening, that's all."

"You should be in bed. You've scarcely eaten or slept for weeks."

"Somehow, Mr. River, coming from you, that suggestion sounds more like a proposition than innocent concern." She mustered a weak smile. "And I'm tempted to take you up on it, though I fear sleep may win over passion tonight."

She made a move to straighten from his protective hold to prove to him her strength and instead staggered against him. The heaviness in her legs became an insidious, aching weakness, spreading over her with frightening speed. Pain stabbed her abdomen, and she clutched an arm to her middle as it forced a gasp from her lips.

Treasure wanted to speak but even the slight effort required to move her mouth proved nearly too much. She tried to focus on Donovan. His voice, triggering alarm somewhere deep inside her, seemed to come from very far away. "I—I don't know what's wrong . . ."

Donovan caught her in his arms as she collapsed.

Chapter Twenty-two

"The water's warm again. Would you please bring a fresh basin?" Donovan wrung out the cloth he'd used to wipe Treasure's brow for the past agonizing forty-eight hours then handed it to Eura Mae.

She draped the linen over her shoulder and lifted the basin from the nightstand, shaking her head. "You gots to get some rest and put somethin' in yo stomach 'fo you's sick too."

Donovan shrugged, his eyes on Treasure. "Maybe you could have Orange Jane send up a tray."

"Sho 'nough. A full belly'll hep you sleep."

"I've been resting. When she rests."

Treasure lay in the newly completed master suite on a beautifully carved bed Donovan and the plantation carpenter had built. Her thin nightdress clung to her damp body. Gently, so as not to wake her, he wiped her face, her arms, her neck, then carefully pulled a light coverlet over her.

He yawned and rubbed bleary eyes. Hours, days—it seemed like months since she'd stirred other than in the throes of a delirium. Settling back into the easy chair he'd moved to the bedside, he watched her as she slept, himself drifting between waking and uneasy dreams.

A tap at the door roused him. Momentarily disoriented, Donovan raked a hand through his hair, trying to clear the numbing fog in his brain.

"It's only me." Eliza slipped inside the room. "How is she?"

"Resting. For hours now. How's Rader?"

"He'll make it, praise the Lord. He's weak as a new-born kitten, but after a few weeks of rest and proper eating the doctor says he'll be as good as new."

Donovan reached out and took her hands in his. "I knew he'd pull through. He has too much to live for." He smiled at Eliza's huge belly. "Especially now."

Eliza patted her stomach. "Yes. This baby needs its daddy, that's for certain." Eliza stepped to Treasure's side. "If the child hadn't taken the responsibility of the world on her shoulders . . ." She leaned down and brushed a lank strand of dulled red-gold hair from Treasure's cheek.

" 'Scuse me, Mastuh River." Solomon paused in the doorway, a tray in his hands.

"Set it over here, Solomon. You're just in time for tea, Mrs. Johnson, and if I'm not mistaken, Orange Jane's famous honey muffins."

Donovan pulled a chair up for Eliza and they chatted quietly, both trying to avoid conversation about the plague-stricken valley. "Bettis must have worked some powerful magic," Eliza said around a mouthful of muffin. "The last time I checked the pantry, there was scarce enough to feed crumbs to the sparrows."

"I had Jared wire me enough to convince Mr. Clement to establish my credit," Donovan admitted, his attention focused on the muffin he was picking to crumbs. He didn't tell Eliza it chafed his stubborn determination never to rely on his family for anything. But the restoration of Rose of Heaven, coupled with the new demands of the plague, had been more costly than he'd anticipated, and right now he couldn't think of a better use for his family's money.

"And you're still alive. Amazin'."

He looked up and met Eliza's twinkling gaze.

"From your expression," she said, "it appears relying

420

on your family in time of trouble is an uncommon notion."

"You may have some Yankee views, Miss Eliza, but that's the Southerner in you talking. Boston is only home because I was born there. And my family is as distant to me in heart as they are in miles. They aren't likely to rescue me from anything."

"Even Jared?"

Eliza's gentle probing made Donovan uncomfortable. He shifted a little in his chair. "Jared knows I'll repay him. But that doesn't mean I have anything in common with him, or any of the Boston elite. I never have. My home is where I lay my head for the night."

"Seems to me you've spent a good many nights right here for a man who claims to be a wanderer," Eliza mused, looking at him over the rim of her teacup.

"Seamus dumped all this on me. I couldn't just leave it in the mess it was. And then, with disaster after disaster . . ." He pushed his muffin crumbs into a little pile then disarranged them again.

"Of course, you're simply bein' responsible, watching out for our poor, helpless Treasure."

"No. I mean, yes, although she could have managed, but . . ."

"Yes?"

"All right, Miss Eliza, you've won." Donovan gave up and shook his head, smiling.

"Why, whatever do you mean, Mr. River?"

"You want a confession. I confess." Donovan got to his feet and paced to the window. He looked out over the winter browns and golds and rust reds of the plantation. The land seemed almost lifeless now. But the promise of it was buried deep, and with care and hope it would slowly bloom again, stronger and more beautiful than before.

"I've become accustomed to this place, this life," he said, more to himself than Eliza. "I never felt a part of anything in my life. But here . . . I feel like I belong.

Staying doesn't seem like a responsibility. It's what I want to do."

The knowledge came to him gently, slowly like a sea change. He stood at the window a long time, thinking about how different he was from the man who had left Boston three years ago. And how a slender sprite of a woman with a vulnerable heart had taught him the meaning of family and love.

When he finally stirred from his reverie, Eliza had gone. But she left behind a piece of paper, propped against his cup, with two words written on it.

Welcome home.

After arranging the fresh basin of water and cloths Eura Mae had brought for the night ahead, Donovan settled back into his chair. He pulled out a thick sheaf of papers from under the bed. He hadn't told Treasure about the book yet. He'd meant to when she returned before Christmas, but the epidemic, with all of the accompanying pandemonium, had made the acceptance of his novel seem trifling by comparison.

There wouldn't be much money in it at first, but the publisher was already talking about a volume of short stories, then another novel. Donovan put ink to his pen and adjusted a few words on the page, glancing at Treasure. He'd fallen into the habit of talking to her, even though he knew she was oblivious. "You know, if it weren't for you, I would never have bothered to try to finish this, let alone publish it. All that nagging paid off, pretty lady."

Absorbed in his work for a time, Donovan started when Treasure gave a weak moan. He was at her side in an instant, trying to soothe her restless thrashing from side to side. "My stomach," she wailed. "Oh, everything hurts. Do something, please do something."

Donovan had never felt so helpless, so frustrated, in his life. It was agony to watch her and be useless to ease her suffering. He grabbed the bucket at the bedside just in time. The disease's furious purging began again and Donovan rung for Eura Mae to lend a hand.

For the next few hours they worked over Treasure, until finally she collapsed, a mere ghost of the woman she had been only days earlier.

"Pray, now, mastuh, all's we can do. Either she wake up or she don't," Eura Mae whispered, tears welling in her dark eyes.

Treasure lay on sweat-drenched sheets, deadly pale in the sallow lamplight. Her eyes were dark hollows in her gaunt face. Still her fragile beauty moved Donovan to bend down and tenderly kiss her face. "You can't die. Not now. Our family needs you. I need you. I can't do it without you."

The force of his emotions rose in a burning, choking wave. He felt his own tears as he lifted Treasure's limp hand in his palm to kiss her fingers, one by one.

Donovan sat beside her, her hand in his, keeping vigil far unto the night, until at last, exhausted beyond measure, he slipped into a tormented sleep, his head atop folded arms at her bedside.

Hours later Donovan awoke to the aroma of strong coffee and freshly baked biscuits. He stretched, wincing at the stiffness in his spine, the pain rebuking him for his awkward sleeping position.

On the bedside table, Solomon was setting down a laden tray. "Mornin', Mastuh River. Orange Jane say you'd be needin' dis."

"I do." Donovan rubbed at his aching neck. He looked over to Treasure and his hand froze in mid-motion.

She lay still, too still. Snatching up her wrist, he frantically searched for the throb of a pulse.' "Come on, damn it! It has to be there." He pressed harder, willing life into her veins as he snapped an order to Solomon to find Eura Mae and Bettis.

"Come on, pretty lady," he pleaded with her limp form. "Don't give up on me now." Unable to discover any beat of blood at her wrist, Donovan pressed his ear to her chest. When he could clear the roaring in his own head, he heard it. Weak, barely audible. The faint throb of her heart.

Bettis and Eura Mae rushed into the room as he gathered Treasure into his arms, cradling her against him.

Without a word, Bettis handed him the concoction of herbs and spring water he'd brewed. It had proved more than once to be the only liquid the very ill could take in the throes of the sickness, more soothing and restoring than laudanum or any other remedy the doctor had tried.

Eura Mae helped Donovan ease the liquid down Treasure's throat a few drops at a time until they'd emptied half a cup. Donovan held her the rest of the morning, alternately feeding her the herbal brew and rocking her in his arms, praying her life would be spared.

For hour after long hour, she made no response, and he detected no pulse.

The sun began its hazy, golden descent over the far horizon and Donovan felt his hope dwindling. Bettis and the doctor had both been in, and he knew from their bleak expressions neither expected her recovery. In a last desperate embrace, Donovan pressed her close, willing his strength to imbue her with life.

Suddenly, Treasure let out a soft cry. Her hand groped weakly against his chest. Giddy with relief, Donovan grabbed her wrist and listened with his fingers. Life throbbed in the tiny blue vein beneath her translucent skin.

"Oh, God — Treasure . . ." Donovan ran his hands over her body in reassurance, burying his face in her hair. He could think of nothing strong enough to express his feelings. They were beyond relief, beyond joy.

A gentle hand on his shoulder drew his attention to

Eliza's presence. "She's going to be just fine. You'll see."

"I intend to make certain of it. For the rest of my life. I swear it."

Tears slid unheeded down Eliza's face. "Honey, I've known that for a long time. I was just waiting for the two of you to realize it."

"I am quite capable of walking to the bottom of the stairs!"

"That's the Treasure McGlavrin we all know and love," Donovan teased as he swept her into his arms.

Treasure wondered at his heady exuberance. All morning he'd been in and out of her bedroom, asking her at least a hundred times if she felt well enough to sit in the garden for a short spell.

"I would rather walk," she insisted, feeling foolish being carried through her own house.

"Sorry, I can't oblige that request. I can't spare another two weeks nursing a broken leg when your knees give out halfway down."

"Stubborn man." Treasure feigned annoyance although she secretly relished his strong support. Something about the way he looked at her this morning made her feel shy and vulnerable. Which was foolish, she told herself. The man had spent nearly two weeks nursing her day and night; they were lovers. Why did she suddenly feel this was any more momentous than the last?

Donovan carried her downstairs and out the back lawns to her mama's garden. Carefully, he set her down at the fountain's edge. "Are you comfortable? If not, I can . . ."

"You're better at fussing than Eura Mae. I'm fine." She leaned back to bask in the mid-morning sun. It was unseasonably mild, almost spring-like, a treacherous warmth in the air. "It seems so long. I'd almost forgotten how I love the outdoors."

"And I almost waited too long to realize how much I love you."

Treasure stared, stock-still. An unbelieving, joyous warmth began stealing over her heart. Had she heard him rightly? Did she dare believe . . . ?

Donovan stood in front of her, looking down, his hands jammed deep in the pockets of his trousers. He looked caught between a smile and uncertainty. "I love you. I have for a very long time. I just didn't want to admit it to you, even to myself. I thought — I thought loving someone meant losing myself, my direction, my freedom. I was wrong." He reached out and took her hands in his, drawing Treasure to her feet. "I could have searched forever and never found what I wanted. But I didn't have to look. It's been here all along. You're everything I've ever needed, everything I'll ever want."

Her tears spilled onto his fingers as he took her face in his hands and kissed her, taking an eternity, as if every touch of his lips to hers was a promise of the heart.

Treasure wondered if it was possible to feel such intense happiness and painful anguish simultaneously. She felt as if her heart would break from the warring storm of emotion. She loved him. God, she loved him. His admission was everything she had longed to hear, for a lifetime it seemed. But she also loved Rose of Heaven. And knowing he cared forced her to make an agonizing decision.

He rightfully owned Rose of Heaven. If she relinquished her beloved land, it would be like losing her soul. But if she continued to live a lie, she would lose him and he was her heart.

"Donovan, I can't — I . . ."

Breaking away from him, she turned to hide the turmoil she knew must show in her eyes. *How can I choose?*

"Treasure?"

Treasure whirled back around. "I can't pretend any-

426

more. I love you too much. Rose of Heaven is yours."

Donovan frowned. "What are you talking about?"

She drew a tremulous breath and looked him straight in the eyes. "I let you believe I went to Louisiana to make peace with Papa's memory. It was a lie. I went to find the truth of how Papa died. I had to know once and for all."

"I see." His expression told her nothing.

"I knew then I loved you. I was afraid—"

"Of loving a murderer?" he finished for her, a bitter smile twisting his mouth.

"Yes. I'm sorry for doubting you now, but I had my family to think about, my heart . . ." Treasure stared miserably at her clenched hands.

"Treasure, you little idiot." Wrapping his arms around her, Donovan cradled her in the circle of his embrace. "It's not as if I ever gave you reason to trust me. I didn't want to admit my reasons for leaving Boston. I arrogantly expected you simply to trust me." He tilted her chin, smiling into her eyes.

"Arrogant? Mysterious? You?" Treasure laughed up at him. "It doesn't matter. None of it matters. I want to forget everything. I just want to hear you say it again."

"Say what, Miss McGlavrin?" Donovan teased a kiss against the corner of her mouth. "That I'm passionately . . ." He kissed the opposite corner. "Desperately . . ." His lips brushed hers. "Completely in love with you?"

The hunger in his kiss drove away Treasure's sense of the garden around them. It was Solomon's voice, loudly calling, that finally penetrated her blissful daze.

"Missy Treasure? Is you in here?"

Treasure exchanged a glance with Donovan, who threw up his hands in good-natured surrender. "Over here, Solomon," she directed.

"I's sorry, Missy Treasure, Mastuh River," Solomon said as he came up the path. "But dis letter jus' come by

427

messenger. Eura Mae says I should bring it right to Mastuh River."

"It's all right, Solomon." Donovan took the letter from Solomon's outstretched hand. His face sobered as he looked at the envelope.

When Solomon had gone, Treasure glanced at the letter, then looked up to Donovan, mystified. "It's addressed to Donovan Radcliffe. Who . . ."

Donovan traced a finger over the neat, precise writing. "Me, pretty lady."

"You?" Treasure stared.

"Me. Donovan Trevor Radcliffe the Third, if you want the whole of it." He heaved a sigh. "I had hoped to explain under more ideal circumstances. But it appears my past has caught up with me sooner than I anticipated."

"That's your name — Donovan Radcliffe?"

"The name I was born and bred with."

Treasure struggled against an angry disbelief. "And when, pray tell, were you going to tell me the real name of the man I love? The man who professes to love me?"

"I'm not exactly proud of the life I left behind in Boston. I wanted to forget it." He flung out a hand. "I planned to tell you, but this morning how I felt seemed more important than detailing my history. If you'll just let me read this, I'll tell you everything. And you'll see how little it matters."

Reminding herself how she'd misjudged him in the past and paid the price dearly with regret, Treasure nodded. They walked back to the fountain and sat together at its edge.

As she watched Donovan tear open the envelope and scan over its contents, a dark burden seemed to settle heavily on his shoulders.

He read silently first, then aloud to her.

My dear brother,
It is with a heavy heart I lay pen to paper to tell

you of the death of our father. Would that I could ease your grief with word of a peaceful passing. But, as you might imagine, his was a fitful end. He was determined to best even the power of death, and profound regrets tormented him to his last breath.

Here lies the most difficult task for me. During his final hours, father spoke of you alone, struggling to reconcile to a peaceful state his role in your long-standing battle. Although never admitting any failure on his part, his request was that I find you and tell you he demanded so much of you, pushed you so hard to follow in his wake because he recognized you had been endowed with a rare talent for knowing the minds of other men and being able put their dreams, and hopes and feelings, into words. It was a talent he coveted, and knew he would never have. When you left, abandoning the future he'd laid out for you, he despised you for nothing other than your selfishness. He saw your departure as betrayal.

The knowledge of his own limitations in his profession destroyed him; his successes offered no comfort, little satisfaction.

In death, he wished only that you would return and succeed him as head of both the family and the business. I understand your feelings in the matter, but I promised I would let you know his last desire.

I know your decision will not be easy. I can only offer you my sympathies and assistance, if you should require it. Godspeed.

Yr. devoted brother, Jared

Treasure wrapped her arms around Donovan's shoulders when he finished. "I am so sorry," she whispered.

"Yes, well . . ." Donovan closed his eyes for a mo-

429

ment. When he opened them again, Treasure saw a deadness had replaced the silver fire. "I've run away from duty all these years. Now, there's no escape from it. He made certain of that."

"What do you mean?"

"I have to go back. I owe it to Jared and my mother. My father's legacy to me is the responsibility of business and family. He knew I couldn't refuse a dying request, even though it's the last thing I want."

Fear gripped Treasure's heart. For the first time, she'd truly found him. He loved her and she him. And now she could lose him to a ghost. "You have a choice. Stay here. With me. This is where you belong."

"I can't." Donovan got to his feet, pacing the ground in front of the fountain. "No matter how much I want to." He made an attempt at a smile. "You're partly to blame, you know. You're the one who showed me how important family is."

"And you've showed me how important following your heart is. Isn't there any other way?"

"Only one, pretty lady." He stroked her cheek gently with the back of his hand.

"What is that? I can't think of losing you now. I love you."

"Enough to share the rest of your life with me as Mrs. Donovan Trevor Radcliffe the Third?"

Perplexed, stunned by his sudden proposal, Treasure could only gape at him.

"Will you marry me, Treasure? Do you love me enough to move to Boston as my wife?"

Treasure gazed into Donovan's deep, searching eyes. "I do love you, and I want nothing more than to be your wife. It's just—"

"Rose of Heaven."

"I—I've never imagined living anywhere else on earth. Leaving it behind, forever . . ."

"I understand." He turned away from her. "And the choice is yours. I've run away from my name and my duty too long. I have to return, or I'll be no kind of man at all. You, at least, should be pleased. I'll finally be the kind of gentleman you've always held in such great esteem."

"I love you just the way you are."

Donovan looked at her, and Treasure knew his question before he voiced it. "But do you love me enough?"

She couldn't answer, and after a long silence, Donovan snapped around and strode down the path, leaving her alone in the quiet garden.

"Well, I for one am certainly glad the dreadful scourge is over," Valene declared over breakfast in the dining hall. "Honestly, my dear, I am just a tiny bit upset at you for your foolishness in allowin' half the valley to invade Rose of Heaven."

Treasure glanced to Donovan. He had showed up at breakfast, at Emmy's request, Treasure learned, but had sat the entire meal in brooding silence. "Mr. River and I agreed to provide a sanctuary for anyone in need of care. I would do the same again, Aunt Valene, without hesitation."

"You risked your life, cousin. That's the sort of chance one can't afford to take." Sitting beside his mother, Ransom shot her a disapproving look over the top of his pince-nez.

Treasure bit back an acid retort. She supposed he meant well. Since he and her aunt had returned two days past, Ransom had been polite, but distant. He appeared to have accepted their broken engagement with a gentleman's restraint, although at times she caught him watching her with an odd, calculating expression that quickly vanished when she met his eyes.

"If you'll excuse me," Donovan said, his voice startling her. "I have to finish packing."

"I'll help," Emmy piped up.

"As a matter of fact, I have a gift for my mother that needs a woman's touch wrapping it."

431

"Oh, I've just the paper and ribbon. May I be excused too, please, Treasure?"

Treasure glanced to Donovan's impassive face, and then back to her sister. "Of course." She guessed how hard it would be for Emmaline when Donovan left.

How hard will it be if you have to watch him leave? Since the morning in the garden, Donovan had never seemed more a stranger. A million times, Treasure longed to run to him and tell him she would go to Boston. Every time, her heart-fear held her back.

"When will you be leavin', Mistuh River?" Valene drawled. She rapped her spoon on the edge of her teacup a few more times than necessary.

"Noon," Donovan answered, his eyes fixed on Treasure.

It struck her that she hardly recognized the man staring at her with love—and pain—hidden behind steely eyes. Freshly shaved and groomed to perfection, he wore an expensively tailored gray coat and black trousers. A more dashing Southern gentleman had never crossed her threshold. Yet he wasn't the man she had fallen in love with.

When she'd tried to explain as much three days ago, they'd argued until, frustrated by her lack of faith in him, he'd walked out. He spent the night in the valley and didn't return until the next evening. It was then he informed her his arrangements to leave were final.

"I've waited as long as I can," he'd said. "I'm leaving Thursday."

"I want to go. I will." Her pleading words didn't sound convincing, even to herself. "I have a few details to attend to, that's all. I must lay out the spring planting for Bettis to supervise, and organize the household. It will only take a week, maybe two."

"You're lying to yourself, Treasure. The truth is your roots are so deep in this Alabama earth you're afraid you'll wither and die if you leave. No matter how much you say you love me, you love Rose of Heaven more."

"That isn't true!"

"It is. And the sooner we both accept that, the better."

He'd left her that day. And now, when he walked away, Treasure knew it would be forever.

She stood in the parlor until noon, pacing and waiting. When the hired carriage pulled up outside, she went out onto the porch as Donovan and Emmy came up. He loaded his bag and trunk, giving Emmy then Abby a long hug before turning to look at Treasure.

Treasure took a step toward him, but his eyes stopped her. For a moment, his pain replaced the faraway coldness of the past days. She wanted to tell him goodbye, to force the words from her mouth. Instead, she could only watch him leave, knowing she no longer had a heart.

Chapter Twenty-three

In the weeks following Donovan's abrupt departure, Treasure's long, lonely days dragged into endless, sleep-starved nights. She constantly kept busy. Replenishing the pantry, planning the spring crops, purchasing new stock; fussing and fretting and overseeing, all the tasks that before had been a substitute for emotion. Then, she never recognized her own emptiness. Now, it dogged her like a relentless nemesis, in wakefulness and dreams.

Worry for Spring and Elijah, and for Camille, plagued her through the long hours. Where were they? Were they safe? It hurt to think her former cold, unyielding attitude was likely the reason she hadn't even received so much as a letter from either of her absent sisters.

Night after miserable night she lay awake, missing them, fretting about them. And missing Donovan.

Treasure hadn't expected the pain of losing him to run so deep. If only she could begin again, with all of them. She would listen with her heart, and never, ever take the gift of love for granted. If only she had the chance . . .

But all she could do now was wait. Wait and pray for Spring and Camille to contact her. Wait for her heart to forget Donovan River.

As if it ever could.

With all her endless duties and worries, it had been a relief to relinquish the responsibility of running the household to Aunt Valene. Treasure knew she had never been as efficient at domestic chores as she was with planting and the business of the plantation. And her aunt clearly reveled in the role of mistress of the house. The slaves working under her, on the other hand, did not.

Valene ran the house with a sharp tongue and a heavy hand, and though Treasure had always been firm, she'd never been harsh. Aunt Orange Jane, Solomon, Mammie Eura Mae, and the others had taken to silent, stubborn resistance. With long faces and slow hands, they went about their work, accomplishing only what was mandatory for that day. *They'll adjust,* Treasure reminded herself to ease her discomfort with the situation. *They'll adapt because they have no choice. None of us do.*

Ransom, to her relief, spent long hours away from Rose of Heaven, engrossed in his law practice. He took only a perfunctory interest in the plantation, making his disapproval clear at Treasure's determination to run the plantation herself.

She'd had only one coolly cordial letter from Donovan, telling her of his arrival and saying he had assumed his father's position as publisher of the *Boston Courier-Journal.* There were no words of intimacy in his letter, nothing to indicate how he felt about his new life. Or her. Was he happy? Was he trying to forget her? Did he even think about the South he'd left behind? She missed him. She missed Spring and Elijah. And she missed Erin.

Sitting in the cart, bound for the Johnsons', Treasure wondered for the thousandth time if her decision to stay behind had been best. There were so many *if*s, *perhaps*es, *maybe*s clouding her emotions, she didn't know anymore.

As Bettis slowed the cart to a halt in front of the Johnsons' store, Treasure tried to shake away her melancholy mood. "I won't be long," she said, climbing down with her basket of baked goods and some of the twins' baby toys she'd brought for Eliza and her new daughter.

"I be waitin' here, Miz Treasure."

Treasure fixed a smile on her face as she pushed open the door to the store. Rader, busy behind the front counter, waved her toward the upstairs. "Go on up. Liza'll be glad to see you."

Eliza sat propped in bed, her new baby at her breast, swaddled in a downy pink blanket. "Why, hello, honey, it's so good to see you." She smiled up to Treasure, but a knowing frown quickly replaced her welcoming expression. "You are a sight. Why, I haven't seen you so skinny since you had that wretched sickness."

"I've been busy." Treasure turned the subject by bending over the suckling infant. "Hello, Annie," she d softly. "You're beautiful. Just like your mama." The void inside her seemed deeper, blacker, as she watched the contented baby sigh and nestle closer to her mother.

"Yours will be just as lovely, when that day comes."

"I've brought some toys," Treasure said quickly, moving away to hide the pain that struck her heart. "Where shall I put them?"

"In the basket next to the hearth if you don't mind. Annie thanks you."

During the awkward silence that followed, Treasure longed to pour out her heart to her friend. But she dared not. Annie's birthing had been long and difficult and now, two weeks later, Eliza was just beginning to regain her strength.

"Have you heard from Donovan again?" Eliza spoke the question softly into the hushed room.

Treasure kept her hands busy with the basket of toys. "I suppose he's terribly busy. I should imagine running a newspaper is a consuming business. It's probably one

436

of those radical publications that constantly condemn Southern planters for slavery," she added with a weak attempt at a laugh.

"I wouldn't put it past Donovan to put his views before God and Boston, that's for certain. Well now, things must be just as you always wanted them up at Rose of Heaven. Your aunt oversees those chores you always hated. You have the most beautiful home in this corner of the county and land primed for a season of bumper crops. You've made peace with the valley, and Donovan's lumber mill project is revivin' everyone's fortunes. What more could you possibly want?"

Treasure sank to the floor near the toy basket and fiddled with a colorful wooden top Donovan had made for Erin. "Nothing, I suppose. Everything is perfect."

"Is it?"

"Of course."

"Oh, Treasure." Eliza sighed, shaking her head. "Child, you are the most heaven-sent liar. When are you going to learn you can't bury your heart with the cotton seed?"

"I'm afraid," Treasure whispered.

"Honey, we all are. Love is a frightening thing. It makes us vulnerable to our needs and desires, our dreams. We have to depend on another for our happiness and that's scary, too. But it's something none of us can be without." Pulling her wrapper back over her breast, Eliza climbed out of bed and gently set her drowsy daughter back in the cradle at her bedside. She went to Treasure and knelt beside her on the floor, taking her hands. "Go to him. Trust your heart."

"What if he leaves? Maybe he's like Papa, a rover who can't stop wandering."

"That's an excuse, and you know it. What you're really afraid of is losing Rose of Heaven. The land is keeping you apart."

"I know it," Treasure cried. "But Rose of Heaven is me, it's all I have to prove I can succeed, that I can take care of my family. What do I have without it? What am I without it?"

"You tell me."

Eliza's question gave Treasure pause. "I — I'm . . ."

"Treasure McGlavrin. A strong, determined, beautiful woman who's kept body and soul *and* her family together despite everything against her. No one can take that away from you. No one except you, Treasure."

"You're right." Suddenly, all the confusion, the doubt, cleared like fog to sunshine. "I don't need Rose of Heaven to prove my worth," she said, feeling an awe-struck amazement. "All I need is my family and friends. And Donovan. I've learned to trust myself. I love Rose of Heaven. But I love Donovan more. How could I ever have doubted that?"

Eliza laughed and threw her arms around Treasure, hugging her tightly. When they pulled apart, smiling at each other, Eliza's eyes sparkled with her old mischief. "So — when do you leave for Boston?"

"Well — as soon as I can arrange it! I'd leave today, if I could, but I have to think of Abby and Emmy."

"What about your aunt? Wouldn't she help?"

Treasure grimaced. "She's so preoccupied playing mistress of Rose of Heaven, she ignores the girls for the most part. Except to remind them of their manners, or when to go to bed."

"It's settled then. They'll stay with Mr. Johnson and me."

"But —"

"Don't say a word, honey. I do have my hands full with Annie, but if you lend me Eura Mae for the time you're gone, we'll manage just fine."

"Are you sure? I could —"

"Are you goin' to argue with me all day or are you going to go home and start packin', Miss McGlavrin?"

Treasure gave her friend another hug. "Packing, Mrs. Johnson. I'm going to start packing."

Sweetie, Treasure's choice to accompany her on yet another journey, shifted for a clearer view from her seat opposite Treasure in the hired carriage. "Lordy, I ain't never seed so many folks in fancy clothes jest out walkin' at midday. And it ain't even Sunday!"

Treasure twined and untwined her gloved fingers. The carriage bounced and rattled along Boston's bustling streets, a myriad of new sights and sounds setting her mind in a whirl and her stomach fluttering.

The nearly two weeks on the train had seemed endless, but now that she was so close to seeing Donovan again, anxiety overwhelmed her. Would he be angry at her surprise appearance? Or worse — unthinkable — would he resent her disrupting the life he'd built here. What if he no longer wanted her? What if he'd forgotten the love between them? What if . . . what if . . . her mind fairly screamed doubts until she thought it would burst from the pressure.

The carriage turned off onto a street leading out of the main heart of the city, to an exclusive area of homes near the sea. It finally pulled to a stop in front of a glorious, sprawling rise of brick and stone that seemed to perch on the very edge of the ocean. A tree-lined circular drive fronted the dazzling view.

Treasure's first thought was that the driver was lost and had stopped to ask directions of the guard at the gate.

"Mercy me, is dat a house or a fancy hotel?" Sweetie asked, her eyes wide.

In the next instant the guard opened the gate and the carriage rolled up the drive. A liveried butler stepped outside massive, carved doors, a curious look on his face. Treasure fervently wished she had sent word ahead of her arrival, even though she risked the chance Donovan might refuse to see her. Now it was too late.

The driver helped Treasure and Sweetie from the carriage. Paying him, she made her way up the elaborate front steps, certain with each step her legs would desert her.

She opened her mouth to announce herself just as an extremely handsome man, smaller in stature but striking in his resemblance to Donovan, appeared in the doorway.

"What is it, Carlan?" he asked the butler.

"I'm afraid I don't know, sir."

"Mr. Jared Radcliffe?" Treasure asked.

The man stepped outside in front of Carlan. He gave Treasure a quick appraisal, then offered her an approving smile. "At your service," he answered with a bow. "I beg your pardon, miss, but I'm at a loss. Have you come to see Fenella?"

"No. No, you see . . ." Treasure drew a deep breath. "I've come to see Donovan."

"Hair the color of the sunrise, flashing green eyes with a temper to match. Of course! With that Southern drawl—why, Treasure McGlavrin, I couldn't have pictured you any better if Donovan had shown me a portrait. My brother does have a passing talent with words," he added with a grin so reminiscent of Donovan, Treasure's heart lurched.

"He told you about me, then," she managed, feeling rather embarrassed by Donovan's avid description. "I am sorry to arrive unannounced, but I didn't want to waste time sending letters."

"Donovan never reads them anyway," Jared said, ushering her inside. He called orders to the butler to escort Sweetie to a room adjoining hers in the guest wing to begin unpacking her mistress's luggage. "I am so pleased you're here. Fenella—my wife—and I have been at wit's end over Donovan. Perhaps you can bring him to his senses."

As he led her into the parlor, Treasure surreptitiously studied him. While the physical resemblance was undeniable, she marveled at the difference in bearing between Donovan and his brother. Donovan's charm was his passion for life, his quicksilver moods, and easy smile. Jared, utterly gracious, impeccable in manner and grooming, seemed his complete opposite. Yet as they chatted over the details of her journey and her impressions of Boston, Treasure caught glimpses of a sharp wit and the same keen perception she admired in Donovan. And remembering Jared's devotion to working with the underground railroad, she knew he must share a measure of Donovan's courage and passion for causes.

At last, emboldened by the warmth of his reception, Treasure ventured to ask, "How is Donovan finding his new responsibilities? Is he having difficulties?"

"Quite the opposite." Jared paused as the butler brought in a coffee tray. He handed Treasure a cup with a wry smile. "Donovan has taken over with a vengeance; he is quite adept at the business. We scarcely see him, and when we do . . . well, he is so short-tempered and brooding, we do best to avoid him."

"I see."

"Do you?"

Treasure hesitated. "Yes," she said finally. "At the risk of being impertinent, I should think you would be more suited to the demands of running a newspaper. Donovan is a wonderful writer, but he has always been quite haphazard about business. In fact, he despises it."

To her surprise, a bitter pain flashed from behind Jared's polite mask. "Yes, I have always known that." He stared into his coffee cup. "Unfortunately, I was never able to prove to our father that while I relished the challenges and disciplines of business, Donovan did not. My brother doesn't belong here, he never has. The sales of his novel prove that."

Treasure felt a quiver of pride. "Is it doing well, then?"

"Very well. Didn't he tell you?"

"We did not part on the best of terms. I hope this visit

441

can remedy that. Mr. Radcliffe — Jared," she amended as he protested the formality. "Have you told Donovan how you feel about the newspaper and his position?"

Jared toyed with the handle of his cup. "Father wanted him to assume control of the business. I am uncomfortable with the idea of attempting to convince Donovan otherwise, and he does not talk about it."

"Then, forgive me, but you are both fools."

Jared's startled eyes flew to her face.

"You are obviously both very unhappy. And yet the solution is so very simple — "

The furious slam of the front door interrupted her. Treasure's heart began to thud against her chest as she recognized the heavy tread in the hallway. The high back of her chair obstructed her view of the parlor door so she at first only heard his dark voice as he strode in without bothering to knock.

"Damn it, Jared, I thought you told me those suppliers were — I'm sorry," he said in a more temperate tone. "I wasn't aware you had a visitor."

"I don't. The visitor is yours," Jared said. With a smile for Treasure, he left them alone in the room, closing the door on Donovan's silent question.

Gathering her courage, Treasure slowly stood up and faced him.

"Treasure . . ." Wary disbelief warred with incredulous joy for command of his expression. "You — you're here . . ." Donovan stopped, staring blankly.

"Amazing," she said softly, putting all her love and passion into her eyes, her tremulous smile. "Donovan River at a loss for words."

The bemusement left his face. In two strides, Donovan had reached her and swept her into his arms, kissing her slowly and deeply as if he were trying to atone for all the desperate days they had spent apart.

When they parted, breathless, Donovan pulled'her down into his lap on a soft-cushioned divan. He ran his hands over her body and loosed her neat chignon of

442

hair, threading his fingers through its silky fire. "I don't care why you're here. But you'd better not have made plans to leave because I don't intend to let you go, ever again."

"Nor I you. I couldn't bear it." She touched his face, hardly daring to believe in the happiness that sang through her veins. "I love you."

"And I love you, pretty lady."

"You know, Mr. Radcliffe," she teased as his mouth began exploring the tender curve of her neck and throat. It's most improper, kissing in the parlor in the middle of the afternoon."

"Oh, no. This isn't improper." She delighted in his raffish grin as he lowered her against the cushions. "But I'll show you what is."

At dinner that evening, Treasure was pleased and relieved that Donovan's family accepted his announcement of her arrival and their plans to marry as soon as possible. Jared's wife, Fenella, congratulated them with unreserved enthusiasm, and his mother, though less ebullient, appeared at least satisfied with Donovan's obvious happiness.

Treasure excused herself early after the meal, pleading weariness from the long journey. In truth, she wanted nothing more than to have an opportunity to be alone and savor her newfound joy. For more than an hour, she sat by the fire, simply basking in contentment. A tap at her door finally roused her from the pleasant reverie and Treasure answered it with a secret smile, knowing who her midnight caller would be.

He was leaning against the door frame, clad only and very obviously in a black silk robe. In one hand he held a decanter; in the other, two snifters. "Care to share a brandy, pretty lady?"

"Don't you have to be at your offices early?" she teased, holding him at bay with a caressing hand. Her fingers teased up and down the deep cleft in the dark silk.

Donovan felt desire smolder low in his body. It had been too long since he'd touched her, embraced her soft skin with his. She wore a dressing gown of purest white, almost absurdly demure. Yet the velvet material was meant to be felt with the fingertips, and any man would have touched her at his peril. "Damn the newspaper," he growled. "If you don't let me in, I can't answer for the consequences."

Treasure stepped aside, just far enough to let him pass, near enough he had to brush against her to enter. "I'm glad you still have a little of the uncivilized river rat I love left in you."

"Perhaps more than is good for me," he said, pouring them each a snifter of brandy.

"Enough to know you're hopeless as a Boston aristocrat. What made you think you should ever run a newspaper?"

"Ah, my love, you never did mince words."

"Well, it's obvious you're miserable. And now that you have made a success of your novel — the novel I knew nothing of, I must remind you — why do you insist on staying where you don't belong?"

"I intended to tell you about the book," Donovan said, deliberately avoiding her question. "But the plague, and then my father's death, made it seem rather unimportant."

"Unimportant?" His nonchalance frustrated her. Treasure set down her glass, facing him boldly. "Jared told me —"

"Jared talks too much," Donovan murmured. Putting down his own glass, he moved around behind her, letting her feel the hardness and heat of his passion. "And so do you. I want you."

"Now?" Treasure melded her body to his.

"Yes, now, and then again," he whispered against her neck. "And again." He kissed the bared flesh of her shoulder as he slipped her wrapper from her shoulders.

"And again." The rich material pooled around her feet. "Any complaints?"

Treasure turned and slowly unfastened the belt of his robe. "Only one." She let her hand dance from his chest downward until he sucked in a fervored breath at her brazen caresses. "Why did you take so long to begin?"

The gurgle and rush of water awoke Treasure early the next morning. Confused, she blinked in the soft half-light, trying to rally her thoughts.

"Good morning." Donovan, propped upon an elbow next to her, stole a lingering kiss. "The servants are drawing *your* bath. I failed to mention I'd be spending the night in the guest wing." He smiled raffishly.

"Mmmm . . ." Treasure closed her eyes again. She nestled against him, absently smoothing her hand back and forth over his shoulder and arm.

"It does seem a waste, though," Donovan mused.

Treasure, still wrapped in a warm blissful fog, loved the rumble of his voice under her ear, but the words seemed insignificant. "Yes, well, maybe later," she murmured, letting herself begin to drift into a light sleep.

In the next instant, her eyes flew open. Donovan flung back the bed clothes, swung to his feet, and scooped her up into his arms.

"What are you doing?"

"Making good use of the bath." He carried her into the small room adjoining her bedchamber and set her on her feet in front of the claw-footed tub. Steam curled off the surface of the water, filling the room with a sultry dew-damp mist. The faint scent of roses twined with the musky heat of desire.

Donovan stepped into the bath, sliding down into the heated water. He held a hand out to her, invitation in his eyes.

Nearly complying, Treasure withdrew her hand before it touched his, a tiny smile curving her mouth. Instead, she picked up the soap lying nearby and knelt beside the tub. With a lazy motion, she dipped it into the water, slowly rubbing it between her hands until the creamy foam slid between her fingers. Her blood raced with a heady anticipation, but she kept her touch deliberately light as she smoothed the lather over his shoulders and chest.

"You're playing a dangerous game, pretty lady." Donovan's eyes moved hot and hungry over her bare skin.

"I thought you liked games. I do recall one in particular . . ." She let one finger draw a line from throat to thigh. "No buttons this time," she murmured as her hand stroked his hardness. The slick glide of water on his skin, the tensing of muscle, the molten silver of his eyes fed her own quickening need until she was breathless, dizzy from the power of it.

Donovan endured her sweet torment for long, fevered moments, torturing them both with the wait for release. Then, when Treasure teetered on the brink of surrendering to him, he reached out and, with swift grace, pulled her up and atop him, joining their bodies in a dizzying thrust of pure sensation.

As they moved together, climbing and falling to the height and fire of ecstasy, Treasure knew, at last, no matter what their destiny, they truly belonged to each other.

"I suppose I should make an appearance at the *Journal* office today." Hours later, Donovan stretched lazily against the propped-up pillows. His hand idly fondled Treasure's tousled hair where it spilled over his chest.

Treasure sighed. "Why? Why are you trying to force yourself to do something you hate?" When he didn't answer, she sat up, forcing him to meet her eyes. "I refuse to let it rest until you explain it to me."

"I'm not sure I can explain it to myself." Tossing aside the bedclothes, Donovan got up and pulled on his robe, restlessly pacing the room. Treasure waited silently till at last he came and sat back beside her. "When I was a boy, I worshipped my father. I would have done anything to command his respect. I was fascinated with the business of writing and publishing. I wanted to be just like him. And he insisted on it. He never stopped demanding, never stopped pushing, even when it became obvious I wasn't suited to the business of newspapering."

"How long did it go on?"

"For as long as I can remember until the day I left."

"And then?"

"Then, we had one hell of a row. I was nineteen and tired of being told I would never amount to anything unless I applied myself to my father's dictates. I told him I was leaving. He just laughed in my face. So, being the responsible man I am, I left."

Treasure couldn't resist a smile. "I confess, I'm not surprised. Where did you go?"

"Here and there." Donovan shrugged. "It seemed a grand adventure. Writing, and a few other odd skills, paid the way. I had no intention of going back to Boston."

"Why did you?"

"I kept in touch with Jared. He asked me to. For my mother's sake." His face tightened. "It was a mistake. To my father, I was a dead man. We lasted an hour in each other's company before I completely lost my temper and walked out again. That was the last time I saw him."

"I am sorry for that," Treasure said softly. "But in truth, you may never have been able to reconcile with him. And it seems you have made peace with your mother and Jared."

"Yes . . . except at times, things between Jared and I seem . . . uneasy."

"Oh, Donovan, for a man who knows so much about people, you've learned precious little about your own

447

family." Treasure turned his face to hers. "Jared belongs in your position. It's what he wants."

"Jared? But he's never said anything to me."

"Of course not. He's as stubborn as you about playing out this charade." Treasure drew a breath, struggling to put words to the feelings in her heart. "You are a writer, not a journalist. And I am a planter, not a Boston socialite. You can't continue to punish yourself for doing what you were born to do. And you can't change, no matter how much your father wanted you to. Let the past go. It's what you have taught me. For your sake, learn your own lesson."

Donovan considered her face. "You want to go back to Rose of Heaven. Don't you? The truth."

"Yes." She said it simply, without hesitation. "I belong there."

"We belong there, pretty lady." Donovan suddenly laughed, a rich, throaty sound that caught Treasure up in its unbridled elation. "I don't know why I've been so stupidly blind. It nearly cost me the only thing that matters to me more than life — you." He took her face between his hands and kissed her, slowly, deeply, giving and taking the fire and silver strength of their love. "Let's go back. As soon as possible."

"To our home?" The word never tasted sweeter.

"Yes." Donovan smiled into her eyes. "To our home."

Two days later, in the midst of a flurry of packing and preparing for their departure, Donovan suddenly announced he wanted to pay a visit to some friends who lived on the west side of the city. With no more word of explanation, he bundled Treasure into the carriage, stubbornly changing the subject each time she asked about their destination.

Now, nervous and perplexed, she stood at his side as he tapped the brass knocker of a modest brick home set among the new green of a half-dozen silver maples.

As the door opened, Treasure clutched his arm to

keep from collapsing then and there on the porch steps. "I don't believe it. Spring!" With a cry of happiness, Treasure flung her arms around her sister. Spring, weeping and laughing at the same time, returned her embrace, hugging her tightly.

"Oh Spring." Treasure finally stood back, holding her sister at arm's length. "I never thought we would be together again. I was wrong, so wrong, to send you away. I don't know how you can ever forgive me," she said, tears welling in her eyes.

"I love you, Treasure," Spring said, pressing her close again. "And we found our way back to each other. That's all that matters."

"I think we'll take this reunion inside," Donovan said, steering the two women into the little house.

Elijah stood waiting for them in the small sitting room. Treasure looked at him a long moment and suddenly realized what Donovan had tried to tell her so long ago. Love chooses its own. Without a word, she walked up to Elijah and held out her hands.

His took them in his and a smile broke over his face. "It's good to see you, Miss Treasure."

Treasure nodded, too overcome with emotion to tell him what was in her heart. He seemed to sense her feeling and gently squeezed her hands.

"I have someone for you to meet," Spring said softly. She ran out of the room and came back carrying a small bundle. "This is Trevor. Our son."

Treasure bent to the baby, catching her breath. Wide blue eyes stared back at her. She reverently touched the dark-gold fuzz on his head, his soft cinnamon skin. "He's perfect. He has your eyes, Elijah, and your strong cheekbones. But that mischievous little twist to his mouth is all you, Spring."

"Personally, I'm rather partial to his name," Donovan put in.

Spring laughed. "I wanted to call him River, but Elijah wouldn't hear of it."

"I always wanted to know why you chose that name," Elijah said.

"No reason actually, except that I was heading South and Southerners are famous for naming people after things. And I have this affinity for water." Donovan glanced to Treasure, eliciting a blush.

To cover her confusion, Treasure let Spring put Trevor into her arms. She sat down on the divan, and he waved a chubby fist at her, reaching up to grab at a strand of bright hair. When she looked at him, she understood all of Spring's determination to be with Elijah. Trevor was evidence of their love, and Treasure longed to share that same fulfillment with Donovan.

Treasure touched his soft, milky-smelling skin again. "He's so happy and content. He reminds me of — "

"Erin?" Spring finished for her. Spring sat down beside Treasure and squeezed her hand. "I miss her, too. When we got Donovan's letter, telling us . . ." Tears glistened in her eyes. "Every time I look at Trevor, I see a little part of Erin. It's almost as if a part of her has come back through him."

"He truly is a perfect gift of love," Treasure said. She turned and smiled at her sister. "For all of us."

The tears in her eyes mirrored Spring's, and for a moment the two sisters sat in silence, hands touching, content to be together. Spring finally broke the quiet by asking, "How are Abby and Emmy? I haven't been able to write because we've been moving around so much. I do want to give you some letters to take back to them, though."

"Of course I will. And your sisters are fine. I've no doubt by this time they've charmed Rader and Eliza into extra desserts and fewer chores. And I do wish you could see Annie, Eliza's baby." Treasure described at length for her sister and Elijah the events that had occurred since they'd left Rose of Heaven, sketching in as many details as she could about family and friends.

"And Camille?" Spring asked. "Have you heard from her?"

Treasure shook her head. "No. But I pray every night she's all right."

Spring reached out and enfolded Treasure in a warm embrace. "We mustn't give up hope. Rose of Heaven is her home, too. I just know she'll come back someday."

"Speaking of homes," Treasure said, forcing herself not to dwell on sad memories. "Yours is lovely. I'm proud of you both."

"Elijah deserves the praise for keeping up the house," Spring confessed with a twinkle. "I'm a hopeless mess. I don't know how he manages with me and Trevor and his job at the *Journal*."

"You work for Donovan's newspaper?" Treasure asked Elijah.

"He's the printing supervisor," Donovan answered for him. "And the way he works, his investments will soon pay him more than the newspaper can, and he'll be in business for himself."

"We never would have made it without your help, Donovan," Spring said.

Treasure looked at her sister. "Has it been terribly difficult?"

"We have few friends, but those who accept us are true. It will never be easy for us, or for little Trevor." Spring's voice held a touch of sadness. "But we have each other, and no one can take that from us."

"We'll make it, Miss Treasure," Elijah spoke up. "I plan to take good care of Spring and our children."

"Jared will help when Treasure and I go back. You don't need to worry. Just don't let him drag you too far into helping with his favorite cause. Robert Purvis has both Jared and Fenella irrevocably involved in the underground railroad."

"Good thing for us," Elijah said. "We never would have made it here without it. And you shouldn't be one to give advice. He managed to get you in, too."

451

"Don't remind me," Donovan said with a sigh. He grinned at Treasure. "I don't know if my Southern wife is going to take too kindly to my Yankee activities."

"Wife? You said you're going back . . ." Spring waved an excited hand. "Are you going home? Are you getting married? Oh, Treasure, you should have told me at once! Honestly, this is just what I hoped for all these months. I can scarcely believe it!"

"You can believe it," Treasure said when Spring stopped to draw a breath. "Nothing is more true."

Elijah's face creased in a frown. "Who is looking after Rose of Heaven?"

"Well, that is a long story, but Ransom is in charge of the plantation and Aunt Valene is running the household."

Donovan laughed. "You won't believe this, Spring, but your sister nearly wed herself to dear cousin Ransom."

"You almost married Mr. Ellis?" Elijah's scowl deepened.

"Why—yes." Treasure was puzzled by his obvious distress. "I realize he's my cousin. But marriages of that kind are common."

"No, not like that one they're not."

"What do you mean?" Donovan asked, exchanging a glance with Treasure.

"I don't like to say it plain like this, Miss Treasure, but Mr. Ellis isn't your cousin."

Treasure stared. "Of course he is. Aunt Valene is my mama's sister and—"

"No." Elijah shook his head. "She may be your mama's sister, but George Ellis wasn't Ransom's papa. Mr. McGlavrin was. Ransom is your half-brother."

A wave of shock mixed with revulsion slapped against Treasure with almost tangible force. "You mean I almost . . . I . . ." She clutched her hands together, trying to focus the sudden turmoil of thought and emotion.

"I think you had better explain," Donovan said, moving to sit beside Treasure. He put an arm around her, letting her draw on his strength.

"I'm sorry to be the one to tell you, Miss Treasure. But your aunt wanted your daddy and Rose of Heaven something furious. I don't know what exactly happened between her and your parents, but I do know when she left the valley, she was carryin' Mr. McGlavrin's child. She married right fast, though, before Ransom's daddy could guess it wasn't his own."

"It's too awful!" Spring cried. "Ransom—our brother. How do you know all this, Elijah?"

"My white daddy did business with Ransom's daddy. When the baby was born three months too early, Ransom's daddy knew he'd been tricked. He hated her and the boy for it. He did his duty by them, but no more. And he told my daddy many a time all about the whore he married and how he had to claim her bastard as his son. I used to sneak out and listen to my daddy tell my mama about it when he came to visit."

"Aunt Valene practically pushed me into his arms," Treasure murmured, sickened. "She must have hung all her hopes on Ransom, even though . . ." She stopped, unable to go on.

"If you had married Ransom, she would have had Rose of Heaven," Donovan said.

"So she hasn't given up, even after all these years." Spring shook her head. "My, how she must have hated your mama, Treasure. And Papa."

"I never could make sense of her ramblings on about patience and time and waiting—oh, Donovan, I left Emmy and Abby. She could have done anything while we've been away."

Donovan stood and pulled her to his feet. "We'll leave this afternoon," he said, his face grim. "I only hope it's not too late."

453

Chapter Twenty-four

Beneath an umbrella of dark water oaks, the bottle-green surge of the Tennessee tumbled headlong downstream, raging against a man furiously poling his heavy oak keelboat the opposite direction. Treasure watched the struggle from her carriage window and thought of the inevitable conflict she must face. The deep bend in the river told her Rose of Heaven, Aunt Valene, and Ransom, were but a mile away.

What are we coming home to?

Disquiet over the answer curled her fingers into a tight knot in her lap.

A warm hand slipped over hers. "This time we're home to stay, pretty lady," Donovan said confidently. The velvet sound touched her frayed nerves like healing salve. "I hope those thoughts you're so engrossed in have something to do with our wedding."

She turned from her window and smiled over to him. "The crape myrtle and red camellias in Mama's garden should still have blooms if we hurry."

"Then we'll have to marry at once, before the blossoms fade." He leaned over and kissed her nape beneath the ribbon that caught her hair. "How does this afternoon sound?"

"Perfect," she murmured, forgetting for a moment everything else the day might bring.

In a now-familiar gesture, he rubbed a finger over

her emerald engagement ring, shrugging at Treasure's knowing smile. He had given it to her just before they left Boston, a symbol of their promises to each other. She teased him about the new habit, and he confessed a compulsion to reassure himself she would soon belong wholly to him. "It's still there," she said, her eyes laughing. "And so am I."

"I've noticed." He changed the topic with quicksilver ease. "You know, the first time I rode up this road, I never imagined I'd be coming to stay. I was sure Seamus had exaggerated or imagined the whole thing. And I certainly didn't expect to be met by a red-haired firebrand who threatened me with a rifle the first time she laid eyes on me."

"I thought you were absolutely the worst sort of barbarian. A dangerous, womanizing gambler." She flashed him a coy smile and lifted her chin. "And of course, I was right."

Donovan pulled her into his arms, heedless of their approach to Rose of Heaven. "And now you, pretty lady, are the one about to gamble your future on me." He melded his lips to hers, kissing her in the slow, hot way that left her breathless with wanting more than just his mouth against her skin.

When he drew back to look deeply into her eyes, she sucked in a tremulous breath. "And are you a safe bet, Mr. Radcliffe? Or will the drifter return to lure you away one day?"

"Safe? Never. But I am a sure bet, Treasure McGlavrin. If you had any idea how much I love you, woman, that question wouldn't even cross your mind. I suppose I'm going to have to prove to you again—"

"Right here?"

"Here, now, anywhere."

The carriage jerked to a halt, and Treasure fell against him, laughing, making a halfhearted attempt to wriggle out of his arms. As always, he'd distracted her from her compulsive worrying, and now she felt much more relaxed and ready to face her aunt and cousin.

The driver opened the door, averting his eyes as Treasure struggled to sit up and make a pretense of smoothing her skirts. Ignoring Donovan's roguish grin, she allowed him to hand her down.

"Treasure, my dear." Valene came down the front steps and her smug, nearly exalted expression gave Treasure her first notion that her suspicions were not unwarranted. Her aunt's smile was graciously welcoming but her eyes were alight with an almost manic gleam. "I do hope your journey was not too taxin'," she drawled. "I was quite distressed when you left so suddenly. Well—I should have guessed . . ." Her eyes flitted to Donovan as he stepped down from the carriage. "I see you managed once again to invite yourself where you're not welcome, Mr. River."

"Stickier than a sweet gum ball in your hair, aren't I?"

Treasure stood firm against her aunt's cutting tone. "He didn't find me, I found him. And Mr. *Radcliffe* is here to stay."

A carefully manicured brow climbed Valene's forehead. "Is that so? No matter. It won't make the slightest difference now."

"I think you had best explain, Aunt Valene," Treasure said, abandoning any attempt at politeness.

"Yes, do tell, Mrs. Ellis," Donovan said, stepping up behind Treasure and putting a possessive hand on her waist.

"What I mean, suh," Valene said, her words bullet-hard, "is that my Ransom has made nonsense of your ridiculous claim to Rose of Heaven, just as I said he would."

"I'm certain Ransom's effort was born of concern, Aunt Valene," Treasure spoke up quickly, trying to keep Donovan's capricious temper at bay, not sure she could control her own. "But it has been in vain. Donovan and I are engaged. We plan to marry at once, so, whether it is his or my name on the deed makes little difference. Rose of Heaven is ours."

"Engaged? To him?" Valene gave a high, tinkling laugh. "How utterly foolish of you, my dear. Still, I am afraid you don't understand. Neither you nor your—fiancé own Rose of Heaven. You see, my dear, I am now truly the mistress of this plantation. Rose of Heaven belongs to me."

Donovan's long strides forced Treasure to run to keep pace with him. Solomon, Eura Mae, Orange Jane, and Bettis had gathered in the hallway to greet them. Donovan marched straight past them, directly to the study. He shoved open the door with a loud crash and hauled a stunned Ransom out from behind the desk by the scruff of his collar before her flabbergasted cousin could utter a single sound.

"I should have kicked you back to Atlanta when I had the chance, you double-crossing son-of-a-bitch. And in your case, I mean that in the truest sense." Donovan made a disgusted sound and flung Ransom against the wall.

Treasure caught his arm as Ransom slowly picked himself up off the floor, drawing a shaking hand across his face. "How could you have done this?" she asked her cousin. "You know your mother has no right to Rose of Heaven. You had to be the one to falsify her claim. You're family. Why would you do it?"

Ransom's thin face pinched in sullen petulance. "You saw fit to disgrace me by breaking our engagement and defiling yourself with—"

He got no further. Donovan, in one swift motion, pushed free of Treasure's hand, and smashed a fist into Ransom's face, driving him against the wall again. As Ransom slid in a graceless heap to the floor, a thin scream sliced the air, turning Treasure and Donovan to the doorway.

Valene, pale and wide-eyed, clutched the arm of

Sheriff Axle, pointing to the half-conscious Ransom with a frenzied thrust of her finger. "You see, he is a madman! I told you, my Ransom told you! You have the evidence he murdered dear Seamus and that other poor man. Arrest him before he murders my Ransom next!"

"You can't be serious." Treasure spun around to look at Donovan, then whirled on the sheriff. "Donovan didn't kill Papa. Although, from the looks of it, Sheriff, you've been lying in wait for us because my dear aunt has convinced you with her lies that Donovan did have something to do with Papa's death. Or has Valene simply been entertaining you on a regular basis?"

"Treasure!" Valene put a hand to her breast. "I simply cannot think you would believe—"

"Now, there, Mrs. Ellis," the sheriff soothed. He glanced at Treasure, not quite able to meet her eyes. "Your aunt is a very—er—generous woman, Miss Treasure. She's had me up for lemonade and meals right regular since you've been away."

"I'm hardly surprised. But no matter what she's told you, if you will listen to us—"

"I'm sorry, Miss Treasure, Donovan." Sheriff Axle shifted from foot to foot. "Mr. Ellis here . . ." He glanced at Ransom, his disdain barely disguised. "Mr. Ellis has two witnesses who claim they saw Donovan murder your papa."

"And I'll bet *my* plantation my cousin gave those so-called witnesses a great deal more than lemonade and a good supper to tell their lies."

The sheriff flushed at the implication in Treasure's words. "Now look here, Miss Treasure, I believed Donovan about Slade Gunter because Gunter left a dirty trail from Atlanta to Baton Rouge. And Donovan's references came back from Boston, strong and clean. Maybe I still believe he killed Gunter in self-defense. But Seamus . . . you believed it once yourself, Miss Treasure."

"No! It isn't true."

"Treasure . . ." Donovan put his hands on her shoulders, turning her to face him. "This isn't helping either of us. Let me go with him. I'll get this straightened out." He looked at Valene and even Treasure quailed at the cold steel in his eyes. Valene turned dead white, her fingers digging into the sheriff's arm. "And then I will settle my business with you and your son, Mrs. Ellis. In the interim, if either of you so much as think ill of Treasure, it'll take more than a rope around my neck to keep me from the two of you."

Valene gave a strangled gasp. "You see there! He's threatenin' us. The man's a bloodthirsty killer!"

Treasure bit her lip to hold back her rage. "I'm going with you." Her tone was intended to leave no chance for rebuttal.

"No." Donovan's jaw set in a hard line.

"I won't leave you now. I'm practically your wife."

Sheriff Axle started. "You're engaged?"

"Yes." Treasure threw back her head, pride and defiance in the straight stance of her body. "We plan to wed within the week. That should tell you what I think of my cousin's bought-and-paid-for evidence."

There was a long silence. Treasure wanted to scream and rail at Valene, Ransom, at Sheriff Axle's indecision, but she bridled her tongue. Her eyes locked with Donovan's, willing him to charm or fight his way out of this nightmare as he always had before.

He stared back, unmoving. And she suddenly knew it was for her. For her, he would try reason instead of acting on the hot emotion she saw flaming in his eyes.

The sheriff's frustrated groan broke the tense silence. Shaking his head in regret, he said, "I'm powerful sorry, Miss Treasure, but I just don't have a choice. I have to arrest Donovan on a charge of the willful murder of Seamus McGlavrin."

* * *

"That's impossibly absurd!" Treasure slapped her palm against Sheriff Axle's desktop. "I was in New Orleans just months ago. I don't care what witnesses Ransom claims to have produced. They're lying. Ransom paid them or threatened them."

The sheriff repeated the sentence Treasure had heard at least a dozen times in the past hour. "You don't have proof of that, Miss Treasure."

She had listened while Donovan told the sheriff about her papa's death, telling the sheriff in turn Judy Rouge's matching version. Sheriff Axle remained passive, jotting down a few notes, but seemingly unmoved by their joint defense. As the minutes passed, Treasure saw Donovan grow exasperated by the futility of his self-defense.

"I don't know what else I can tell you," he said, flinging back against his chair. He shoved his slouch hat back from his brow, his free fingers drumming restlessly against the arm of the chair. "I don't know who these two people are who Ellis claims saw me push Seamus off that damned balcony, and I don't care. If you had any sense, you'd realize he and that mother of his are just using this to get control of Rose of Heaven."

"Now, look here, Donovan . . ." Sheriff Axle began.

"Donovan's right," Treasure broke in. "Aunt Valene wants Rose of Heaven, and she obviously doesn't care how she goes about getting it. Are you prepared to make another arrest when she and Ransom concoct some charge against me?"

"I'd just as soon send the both of you out of here now and wipe my hands of it," the sheriff said grimly. "But it's not up to me to decide." He looked at Donovan. "You're gonna be my guest until I get word back from Louisiana on the charges. If the extradition hearing here proves there's enough evidence to warrant a trial, then it's back to New Orleans for you. And you" — he turned his gaze on Treasure — "had best get your fiancé the finest damned attorney his and your money can buy."

Donovan watched the door to the jail cell swing slowly closed. He suppressed a flinch as it locked with a final thud and click.

He'd been in worse holes. Of course. And gotten out of them, too. He just couldn't remember when and how.

Donovan Radcliffe, an impossible cause himself. Ironic, deserving perhaps.

Yet it wouldn't have been so hard, quite so painful, if it wasn't for the woman — the only one ever to believe in him, to have enough faith in him to trust him with her future, her fragile heart — now parted from him by iron and steel.

Through the bars, she reached out her hand and touched his cheek. River green eyes misted with unshed tears, and she blinked them back. He almost wished she would cry, or at least rail and rant. This anguished quiet tore at his soul. His reckless gamble in New Orleans, his unbridled temper, had brought them to this tortured impasse. And it drew those tears to her eyes.

"Perhaps you should go home now," he said softly. "You've had no time to talk to the girls."

Her lips trembled. But the strength he knew so well kept her voice firm. "The children are still with Miss Eliza and Rader. I couldn't trust to leave them at Rose of Heaven with Aunt Valene . . ." Her tone faltered, then firmed. "I'll send a wire to Jared. Perhaps he can recommend an attorney nearby. And I'll speak with Rader. He can go down to New Orleans —"

"Treasure, stop it." Donovan slammed both hands against the cold metal, releasing some of his frustration. "I have to know . . ." He drew a long breath. "Do you believe what those witnesses said? Any of it?"

The stricken expression on her face made Donovan

461

immediately regret his impulsive question. She whirled away from him, and when she turned back, her eyes burned with tears and anger. "How can you even ask me such a thing?"

"I'm sorry. It's just . . . Hell, you don't deserve this."

"Neither do you. And we'll prove it. To everyone."

The lightning thrust of her response stabbed his conscience and his heart. "I never thought I could love you more than the day you found me in Boston. I was wrong." He reached out a hand to her through the bars.

She put hers into it. He felt her tremble. One tear slid down her face. "I love you, Donovan Radcliffe. And we won't be beaten." She gave him a small smile and he felt himself grinning foolishly in return.

"Then get ready, pretty lady. Because there's nothing I like more than a good fight."

Treasure crossed the street, and Rader met her at the doorway of the general store. Without a word, Eliza took her hand, led her inside to their upstairs sitting room, and guided her to a chair. "News travels fast. Is it that bad, honey?" She bent to hand a wooden rattle to Annie, who lay on her tummy on a quilt in the center of the room.

Treasure nodded. In terse detail, she gave the Johnsons an account of her and Donovan's disastrous homecoming. "I should never have trusted Aunt Valene. Donovan warned me from the beginning. But I trusted that family would never . . ." She made a cutting gesture. "It doesn't matter. Ransom has claimed Rose of Heaven belongs to him, the family's only male heir, because Donovan murdered Papa to get the deed, a deed Ransom says is now worthless. There is only one way to disprove Ransom's evidence. I have an idea, but I need Rader's help."

She told them everything about Judy Rouge, about her testimony. Before she could ask the favor, Rader volunteered. "I'll leave for New Orleans as soon as I can book passage," he said. "What was the name of that hotel?"

"Maison des Rois in the French quarter. How can I ever—"

"Hush now, honey, Mr. Johnson is delighted to be of service. Aren't you, my darling?" Eliza bestowed a sweet smile on her husband.

"I'd gladly do anything for you and Donovan, Miss Treasure, you know that." Rader patted her hand.

Settling back in her chair, Treasure tried to fight the burden of worry settling over her. "I know. I just hate the frustration of having to wait. It could be weeks, even months . . ." She talked slowly, more to herself than to the Johnsons. "Sheriff Axle is sending a request for bail to Louisiana. I'm sure it will be approved. But even if it is, after the hearing . . ."

Treasure stopped, unable to give the words a voice. Bail or not, if Ransom's lies were strong enough, there might not be anything she could do to come between Donovan and a hangman's rope.

She clenched the arms of her chair to subdue her inner terror and deliberately focused her thoughts away from the too-real image. "Where are Emmy and Abigail? I've missed them, and we've a lot to catch up on."

Rader and Eliza exchanged a glance. Treasure looked from one to the other, questioning. Finally Eliza sighed. "Perhaps you should talk to Emmaline first, alone."

"Emmy? Whatever for?"

"Well, I just hate heaping trouble on you, but I think that child is hiding something. She's been distraught and moody ever since you left for Boston. I can't get a word out of her. I think she's been spending time with Jimmy Rae Stanton. That boy is trouble, Treasure, big trouble. I'm afraid he'll ruin her." Eliza's voice trailed off to a whisper. "Lord in heaven, I hope he hasn't already."

"I have to do something." Treasure quickly got to her feet. "Do you think she's with him now?"

"I'm afraid it's mighty likely."

After a hasty recount of her reunion with Spring and Elijah, Treasure left, knowing her friends understood her rush. She flew down the stairs and out the back door of the store, taking a path often used as a shortcut between the valley and Gold Meadow. Halfway to the Stanton plantation, she found Emmy and Jimmy Rae standing close together under a large red cedar. Without preamble, she walked up to them.

"Treasure. You're home." Emmy's face reflected both pleasure and fright.

"Yes." Treasure let the word hang between them and used the silence to study Jimmy Rae. Pale and thinner than last she remembered, he stood scuffing the toe of his boot in the dust, a muscle twitching at one corner of his mouth. Dark circles rimmed bleary eyes. "What's wrong, Emmy?" she asked finally.

Looking from Treasure to Jimmy Rae, Emmy appeared ready to burst into tears. "We've just been talking." She glanced in appeal at Jimmy Rae, who held her eyes for a moment, then dropped his gaze down. "Oh, Treasure! It's—"

"Nothin'." Jimmy Rae eyed her defiantly. But Treasure sensed a wavering behind his glare. The usual brash insolence was lacking in his stance. "We've just been talkin'. No harm in that, is there, Miss Treasure?"

"Why don't you tell me, Jimmy Rae? Is there harm in the subject you are discussing with my sister?"

For a split second, Treasure saw an uncharacteristic fear cross his face. Then, it was gone, and he put on a shadow of his usual swagger. "I was just sayin' what a shame it is those folks saw Mr. River kill Miss Emmy's daddy. They'll hang him for sure now and people'll be talkin' about how proper Miss Treasure was ruined by a murderer."

Treasure slapped the smirk from Jimmy Rae's face. Too shocked at first to respond, the boy drew back and rubbed his cheek. She took Emmy's unresisting hand and led her aside. "What you are, Jimmy Rae Stanton, may not be entirely your fault. But what you do about yourself from here on is up to you. If you ever want to show you're something more than an ill-tempered child, I suggest you prove you can do more than create trouble and empty a bottle."

May, with its capricious fits of cool and hot, turned out a day of blistering heat the morning Treasure prepared to go to the courthouse. It had been nearly a month since Donovan's arrest, and Treasure, mired in frustration and growing desperation, began to doubt her own faith in his eventual release and their reunion. The proceedings to secure his bail were hopelessly delayed, tied up in paperwork with the authorities in Louisiana.

She tried to hold on to the hope that Spring and Elijah and Jared had all expressed in letters, lending their love and support. Jared, on the recommendation of his family attorney, had enlisted a lawyer from Birmingham to come over to McGlavrin's Valley to defend Donovan's case.

Emmy, and even Abby, sensed her distress and tried to find little ways to please her or help with her chores in town. Treasure longed to have them near, but stood firm by her decision to leave them at the Johnsons. There, at least, she knew they were loved and cared for; she couldn't trust leaving them alone for even a minute with her aunt or cousin.

Besides, they both missed Donovan and, by being in town, were able to visit him more often. Those visits, Treasure knew, went far to lift Donovan's spirits.

And Miss Eliza. Dear Eliza, always believing, always a smile or a word to cheer her. *What would I do without her? Without any of them?*

They'd all tried their best to help. And she'd tried to keep her spirits up, tried to smile. Except when she was alone in the bed meant for them to share as husband and wife. Each night she cried into the pillow where his head should have lain, wondering how she could bear the loss.

But when morning came, she did go on, forcing herself to hold her remaining family and plantation together.

Treasure decided to stay at Rose of Heaven after both she and Donovan agreed it was best for her people and the future of the plantation. And because they both were determined to fight Valene and Ransom.

Despite her aunt and cousin's claim, Treasure comforted herself with the knowledge Donovan had taken possession of the deed the day he settled her papa's debts. As much as she felt Valene's hatred and Ransom's disdain, she wouldn't abandon Rose of Heaven to them.

And Valene could hardly throw her off the plantation without inciting the outrage of the whole of McGlavrin's Valley. The majority of the townspeople supported Donovan and Treasure, and Valene would suffer the insult of being completely ostracized if she forced her niece to leave.

Besides, to take control of Rose of Heaven, Valene and Ransom would have to prove Donovan's guilt. Treasure didn't intend to give them the chance.

So she went about her chores, waiting and praying, trying to hold on to her faith that their nightmare would soon end. In a numb daze she went about daily life, planted the May garden: cimbelines, snaps, salsify, sugar beets; supervised the cotton and corn. But it only made her separation from Donovan more painful. Every chore, even the most mundane of tasks, brought him to mind. When she planted, she felt his fingers take the seeds from her palm. When she chopped weeds, she saw the copper of his bare, muscular back glistening beside her in the sun. When she scalded the beds, she saw him lifting and turning the sick with the hands of a gentle giant.

Those months they'd grown closer now haunted her—specters of a love that each day he seemed more determined to deny. Slowly, subtly at first, he began to distance himself from her, as if he, too, doubted the final outcome and wanted to spare her as much grief as possible.

He discussed his defense with her, but spoke less and less about the future, his feelings. Yet Treasure knew too well the anger and despair eating away at his hope like bitter poison.

Despondency, creeping and insidious in its penetration, put an invisible barrier between them, dividing them not only physically but, more and more, in spirit. Though unseen, it was as tangible as the bars separating them.

As Treasure adjusted her simple blue bonnet, she wished the pale image gazing back at her from the glass didn't reflect all her distress. She had once been so adept at hiding her emotions. Now her pain, her worry, was plainly written in the clouded green of her eyes. It hurt to love so deeply. But she wouldn't trade one moment of it to return to her safe, dispassionate aloneness, even if following her heart meant having it broken.

In the courtroom today, she wanted to be his strength, not a weakness he would have to contend with. She ached to be as close as they had been before his arrest, so he would feel her support, her faith in him. Only now, with so much between them, so much against them, they needed more love, a stronger union . . . yet how could she reach him?

With a sigh, Treasure straightened her skirts, pulled on her gloves, and as she did, an impulse struck her. She lifted her chin. She glanced again into the glass. A different woman, resolute, strong, returned a small smile.

Today she and Donovan would face the verdict as one.

"I have never been more serious, Donovan."

"Damn it, we can't get married now! I'm practically a condemned man. Listen to reason."

"Reason! You're a fine one to talk about reason, Donovan Radcliffe." Treasure gripped the bars between them. "How long have I listened to you badger and cajole me about trusting my heart?"

"Ex-excuse me, Miss Treasure, but the sheriff said we only had a few minutes." The pastor gripped his Bible to his black coat. "Is there going to be a wedding?"

"Yes."

"No!"

"Yes, damn it, there is!" Treasure snapped at Donovan, then immediately turned contrite eyes to the pastor. "I'm sorry. He's just being difficult."

"I'm not being difficult. For once I'm being sensible. Just like you always wanted."

"I don't want sensible and reasonable. I want you!" Treasure stopped, knowing she was losing control of both her emotions and the battle of wills between them. Donovan turned away from her, shoving a hand through his hair. She watched him pace the limited confines of the cell, feeling his frustration and anguish as surely as if it had been her own. He hadn't bothered with the coat she'd sent along today; his loose shirt was unbuttoned at the throat and he looked ruffled. But it was the air of tired defeat that struck her hardest and gave her the resolve she needed.

"You asked me to be your wife," she said, meeting his eyes, unflinching. "I accepted. This"—she waved a hand around them—"doesn't change that. You either prove you meant your proposal, or I will turn and walk out of your life."

Donovan cocked his head slightly. "I do believe you're threatening me, pretty lady."

468

"I'm not above it. I love you. I want to marry you. To-day. Right now."

"Treasure . . ." Donovan looked at her and she saw the struggle in his face. "Do you realize what you're do-ing?"

In the barren, dusty gray jail, separated by iron and lies, knowing none of their tomorrows were certain, Treasure had never felt as confident of anything in her life. She nodded and held out a hand to him. "I do."

A heartbeat of silence hovered between them. Then Donovan reached out and twined her fingers in his.

As the minister opened his Bible and cleared his throat, Sheriff Axle walked around Treasure and opened the door to Donovan's cell. "Make things a little easier," he mumbled, flushing under Treasure's know-ing smile.

He stayed as the only witness as the pastor solemnly read the simple service. When the final words, naming them man and wife, were read, the sheriff took the pas-tor's arm and quietly led him to the front office, gifting Treasure with a brief moment alone in her husband's arms.

Tears spilled unheeded down her face as Donovan kissed her, deeply, desperately, with all the passion and fire of his love for her.

When they parted, Donovan took her face between his hands and looked at her for a long moment. "Thank you," he murmured, stopping her protest with a finger to her lips. "For teaching me to believe again."

The air inside the courtroom was still and musty. A fly buzzed incessantly among the ceiling cobwebs. It smelled of dank wood and dust and sweat. Spectators crowded onto the benches behind the dock, all watch-ing her, watching Donovan. Emmy. Ira Stanton and Jimmy Rae. Valene. Ransom. Eliza and Rader. Judy Rouge.

And Donovan's accusers. Across the courtroom, Treasure recognized them at once as the proprietor of the Maison des Rois and her shifty-eyed cohort.

Directly in front of her, Donovan sat next to the lawyer Jared had recommended. He turned back to her and smiled, an echo of his old, raffish grin. For a moment, the room faded and there was nothing but the two of them, together.

Only after Donovan turned away did Treasure release the tears she'd kept carefully secreted behind her brave facade. He needed her strength now, not her fears.

Beside her, Rader took her hand, squeezed it hard, then dropped it. "Lisa and I believe him. Not much help, I know—"

"It's more help than you can guess." She put on a smile for him. "You tracked down Judy Rouge. At least we'll have her testimony to counter the lies."

"And her friend's, I hope. Judy Rouge said she'd convince the other woman who lives with her, the one who knew Donovan, to come along. Doesn't seem to be here yet, though . . ."

The sharp crack of a gavel against wood brought their discussion to an abrupt halt. Treasure sat straight on the hard wood seat, her hands balled in her lap. The judge droned on with the opening words of the hearing, words that reached her ears only as an ominous rumble. At any moment it would begin.

Or end.

The judge's voice grumbled toward a close when a confusion at the rear doorway interrupted. The door flung open, and Treasure heard a collective gasp ripple through the crowd.

"Well, well, such a fine hearin' we've got this mornin'. It's just entirely too bad the wrong man is going to end up at the hangin'."

In a flash, Treasure leapt to her feet. "Camille!"

Donovan was up and at her side, putting restraining hands on her shoulders.

470

"My, my, honey," Judy Rouge drawled. "If I had known this was what you had in mind, I'd have brought friends to see the show."

Camille stepped boldly to the center aisle of the room. Treasure stared at her stepsister, recognizing the voice, but hardly the woman standing, hip slung, eyeing the crowd with malicious pleasure.

Dressed in royal blue satin and black lace, Camille's tightly fitted gown revealed more creamy flesh than it covered. Bright blue ribbons twined in her dark hair and her face paint was more a mask than an enhancement. In her hand, she held a pistol.

She waved the tiny gun at Donovan and Treasure. "I did so want to pay my respects to my dear sister and you, Mr. Donovan River. Although I do hear you've changed your name and become quite respectable. A pity, honey. Such a waste. You know, I do still nurse thoughts of inflicting a little sufferin' on the two of you." Camille pointed the pistol directly at Treasure. Someone near them screamed.

Donovan quickly stood in front of Treasure. "Don't be a damned fool, Camille."

"Oh, its far too late for that, Mr. River." The muzzle of the gun didn't waver as she aimed it at Donovan's heart.

"Then shoot. If you've got the nerve."

Treasure tried to force her way past Donovan's arm, but he barred her way. "No! Camille —"

"My, how noble. You are both making me quite nauseated. And I do have the nerve, honey. I have all the nerve I need to kill the man who murdered my baby sister."

Before anyone could react, Camille whirled, aimed, and pulled the trigger.

As he clutched a hand to the spreading red stain on his shirt front, Ira Stanton stared at her in stunned disbelief. Slowly, his knees crumpled and he fell forward onto the floor. Jimmy Rae gave an anguished cry and dropped to his knees, bending over his brother's body.

Judy Rouge jumped to her feet. "Camille," she shouted. "Run!"

With a wild laugh, Camille ran toward the open door, firing a shot backward above the crowd to deter any pursuers. Treasure heard shouts and the frenzied clatter of a horse's hooves before the courtroom erupted in chaos.

"Hell and damnation," Sheriff Axle cursed. "That girl's plumb crazy." Motioning to his deputy, he managed to push his way through the crowd, following in Camille's wake. "We'll have a helluva time following her now," he said, shaking his head in disgust as he shoved outside the courtroom.

Donovan, pushing his way through the milling mass of bodies, knelt at Ira's side. Gently, he moved Jimmy Rae aside. His fingers probed for any sign of life.

Treasure waited beside him. He looked up at her. "He's dead."

"No." Jimmy Rae shoved away from him, careening off several persons in a tortured dance, holding his head between his hands. "No, it wasn't Ira. It wasn't Ira. Ira didn't do it."

"What wasn't? Jimmy Rae . . ." Donovan caught his shoulders, shaking him a little. "What didn't Ira do?"

"The fire. At the house. I told her—"

"Told whom?"

"It is quite obvious the boy is in distress," Valene cut in, stepping close. "I do believe someone should take him home where he can be seen to."

Donovan ignored her, forcing Jimmy Rae to look at him. "Whom did you tell?"

"Her." Jimmy Rae pointed a shaking finger at Valene. "She wanted the fields burned. Ira said so. To scare Miss Treasure off Rose of Heaven. I did it. But not the house. I didn't mean the house. It was an accident. I told Emmy. I tried to explain to her. It was an accident.

472

I stopped, just for a minute, with the lantern. I dropped my bottle. I just had one drink, maybe two. Then I dropped it. And it caught fire. I tried to stop it, but it was too late. The wind — I didn't mean the house. Not the house." He broke down, sobbing, held up only by Donovan's arm.

"This is absurd." Ransom, moving up behind Valene, readjusted his pince-nez several times. "This boy is obviously a drunkard trying to affix his blame elsewhere."

"Of course, of course." Valene nodded her head several times. She stood still except for her fingers. They worked frenziedly, shredding the edges of a lace handkerchief. "My Ransom knows. My Ransom can tell you. He can set this all right."

"Does your Ransom know you urged him to marry his sister?" Treasure blurted out the words before she considered their impact. She knew at once from the look on Ransom's face he thought she'd gone mad. The crowd seemed to draw a single sharp breath in disbelief. "It's true."

"W-why of course it isn't," Valene faltered. "Of course it isn't. Why should I consider such as thing? Even if it were true."

"Because you wanted Rose of Heaven," Donovan said. "And you would do anything to get it. Including arranging a marriage between Seamus's daughter and his alleged son."

"Ransom is Seamus's son!"

"Mother!" Ransom stared at her, suddenly white to the bone.

"Oh, I tried to tell him, again and again. He just wouldn't believe me." Valene stared straight ahead, seeing images no one else could envision. "He jilted me. Me. Valene Peyton. The belle of McGlavrin's Valley. For my sister, dear little Claire, so sweet, so stupid. I should have been mistress of Rose of Heaven. It belongs to me and Seamus's only son, not Claire's wretched daughter. When I heard he was dead, I was glad. I was so glad. Because I knew my Ransom and I could finally get what was ours. We couldn't while he was alive. No, he would never, never let us have our due. He didn't believe me. No one believed me." She shook her head, sadly, as if she were describing a trifling social oversight.

"It can't be the truth. Mama . . ." Ransom limply extended a hand.

Valene frowned at his hand and Ransom let it drop. "No one believed me," she repeated softly. "Just as no one believed you, Mr. Donovan River." She laughed, a shrill, high sound. "It was so simple, wasn't it, Ransom? Why, a few dollars can buy the truth from anyone's lips."

"But Mama—"

"Oh, do be quiet, Ransom! It's all over now, isn't it? All over now." Valene trailed off, smiling to herself, as her fingers tore the lace scrap into tiny pieces. They drifted to the floor like fallen petals from a dead bloom.

Ransom, with a piteous bewilderment, looked around at the circle of faces surrounding them. Valene only smiled her vacant smile, her eyes dead.

Sheriff Axle stepped forward, pushing back his hat with his thumb. "Is it true, Mr. Ellis?" he said, staring hard at Ransom. "Did you buy the evidence against Donovan?"

"I . . ."

"Of course he did." Judy Rouge shoved her way into the center of them. "Donovan didn't kill Seamus. I was there. The old man was drunk and he fell off the balcony, just like I told her." She pointed a finger at Treasure. "And those two . . ." Judy swung around, waving a hand at Ransom's pair of witnesses, who were making a hasty retreat toward the doorway. "Those two damn well know Donovan's innocent. Seamus owed them a tidy debt, and if Donovan hadn't paid it, they'd have

474

gladly pushed the old man off that balcony just for the satisfaction."

Several men in the crowd had blocked the doorway, keeping Ransom's pair from leaving.

"He didn't pay me enough to spend no time in a jail cell," shouted the woman Treasure remembered from the New Orleans boardinghouse. She was still screaming obscenities at Ransom as the deputy, aided by two men standing by, escorted the woman and her companion from the courtroom.

Treasure reached for Donovan's hand as she saw Axle walk over to say a few whispered words to the judge.

When the sheriff walked back, there was apology and a touch of chagrin in his eyes. "The charges have been dropped. You're free to go." He extended a hand to Donovan.

Donovan, after a moment's hesitation, returned his grip.

"What about my sister?" Treasure asked. She looked toward the open door. Camille had murdered a man, but Treasure couldn't find it in her heart to despise her stepsister. She understood, in small part, the passion and pain that had led Camille to avenge Erin's death. And she hoped, somehow, Camille might have finally found a measure of peace.

"She killed a man, Miss Treasure," Axle said. "Whether it was justice or not, that'll be up to a judge to decide. If and when we can find her, that is."

Donovan gently squeezed Treasure's hand. "I think we both hope that doesn't happen, sheriff."

"I confess, I've got more than enough to tend to here." Axle glanced to Ransom, standing helplessly by his mother, watching her twist and untwist her now-empty hands. "They're a sorry pair, I'll say that. If you want to press charges, Miss Treasure, Donovan, I'd say you got more than enough reason."

Treasure bit her lip as an unexpected pity welled up in her. She could hate them both, but all she felt was a sad emptiness. They were, in their own ways, pathetic and their misery was their punishment.

"No," she said softly. "I think Ransom will agree to take Aunt Valene back to Atlanta. They'll be out of our lives and that's all I want."

"I had Jimmy Rae taken down to the jail." Axle shook his head. "The boy's in heap of trouble. I'm afraid there's not much I can do but see that he gets a fair trial." Tugging his hat back down over his brow, the sheriff nodded to them. "I best be gettin' along. I've got long day ahead cleanin' up this mess."

"Emmy was secretly meeting Jimmy," Treasure murmured when Axle had left. "She'll be crushed."

"You'll be there to help her over it," Donovan said. "We both will." He turned to guide her from the courtroom, but Treasure held back.

"Just one moment." Treasure walked up to Judy Rouge, where she leaned against one of the benches. "You know Camille?"

Judy nodded. "She came to New Orleans, looking for the place your papa and Donovan had been. She needed a room, and I needed help with the rent. When your friend came lookin' for me, I told Camille and she decided to come back on her own. She didn't want your Mr. Johnson to know what she'd become."

"It wouldn't have mattered to me or to Donovan," Treasure said, staring blindly down at the floor. "All I ever wanted was for her to be safe." She looked back at Judy. "If you see her again, tell her — tell her we all love her. I know she can't come home to us, but tell her there's nothing to stop us from going to her. And we intend to do just that."

As Treasure gazed up to her husband, Donovan smiled. "Yes, we will. But now, my wife and I are going to do something I've wanted to do since the day we left Boston." Gathering Treasure in his arms, he gently kissed her willing mouth. "We're going home."

476

"I was beginning to believe we would never come to this." Treasure sighed and leaned against her husband's heart, watching the twilight settle over Rose of Heaven in a dusky-lavender mist.

Donovan nuzzled the curve of her neck, his mouth wandering over her soft skin. "We're here now. And you had best get used to it. I don't intend to let you stray too far from my arms again."

"I do hope you mean that, Mr. Radcliffe. It's time to fertilize the north fields and put in the cabbage and corn. And everyone in the valley is talking about expanding the mill." Treasure stopped suddenly and pulled a little away, a shadow crossing her face.

"What is it?"

"Nothing. It's just . . ." She shrugged, avoiding his eyes. "Rose of Heaven is yours. You should be making these decisions."

"Ah, I see. The lady still can't forgive me for winning her plantation."

"It's not that . . ." she began hotly.

"It is that. But . . ." Donovan held up a hand. "I think I have something that will resolve this rather quickly."

He took her hand and led her into the parlor over to the piano. On the top lay a folded paper, tied with lavender ribbon to a single silver rose. "Go ahead," he said, nodding to the package.

Surprised and curious, Treasure looked questioningly at his secret smile. He merely shrugged and grinned. She turned to the package and, with trembling fingers, pulled open the ribbon and unfolded the paper.

It was the deed to Rose of Heaven. With her name, Treasure McGlavrin Radcliffe, as sole owner.

Her eyes flew to Donovan.

"It always belonged to you, pretty lady. I just wanted to make it official."

"But Papa . . ."

"Seamus died trying to hold on to an illusion. You're the one who made Rose of Heaven your heart and soul. Besides, you always told me I was never much of a farmer."

"Maybe not," Treasure said, tears shining among the laughter in her eyes. "But there are some things you're very good at." Reaching up, she pulled his body close to hers. "You've given me the rose," she said, nodding at the silver bloom. "There's just one thing left."

"And what might that be, pretty lady?"

Treasure smiled and, closing the final distance between them, whispered against his mouth, "Show me heaven."

Author's Note

The setting for *Alabama Twilight* — Treasure Mc-Glavrin's Rose of Heaven plantation and McGlavrin's Valley, Alabama — was inspired by the plantation house of General Ira Foster. The house itself was recently destroyed by fire, but traces of the original homestead site remain on Georgia Mountain, in Guntersville, Alabama. Descendants of the Foster and Ayres family have lived on the mountain since the mid-1800s.

"Whisper in the Twilight," the song that Donovan River sings to Treasure, was written in the 1800s by George May and Anthony Nish. A yellowed and tattered book of sheet music, discovered in a piano bench in a room of the old house, suggested a theme of music throughout the book. Although many of the songs in the story were written by the authors, the words to another song in the music book, "Evening Bringeth My Heart Back to Thee," are also used.

Among the historical sources tapped during the research for *Alabama Twilight* was the diary of Albert M. Ayres. Albert Ayres was born in Macon, Georgia, in 1843 and, after his death in 1922, was buried in the family cemetery on Georgia Mountain. His memoirs provided an intriguing perspective on Southern society, plantation life, and the events surrounding the Civil War.